BRIDE OF THE FAT WHITE VAMPIRE

Also by Andrew Fox

FAT WHITE VAMPIRE BLUES

BRIDE OF THE FAT WHITE VAMPIRE

A NOVEL

ANDREW **FOX**

BALLANTINE BOOKS • NEW YORK

Bride of the Fat White Vampire is a work of fiction. Names, places, and incidents either are a product of the author's imagination or are used fictitiously.

A Ballantine Book
Published by The Random House Publishing Group

www.ballantinebooks.com

Grateful acknowledgment is made to Jon Sanborne for permission to reprint "Smoke Stack" by Jon Sanborne.

LIBRARY OF CONGRESS CATALOGING-IN-PUBLICATION DATA
Fox, Andrew (Andrew Jay), 1964–
Bride of the fat white vampire / by Andrew Fox.
p. cm.
ISBN 0-345-46408-7 (alk. paper)
1. Overweight persons—Fiction. 2. New Orleans (La.)—Fiction. 3. Taxicab drivers—Fiction. 4. Vampires—Fiction. I. Title.
PS3606.O955B75 2004
813'.6—dc22

2004049398

Manufactured in the United States of America

9 8 7 6 5 4 3 2 1

First Edition: August 2004

Text design by Julie Schroeder

for Dara, my bride

ACKNOWLEDGMENTS

Very few writers, I think, write their books without a mighty impressive support team backing them up. Dara, thank you for putting up with all the late nights, for making all those road trips with me so enthusiastically, and, most of all, for giving me such a beautiful son. Thanks are due again to the members of the George Alec Effinger Memorial Writing Workshop, who patiently steered me around the pits of poor plotting or murky characterization many times. Thanks to Maury for being such a fan of Jules, and to Ric and Robyn for being supportive in so many ways. And to all the members of my family who hawked *Fat White Vampire Blues* to bookstore managers—keep it up, guys!

Getting better acquainted with the community of book lovers has been a tremendous pleasure. Some book people have been especially wonderful to me; thank you Judith and Tom of Octavia Books, Susan of Bookends, and Carol of Loyola University Bookstore. I wish I could list all the gracious hosts of the conventions I attended in 2003; thank you for being so welcoming to Dara and me. And big thanks to my agent, Dan Hooker, who enchanted my family with anecdotes about A. E. Van Vogt and Forry Ackerman at my wedding; to my editor, Chris Schluep; and to Colleen Lindsay and Fleetwood Robbins of the Ballantine staff.

Finally, I couldn't publish a book celebrating New Orleans and its characters without mentioning my dear friend Robert Borsodi. Bob likely holds the record for greatest number of coffeehouses personally operated in a lifetime; he ran thirteen of them between 1960 and 2003, the first in New Haven, the last three in New Orleans. Bob loved theater, poetry, and cappuccino, and his greatest joy was creating a warm, welcoming space for unusual folks, "bringing artists and the community together," in his words. Bob and his coffeehouse were two major draws that brought me back to New Orleans years ago. He saw me through some rough times, and I tried to do the same for him. He died in October 2003, following a run-in with cancer. Bob's motto was, "Slow is beautiful," and he exemplified it. Bob, I hope you're on a slow cruise to some place good.

"Yes . . . a woman. That should be really interesting."

—Ernest Thesiger as Dr. Pretorius,
Bride of Frankenstein

"She's alive! ALIVE!"

—Colin Clive as Henry Frankenstein,
Bride of Frankenstein

and you said
"i know what that thing is
and i know what it's doing,
but i still can't help
thinking it's beautiful."

no, no
there's no helping
the things we love

—Jon Sanborne, "Smoke Stack"

BRIDE OF THE FAT WHITE VAMPIRE

PROLOGUE

It was a good night to be a rat. The early March night air was brisk, just cool enough to make the white fur on his long, plump body tingle deliciously whenever a breeze gusted through the French Quarter alleyway where he waited impatiently for his dinner. The breezes brought the scents of the city to him, emissaries bearing gifts for a king: spilled beer, fermenting enticingly in the sticky gutters of Bourbon Street; andouille sausage and crabmeat and spiced rice baking in the restaurant kitchen that backed onto this alleyway; the pungent, fruity perfumes worn by exotic dancers on Iberville Street, wafting out open doorways, an aroma that made the rat mysteriously nostalgic and sad.

He wasn't the only rat waiting for his dinner. He never was. Waiting behind him, in the crawl spaces beneath the centuries-old Spanish town homes, in the dark, drafty spaces within the walls of those venerable buildings, were his brothers. Many, many white rats. He'd known how many there were, once. There had been a time when he could count, when he'd known what numbers were. He'd lost that knowledge somehow; it had drifted away from him in the sleeps that came between nights, when he'd been curled up with his brothers in lightless crevices, dreaming of the sweet, metallic, intoxicating taste of blood. But he vaguely remembered a time when he'd continuously counted his brothers, terrified that one of them might have gone missing. Almost as if he'd been afraid of losing part of himself.

The light above the kitchen's screen door flickered on. Dinnertime! The rat's hairless, pinkish white tail twitched happily. He heard a rustling behind him, the sounds of his brothers massing for their nightly Charge of the Rat Brigade. He steeled himself, tensing his muscles and gnashing his tiny fangs—every night, there was at least one who tried to butt ahead of him.

The screen door swung open. A slender young man, wearing a purple apron, grunted as he dragged two overloaded garbage bags down two steps and across the alleyway. The rat heard his brothers squeaking excitedly behind him. He turned and hissed at them, sending them scurrying back beneath their shelter.

The young man lifted the Dumpster's metal lid, letting it fall open with a deafening clang. His face puckered with distaste as the odors inside the Dumpster belched forth. "Fuckin' garbage," he muttered. "Bane of my existence. But somebody out there likes it." He grabbed the first of the two garbage bags by its knotted neck and heaved it into the air. It landed inside the Dumpster with a flatulent clatter. He did the same with the second bag. Then he carried a plastic bin to the edge of the Dumpster and tipped it over, thumping it to make sure that no glob of greasy food waste clung inside.

The busboy checked to make sure nobody in the kitchen was looking out into the alley. Then he lifted the Dumpster's heavy lid as if to close it, but he released it, letting it fall open again. He backed away from the Dumpster, his eyes scanning the corners of the alleyway. Just before he went inside, he said in a muted voice, laced with morbid fascination, "Come out, come out, wherever you are . . ."

The screen door swung shut behind him. Its clatter was the signal. Go! Go! The rat scrambled up a pile of flattened corrugated boxes to the lip of the Dumpster. But several of his brothers were close behind. The rat jumped onto the rim of the Dumpster, turned, and hissed. Several of his pursuers backed away to a lower shelf of soggy cardboard. Three, however, peered at one another, gathered their communal courage, and rushed him.

It wasn't much of a contest. He weighed as much as any two of them put together, and he was faster and meaner, besides. He head-butted the first of his challengers, knocking the smaller rodent silly and tumbling him onto a pile of mildewed newspapers near the Dumpster's wheels. The second challenger tried to sneak around to the side, but the alpha rat quickly pivoted and bit his rival on the flank. Not hard enough to draw blood (although that notion seemed oddly appealing), but hard enough to leave a lasting memory.

The bitten rat squealed, then slithered back down the cardboard staircase. As he passed, the third challenger's tail went limp. The alpha rat stood on his hind legs and bounced a victory jig, clawing the air with triumph. Then he turned and leaped into the Dumpster's maw, satisfied that he'd earned at least a minute or two of dining peacefully alone.

He landed, snout-first, in a pool of garlicky cream sauce. His whole body tingled with pleasure as he half crawled, half swam through the thick mixture, which had pooled in a concavity atop a garbage sack. He nibbled at smoky crabmeat and tore a slab of spicy breading from a chunk of okra. He licked cream sauce from his fur, then rolled lustily in it, tumbling round and round, so he could lick himself clean again and still discover flavorful crannies and orifices hours from now.

He slashed the plastic bag with sharp foreclaws. Burrowing inside, he discovered that a diner (probably some Yankee with a timid palate) had discarded practically an entire Creole sampler plate. Andouille and chicken gumbo, shrimp Creole, peppery jambalaya, bread pudding laced with rum—the rat opened his mouth wide and wiggled deeper inside the sack, barely bothering to chew before swallowing.

Tiny feet drummed against the Dumpster's rim. Within seconds, dozens of his brothers began smacking into lumpy garbage sacks, a small army of rodent paratroopers leaping into action. The alpha rat weighed his options. His stomach was already stuffed to the size and roundness of a ripe cantaloupe. If he stayed any longer, he'd have to fight off a multitude for the choicest morsels, and he was too food-drunk and sluggish to engage in combat. Worse, if he ate much more, there was the chance he'd get so sleepy that he'd doze off inside the open Dumpster. An instinctual clock told him dawn wasn't more than six hours distant. That same instinct told him he'd better get his pink tail inside lightless walls well before then.

So he reluctantly burrowed his way out of the garbage sack, hissing irritably as his brothers scurried over him. The big rat, having sated his own hunger, now found himself faintly disgusted with his brothers' behavior. He needed his space.

The damp, dark, slumberous spaces within the Vieux Carré's walls tugged at him. But he fought the instinct to call it a night and surrender to sleep. He vaguely remembered a time when nights had been electric, when the thrill of the hunt had made the blood fizz within his veins like a well-shaken Dixie beer. Women. There had been lots of women. Where had he found them all? He had invited them into a little house, a house on wheels.

He missed that little house. Nostalgia and loss washed over him in waves. But then he remembered something else. Something he remembered a few times a week, then forgot again. His house on wheels would be parked near the front of the restaurant. It was there almost every night. He could go and look at it.

Sticking instinctively to the shadows, the rat scurried along the drainage culvert at the edge of the alley and headed for the street. Half a block away, he found it. It was so much *bigger* than he remembered! Its tall, straight white sides, culminating in those distinctive chrome-tipped tail fins, seemed to stretch on forever. The rat remembered the comforting scent of cracked leather seats, marinated by decades of aftershave, hair tonic, and sweat. What he couldn't remember was how he'd gotten inside, and why the house on wheels was no longer his to live in.

The rat heard soft laughter behind him. A woman's laughter, then a man's. He hid behind a tire and peered out to see who it was. The front doors of the restaurant swung shut behind them, scattering amber light and old jazz and the scent of bread pudding onto the sidewalk. The man had his arm around the woman's waist. He was nearly as wide as he was tall. His dark skin had a healthy, oily sheen to it, almost matched by the sheen of his dark suit. His big round head was smooth and bald; it reflected the orange neon of the bar across the street. His cologne was heavy on the musk. He wore gold-rimmed spectacles looped around small ears, and his thick fingers were made weightier by blocky rings encrusted with jewels. He looked very, very happy. The rat liked the sound of his laugh.

But the one who really captured the rat's attention was the woman. She was slender and tall, a full head taller than her companion. Her skin was every bit as white as her companion's was dark; as white as the rat's own fur. Her long, straight hair was whiter still, white as the moon. Her perfume was delicate and flowery, but beneath it, the rat could smell the faint scent of earth, the tang of decaying humus. She laughed and ran her long, slender fingers along her companion's back as they walked. But between laughs, her smile faded, and the rat saw her cast sidelong glances at the man's thick neck, glances that were feral and hungry.

The rat was suddenly afraid for the man. He began to follow the couple, sticking to pools of shadow. He didn't understand *why* he felt afraid for the man, whose eyes looked so happy and who laughed with such warmth. But deep inside, in the human portion of his minuscule brain which he accessed with less and less clarity as the nights passed, the rat understood only too well.

The couple had turned their backs on the clamor of nearby Bourbon Street. They walked toward the empty stretches of Burgundy and North Rampart Streets, gloomy blocks of Creole cottages and brick townhouses. The rat followed. The woman . . . he was pretty sure he'd never seen her before. But he tingled all over with a certainty that she and he had something in common, something basic and important, and that by following her and watching her he could remember things about himself that he'd forgotten.

The couple stepped off the sidewalk into an alleyway. The alley was open at both ends. It was cluttered with piles of dirty plywood pallets and stacked cartons of empty beer bottles. The smiling black man leaned against a wall, putting a pile of pallets between himself and the sidewalk. The rat hid between a garbage can and a bundle of mildewed newspapers. The woman kneeled in front of the man, her back to the rat. The man's arm stretched low, and the rat heard a high-pitched *zzzzz-zup!* sound. The sound made the rat want to pee. The woman, still kneeling, did something with her hands, but the rat couldn't see what. Then she moved her head forward. The man's smile grew much wider. His eyes half closed, and a sigh like a baby's cooing slipped from his lips.

The woman began moving her head forward and backward. The man sighed again, this time at a lower pitch. The rat felt his entire body, whiskers to tail tip, grow stiff, his tiny heart beating triple-time. It was an exhilarating sensation, strangely familiar. He watched the man bite his lower lip and run his fingers through the woman's platinum hair. Then she stopped moving her head.

"Bay-*beee,*" the man moaned, "don't you go stoppin' now. Not *now.* Not when you're doin' so damn *nice.*"

She looked up at him. "I'm not stopping," she said, her voice sweet and chill as an autumn wind through an apple orchard. "I'm *teasing.* Now close your eyes and lean back."

She changed the angle of her shoulders and head. The man's moaning began again, louder and more musical. "Now that's *dif'rent,*" he said, eyes closed but smiling. "*Cree-AY-tive.* You can keep that up all night, all night long—"

Her head jerked. The man's eyes popped open. Wide, like eggs sunny-side up. "What the *fuh*—?"

His last word was an almost ratlike squeak. His eyes stayed wide-open as his body stiffened and he began to slide down the wall. Muscles in the woman's neck stood out like rope as she sucked furiously. She used her hands to keep him from sliding any lower. The rat heard slurping noises, noises that made him dismayed and wistful, jealous and sick at heart all at once.

Then she pulled her head away and let the man slump to the ground. The rat's nose twitched as the air took on a metallic tinge. The woman stood and stretched. Dark liquid oozed down her chin. Her tongue flicked out, lizardlike, and swept up the droplets before they could fall to the ground. Then she leaned over him again, this time burrowing her white face into his fleshy neck. And she began once more to feed.

Someone entered the alleyway's more distant mouth. Were it not for the rat's extremely sensitive ears, he wouldn't have detected the man's catlike steps. The intruder was tall and slender and wore a gray hat and a long gray overcoat. A woolen muffler was wrapped around the lower part of his face, and his eyes were hidden by dark glasses. His scent—cologne? hair tonic?—was comfortingly familiar to the rat, whose pink tail wagged tentatively, hopefully.

The newcomer approached the woman from behind. Her face was still buried in the black man's neck. The intruder pulled a gloved hand out of his overcoat pocket. He held something shiny that had a skinny, silvery protrusion. He plunged the protrusion into the woman's neck. She cried out, but her cry was muffled by the black man's wet neck. Then her body went soft and doll-like, as if she'd fallen asleep.

The intruder pulled the silvery protrusion from the woman's neck and placed it back in his pocket. He crouched down, rolled up the sleeves of her blouse, and ran a gloved finger across her smooth, unblemished white arms. Then he lifted her up from the alley's floor as easily as if she were made of paper.

He stood with the woman in his arms and turned toward the entrance he'd come in. The rat emerged from his hiding place, eager to follow this familiar-smelling man and the sleeping woman whose lips were glistening and dark. Then the man turned back. The rat froze. The man slung the woman over his shoulder and took something out of his other pocket, something snub-nosed and black and hard-looking. He leaned down next to the black man, whose eyes were still open and glassy. He placed the snub-nosed object (*a gun?*) against the back of the black man's bald head. A sharp crack made the rat jump a foot into the air. The black man's chin was now buried deeply in his disheveled polka-dotted necktie.

When the rat landed on slick cobblestones and looked up again, the man with the muffler and the woman with the glistening mouth were gone.

ONE

Rory "Doodlebug" Richelieu shivered as he walked up the dark gravel path toward the fifteen-foot-high walls surrounding the High Krewe's compound. A vampire shouldn't be afraid of the dark, he told himself. Yet the short walk from where a cab had let him off on Metairie Road through these gloomy woods, barely lit by a weak moon, had seriously creeped him out. He wished he'd worn a shawl. His lightweight linen dress and lace hosiery were fine for the Quarter, but here they left him feeling chilled. And the heels of his pumps sank into the gravel, nearly causing him to twist an ankle several times.

When he was ten feet from the gate, something scurried near his feet. He saw something run into the underbrush, a mouse or squirrel or maybe a small rat. Doodlebug smiled a wistful smile. The tiny mammal had made him think of Jules. As he had innumerable times during the past eight months, Doodlebug wondered how the Fates had been treating his vanished friend. He hoped with all his heart that Jules had found happiness.

The iron gates towered before him like the entrance to one of Dante's inner circles of Hell. Doodlebug pressed the cold steel button that protruded from the marble gatepost. A disguised panel slid open, revealing a video screen. A dignified, somewhat haughty face appeared; a computer-generated image, Doodlebug realized, since the butler was himself a vampire and could not be photographed. Above him, at the top of the entrance archway, a small camera tracked his movements. All it would reveal to the viewer on the other end was a knee-length black dress, pale ivory lace hosiery, sensible black pumps, earrings, and lipstick of a modest shade of red.

"I'm Rory Richelieu," Doodlebug said. It felt odd to call himself by his birth name; normally he went by Debbie, and whenever he'd returned to New Orleans to see Jules or Maureen, he'd always slipped back into his childhood nickname, Doodlebug. "I flew out from California. Georges Besthoff asked me to come." *Asked* was too pale a word; *demanded* was more like it.

The face on screen appeared to be examining a list. "Yes. Mr. Richelieu. I've been told to expect you. Master Besthoff is awaiting you in the library."

The massive iron gate swung open as smoothly and silently as silk on silk. The scent of pomegranates reached him on a cool breeze. Blood apples. High above, at the center of a cloud-dimpled sky, a half-moon illuminated stately groves and manicured gardens, all of which would appear quite at home surrounding the ancient fortress-estates of Moravia or Romania. Doodlebug had not set foot within the gates of the compound of the High Krewe of Vlad Tepes in decades. Not since 1968, just after he'd completed his thirteen years of study in Tibet, when he'd been planning to leave New Orleans for California to establish his Institute of Higher Alpha-Consciousness.

As grand and beautiful as this walled assemblage of mansions and gardens was, he'd never felt any fondness for this place. Most of the vampires here were far older than he was, immigrants from Eastern Europe, one of the cultural hearts of world vampirism, and had amassed their impressive fortunes over hundreds of years. The wisdom of their collective centuries had not brought them enlightenment, as it had to Doodlebug's Tibetan monk teachers; instead, it had taught them to pursue their own narrow interests with scientific precision. As a fledgling vampire, he'd considered himself a catfish among tiger sharks in his dealings with the masters of this place. He'd always suspected they'd granted their support to his California project only because they'd judged him to be an interesting, potentially useful freak.

Doodlebug hadn't heard a peep from the High Krewe's masters in a quarter century. What did they want with him *now*? Besthoff certainly hadn't ordered him to fly across the continent for a social call. He had been infuriatingly evasive in his communiqués, as he always was. But he'd left no doubt that he was willing to pound the stake through Doodlebug's most precious aspirations if Doodlebug failed to comply.

Doodlebug walked briskly past fountains illuminated with beams of green, red, and white, the colors of the old Hungarian monarchy. He sensed an unfamiliar dampness under his smooth arms, despite the chill in the air; he was thankful that he'd chosen to wear black. Apprehensive as he was about the nature of his mysterious task, he was eager to get the undoubtedly sordid business over with as quickly as possible.

He climbed the broad marble stairs that led to the compound's central building, an Italianate mansion easily twice as large as the grandest home on St. Charles Avenue. Twin twelve-foot-high doors opened soundlessly before he could knock.

"Mr. Richelieu. Welcome. It is a pleasure to see you again after all these years."

The sentiment sounded as sincere as a local politician's promises to fix the potholes. Doodlebug stared up at the long, sallow face of Straussman the butler. He was even haughtier and more austere than his computer-generated image; Doodlebug, an avid fan of the films of the forties, thought Straussman made Erich von Stroheim look like Lou Costello. Nevertheless, he smiled and answered Straussman's stiff bow with a polite curtsy.

"Thank you, Straussman. The years have been good to you."

"You are too kind, sir."

Straussman closed the doors, polished oak eight-inches thick, with little discernible effort. "Please allow me to escort you to the library."

They left the entrance foyer and entered a tall, wide hallway decorated with tapestries large enough to cloak elephants. Doodlebug remembered these tapestries well. Each depicted a victory of King Vlad Tepes over the marauding Turks, who were portrayed as beasts with barely human features. The largest of the tapestries showed Vlad Tepes holding court in front of a panorama of severed Turkish heads impaled on tall wooden spikes.

Just before they reached the library, Straussman paused and turned back toward Doodlebug. "We have been experiencing unsettled times within our household," he said in a low voice, almost a whisper. Doodlebug detected a slight change in his normally imperturbable face, a hint of what might almost pass for concern. "The young masters . . ." His voice trailed off. It was fascinating and unsettling to watch Straussman struggle for words. "I do hope, sir, that you will be able to assist Master Besthoff in bringing certain matters to a satisfactory close. Bringing certain . . . foul parties to the justice they richly deserve."

Then he turned away again, and Doodlebug watched him straighten his neck and torso to their habitual lacquered stiffness before he opened the doors of the library. "Master Besthoff," he said, "if you would kindly forgive the intrusion, I have the pleasure of presenting Mr. Rory Richelieu."

"Thank you, Straussman," a deep, fine-grained voice, tinged slightly with a Rumanian accent, answered. "You may show him in."

Doodlebug hurriedly smoothed the wrinkles from his dress and entered the library. Of all the compound's hundreds of rooms, this was the one that had always fascinated him the most. He was greeted by a seductive perfume of polished teak and aged paper. His mouth fell open as he craned his neck to take in the thousands of volumes, most of them more than a century old. The inhabitants of this compound had millions of empty hours to fill, particularly since they had "advanced beyond the primitive hunting and gathering stage," to use Besthoff's memorable phrase. What better place to spend some of those millions of hours than this cathedral of literature, open all night long?

However, apart from Doodlebug and Straussman, who hovered near the entrance in readiness for additional tasks, the library held only one occupant. Georges Besthoff sat in a high-backed, gilded Queen Anne chair beside a tall Tiffany lamp and a coffee table decorated with the wings and clawed feet of a gryphon. He was as tall as Straussman, but far broader through the chest. Untold centuries in age, he didn't appear any older than his midforties, with only an occasional strand of silver flashing within the midnight blackness of his immaculately groomed hair. His eyes were coals that had been compressed by unnatural gravity into onyx diamonds, glowering with negative light.

Doodlebug frowned slightly as he remembered how Besthoff and the others had built their fortunes in Europe. Among the oldest of that region's vampires, they had gradually seduced many of the neighboring noble families into the blood-sucking fraternity, convincing them to leave one aristocracy for another; then they had taken advantage of the nouveau vampires' junior status to appropriate portions of their holdings. If it hadn't been for the antiroyal revolutions of 1848, Besthoff, Katz, and Krauss would never have left the enriching embrace of their ancestral lands for New Orleans.

Besthoff's smile was well rehearsed, the practiced smile of a diplomat from the age of dynastic empires. "Mr. Richelieu," he said, gesturing for him to sit in the chair on the far side of the gryphon table, "I believe the last time you visited us, that Texan excrescence, Lyndon Johnson, was still in the White House. It has been too long." He looked Doodlebug over with a coolly appraising glance, his eyes lingering on the swellings of his guest's hips and bustline. "I see that you have honed your talents considerably since the last time we met. Were I ignorant of your natural sex, I would be most aroused by your display of lush, young femininity."

Doodlebug felt hot blood rush into his face. It wasn't a sensation he felt often. He'd grown used to being around people who accepted him as a woman, who didn't know differently. Now, in the presence of this man who knew him to be a fellow man, who could take away his independence with the snap of his fingers, Doodlebug experienced for the first time the sense of relative powerlessness that so many women suffered. "Maintaining continual control over my form," he said too quickly, "is a useful exercise in spiritual discipline."

"Yes," Besthoff said, smiling. He interlocked his long fingers, flexing the powerful muscles of his hands. "That must be so, I am sure." He glanced toward Straussman and signaled with a slight tilt of his head that the butler should attend to him. "But I forget my obligations as host. You are famished after your long air journey. All those distressing changes in air pressure. Would you prefer blood or a glass of wine?"

Doodlebug took a moment to consider this. With men such as Besthoff, there were no gifts; accepting even the smallest of boons meant allowing the cords of obligation to be pulled ever tighter. There was good reason he'd air-shipped his coffin and a week's supply of blood to a New Orleans bed-and-breakfast inn where he'd stayed before, rather than accept Besthoff's offer of lodging in the mansion. Truthfully, a long drink of the life-giving ichor would restore his strength and possibly settle his nerves. But he couldn't bury the thought that the less obligated he was to the High Krewe, the better off he'd be.

"Well?" Besthoff said, raising an eyebrow, a hint of amusement in his dark eyes. "What will you have, Mr. Richelieu?"

"A pot of herbal tea would be *lovely,*" Doodlebug said. He glanced up at Straussman's unreadable face. "Could you fix me some chamomile?"

"I will check the pantry, sir," Straussman said.

"Very well," Besthoff said. He frowned and waved Straussman away. "Bring me my usual midevening cocktail." He turned back to his guest.

"How fares your Institute?" he asked, a polite smile reaffixed upon his predatory face.

To Doodlebug's ears, his host's expression of interest was wrapped around a core of cold condescension. It wasn't at all surprising that, after Doodlebug declined his host's offer of blood, Besthoff would focus on the vulnerability that granted him the greatest degree of leverage over his guest. Doodlebug closed his eyes for a second and attempted to picture a perfectly calm sea. "It fares very well, thank you," he said, his eyes open again. "I currently have forty-two students. Twenty-three reside on my campus. The others commute from surrounding towns."

"So the passion for Eastern mysticism has not subsided in your part of the country?"

"Apparently not, no."

"Your students," Besthoff continued, "they still make their monthly 'donations' of blood during their periods of study?"

"Every six weeks, yes. It's part of their cycle of cleansing and purification. All of my students are strict vegetarians. The blood-letting complements their regimens of fasting and ascetic yoga."

"Very clever," Besthoff said, a hint of genuine admiration in his voice. "I always expected that our investment would return interesting dividends. Have any of your students expressed any opinions regarding this regimen of 'blood-letting,' as you call it? Do you think they suspect vampirism might be the motivating factor?"

"California is different from the rest of the country," Doodlebug said, shifting in his seat. He pulled the edges of his dress well below his knees, then chided himself for doing so. "A combination of widespread Wiccanism and Hollywood liberalism means that blood-drinking is not as stigmatized as it would be here. All that aside, my students accept me as what I present myself to be—a spiritual mentor and a fellow learner. I've never overheard any whisperings of vampirism. Such suspicion and distrust are the opposite of all that my students seek to achieve."

"Yes. Of course." Straussman returned with a silver tray. A white china teapot, embossed with twirling roses, emitted a strong aroma of Earl Grey through its spout. *Oh, well,* Doodlebug thought. *Close enough.* Straussman set the tray down on the gryphon table and served Besthoff his cocktail, which, Doodlebug guessed from its scent, was a mixture of sherry and blood.

Besthoff took a sip of his cocktail and eyed Doodlebug evenly over the rim of the expansive goblet. "Would you expand the Institute, if you were able? Do you feel you could attract a larger number of students?"

"It's . . . possible," Doodlebug said, measuring his words carefully. What was Besthoff driving at? "Although I couldn't handle many more students myself. If I allowed more students in, I'd need to train additional instructors. Additional instructors would require expanding my physical plant."

"That could potentially be arranged." Doodlebug felt Besthoff's eyes drilling into his. The tall man set down his goblet and leaned closer. "Our household has been experiencing some disquietude of late. Some of the younger members have begun to . . . chafe within what they feel to be unreasonable restrictions on their liberties. You were once the child protégé of that Duchon person, were you not?"

The mention of Jules's name brought a flood of memories. Only eight months had passed since he'd taught his friend and blood-father the skills he needed to overcome the deadly challenge posed by a group of new, young black vampires.

The distaste in Besthoff's voice when he uttered Jules's name was unmistakable. "Yes," Doodlebug said. "Jules turned me in 1943, during the war. He wanted a sidekick to help him protect New Orleans's munitions plants from Nazi saboteurs."

"But you did not stay with him long after the war was over, did you? You began your spiritual quest, which eventually led you to Tibet. Correct?"

"That's true. But I might have stayed longer with Jules in New Orleans if he hadn't been so uncomfortable with my, ah, proclivities." Doodlebug stared at the crimson-painted nails that adorned his slender fingers, now interlaced tightly on his lap.

"In any case, I expect you have some understanding of the rebellious impulses that often accompany youth. A need to break away from the often sensible lifestyle of one's elders, to establish one's own identity and autonomy."

"That's a common preoccupation of youth in all societies. Even vampiric ones. It's not unhealthy."

"In many cases, perhaps." Besthoff took another sip from his goblet. He let it linger in his mouth before swallowing. "But in the case of my little society, my High Krewe, youthful rebellion and indiscretion have led to outcomes *most* unhealthy." The dark red tip of his tongue brushed his lower lip. "Tragic outcomes. Events which I deeply regret, and which I cannot allow to go unaddressed."

Doodlebug waited for him to continue. He picked up the cup of tea Straussman had poured for him. The liquid burned the roof of his mouth.

"I will speak more of this in a moment," Besthoff said after many long seconds. "The restless energies of youth are difficult to contain, even in the face of tragedy. I may need to find a safe haven for several of our youngsters away from this compound, in a place where they can feel they have broken away from the nest, and so will not be tempted into dangerous pursuits. I believe your Institute would be an ideal place for them to 'find themselves' without endangering themselves."

Doodlebug's face tightened as the reason for his summons to the compound of the High Krewe of Vlad Tepes became clear. The Krewe had never interfered in his running of the Institute before. They'd never had reason to. Until now. But now, from the sound of things, he was expected to take in a bunch of spoiled, aristocratic vampires, most of whom probably had zero interests outside of sex, leisure, and a good meal, and try to guide them on a path toward enlightenment. "You want me to take them on as students? How would I keep them fed? Even with strict rationing, the blood donations provided by my current students would barely sustain me and one other vampire."

"I don't expect you to take them on as *students,*" Besthoff said. "I expect you to take them on as instructors. Each will need to be provided with a complement of students adequate to supply him with a steady diet. The High Krewe will provide financial support for the construction of expanded facilities, advertising to attract additional students, et cetera."

Doodlebug's alabaster skin turned a sicklier shade of white. His dream. The great spiritual project that gave his undead existence meaning. They wanted to pervert it, to take it in their filthy hands and reshape it in their own cruel, selfish image. He'd known, of course, when he'd first acquired the monumental loan from the High Krewe to buy his twenty-five acres of oceanfront property and construct his austere campus, that a quid pro quo was likely. But he'd spent decades avoiding that possibility, pushing it into the dustiest corners of his mind.

"You ask . . . very much of me," he managed to say at last. "This is the reason you demanded I come here? To recruit your youngsters?"

Besthoff smiled tightly. "Not exactly, no. That is more of a long-term goal. I recognize that such arrangements as I have spoken of will take time. You will need to make plans. The more restless youngsters will need to be convinced that a move to Northern California is indeed what they want."

Besthoff stood, rising to his imposing full height of six feet and five inches. "No, Mr. Richelieu, the reason I had you come is far more pressing. Follow me, please. What I am about to show you will make my needs and your responsibility abundantly clear."

He walked to the library's entrance. Doodlebug set his teacup down (caffeine was the last thing he needed at this point, anyway) and followed. Besthoff motioned for Straussman to accompany them. The butler opened a set of tall French doors that led to a courtyard of formal gardens and hedges trimmed as exactingly as a nobleman's mustache.

At the far end of the gardens, beyond the ponderous wings of the main mansion, sat a separate building much more plain and simple than the one Doodlebug had just left. Not that it was not ornate; it reminded Doodlebug of the redbrick Catholic schoolhouse he'd attended before he'd met Jules. They climbed three steps to a broad porch lined with white wooden posts. Straussman removed a large ring of keys from his coat pocket and unlocked the door.

They stepped inside the entrance foyer, and Straussman locked the door behind them. Doodlebug crinkled his elfin nose. The odor he smelled wasn't repulsive, at least not overwhelmingly so. He remembered the odor from years ago, when he'd been a small child and a broken arm had landed him within the crowded wards of Charity Hospital for a week. It was the collective scent of dozens of people who spent their days and nights confined to bed, who bathed infrequently and changed their garments less often than they bathed and who relieved themselves in bed pans.

"You may remember our farm," Besthoff said. "I can't recall whether I granted you a tour the last time you visited."

"I've never been inside here, no," Doodlebug said.

"But you're aware of the economic underpinnings of our compound, of course? Our blood-cows?"

Blood-cows. Doodlebug frowned slightly. It didn't seem right to refer to human beings that way. Not even human beings of the sort who lived here. "So this is where the, uh, mentally handicapped individuals are cared for?"

"Yes." He gestured for Straussman to turn on the lights in the next room. "Please forgive the slight stench. Over the past year, it has become harder and harder to get our young people to fulfill their obligations here. We threaten them with cutting back on their blood rations if they miss shifts. But one can only take such threats so far without it becoming counterproductive. And Straussman and the other household staff are limited in how much time they can take from their primary duties to tidy up here."

They walked into the main room. The building was much deeper than it had looked from the outside, Doodlebug realized. This dormitory contained four rows of thirty beds each; the beds were about eighteen inches apart, and the aisles between rows allowed two people abreast to squeeze through. The only light was provided by three bare hanging bulbs and four video monitors, each mounted on a different wall. The monitors all played the same Woody Woodpecker cartoon. Doodlebug watched the dim primary colors play over the broad, flat faces of the men and women in the beds. They were strapped down; most had plastic tubing protruding from their arms, although whether the machines were injecting liquid nutrients or extracting blood, Doodlebug couldn't tell. Their widely spaced, small eyes followed him as he walked past. A few smiled, revealing mouthfuls of teeth like broken shells on a dirty beach.

"This is only half of the herd," Besthoff said. "In 1882, when we took over their care from the soon-to-be-disbanded Little Sisters of the Blessed Bayou, we started with only twenty-six. Since then, we've bred seven generations. They eat strictly balanced diets, to ensure that their blood is as healthful as possible. They are walked around the grounds every other evening. Due to their high fluid and nutrient intake, they can be blooded every two weeks. Every so often, we are able to train a few of the more high-functioning ones to provide basic sanitary care for their fellows."

"Given the current situation with the young masters," Straussman said solemnly, "perhaps it would be wise to accentuate our training efforts with the more clever of these creatures. If I may say so, I believe such a course of action would be greatly preferable to bringing in outside help."

"That is so obvious as to be barely worth mentioning," Besthoff snapped, irritation coloring his usually imperturbable voice. He clasped his hands behind his slender waist and took a lingering look at the hundred-and-twenty beds and their occupants. Pride and apprehension seemed to battle for control of his sharply handsome features. Pride won.

"How ironic," he said, "that the Vatican, when they shut down one of their faltering nunneries here in the hinterlands, should have provided our High Krewe with the greatest boon we ever received." His smile faded, and he slowly shook his head. His next words were so low that Doodlebug barely heard them. "How they could even consider leaving this behind . . . I cannot understand it."

Doodlebug wasn't sure which *they* Besthoff referred to. He didn't have long to ponder, however, because the grim-faced vampire motioned them forward again. "Come, Mr. Richelieu. This is not what I brought you to see."

They reached the far end of the dormitory. Three doors were set within the blue plastered wall. Besthoff directed Straussman to unlock the far-right door. Doodlebug noticed that the key to this door was on a separate, smaller key ring that Straussman removed from a buttoned pocket inside his coat. Both Straussman and Besthoff ducked their heads upon entering the room. Doodlebug was able to walk through the doorway without ducking, although barely two inches separated his pulled-back hair from the beam above.

The space they entered was completely dark. The air smelled dusty and stale. Doodlebug heard the sound of a light fixture's chain being pulled. A forty-watt bulb dimly illuminated what was originally a storage room, bare brick walls windowless and gloomy. Only now it was being used as a bedroom, or perhaps an infirmary.

Two young women slept within coffins placed on narrow iron beds identical to those in use outside. Or they appeared to sleep. Doodlebug walked closer to one of the women, a pale, pretty brunette whose mouth looked hard, even in slumber. Her breathing was so shallow and so slow that she seemed not to breathe at all. She was covered, from the neck down, with a light linen blanket. Doodlebug noticed that an intravenous-drip machine, the same type that stood next to many of the imbeciles outside, fed a dark red substance through a plastic tube that disappeared beneath the blanket. But that wasn't all that disappeared beneath the blanket. Doodlebug's eyes followed the graceful curves of her torso from her bust to her flat stomach. Below her pelvis, the blanket fell to the floor of the coffin. As if her body suddenly . . . ended.

Doodlebug felt Besthoff's eyes on him. "Go ahead," his host commanded. "Lift the blanket and look. You will not awaken her."

Doodlebug held his breath as he lifted the blanket's lower edge. The woman was dressed in a plain white nightgown. Its unoccupied lower reaches lay flat on the thin layer of earth at the bottom of the coffin, like an airless balloon. She had no legs.

Doodlebug let the blanket fall and stepped back from the coffin. "How—how long has she been like this?"

"Little less than a week," Besthoff said. Doodlebug detected a note of weary sadness in his voice; of mourning and of anger. "Victoria was one of our finest dancers. So graceful; you should have seen her pirouetting through the gardens, making leaps that would shame a gazelle. Watching her dance was one of my most reliable pleasures. Unfortunately, the two dozen of us here within the compound were not audience enough for her. She insisted on seeking thrills and pleasures beyond our walls. And now she will dance no more."

"Do you have any idea what happened to her?"

"She went outside," Besthoff said. "Like so many of the young ones have been doing of late. It is impossible to stop them. The lure of that damnable *city*"—Doodlebug saw his host's face darken like a thundercloud—"is too strong. Straussman took a call last Thursday. The anonymous caller instructed him to enter the woods outside the gates, that there was a 'lost treasure' waiting there. He went outside with two of the other servants. They found her, wrapped in a bed sheet. As you see her now."

"Has she regained consciousness? Spoken to anyone?"

"No. She seems to be in a very deep coma. Extremely deep. Not even my powers of hypnotism—not even the combined powers of myself, Katz, and Krauss—have been up to the task of bringing her out of the mental cavern she has been forced to retreat within."

Doodlebug took a second look at the blood-drip apparatus. "A mutilation of that magnitude"—he shivered, then blushed with embarrassment—". . . she must have lost a tremendous volume of blood."

"You would not have known it, sir," Straussman interjected, "from her condition when we found her. Her wounds were sealed. Completely. The flesh at the bottom of her, ah, pelvis, it was without blemish or scar. As though she had been born . . . legless."

"Show him Alexandra," Besthoff commanded.

Straussman approached the open coffin of the other woman, who was elegantly tall, with long platinum tresses and striking Eurasian features. She made Doodlebug think of a Siberian wolf, white-furred and gorgeously savage. Straussman pulled back her blanket. Unlike the first woman's mutilation, Alexandra's was not hidden by her nightgown. Lacy spaghetti straps rested on pale, beautifully formed shoulders that simply *ended.* The slight protrusions of her shoulder blades sloped in a graceful, unbroken curve into the concavities of her armpits, and then into the swellings of her breasts and the subtle undulations of her rib cage.

"Two nights ago," Besthoff said, "we received a second call. This time, Krauss and I accompanied Straussman outside the walls. Alexandra was left for us farther away from the compound than Victoria had been. The assailant must have suspected that we would line our walls and the surrounding woods with surveillance cameras, as we indeed had done. She was left for us in the Metairie Cemetery, to the north of Metairie Road. We found her next to the crypt of a Confederate captain of artillery."

"She was left the same as Victoria?"

"Yes. Wrapped in a bed sheet, unstained with blood or any sign of violence. Trapped in the deepest of comas."

Straussman carefully rearranged the blanket beneath Alexandra's chin. With the blanket covering her shallowly breathing form, she looked virtually normal; certainly more so than Victoria. Doodlebug was not as surprised by the absence of fleshy derangement where the women's limbs were missing as he imagined Besthoff and company had been. His thirteen years with the monks in Tibet had taught him much about the wonders of vampiric physiognomy, the astounding supernatural plasticity that was not at all limited to the traditional European transformational varieties of bat, wolf, and mist.

"Who knows about this?" Doodlebug asked.

"Straussman and two of the other servants," Besthoff said. "And Katz, Krauss, and myself."

"The police haven't become involved?"

"Of course not," Besthoff snapped. "Who here would have called them?"

"No one, I'm sure," Doodlebug said; Besthoff's fierce gaze had him feeling defensive. "But it's possible that an outsider could've seen you removing Alexandra from Metairie Cemetery and alerted the authorities."

"We were exceptionally discreet."

"I see," Doodlebug said. "So what are your plans for investigating . . ." The question died on his tongue. *He* was their plan. Determining who was behind this violence and, presumably, ensuring that it wasn't repeated—*this* was the reason he'd been summoned from California. The High Krewe couldn't dirty their hands with such matters. More likely, they simply weren't up to the job—they'd spent so many decades living in splendid isolation behind these high walls, they'd lost the ability to deal effectively with the outside world.

He glanced back at Victoria's legless figure. Detective work certainly wasn't his strong suit. But if he could hunt down the culprit, deliver him to justice (Doodlebug did not want to imagine what the High Krewe would consider "justice" under these circumstances), and restore these young women, he might be able to avoid having his Institute overrun by amoral, spoiled refugees. He turned back to Besthoff, who was still waiting for him to finish his earlier question. "I take it that you'd like me to investigate these crimes," Doodlebug said.

"Actually, no."

"No?"

Besthoff smiled slightly. "No. You are too valuable to us. Investigating this villain's crimes is likely to be a hazardous business. There is also the factor of your unfamiliarity with the city. Although you grew up here, you have been mostly absent from New Orleans for the past fifty years. We need someone who knows this filthy, misbegotten city intimately. Someone who has trafficked with the lower classes of both races, who frequents the despicable taverns and brothels, who knows the trash-strewn alleyways because he regularly dines in them. Someone powerful, in his way. But expendable."

"Who?" Doodlebug asked in a small voice. His spirits sank. He already knew the answer.

"We need Duchon. Jules Duchon." Besthoff's iron gaze belied the polite cordiality of his smile. "He has not been heard from in eight months. Our efforts to locate him have failed. Your mission is to bring him here and convince him to work for us."

Doodlebug remembered his last glimpse of his friend—transformed into hundreds of plump white rats, scurrying from the open window of a French Quarter hotel, then disappearing into the crawl spaces beneath Bourbon Street's strip joints and daiquiri bars. Sad as he'd been to lose him, Doodlebug had been incredibly proud of Jules for that splendid act of self-dissolution. "That . . . that's not possible," he said.

"Why not? He is still among the living, isn't he? Relatively speaking? We know through channels that the Negro upstart, Malice X, did not slay him. In fact, the salutary way Duchon handled himself during that sorry affair makes him all the more desirable for our purposes." Doodlebug remained closemouthed. Besthoff rubbed the space between his eyes, as if pondering the reason for Doodlebug's reluctance to speak, then took an intimidating step closer. "Answer me, Mr. Richelieu. Is he alive or is he dead? And don't even consider telling me falsely. Believe me . . . I will know it."

Was Besthoff bluffing? Doodlebug had no doubt that his host could determine the veracity of a mortal's statements quite easily, but peering into the mind of another vampire—? Still, given Besthoff's centuries and his vast experience in utilizing his abilities, such a power might not be beyond him.

"Jules is alive," he said reluctantly. "But not in the way you think."

"Is he still in New Orleans?"

"To the best of my knowledge, yes."

"Then you should have no difficulty in carrying out my directive."

"Mr. Besthoff. Georges. May I call you that?" Doodlebug materialized his most gaminelike smile and made his large, liquid eyes even larger and rounder. "Please let me undertake the investigation. Jules isn't right for this at all. I hate to admit this to people, given the fact that Jules was my blood-father and first mentor, but he isn't terribly, well, *smart.* Good-natured, yes. Smart, no. Whoever has committed these crimes against your clan has shown himself to be both brutal and intelligent. I fear Jules would find himself outmatched. *I,* on the other hand—"

"Our minds are quite *firm* on this matter," Besthoff said harshly. "Why are you shielding Duchon?"

Doodlebug was loath to reveal his friend's secret. But Besthoff wasn't leaving him any alternative. "He is . . . incapacitated. In his present state, he's no good to you at all. I doubt he'd even recognize me."

"Explain."

"He has attained nirvana," Doodlebug said, his words racing. For the second time tonight, blood rushed to his face; with each word, he felt himself closer to betraying his friend's achievement. "He has unshackled himself from his blood-lust. He's found a way to live in this world and enjoy the things he loves without harming another soul."

Besthoff took another step closer. "This means nothing to me," he said darkly. "Leave the spirit talk to your monks and speak plainly."

"He has transformed himself," Doodlebug said, forcing each word from his lips like a hostage being thrown from an airplane, "into approximately two hundred white rats. They are living in the sewer drains and inside the walls of the French Quarter, protected from the sun."

For the first time, Doodlebug saw shock on his host's face, however brief. "That is . . . quite impossible. No vampire on earth could manage such a feat."

"You told me you could separate truth from falsehood. Am I lying?"

The question hung between them for several long seconds. Doodlebug turned his senses inward, trying to determine whether his mind was being probed. Sensitive as he was, he couldn't detect any mental incursion. "No," Besthoff said at last. "I believe you are telling me the truth."

Doodlebug half sighed with relief. "Then you'll permit me to investigate these crimes in Jules's stead?"

"This changes nothing. All transformations can be undone. Even a transformation into two hundred scurrying vermin."

"But what you ask of me—for Varney's sake, *listen* to me, he's found his peace at last—"

"This interview is concluded." Besthoff turned his back on Doodlebug with a dismissive turn of his head. He walked to the door and directed that Straussman open it, then deigned to look back at his guest. "You have four nights to bring a compliant Duchon to me here. Or the High Krewe will foreclose on your Institute."

Few sounds registered for Doodlebug as he followed Besthoff and Straussman through the courtyard and the shadowed halls of the mansion; not the agitated babbling of the imbeciles, not the tinkling of fountains, not the now-ominous hiss of gas lamps. The word *foreclosure* rattled through his mind like a garbage can knocked over by hungry rats, drowning out all other stimuli. Walking out the front gate, he barely heard Besthoff's final words to him: "Four nights, Mr. Richelieu. I suggest you purchase large quantities of cheese."

TWO

Doodlebug could, without risking immodesty, consider himself an expert on many subjects. Rodent behavior was not among them. Loath as he'd been to involve one of his students in his personal business, in this instance he'd had no choice.

Daphne Petruko had never been one of Doodlebug's more promising students. Not that she wasn't devoted to her studies, punctual in her attendance, respectful to her instructor, and kind to the other students, particularly any newcomers. She was all of these things.

So why has she failed to progress? Doodlebug asked himself as he stood next to her, waiting for the cab that would take them to the French Quarter, staring at her stained lime-colored sack dress and lightly clucking his tongue. The answer wasn't complicated. She lacked the confidence needed for spiritual breakthroughs. Her deficit of self-regard prevented her from scaling the walls of everyday illusion that separated the mundane from the essential. Perhaps the failure was as much his as it was hers. He wouldn't be honest if he failed to admit that the more assertive students monopolized much of his face time. Maybe devoting more individualized time to Daphne would be a side benefit of bringing her to New Orleans.

But right now, the most important thing about Daphne Petruko was that she knew rats.

They stood together in front of the bed-and-breakfast inn where they both had cabins, watching for the cab. Doodlebug noticed his young companion shivering in the brisk breeze; he took his wrap off and placed it around her bare shoulders.

"Oh, Miss Richelieu, you shouldn't," she said, trying to hand it back.

"No, dear, you wear it," he said, taking her small, delicate hand between his. Her nails were uneven and dirty, he noticed; chewed, from the look of them. "I can't tell you how much I appreciate your coming on such short notice."

"But . . . but of *course* I'd come," she said in a breathless voice, halfway between a swoon and a whisper. Her face, only a few years beyond the ravages of teen acne, was dominated by a pair of large, light blue eyes, which looked perpetually startled. Her short, mousy brown hair looked as though it had been styled with a weed whacker. "You sent me airfare, didn't you? I was so, well, so *happy* that I actually know stuff that can help *you.* Imagine that! And I've never been in New Orleans before." She pronounced it "OrlEEEns," which grated on Doodlebug almost as severely as if she'd recited a Hail Mary.

Their taxi, an ancient Ford Country Squire station wagon, wallowed onto the oak-shaded gravel driveway and squealed to a stop. Doodlebug opened the rear door for Daphne, then slid in after her. Even though he'd passed himself off as a woman for the majority of his seventy-plus years, he'd never managed to slough off his childhood training of chivalry toward the fairer sex.

Doodlebug gave instructions to the driver, a Jamaican man with a glistening bald head. He realized, wistfully, that every time he would climb into a taxi in New Orleans, he'd always expect to see Jules in the driver's seat. The cab rumbled off along Bayou Road, dimly lit by nouveau-antique gas lamps, then turned east on Esplanade Avenue and headed for the French Quarter.

Doodlebug opened his purse and touched up his makeup. He really didn't need to look beautiful to go rat hunting, but one could never look too fresh. "Daphne, dear, we've never had much time to talk about your professional life. Working on movies must be so fascinating. Tell me again which films you've worked on?"

Daphne turned away from the window, where she'd been watching antebellum Creole mansions pass by, some restored, some crumbling; her smudged fingerprints marked the window like a child's finger painting. "My movies? The first one I ever worked on was *You Dirty Rat.* That was back in high school, six years ago. I'd been raising rats and mice and selling them, and I got friendly with a rodent wrangler, Mr. Busby, and he took me on as his assistant. I worked on a bunch of pictures with Mr. Busby before he passed away. *Pied Piper Versus Rumpelstiltskin;* that was fun, even if the computer-animated rats looked nothing like the real rats we used. Let's see . . . there was *Dr. Doolittle IV: When Animals Attack.* And *SQUEAK!*"

"*SQUEAK!?* I never heard of that one."

"Hardly anybody has. It was direct-to-video. Good story. Terrorists breed superrats to spread plague in New York City. Pretty low budget. We had to use downtown San Pedro to stand in for Manhattan. I got to play a corpse."

Doodlebug took a long look at her. He imagined her lying on an evacuated street, her face smudged with makeup rather than dirt, trying not to breathe. Then he thought about the two women lying in their coffins in the storage room on Bamboo Road. He hoped Daphne wouldn't be playing a corpse again for a very long time.

"So it sounds like you've had plenty of experience working with big groups of rats," Doodlebug said. "You know how to round them up and safely catch them?"

She nodded her head eagerly. "With the right equipment, sure! You said you'll take me to a supply house and let me pick out whatever I need?"

"Of course."

Among his students, Daphne had been famous for her naïveté. Doodlebug recalled the time he'd announced that a guest lecturer would be presenting a talk on "The Cultural Implications of Euthanasia." The next evening, not wanting to be ill-prepared, Daphne had appeared with a stack of children's *manga* books. Loath as he was to take advantage of people's weaknesses, Doodlebug couldn't help but think this quality of Daphne's would be essential to his plans for the next few evenings.

"So this college friend of yours," Daphne asked, "he's been doing a study of rat colonies in the French Quarter?"

"That's right. Eighteen months ago, he released ten breeding pairs into the Quarter. All tagged with tiny radio transmitters under their skin. Unusual rats, specially bred. Pure white and quite large."

"Roof rats or Norway rats?"

"Which ones are bigger?"

"Norway rats."

"Norway rats, then. Anyway, he's been utilizing the radio transmitters to track and map their movements. Now his study protocol dictates that he round up their colonies, to determine how quickly they've been able to reproduce in the unique environment of the Quarter. However, at the worst time possible, a family crisis erupted. In New Zealand. The poor man, knowing my connection with you, asked if we could round up his rats and safeguard them until he returns."

Daphne's eyes grew large, and her mouth (whose chapped lips cried out for even a touch of lipstick) puckered into a worried frown. "He won't be experimenting on them when he gets back, will he? Sticking electrodes in them and cutting them up when he's done with them?"

"Oh no no no," Doodlebug said, grasping her hand again. "Nothing like that. He just wants to count them and see how they've been getting along. After he's done, he'll, uh, he'll be sending them to a special rat preserve in the bayou country. A kind of rat retirement home."

He chewed his lip while waiting for her to respond. Aside from her familiarity with rats, the other essential quality of Daphne's in this matter was her trusting nature, particularly when paternal (or in his case, maternal) figures were involved. He hated to use the term *gullible* . . . Doodlebug sighed. Between the series of lies he was telling Daphne and his planned abrogation of Jules's nirvana state, he'd be sweeping up his own bad karma for years to come.

"All right," she said at last. "Just so long as he doesn't plan to hurt any of them. Are the rats spread out all over the French Quarter?"

Doodlebug took a deep breath and smiled. "To the best of my knowledge, no. These rats are exceedingly social, but apparently they prefer to stick with their own kind. I'm told all their colonies should be fairly close together. Sort of like a New Orleans extended family, with uncles and aunties and cousins all living on the same block."

"That sounds so *sweet,*" Daphne said dreamily.

The cab turned onto North Rampart Street. Doodlebug was interested to see that the entertainment corridor that he remembered from his younger days, badly faded since, was showing signs of life again; crowds of young people loitered on the sidewalks in front of Donna's Bar and Grill and the Funky Butt jazz club. They passed the entrance to Louis Armstrong Park, a three-story white arch that spelled out *Armstrong* in golden bulbs, beaux arts style.

Daphne turned to him excitedly. "Is that where Louie Armstrong lives?"

Doodlebug smiled. *Yes, right about now he's smoking cigars by the fountain with Buddy Bolden and Jelly Roll Morton.* "No, dear. Louie lives with us only in spirit nowadays."

The cab turned left at Conti Street, heading into the western fringes of the French Quarter. It rolled past two Creole cottages in need of tender loving care, their twin dormer windows, peeking out from behind sagging green wooden shutters, staring forlornly from steep black-shingled roofs. Doodlebug wondered what the cottages would look like in the daytime, illuminated by a bright sun rather than a light-miserly moon. He hadn't walked through the Quarter in the daytime since he was twelve years old, about sixty years ago. Thanks to Jules, Doodlebug would have the body of a lad of twelve forever. It wasn't something he begrudged his friend. However, it had been much, much more pleasant spending the past half century as a woman than it would've as a twelve-year-old boy.

The taxi turned upriver onto Dauphine Street, and half a block up from the Château LeMoyne Hotel, Doodlebug spotted the car he was looking for—Jules's old Cadillac taxicab, which he'd left a note on the night before. "Stop here, please," he told the driver. "We'll get out here."

Doodlebug settled up with the driver, leaving him a tip that brought a smile to the man's otherwise stony face (having been regaled with years of Jules's bitter complaints about tightwad fares, Doodlebug always left a sizable tip whenever he traveled by taxi). The intersection of Dauphine and Bienville still retained some of the character of the French Quarter Doodlebug remembered from his childhood, decades before most of the Quarter metamorphosed into a tarted-up tourism gold mine. It was a picturesque dump. A gray granite-block building with padlocked, peeling green shutters dominated the corner, its sign so faded that Doodlebug couldn't tell what kind of business it was, or whether it was even still in business at all. The boarded-up doors and windows of its crumbling Edwardian neighbors offered no such uncertainty.

The big white Cadillac was parked in front of what used to be a shoe-repair store, the kind of blue-collar business that once predominated in the neighborhood. The note he'd left on its windshield last night was gone. So was the twenty-dollar bill he'd left in an envelope.

Daphne craned her neck looking at the upper stories of the boarded-up buildings, her expression a mix of fascination and foreboding. "Is this where the rats live?" she asked.

"I don't know," Doodlebug admitted. "But I think the driver of this Cadillac might be able to help us find them. Last night I left a note on the car, asking for its current owner to meet me here tonight at eleven-thirty. Which is right about now."

Eight months ago, in wolf form, Doodlebug had followed Jules from the Warehouse District to this very intersection and had watched him give away his car. That occurred little more than two hours after Doodlebug had led a pack of Jules's wolf-dog "children" on a calvary charge into the underground lair of black vampire Malice X. Doodlebug had arrived just in time to prevent his friend's death by stake, giving Jules extra seconds to turn the tide and conclusively defeat his nemesis. Jules had thought himself alone when he'd marched into Malice's lair. Even though Doodlebug had wanted Jules to have an opportunity to triumph on his own, he'd been unable to abandon his blood-father completely to the Fates.

And now, in a turnabout that made Doodlebug quietly ashamed, he was forced to ask his old friend to return the favor.

A tall young man, dressed in black pants and a stained white button-down shirt, carrying a wadded-up apron in his fist, crossed the street. He approached Doodlebug and Daphne warily, as though he were a john caught between desire for sex and suspicion the two women staring at him might really be vice-squad decoys. He stopped ten feet away and stuck his hairy chin out. "One of you Debbie Richelieu?" he said.

"That would be me," Doodlebug said, stepping toward him as unthreateningly as possible. "Thank you for agreeing to talk with me."

"Who said anything about talking with you?" He sneered and puffed himself up like a blowfish, crossing his arms in a defiant pose copied from a hundred rock videos. "Show me those five Jacksons you mentioned in the note, and I'll maybe think about it. Maybe."

Doodlebug opened his petite leather purse, removed five twenty-dollar bills, and spread the bills on the Cadillac's trunk. "I'm looking for information concerning a friend. This used to be his car. I have reason to believe he gave it to you, and I'd like to find out why."

The young man's arrogant facade melted like an outdoor ice sculpture in August. "Shit . . . I *knew* that dude was trouble. I just *knew* it!" He stared at the bills on the trunk, then stared at Doodlebug with a smile that strained to be conciliatory. "Look. I don't want any problems. Is the car hot? Are you guys cops, or what? The big fat dude, I swear, I just met him one time, and that was, like, eight or nine months ago—"

"Miss Richelieu," Daphne piped up from the far end of the Cadillac, "I thought you were going to ask him about the rats."

Doodlebug turned to her. "First things first," he said. When he turned back to the young man, Doodlebug saw him staring at Daphne with an expression equally puzzled and surprised. "You aren't in any trouble," Doodlebug reassured him. "We're just seeking information. My friend's name was Jules Duchon—"

But the young man wasn't paying any attention to him. "That's so weird. What she just said, that's so *incredibly* weird," he muttered, staring at Daphne. "See, when the fat dude gave me the car, the only thing he asked in return was that I leave open the restaurant Dumpster every night. Didn't make any sense to me, but I figured, 'What the hey—free Cadillac, right?' But it bugged me, y'know—why he'd ask me to do something so screwy. So one night, out of curiosity, after the kitchen closed, I hung out by the back door and watched the alleyway. And then *they* started pouring in."

"Who?" Doodlebug and Daphne asked in unison.

"Rats. Like *millions* of them. I almost freakin' lost it that first time—it was like a scene outta some whacked-out midnight movie—"

"SQUEAK!?" Daphne asked excitedly.

"What? You mean the one with the terrorist superrats in New York City?"

Daphne clapped her hands together with genuine delight. "*Yes!* I played a corpse!"

"No shit?" The young man looked impressed. "That movie was *boss.*" He turned back to Doodlebug. "Look, you wanna see them? I opened up the Dumpster maybe five minutes before walking over here. Some of them doobers are probably still chowin' down."

"Definitely," Doodlebug said, a confident smile spreading on his face. "We'd like very much to see them."

The young man eyed the money sitting on the Cadillac's trunk hungrily. "You, uh, you aren't gonna just leave those Jacksons lying there, are you? This is a rough neighborhood. I'd be happy to, y'know, look after them for you . . ."

Doodlebug handed him forty dollars and placed the remaining sixty back in his purse. "Keep cooperating and you'll get the other three," he said. "You can start by telling me your name."

"Hank," he said. "Hank Octavio." He turned to Daphne, smiled politely, and tipped an imaginary hat. Daphne smiled back for half a second, then looked away, popped a finger in her mouth and began chewing.

Hank led them a half block east along Bienville to Arnaud's Restaurant. The restaurant, a motley collection of well-preserved two- and three-story nineteenth-century buildings, took up three-quarters of a block just off bustling Bourbon Street. The owners of the restaurant certainly liked bright colors, Doodlebug mused; the cottage portion was a warm peach with green trim, and the adjoining buildings were yellow, tan, and a striking mauve stucco. The faceted crystal windows framing the now-darkened entrance looked like freeze-dried snowflakes.

Hank furtively looked back over his shoulder at Daphne, trailing fifteen feet behind them. "So what's the story here?" he asked. "That girl—is the big fat dude her father or something? Is that why you're lookin' for him?"

"Oh no, nothing like that," Doodlebug said. Jules and Daphne didn't look the slightest bit alike, aside from a shared lax standard of hygiene. "What made you think that?"

"Oh, I dunno . . ." Hank sneaked another glance behind him. "She just seems so, well, so sweet or something. Like she's kind of lost and, y'know, lookin' for a parent maybe. I can't really imagine her being tangled up in something nasty, like a drug deal gone bad or people getting chopped up into little bits."

Doodlebug stopped walking. " 'People getting chopped up?' What put that into your head?"

Hank snickered nervously. "Just a figure of speech, y'know? Don't worry—the only things I see gettin' chopped up around here are crawfish, shrimps, and alligators."

Maybe the busboy had an active imagination, Doodlebug thought. Or maybe he knew more than he was letting on? Doodlebug filed the notion away for later use. One more bit of information to hand off to Jules. Assuming he could put Jules back together. Assuming a reconstituted Jules would be willing to work for the High Krewe at all.

Hank led them to a long, narrow alleyway, partially roofed by the overhangs of the neighboring buildings. The alley's major tenant was a grime-encrusted, wheeled Dumpster.

Doodlebug waited for Daphne to catch up, and they walked into the alleyway together. The Dumpster's lid was open. Doodlebug heard a cacophony of scurryings and squeaks from within; some of the squeaks sounded almost orgasmic. He was almost positive he heard a series of tiny but raucous belches. They peered over the Dumpster's rim. "Oh . . . my God," Daphne said breathlessly. "They're . . . they're *magnificent.*"

Magnificent was not the first word that came to Doodlebug's mind. Each of the rats looked as though it had swallowed another rat whole.

They were uncountable, lying atop one another like happy winos; others had burrowed partway into any of a dozen garbage sacks, their tails twitching deliriously. His old friend had truly found a way around his longtime dependence on blood and his accompanying inability to tolerate solid foods. How Jules had pined for the jambalaya and muffalettas and andouille-laden red beans of his youth! Now, night after night, he could stuff nearly two hundred separate stomachs with the finest discards New Orleans had to offer—and *stuff* he certainly did.

Hank walked up behind them and looked inside. "That's not all of them, not hardly," he said. "These're the diehards. The ones that didn't overeat have already crawled back into the woodwork."

"I've never seen rats so *huge,*" Daphne said excitedly. "My hand-fed Norway rats, bred to be big—they didn't come anywhere close to these. Look! Even their little claws are fat! Like itty-bitty sausages! Aren't they simply precious?"

"Just darling," Doodlebug mumbled.

"We could get a good start on rounding them up right now," Daphne said. "I'll close up the Dumpster, and in the morning we could buy some equipment and come back. I'll bet I could bag at least fifty of them tomorrow morning."

"That would *not* be a good idea," Doodlebug said quickly. Images of dozens of piles of powdered rat danced before his eyes.

"Why not?"

"All rats are nocturnal creatures. These rats, particularly so. My friend explained it to me. If we force them to experience daylight, we will do them irreparable harm."

Daphne thought about this for a moment. "Okay . . . it still seems a shame to pass up such a good opportunity." She stared longingly at the curled-up rats, many with their eyes barely open, some still weakly nuzzling morsels of food. "If we caught some tonight, would you have a safe place to put them?"

"Yes. I've rented an old veterinary clinic here in the Quarter. It's out of business, but it still has an impressive supply of cages."

Daphne's face lit up. "Great! Is there any place I could grab some gloves and canvas sacks, and maybe a cheap pair of jeans?"

♠

Following a quick drive to a GoodiesMart located in the suburbs on the far side of the Mississippi River bridge, they returned to the alleyway.

"I can't believe it," Hank said, shaking his head, a slightly dismayed grin on his face. "I can't believe you're thinking about climbing into that Dumpster with fifty or sixty rats."

"I'm not thinking about it," Daphne said, smiling brightly. "I'm *doing* it. With your help, of course." She reached her skinny arms out to Hank. The prospect of interacting with her beloved rats had transformed her, Doodlebug noticed. Now she brimmed with confidence and eagerness. "How about a hand up?" He frowned and stood his ground. "Oh, come on," she said. "I've been doing this kind of stuff since I was six years old."

"Climbing into Dumpsters?"

"Not Dumpsters, no. But I've climbed out onto tiny little spaces on movie sets, roofs and eaves, and tree branches, to rescue actor rats that wouldn't come down. I started feeding rats with baby bottles when I was barely off the bottle myself. I've slept with rats when they were sick—"

"All right, enough already!" Hank said. He walked over to her, laced his hands tightly together, and held them at knee height like a stirrup. "I hope you've got some place where you can hose the stink off you. Just be careful, okay?"

"When you work with animals," she said, hopping onto his grip, "you learn that 'stink' is a very relative concept. And thank you for the lift." She grabbed the rim of the Dumpster and scrambled over the edge. Doodlebug saw that she took great care not to step on any diners; she hung on to the edge and slowly lowered herself, successfully avoiding crushing any tails or breaking tiny bones.

Doodlebug picked up a sack, readying himself to receive the first rodent. *A journey of a thousand miles begins with one rat,* he told himself.

Daphne cooed inside the Dumpster like a nanny in a nursery of sleeping angels. "Here comes the first little darling," she said, handing him a hairy white football that he placed in the sack as gently as he could. As his sack began filling up with fat, drowsy rats, he thanked the blood saints for his unnatural strength . . . even a portion of Jules was a lot to handle.

♠

They returned early the next evening with fifteen Luv-'Em rotating traps, large wire-mesh boxes with two rotating entrances that allowed small animals to enter but not exit. Daphne directed that they deploy the traps several hours before the rats' usual dinner hour, so the suspicious rodents would have a chance to get used to the traps' presence in the alleyway. An hour before Arnaud's closed for the night, Doodlebug shelled out for plates of shrimp Creole, oysters suzette, filet mignon au poivre (which translated to expensive steak swimming in French brandy cream sauce), and several large side servings of smothered okra. He and Daphne baited the traps with these savory, five-star delicacies. And then they waited.

Eleven-fifteen came and went. Hardly any rats entered the alleyway. Doodlebug, standing behind the kitchen's screen door with the others, saw a pair of them creeping along the top of the Dumpster, sniffing at the edges of its closed lid, but then they disappeared. "They aren't taking the bait," he said forlornly. It was hard for him to believe that Jules, in any form, could pass up such fresh, rich food.

"I think we changed their environment too much, too fast," Daphne whispered. "It'll take them a while to get used to those traps. Maybe if we leave them there a full day—"

"But we're running out of time," Doodlebug said, thinking uneasily about Besthoff's deadline. He was supposed to present Jules to Besthoff, ready to cooperate, by tomorrow night.

They needed something that would override the rodents' natural caution, something Jules loved but hadn't been getting . . .

He turned to Hank. "Would it be possible to brew up some pots of chicory coffee?"

"I guess so. Why?"

"I happen to know that these rats are extremely fond of it." He noticed Daphne's quizzical stare. "Their, uh, breeder raised the original cohort with coffee as part of their diet. Part of the experimental protocol."

Hank brewed three pots of coffee, and they placed pans of the steaming, aromatic brown liquid inside the cages. Then Hank performed a pantomime of his nightly routine, clanging the Dumpster's lid, although tonight he kept the lid shut.

Tentatively at first, the rats began emerging. Their noses probed the air, seeking the source of the tantalizing, if dimly remembered, aroma. A half dozen surrounded the trap farthest from the kitchen doors and, their snouts through the wire mesh, futilely tried to insert their tongues into the pan of coffee. Then one rat crept through the trap's doorway. He paused, as if astounded at his audacity and good fortune; then he shuttled rapidly between the coffee pan and the plate of shrimp Creole and okra, his tongue working more rapidly than the eye could follow. The others, violently agitated at seeing their brother feasting alone, quickly figured out the doorway and joined in. Very soon, all fifteen traps began filling up with hungry rats.

Ten minutes later, Doodlebug and Daphne emerged from their hiding place to retrieve the cages, now stuffed so full of rats that each seemed to hold only one amorphous animal with multiple tails and dozens of twitching legs. Doodlebug knelt down by one of the cages and tried to soothe several of the rodents who seemed especially perturbed at their squished confinement; he wondered whether any of these fragments of his friend retained some memory of him.

Above them, something metal rubbed against brick. They looked up. Daphne pointed at an impressive white rat clinging to a sagging, rusted-out rain gutter above their heads. Oblivious to the fact that its weight could cause the gutter to collapse at any second, the rat stood defiantly on its hind legs and stared down at them with what seemed like a nascent, wary intelligence.

"Look at *that* one," Daphne said. "Gorgeous, isn't he? A leader among rats, I'd bet. I'd also bet he won't be an easy one to catch."

♠

They changed tactics the next night, neither Daphne nor Doodlebug being comfortable with the seemingly painful overcrowding the captured rats had temporarily endured in the Luv-'Em traps. They resolved to catch any remaining rats in the same fashion they had their first night together, but with adjustments to make the process more efficient. Daphne adulterated the evening's food garbage with small quantities of a mild animal sedative. Doodlebug arranged for a waste-management firm to truck the Dumpster to his rented veterinary clinic, then return it to Arnaud's in the morning.

Once the night's catch was removed from the Dumpster and deposited in cages at the clinic (whose windows had been carefully sealed against the sun), Doodlebug and Daphne weighed each of their 186 reluctant guests. The rodents' combined body mass added up to 503 pounds, at an average weight of 2.7 pounds apiece. Doodlebug tried to recall how much Jules had weighed during their most recent encounter. The figure "450 lousy, knee-grindin' pounds" stuck out in his memory, which would mean that the rats' combined mass could account for all of Jules, at least Jules as he had been eight months ago. What was impossible for Doodlebug to account for, however, was just how much weight the rats had gained during those intervening eight months. He and Daphne had waited an hour after the last rat crept into the Dumpster before shutting the lid, searching the crawl spaces beneath the adjoining buildings for any laggards. There was a reasonable chance that they'd captured all the Jules rats over the past three nights. And if they'd missed one or two . . . ? It might not turn out too badly; Jules could certainly live bereft of a few square inches of belly fat. Living without his heart, on the other hand . . .

Doodlebug forced the thought from his mind. He'd cross that rickety bridge when and *if* he'd come to it. In the meantime, he had more immediately pressing issues to attend to. Such as ditching Daphne for the rest of the night, and then determining the best way to reconstitute Jules (if only it were as simple as reconstituting powdered milk!).

He washed his hands in a huge aluminum sink, then turned to his companion. "Daphne, dear, how about we call it a night?"

She wiped her face with a paper towel. Retrieving, then weighing, 186 rats had been grueling work. "But we haven't fed the ones we caught the last two nights yet—"

"You let me worry about that," Doodlebug said. "I'll handle it. You know I stay up all night. You, on the other hand, haven't quite adjusted to our nocturnal schedule—"

"I'm *fine,*" she insisted.

He took a hundred dollars out of his purse and handed it to her. "Call yourself a cab and go back to the bed-and-breakfast. Wash up and go to bed. Guru's orders. After you get up, go out and have a big, sinful brunch and see the town. There's more to New Orleans than a garbage alley next to Arnaud's, after all."

She stared at the hundred dollars in her hand, then reluctantly put it in her pocket. "Well . . . okay. But you call me at the bed-and-breakfast if you end up needing help, all right?"

After he put her in a taxi, Doodlebug returned to the clinic's animal-storage room. He stared at the dozens of cages, lined with newspapers and soil, each holding five to ten rodents. Staring at them all, he realized, with a sinking heart, that despite his thirteen years of learning the intricacies of vampire lore with the vampire monks of Tibet, he had no idea whether his plans for reintegrating Jules would work.

He turned his gaze to the large wire-mesh cage in the center of the room. It was six feet square, large enough to walk in; Doodlebug assumed it had been used for big dogs, or possibly some large, exotic pets (tapirs? orangutans?—he put nothing past the denizens of the French

Quarter). There was a slim possibility that if he put all the rats in the big cage together, their close physical proximity would cause a spontaneous reversion to their original form.

He frowned. The rats had been bunching up together in the Dumpster every night for eight months, and Jules hadn't reappeared. Still, it was worth a try. He took some of the take-out bags of shrimp Creole, alligator sausage, and oysters Bienville he'd brought from Arnaud's and spread the food out in a trio of pans at the center of the cage. Then he began emptying the dozens of smaller cages into the big cage.

Nothing. Zip. *Nada.* The rats crawled over one another to get at the food, certainly comfortable and familiar enough with one another to be parts of the same body; but they stubbornly remained 186 separate squealing rodents.

If only he had some way to remind them who they once were. A photograph of Maureen, Jules's lost love, would be ideal . . . but unless she'd had one taken before she'd become a vampiress, no such photograph could exist. But he had another, more promising idea. Maureen's house wasn't far; just at the other end of the Quarter. He was fairly certain that the house had been sitting empty and unused for the past eight months, ever since Maureen had been murdered. Her belongings should still be there. And Jules's belongings, too, since he'd briefly lived with her during the weeks before his dissolution into 186 rats. Doodlebug could bring some of her clothes and Jules's clothes to the clinic and hang them inside the cage. With any luck, some hints of Maureen's perfume might still cling to one of her nightgowns or stripper costumes. A rat's nose was its most potent sensory organ; if anything could jolt the rodents into remembering the man they'd been, it would be a whiff of Maureen's scent.

He took his cell phone out of his purse. No dial tone; just a pathetically weak beep. Its battery had gone dead, and he'd left the charger at the bed-and-breakfast. The phone hanging on the wall was even more dead. Well, he'd just have to flag down a cab on the street.

He locked the clinic's front door and stepped out onto Esplanade Avenue. A light fog swirled around the cracked masonry of the Creole mansions that lined the avenue. An oak-studded neutral ground separated Esplanade's lanes and divided the French Quarter from Faubourg Marigny, the city's earliest suburb. White smoke spewed from the exhaust chimneys of the Port of Call Restaurant, still serving up giant burgers to nighthawks at almost two o'clock in the morning. The smoke mingled with the fog and made the air around Doodlebug smell like charbroiled grease.

A big Lincoln painted purple, green, and gold pierced the fog. The light on its roof glowed a dull yellow. Doodlebug stepped between two parked cars and waved imploringly. To his satisfaction, the cab immediately slowed and pulled over to the curb. Appearing to be an attractive young woman sometimes came in handy.

Doodlebug got in. "I need to go to Bienville and Burgundy, please," he said. "And would it be possible for you to wait a few minutes there while I gather some things?"

The driver turned around. "Sho' thing, miss." He was a light-skinned black man, middle-aged, moderately portly, with a lazy eye. He looked vaguely familiar. That bloodshot lazy eye was hard to forget.

The cabby started to put his transmission into drive, but then he shifted it into park again and turned back around. "Say, don't I know you from somewheres . . . ?" His face suddenly became animated, and even the lazy eye popped into alignment. "Sho' nuff I do! You're Miss Doodlebug, ain't cha? Jules's friend?"

It was a shock to be recognized. "Y-yes, I am," Doodlebug stammered. He remembered the man now. Jules's fellow taxicab driver, one of his few human friends. "I'm so sorry, but I can't remember your name—"

"Erato." The man smiled, and Doodlebug realized he was handsome, in an offbeat way. "We met almost a year back, last summer, when Jules was havin' lady troubles of some kind, and he hid in that big black box for days on end. You came to the Trolley Stop to find a buddy of his to git him outta there."

"Of course. I remember it all now." Jules had gone into a three-night funk, confining himself to his coffin, after he'd learned from Maureen's own lips that she'd been the one responsible for turning Malice X into a vampire. "Thank you for what you did. Your talking to him got Jules back on his feet."

"What else're buddies for, huh?" His face turned somber. "Look, I'm so glad I'm meetin' up with you. Maybe you don't know this, but Jules brought me the ashes. Maureen's ashes. He wanted me to keep 'em, like he expected to die or somethin'. But he wouldn't tell me nothin', *nothin'* about what was goin' down with him, and me and him been knowin' each other fifteen years. These last eight months, it's like he done vanished off the face of the earth. Ain't nobody heard from him. Ain't been nothin' in the papers about him. Do *you* know what happened?"

Doodlebug hated to lie to this man. Jules wasn't always an easy person to be friends with, and Erato had clearly stuck with him for, in human terms, a very long time. But it was equally clear that Jules had never confided to Erato about his blood-sucking ways, and Doodlebug was constrained by the unspoken rule he shared with his fraternity—to mortals, whenever possible, vampires must remain mere urban legends. "I wish I knew myself, Erato," he said. "That's the main reason I'm back in New Orleans. To try to find out what happened to Jules."

Erato headed back toward North Rampart Street. At the intersection, he turned uptown, ignoring the "No Left Turn—Buses Only" sign. Doodlebug realized he was repeating the same route he'd taken three nights earlier; Maureen's house wasn't far at all from Arnaud's. He wondered whether, when Jules made his arrangement with Hank to feed the rats each night, he'd picked Arnaud's because of its proximity to his dead lover's home.

When they turned onto Bienville, Erato pointed and said, "That's Maureen's house, ain't it?"

Doodlebug stared at the two-story-tall mustard-colored building. Several tiles were missing from its mansard roof, and vandals had spray-painted indecipherable graffiti on all four of its dark green shutters. But the shutters were still solidly in place, as was the massive front door. "Yes. That's where I'm going."

"You inherit the property or somethin'?"

"No. But I'm a caretaker of sorts. At least until Jules shows up."

In the rearview mirror, Doodlebug saw Erato's eyebrows suddenly rise. "So you think he will?"

"I have every hope."

Doodlebug got out of the cab, assuring Erato that he'd only be a few minutes inside the house. Maureen had always kept a spare key in a box beneath the three steps leading to her front stoop. The front lock was balky, but no real trouble for someone with Doodlebug's strength. The air inside was stale and musty. He felt along the wall for a light switch, found one, and clicked it on. Nothing happened. Of course; the Energy bill hadn't been paid in at least seven months. He hadn't thought to bring a flashlight with him. Well, he'd just have to resort to other methods of getting around in the dark.

He focused all his attention on his eyes. Transfiguring only part of his body was actually more difficult than a total transformation; it called for a greater degree of purposeful concentration, both initially and to maintain the change. But this particular trick was a favorite of the monks during the nineteen-hour nights of their Tibetan winters, so Doodlebug had learned it well. He thought cat thoughts, but limited those thoughts to the visual . . . new and fascinating wavelengths; shimmering waves of heat absorbed and released by walls and furniture, outlining them in violet fuzz . . . And although he couldn't look at himself in a mirror, Doodlebug knew that he now had cat's eyes.

Seeing Maureen's parlor and living room brought on a wave of sudden sadness. He'd spent many happy hours here as a young vampire with Jules and Maureen. After Jules had divided himself and disappeared into the Quarter's crawl spaces, Doodlebug had come here, looking for answers. When he viewed the videotape that had recorded Maureen's final, agonized seconds, he knew he'd discovered the reason Jules had abandoned his identity and memories.

He climbed the stairs to Maureen's bedroom. He went to her closet and pulled down a billowy nightdress (large enough for four of him to wear, although he never would've told Maureen that) and one of her stripper costumes, an hourglass-shaped affair with green silk fish scales, probably a mermaid outfit. In a hall closet, he found some of Jules's clothes.

Just before leaving the house, he remembered to return his eyes to normal; he didn't want to shock Erato. He put the door key in his purse, rather than back in its box beneath the steps. Then he pulled the bundle of clothing with him into the backseat of the Lincoln. "How'd you get around in there?" Erato asked. "I didn't see no lights go on."

"There was a flashlight inside," Doodlebug lied.

"What're all them clothes for?"

"Maureen would've wanted her things donated to a good cause. I'll be donating these to, uh, People for the Ethical Treatment of Animals."

"Huh. Two-thirty in the A.M. is a weird-ass time to be makin' a donation. But then, I guess you and Jules always been night people, huh? Not me. If I wasn't gettin' ready to send a kid to college, I'd be home in my bed right now, sawin' logs."

He dropped Doodlebug off in front of the veterinary clinic. Doodlebug opened his purse and pulled out a ten and a five, but Erato refused it. Instead, he handed Doodlebug his card. "You wanna pay me for this ride? When you find out somethin' about Jules, you call that number there. That's my cell phone. That'll be payment enough."

"Thank you," Doodlebug said. "I'm glad Jules has a friend like you."

"And you gimme a call if I can help in any way, understand? A ride, help with the cops—lots of 'em drink coffee with me at the Trolley Stop, so I knows 'em—*anything,* okay?"

"I will," Doodlebug said, his voice muffled by the pile of clothing sprouting from his slender arms.

Erato pulled away, turning left on Bourbon Street and disappearing into Faubourg Marigny. Standing alone on an empty, fog-shrouded Esplanade Avenue, Doodlebug felt a sudden surge of desire to see his friend restored to his old self again. Not only so the threat Besthoff had hung above his head could be averted. But also so he could talk with his blood-father again, maybe share a cup of coffee at an all-night coffee stand.

Back inside the clinic, he hung the clothes on the wire-mesh walls of the big cage. If he were successful, what would he tell Daphne? He supposed he could say he accidentally left the door to the cage open, and the rats escaped; but then how would he explain why he placed them all in the big cage? Oh, he'd think of something . . .

Doodlebug held his breath as more and more of the rats scurried to the side of the cage where Maureen's dresses hung. They sniffed the fabric, tails a-twitter. They climbed over one another, their eagerness to reach the dresses so electric that Doodlebug felt his hair begin to frizz. Any second now, he prayed, he'd see the gray smoke spill from their bodies, witness the rats begin to devolve into proto-matter before recombining into Jules . . .

Any second now . . .

Any second—

Nothing.

Maybe the rats' memories of Maureen were too diffuse, too tenuous. Or maybe yearning and nostalgia weren't strong enough emotions to trigger the change. Perhaps a more visceral, primitive emotion was needed.

Doodlebug stripped off his jeans, blouse, pumps, bra, and panties. He placed his rings and earrings on a table. Then he unbolted the cage and stepped inside. About twenty of the rats were distracted enough by his entrance to pull their noses away from Maureen's clothing and come sniff around his feet (which were gorgeously pedicured, but, given the night's activities, Doodlebug wouldn't be shocked if the rats might detect a wee bit of interesting odor). Staring up, the rats would see a fashionably slender but curvy young woman, blessed with flawless white skin and perky breasts that laughed at gravity; even though, at the genetic level,

Doodlebug remained the twelve-year-old boy he'd been since 1943. He'd been presenting himself as a woman for so many years that holding that form had become effortless, requiring no more conscious thought than breathing.

Well, what he was about to change into would have balls. Big, hairy balls. He began imagining the biggest, nastiest tomcat he could. A street-tough orange tabby that hadn't eaten in days; a cat from a 1950s atomic-attack movie (*Panic in the Year Zero,* or *Beginning of the End*) that had soaked up radiation like a feline sponge and mutated to ten times its original size.

Fur. Claws. Carnivore's teeth. He thought of these things, and his bones began to melt like baking butter, and his skin turned to gray, oily smoke. His legs bent in unaccustomed ways as his hands and feet gained pads and deadly retractable claws. His spine grew supple. Hair sprouted from his new flesh like grass force-fed with Miracle-Gro. During the four-and-a-half seconds it took him to change, his most trying task was to hold on to all of his mass, to not permit a single pound of himself to escape to his coffin as proto-matter. He needed to become these rats' worst nightmare.

The initial evidence of his success was a sudden change in pitch of the rats' exclamations, from bewildered squeaks to panicked squealings. He tried a hiss. It came out so loud and menacing that it hurt his own newly sensitized ears. Most of the rats ran immediately to the far side of the cage, trampling one another in search of a nonexistent exit. A few tried bolting around Doodlebug to get through the cage's slightly ajar door. Doodlebug slammed the door closed with his hind leg, then swatted three of the rats against the walls of the cage, his paws moving like furious quicksilver. He didn't want to hurt them (he forced himself to keep his claws sheathed, as much as the feline part of him wanted to skewer a few dozen rodents, then shake them in his jaws until their brains turned to jelly). But he needed to make this look deadly real.

The rats that he hadn't batted into near unconsciousness retreated with their brethren to the far side of the cage. Doodlebug advanced slowly. He arched his back and made every orange hair along his six-foot length bristle, making him appear twice as big. He hissed and yowled and spat, showering the trembling rats with hot spittle.

And then it started. Gray smoke began seeping from the rodents' bodies, as though an invisible match had ignited their fuses. Their forms started quivering; their outlines became fuzzy, indistinct, like television images seen through a murky aquarium tank. Doodlebug's rapidly beating heart took flight. It was working! He was forcing Jules to return—

"Miss Richelieu? I couldn't sleep, so I decided to come back and help—"

Doodlebug swung his whiskered muzzle around in time to see Daphne enter the room. Her eyes grew wide and her mouth fell open when she saw him in the cage. But then her shocked gaze shifted to something behind him. She flung her hands over her face and shrieked.

"Ohhh man . . . what the hell's goin' on . . . who's the noisy dame?"

Doodlebug turned back toward the deep, gravelly, and very familiar voice. Jules slowly picked himself up from the floor of the cage. The rats were gone, as though they'd never been there at all. Jules's hair, once jet-black, was now completely white. He was a blunt-headed mountain of alabaster flesh. Seeing Daphne, Jules instinctively covered his privates with his hands. Doodlebug heard a loud *thump* behind him, presumably Daphne falling to the floor in a dead faint. His job of explaining matters had just gotten considerably more complicated.

He steeled himself to change back to his womanly form and begin the task of bringing Jules up to speed. But he paused when he saw the look on Jules's face. It was a profoundly distressed look. His friend, whose hands remained below his huge belly, groped frantically beneath his hanging rolls of fat, as though something had gotten lost.

"Hey! Where's my *dick*?"

THREE

"AAHHH!!! MY DICK! WHERE IS IT?!? I'M A FUCKIN' KEN DOLL DOWN THERE!!!"

Jules groped lower and lower, until his fingers nearly reached his asshole, but his equipment was nowhere to be found. Not only that, but he was naked, in a cage, surrounded by Maureen's clothes (which he recognized) and a passed-out girl on the floor (whom he didn't). And in front of him, the giant tomcat that had nearly given him a heart attack was dissolving into oily smoke.

Seconds later, the smoke congealed into Doodlebug. Equally as naked, and flagrantly female. Under less distressing circumstances, Jules would be utterly disgusted by this shameless display of his one-time protégé's transvestitism (or transsexualism, or whatever; he'd never asked, and Doodlebug had never told). But right now, having Doodlebug's uncovered titties staring him in the face was the least of his concerns.

"You!" Jules bellowed. "I mighta known it! What is this? Some kinda twisted conspiracy so that nobody can have the genitals they was born with?"

"Calm down, Jules," Doodlebug implored, gesturing with open hands in a futile effort to soothe him. "I'll explain everything. Tell me—what's the last thing you remember?"

The question stopped Jules's rampage in its tracks. He could remember things, all right, but the images were all crazy . . . like he'd had a thousand pairs of eyeballs, all looking at different things at the same time. His brain nearly short-circuited when he tried thinking about it. He clenched his eyes shut and fought down a wave of vertigo and nausea. "Holy mackerel . . . what the hell *was* I? I can't even think about it. It's like that scene from *The Fly,* where we're seein' things through David Hedison's fly eyes—he's lookin' at his wife, who's screamin' her head off, but we see a hundred little pictures of her at once. Ooowww."

Doodlebug helped to steady him. The little pip-squeak was surprisingly strong. "Do you remember the last thing you did while you were in your human form, eight months ago?"

"Eight *months* ago—?" The memories started coming back. Had it really been that long? The food, the endless universe of smells, the damp spaces between walls . . . it could've lasted a couple of nights, or a hundred lifetimes. "Let's see . . . the last thing I remember seein' with my own eyes was Veronika. That government bitch who tried setting me up to take a fall. The one who ratted out Maureen to Malice X and got her killed. I was on top of her, in a hotel room, stickin' it to her but good. Not enjoyin' it, y'know, but doin' it anyway. She kept tellin' me over and over again that she wanted to be my vampire queen, that she wanted me to turn her so the government could relocate us to Guatemala or someplace and we could fang a bunch of narco-gangsters. She'd been cock-teasing me for weeks, then pullin' shit like tryin' to boil me in a hot tub laced with holy water. But I fixed her wagon. I drained her almost all the way, maybe four-fifths empty. Then I changed into a whole messa rats and ran out an open window, figurin' that was the best way to avoid the Feds and Malice X's crew and still stay in New Orleans . . ."

He opened his eyes, startled as the truth of his situation sank in. "So you're sayin' I been runnin' around as, like, two hundred rats for the last eight months?"

"That's the upshot of it, yes."

"Holy shit."

Doodlebug draped Jules's pudgy arm over his own slim shoulders. "Let's get out of this cage and put some clothes on. I've got a lot to tell you."

Jules took an unsteady step, then immediately noticed that his knees were aching again. He looked down but couldn't see his feet. He'd definitely gained some weight since the last time he'd examined himself. He must've spent much of the past eight months chowing down. And the worst thing about it was, he could hardly remember enjoying it. "Lots to tell me, huh? You can start by telling me where my dick went. And who the girl on the floor is."

Doodlebug sighed. He pulled the door of the cage open, sat Jules down on a sturdy-looking metal chair, and handed Jules the safari suit and trench coat that were hanging on the side of the cage. "That's Daphne," Doodlebug said, staring at the girl with a look of embarrassment on his face. He grabbed his own clothes and began dressing. "She's one of my students. I got her involved in this because she has experience working with rats. Movie experience. I needed her to help me trap all the rats you'd changed into. But she wasn't supposed to know . . . I didn't mean for her to see . . ."

"All them rats change back into me, huh?" Jules said, finishing the thought. The safari suit was a bust. He couldn't zip up the pants more than halfway, and the vest wouldn't button across his chest anymore. The trench coat still fit okay, though. "She's got no idea you're a vampire?"

"No, she doesn't. At least, she didn't."

"So where did my pecker go?"

Doodlebug smiled weakly. "We thought we'd collected all the rats. I guess we, uh, missed one."

Jules sensed the tight polyester pants pressing flush against him in a spot where they shouldn't be flush. "Yeah. I guess you did." Now that his initial disorientation and nausea were receding, he felt a groundswell of resentment building in his gut. Fury, even. Why had Doodlebug brought him back? Had the rats been bothering anybody? He hadn't been fanging anybody, had he? Why couldn't people just leave him the hell alone? Now he was stuck thinking about Maureen again, when before he'd been able to forget.

The girl on the floor moaned softly. Jules put his growing sense of grievance on hold and looked at Daphne. Her head was at an awkward angle on the floor, and she was drooling. She looked kind of sweet, like a homeless puppy that needed a bath and a saucer of milk. "So what're you gonna do with her, D.B.? Fang her?"

Doodlebug looked horrified. "Of course not! She's my student! Besides . . . we need her to catch your missing rat."

"Yeah? Well, okay, then. But you get to do the explainin'." Jules felt another stab of pity for the unconscious young woman. "Anyway, you just gonna let her lie on the floor like that? Go pick her up. Get her a glass of water or something. You probably scared her outta a year's growth, you dumb-ass."

Doodlebug finished pulling on his jeans, then silently did as Jules instructed, pouring bottled water into a Styrofoam cup and kneeling by Daphne's side, looking thoroughly mortified. "Daphne, dear. Wake up. It's Miss Richelieu. You've had a shock."

Daphne opened her eyes. Unfortunately, when she opened them, she was looking directly at Jules. Her eyes grew big as jumbo eggs, and she shrieked again. "*Aaahhhh!* He's still there! He's still there!"

Doodlebug pulled Daphne onto his lap. "It's all right, dear. Jules is a friend. He won't hurt you."

"But the rats—he dissolved all the rats—"

"I *am* the rats, sweetheart," Jules said as kindly as he could.

Ten minutes of convoluted explanation followed. Jules got some bitter satisfaction from seeing his know-it-all ex-protégé, usually so glib, struggle for words. What he didn't enjoy was watching Daphne's reaction. She seemed nearly comatose at times, her mouth hanging open, her pretty eyes staring into space. The worst was when Doodlebug, in an effort to prove his supernatural bona fides, transformed himself into a much smaller and cuddlier version of his earlier tomcat. The way Daphne screamed, it was as if he'd changed himself into Godzilla.

It took Jules and Doodlebug another five minutes (plus three more cups of water, two of which ended up spilled on the floor) to calm her down again. Daphne grew progressively less horrified of Jules, but progressively more so of Doodlebug. "So, so, the blood we donate every month at the Institute," she asked Doodlebug in a tight, tiny voice, "you don't give it to the American Red Cross, like you said?"

"No, dear," Doodlebug admitted.

Jules chuckled, then scowled at his friend. "The only blood bank he donates to is the one at the bottom of his gullet."

Daphne's chin began trembling, and her eyes filled with water. "I . . . I want my *rats* back."

"The lady wants her rats back," Jules said sharply to his friend. "And I'm of a mind to *give* her her rats back, unless you come up with a world-class 'fess-up of why you tried puttin' Humpty Dumpty back together again."

"You aren't going to like the answer," Doodlebug said quietly.

"Try me."

Doodlebug looked uneasily at Daphne. "Jules, I'd rather keep this just between you and me. Some of this concerns my Institute, matters I'd rather keep confidential from the student body—"

Jules laughed. It felt good. Maybe when you didn't have a dick anymore, laughing was the best thing left to you. "You think she's ready to sign up for another semester? Could be I'm still stuck with a rat brain, but I'm pretty damn sure that's down the toilet. Whatever I can hear, she can hear."

Jules sat, and Doodlebug told them about his summons to the compound of the High Krewe of Vlad Tepes. He told them about the comatose young women missing arms or legs. He told them about Besthoff's threat to foreclose on the Institute's mortgage unless Doodlebug could persuade Jules to investigate the disappearances and dismemberments.

Doodlebug pulled his hair away from his forehead, then wiped away the sheen with the sleeve of his blouse. "So that's why I did what I did, Jules." He spoke these last words softly, as though Jules were a bomb that might be set off by too loud a vibration.

Jules had sunk lower and lower in his chair during Doodlebug's recounting. Now he leaned his head onto the thick, fatty pads of his palms. "You've got to be fuckin' kidding me." Strands of his hair, loose and greasy, fell in front of his eyes. It had been black before Maureen's death and his months as hundreds of rats. Now it was stark white, too white for even Grecian Formula to fix.

"I'm not proud of what I've done and what I'm asking. Under any other circumstances, I never would've disturbed the peace you found for yourself—"

Jules felt his face grow hot as a floor furnace. "Is that what you call what you did to me—*'disturbin' the peace'*? 'Disturbin' the peace' is tossin' water balloons at a carnival parade. 'Disturbin' the peace' is playin' jungle rap music at three in the morning. But this—this—*this*—"

"Breathe," Daphne said fearfully.

"This is a crime against nature! *My* nature! You yank me away from a life where I was botherin' nobody, a life even the priest at Saint Joseph's couldn't have faulted me for, where I was enjoyin' myself and able to forget about Maureen, even—and what for? What for? To help those assholes with the High Krewe, those goddamn snooty assholes what couldn't even give me the time of day when I went to *them* for help? Maybe if they hadn't given me the bum's rush, maybe if they'd leaned on Malice X and his goons when I asked them to, then maybe what happened to Maureen never woulda happened. You're a pretty smart kid, Doodlebug—you really think I'm gonna raise a goddamn *pinky* to help the High Krewe?"

"It's not helping them," Doodlebug said softly, his eyes downcast. "It's helping me."

"And why should I help *you*?" Jules regretted the words as soon as they popped out of his mouth. But it was too late to take them back now.

"Because I'm your friend." Doodlebug's face, normally a doll's porcelain white, was now stricken with a dull pink blush. "Because if I hadn't taught you what I did, you never could've transformed into multiple bodies and found even eight months of peace. Because . . ." He raised his eyes, glossy with held-back tears. "Because you're my daddy, Jules. You made me. And helping is what daddies do."

"You hadda go and remind me of that fact." Much as Jules hated to admit it, Doodlebug had struck a nerve. The kid was as close to a son (or daughter) as he'd ever have. *Daddy.* Doodlebug had never called him that before, not in all the sixty years they'd known each other. The shoe fit, even if it pinched his toes something awful. Doodlebug was family. And despite the fact that Jules's own father had left him, or maybe because of that fact, Jules had never been one to turn his back on family.

Jules rubbed his temples with his palms and sighed, a raspy sound like a Vega with a loose fan belt. "Hell . . . you stuck by me, kid. You came back to New Orleans and tried to help me through that Malice X thing, even though I sure as heck pushed you away. If you stuck by me, I guess I can return the favor. Buy me a big clothespin to pinch my nose shut, and I'll go kiss the High Krewe's ass for you."

Doodlebug made a visible effort to compose himself, blinking rapidly four times. He hesitantly smiled. "Thank you, Jules."

"Don't thank me yet. If I'm gonna pull your girlie tail outta the fire, there's something you gotta do for me."

"Of course, Jules. I'll do anything I can."

"It's Maureen." Jules's voice cracked slightly as he said his lover's name. He cleared his throat. "I saved her ashes. The dust she turned into after Malice X staked her through the heart. I put it in a flower vase and gave it to Erato to keep safe. You're the smart one. You gotta find a way to bring her back."

Doodlebug crossed his arms tightly over his chest, as though he were shielding himself from a blow. "That may not be possible, Jules. If she'd just been killed, say a few hours or even a day ago—"

"I don't care if it's easy or not. Just do it. Get ahold of them vampire monks in Timbuktu if you have to. There's gotta be a way. You brought me back, didn't you?"

"That was different. You hadn't been dead for eight months. This could backfire horribly, Jules. There might be a ceremony, yes. There might be a technique we could use. But the Maureen we'd bring back—she could end up hating you throughout all eternity."

Jules slowly stood up, ignoring the shooting pains in his knees. "I'll take that chance. Bring her back, Doodlebug."

"But—"

"No buts. You don't agree to bring her back, I don't agree to see Besthoff. And then you can paint yourself a nice little sign to hold while you're standin' on a street corner—'Will Work for Blood.' *Kapeesh?*"

Doodlebug's shoulders slumped. "I loved her, too, you know," he said quietly. "All right. I'll do everything I can, Jules. I promise."

"Good," Jules muttered. He jutted his accordion chin at Daphne, who was still sitting on the floor in a daze, chewing slowly on her index finger. "How about her?"

"Daphne?"

"No, the Tooth Fairy. Looks like you messed up her head pretty bad, whether you meant to or not. It's always a bad idea to get normals too involved in your business. That's how come I never 'fessed up to Erato, much as I wanted to. Anyway, I guess there's not much chance of gettin' her to hunt down my missin' part like you said, huh?"

"Is that part of your deal, too?"

Jules rolled his eyes. "Don't make me out to be as bad as Besthoff, all right? She's just an innocent kid who got dragged into this. I got nothin' to hold over her head, and I wouldn't want to if I did. But if you could maybe talk her into findin' the missin' rat, I'd sure appreciate it. Runnin' around town lookin' for bad guys without my codpiece on—it just ain't dignified."

Doodlebug knelt by Daphne's side and lightly stroked her arms. The young woman didn't appear to respond. "Daphne. I realize I've greatly upset you, dear. I'm terribly sorry. I never meant to hurt you in any way. What would you like to do now? Would you like to help Jules find his missing rat? Or would you rather I send you back to California? You're welcome to stay at the school, although I realize you may not want to anymore. Of course, if you do go back to the school, I'll have to ask you to promise never to say a word about what you've seen here tonight—"

"Oh, cut that out, will you?" Jules said, a disgusted grimace on his face. "Don't bug her with that now. Move aside, gimme a shot here." He pulled over the steel chair and straddled it. "Hey, Daphne?" She pulled her finger out of her mouth and looked up at him. She struggled to focus on his face, as though she were coming out of a dream. "I hear you like rats, huh? How'd you like to help me find a special rat? A *really* special rat?"

"I . . . I think I know the one you mean," she said hesitantly. "I saw him. Last night. He was standing on a rain gutter above my head."

"What'd he look like?"

"He was really big. He had a long body, and a big head. He wasn't doing what all the other rats were doing. He had a mind of his own."

"Yeah, that's the one," Jules said. "So how about it? You wanna help Uncle Jules find his rat?"

She leaned close to his massive thigh, encased in severely stretched double-knit polyester, closed her eyes, and sniffed him. A tiny smile appeared on her face. "I . . . I'll think about it. Okay? Right now, I have to sleep. So tired . . . I just wanna lie down . . ."

"Good girl, you think about it," Jules said, raising an eyebrow when she sniffed him for a second time. "We'll get you back to where you're staying so you can get some shut-eye."

They went outside, found a pay phone near a Circle K Food Mart, and Jules called a cab. Not Erato's cab; Jules wasn't quite ready to reveal himself to his friend yet. The cab pulled up a few minutes later, a Chevy Astro van. Jules opened the sliding side door and took a look at the hanging plastic grab handle meant to help him make the big step up. Maybe if he were a hundred pounds lighter . . . Instead, he sank his fingers into the headrest of the front bucket seat and pulled himself onto the running board. The van heeled to one side like a torpedoed freighter about to capsize, its springs groaning with sudden compression.

The driver, a swarthy man with a long, shiny mustache, gaped at Jules with alarm. "This vehicle—I only lease it—!"

"Don't blow a gasket," Jules said. "You'll be fine once I'm in. General Motors don't build no junk." He pulled on the headrest again, yanking it from its mooring, but he managed to get himself inside the van. Daphne climbed in next. She surprised Jules by sitting next to him, even though there were two other benches, and he took up four-fifths of the front one.

Doodlebug sat on the next bench back and gave the driver instructions to the bed-and-breakfast. Five minutes later, when the van passed between the graffiti-scrawled concrete pillars of the elevated highway at Claiborne Avenue, Daphne was leaning on Jules's shoulder, softly snoring.

Jules glanced at her and grinned in spite of himself. "Huh. Guess I have that effect on women." *Especially now,* he thought.

"Speaking of sleeping," Doodlebug said, "where should we put *you* before sunrise? Should I fix you up something at the bed-and-breakfast, like I did the last time I was in town? I doubt we could get you a piano box at this hour of the morning. The veterinary clinic is sun-proofed, if you wouldn't mind camping out there for a day . . ."

Where did he want to sleep? In the best of all possible worlds, he'd want to sleep in his own familiar old coffin, in his own house, surrounded by a century's accumulation of jazz records, comic books, girlie magazines, and his mother's dusty Victorian bric-a-brac. But that haven was gone, burned to the ground by Malice X and his goons nine months back.

There was one other place that had been his home. The house that provided him sanctuary after his own house was destroyed. He hadn't always been welcome there, and it would be harder than ever for him to return now. But he couldn't imagine resting his head anywhere else.

"I'll stay at Maureen's," Jules said.

"Are you sure?" Doodlebug asked. "Won't that be . . . painful for you?"

"Sure. Maybe. But not for long, not if you do your job. I can fix up the place some before she gets back. Tidy things up. She'd like that."

The van turned onto Bayou Road, then pulled onto the bed-and-breakfast's long gravel driveway. It drove slowly past the main house, a Creole mansion with a wide skirt of sheltered porch, and came to a stop near the cabins at the back of the oak-shaded lot. Doodlebug got out first. Daphne remained asleep on Jules's shoulder.

"Hand her to me," Doodlebug said. "I'll carry her to the cabin."

Jules frowned. "Naww. You'll wake her up. Lemme get out, then you hand her to me."

Doodlebug unlocked one of the cabins, and Jules laid Daphne on top of the high four-poster bed, pulling down the rose quilt first. She barely stirred. "Where do you sleep?" Jules whispered to Doodlebug.

"My cabin's on the other side of the frog pond."

"You got your coffin in there?"

"Of course. Shipped FedEx, just like before."

Jules motioned that they should exit and leave Daphne to sleep. Outside, he said, "You've got your coffin in that cabin, and you didn't think she was gonna suspect something?"

"I was discreet," Doodlebug said. "And never underestimate a mortal's ability to rationalize away things they think are beyond belief."

Jules glanced back at Daphne's cabin. "Yeah, I'm sure that little girl's doin' *lots* of 'rationalizing' right now," he grumbled.

They returned to the van. The driver had put the passenger seat headrest back in place. His eyes pleaded with Jules not to wrench it loose again. So Jules wrapped his fist, a bit dubiously, around the grab handle instead. It held—a tribute to American manufacturing skill that made Jules misty-eyed with patriotism.

Doodlebug gave the driver instructions for bringing them to Bamboo Road. *The High Krewe,* Jules thought darkly. What steaming pot of horse manure was Doodlebug asking him to stick his head into? He stared down at his big, calloused hands and the white belly that insisted on peering out between the buttons of his trench coat. He could hardly believe he was back, as himself. *Mostly* as himself. Had he just dreamed it, that he'd been a couple hundred rats? Or were a couple hundred rats right now dreaming they were Jules?

He glanced at his companion. How had Doodlebug found him? How had he known what had happened to him? Only one answer seemed to make any sense. "Eaten any dog chow lately?" Jules asked.

"What?"

Jules shifted in his seat so he could face Doodlebug more comfortably. "Lemme tell you a little story. Eight months ago, right after I saw the video of what he done to Maureen, I went down to Malice X's secret hideout underneath the big casino on Canal Street. I figured there wasn't a whole lotta chance I'd beat him, especially not with all his men around. But right then, I didn't really care. It was him or me. Besides, with what you'd taught me, I thought I might have an edge, might be able to trick him into fuckin' up. As things turned out, *I* was the one who fucked up—no big surprise, right? Anyway, just as I was about to get a stake shoved through my ticker, the cavalry showed up. A pack of wolf-dogs—not just any wolf-dogs, but *vampire* wolf-dogs—crashed through the glass ceiling and gave me time to light Malice X's coffin on fire. Some coincidence, huh?"

Jules stared at his friend, watching for a reaction. Doodlebug opened his purse and rearranged its contents, avoiding Jules's gaze. Jules continued. "So I figured, these wolf-dogs, they coulda come from one of two places. Either they were my 'puppies,' the litter from that stray bitch I accidentally screwed in Baton Rouge. Or they were *you.* You got an opinion?"

Doodlebug turned toward the window. "It—it certainly wasn't me. I'd gone back to California, remember? I left you that good-bye note."

"I remember. It said you wanted me to have the satisfaction of solvin' my problem myself. But I'm havin' a little trouble 'rationalizing' that you had nothing to do with those wolf-dogs."

Doodlebug said nothing.

"You still want me to think I did it all by myself, don't you? That I won my big victory on my guts and smarts alone, maybe helped by the fact that I was nice to a stray dog in a bummy part of Baton Rouge. It's okay for me to know otherwise, y'know. My ego ain't that fragile." He waited a few seconds for his companion to respond, but Doodlebug continued staring at the window. "Keepin' quiet like that, you're still tellin' me what I want to know."

They drove on a while longer in silence, passing the marble tombs of Metairie Cemetery. Statues of Confederate heroes stood atop the tombs, their white eyes staring out at a city that was seventy percent black, whose last three mayors had been black, whose biggest cultural export, jazz, was the gift black musicians had given the world. Jules wondered, briefly, what those Confederate heroes would think about all that.

Looking back at Doodlebug, he realized something else. "You coulda held that over my head, couldn't you? The fact that you'd pulled my fat outta the fire. The fact that you'd didn't let me end up like Maureen, staked through the heart. You coulda told me that to force me to do this job for you. But you didn't."

Family. He'd never had much of one. Without his mother and Maureen, he had even less now. Whatever shit-storm might lie ahead, he'd just have to weather it. For Doodlebug's sake. That's what you did for kin.

"You're a good kid, Rory. A good kid."

FOUR

The tall iron gates swung open. Jules's memories of the last time he'd walked through them were bitter as rancid lemons. He and Doodlebug walked between groves of darkly fertile fruit trees. They approached one of the High Krewe's marble fountains. A stone wolf shot a plume of crimson water from its mouth in an arc twenty feet high. Its pups, arranged around the fountain's rim, expelled smaller jets from their jaws. *I'd sure love to turn that red water orange,* Jules thought, but he squelched his desire to piss in the fountain. Not out of any sense of propriety; he simply wasn't sure he *could* piss.

Straussman opened the mansion's front doors before Jules or Doodlebug could knock. Jules looked up a few inches into the eyes of the six-and-a-half-foot-tall butler. *Bet he's wearin' heels,* he thought. "If it ain't tall, light, and ugly," Jules muttered.

Straussman gave no indication that he had heard Jules's remark. "Mr. Richelieu. Mr. Duchon. Master Besthoff is pleased that you have observed his deadline."

Jules and Doodlebug stepped inside the foyer. "They still stickin' starch in your blood ration, Straussman?" Jules asked, roughly shrugging off the butler's silent offer to take his trench coat. "Bet this time you're not in such a hurry to grab me by the lapels and pitch me out the gate, huh?"

He felt a sudden yank on his trench coat. "Jules!" Doodlebug, his hair now tied up in a bun, looked like a scolding librarian. "Could you *please* try not going into this with a chip on your shoulder the size of Alaska? *Please?*"

"That's quite all right, Mr. Richelieu," Straussman said. "It's no secret that we treated Mr. Duchon most discourteously the last time he visited us. I am at full liberty to say so."

This admission of guilt, completely unexpected, let the steam out of Jules's temper tantrum, at least for the moment. He felt like he'd just been judo-tossed, his own weight and momentum turned against him. "Well . . . okay, then. Just make sure it don't happen no more. I'm a pretty important guy nowadays."

"Of course, sir," Straussman said.

The butler led them past the doors of the library. *Guess I still ain't important enough to rate a goblet of blood in the fancy library,* Jules thought. He wondered how long Straussman had been the High Krewe's butler. All the way back to their years in Europe? Given Straussman's vague Rumanian accent, it would seem so. That was a long, long time to be somebody's flunky . . . especially when you were a vampire yourself.

Straussman opened a pair of French doors, and they walked outside into a long courtyard garden that Jules remembered. The butler led them toward the two-story dormitory building where Besthoff had gloated to Jules about his blood farm almost nine months ago. Maybe that's why Straussman hung around—the easy blood? Jules wasn't sure he could do it himself . . . be a bootlicker in exchange for nightly draughts of the red stuff. But then, wasn't that what most average Joes in America did? Lick someone's boots so they could put chow on their plates, and on their families' plates? Thinking of it that way, driving a cab hadn't been so bad. Sure, he'd had to kiss a lot of fares' butts, put up with their bitching and their lousy tips. But he'd gotten his "pound of flesh" back, in spades; at least one in twenty of those fares ended up sucked dry, at the bottom of Lake Maurepas or floating south on the Mississippi.

Straussman led them up the steps to the dormitory. "Master Besthoff is waiting inside," he said.

The first thing Jules noticed when he entered the dimly lit hall was the stink. The place smelled like a cross between an NBA locker room and a baby-changing station in a Greyhound bus terminal. It hadn't smelled this bad nine months ago. "Hey Straussman, what's the deal here? The housekeeping crew go on strike or something?"

The butler's face betrayed its first sign of emotion—a barely discernible tightening of the lips. "Our household has been undergoing some . . . transitions. This is a stressful time for us, Mr. Duchon. I'm certain Master Besthoff will explain."

They walked between the long rows of beds. Jules found the soft gurglings and grunts rising from the beds' occupants, most of whom were restrained with leather straps, eerie, somehow not right at all. *Weird that a vampire should get creeped out by a room fulla retards,* he thought, trying to shrug the feeling off. But he hadn't liked this setup nine months ago, either, when the place had been cleaner.

Straussman unlocked a door at the back of the hall. Jules immediately felt claustrophobic when he stepped through the door. The ceiling was much lower in here; he had to duck underneath a hanging lightbulb. Worse, the tight, dusty room had the feel of a death house. Jules knew that feeling; he'd worked enough years with Doc Landrieu in the city morgue, before Doc Landrieu lost his last race for coroner and Jules had been forced to take up driving a cab. Two coffins sat atop cots in the middle of the room. Based on what Doodlebug had told him, Jules had a pretty good idea what was inside them.

"Welcome back to the world of Homo sapiens, Mr. Duchon." Besthoff stepped into the small circle of light. Jules thought the leader of the High Krewe looked thinner, older than when they had last met; worry lines had appeared around his eyes and mouth, tiny fissures in a marble mask. *Couldn't have happened to a nicer guy,* Jules thought.

"So I hear you need me to hunt down some bad guys," Jules said. No wisecracks sprang to mind, not even one about how, pound for pound, he was the best vampire-detective around. Besthoff's presence killed any humor in its crib.

"That is an admirably succinct summation."

"You gotta realize I don't come into this job with a bucketful of enthusiasm."

"Given our history, that is not surprising," Besthoff said. "But you are known for your strong loyalties. You will not allow your friend and protégé to suffer loss on your account."

Jules glanced over at Doodlebug. His friend quickly looked away. "Yeah. That stinks, what you're pullin' on Doodlebug. If I had known thirty-five years ago that the kid was thinkin' of doin' a deal with you, I woulda warned him off. Lie down with dogs—" Actually, *he'd* lain down with dogs, or a dog, and things hadn't turned out too badly. Better change the aphorism. "Well, uh, lie down with snakes, get up with, uh, snake bites."

"The morality of our treatment of Mr. Richelieu is quite immaterial. The sole pertinent issue at hand is this—only your swift and thorough cooperation can avert a disaster for your friend."

"I ain't doin' this job for you only so that you don't screw over Doodlebug. I got conditions."

"Name them," Besthoff said.

Jules took a deep breath. "First off, you gotta supply me with a decent blood ration while I'm on the case. You don't want me spendin' all my nights huntin' down meals. I'll need a pint a night, for as long as the job takes."

"Agreed. What else?"

No argument? A pint a night was actually twice what he needed; he'd be able to stockpile some for when the job was over. "I need my expenses paid, with some up front. I'll probably have to shell out for information on the street. Two grand should get me rolling." Besthoff's expression remained tightly neutral. Push for more. "After the first four nights, I'll need two hundred a night."

"Straussman will provide you with one thousand dollars in small bills. You will be given a second thousand dollars upon providing evidence of progress toward locating the culprit. An additional fee of two hundred dollars per night worked, beyond receipted expenses, is acceptable, again contingent upon acceptable progress. What else?"

This was going much better than Jules had anticipated. Maybe he held a stronger hand than he'd thought. It was time to hit Besthoff up for the big score. "I need wheels. Hailin' cabs all the time is a pain in the ass, and I sure as hell ain't playin' detective ridin' no bus."

"Very well. You may borrow one of the Mercedes sedans the servants use."

Jules's face puckered with disgust. "Hell, no! I ain't drivin' around in no damn Kraut car! I didn't spend three years of my undead life puttin' the bite on Nazi saboteurs to start drivin' Krautmobiles in my own country. Jules Duchon sits *his* ass in the 'Standard of the World.' And that's *Cadillac*!"

Besthoff's face remained unperturbed. "We have no Cadillacs in our motor pool, Mr. Duchon. You will have to accept the loan of a Mercedes."

Doodlebug lightly grasped his arm. "Jules, please be a little reasonable—"

"Reasonable? *Reasonable?!!*" Jules saw red. The Germanic tint of Besthoff's accent when he said *Mercedes* made the issue even more volatile. "How 'reasonable' was it to yank me away from some of the only peace I've ever known? How 'reasonable' was it to jam me back together again without all my plumbing intact? You wanna know reasonable? I'm being fuckin' reasonable just walkin' in here and sharin' the same air with these hoity-toity pinheads. Unless the High Krewe buys me a Cadillac, I ain't doing SQUAT!"

He hadn't meant to cause the hurt he saw in his friend's face. But maybe his tantrum had served a purpose. The only way to keep dick-heads like Besthoff or Malice X from walking all over you was to show them right up front that you could be just as ruthless and selfish as they were.

"I see this is an issue that has great emotional significance to you," Besthoff said evenly. "An immediate purchase is out of the question." Jules opened his mouth to protest, but Besthoff cut him off. "However, I will have Straussman accompany you to the downtown dealership, and he will arrange for a short-term lease of the vehicle of your choice."

"*Short*-term—?"

"Then, should you complete the investigation in an expeditious and satisfactory manner, I will give serious consideration to converting the lease to a purchase. Consider this an incentive clause, Mr. Duchon."

Jules thought it over. It wasn't that bad a deal. At the very least, he'd get to tool around for a while in a brand-new Caddy he'd never be able to afford himself. He had just the car in mind, too. An Eldorado convertible. A modern version of Elvis's car. Twenty-five feet long, plenty of flashy chrome, a big V-8 with at least five-hundred cubes of rompin'-stompin' torque. And when Doodlebug brought Maureen back . . . well, she'd just *love* it. Riding in that big open car, the warm breeze would make her long blond hair float behind her like an angel's wings.

"Will that be acceptable to you, Mr. Duchon?"

"Uh, yeah. That'll work. Hey, shouldn't we be gettin' all this down in writing? Maybe Straussman there can write us up a contract, since you got him doing everything else."

Besthoff's nose twitched, as though a gnat had flown up one of his nostrils. "That will *not* be necessary, Mr. Duchon. My word is my bond.

I am surprised and disappointed you would presume otherwise. Now, do you have any other stipulations, or is the matter settled?"

Doodlebug stepped closer. "Jules, don't forget what we spoke about in the cab."

"Oh, yeah. There's one more thing."

"Name it," Besthoff said, an impatient edge surfacing in his voice, like the fin of a shark slicing a placid sea. "The night is growing short."

"Eight months ago, somebody real special to me got murdered," Jules said. "Maureen Remoulade. I know you remember her, 'cause she originally came from here."

Besthoff's face showed no trace of emotion at the mention of Maureen's death. "Yes. Miss Remoulade. Our breakaway. An unfortunate woman. We had noted her apparent disappearance some months ago. You have our condolences."

"Yeah. Well, Doodlebug thinks he may have a way to bring her back. But to do that, he needs about a pint of blood donated from the guy who made her a vampire. She never would tell me who that was. But she lived with the High Krewe before she took up living in the French Quarter, back in the teens. So I figure her blood-daddy is somebody here."

Jules stared at Besthoff, waiting for an answer. The tall vampire looked beyond Jules's shoulder, and his gaze narrowed slightly. Jules turned around. Straussman stepped away from the door and joined them in the faint circle of light. "That would be I, Mr. Duchon," the butler said. "I was Miss Remoulade's blood-father."

"You?!?" Was the butler kidding? Not likely—Straussman looked like he'd never heard of the concept of humor. "But, but—but I thought it had to be one of the Big Three—Katz, Besthoff, or Krauss." He turned to Besthoff. "Since when have you guys let the hired help make more vampires?"

"The story behind Miss Remoulade's creation is inconsequential," Besthoff said. "Straussman may choose to tell you, if he is so inclined. However, I will vouch for the fact that he was, indeed, her blood-father." He turned to his servant. "Straussman, you will provide Mr. Richelieu with what he requires. Your weekly blood ration will be increased accordingly."

"Of course, sir," the butler replied. "I was . . . not aware that Miss Remoulade had passed. I will do whatever I can to help Mr. Richelieu's project succeed." Jules thought he detected a flicker of actual sorrow in

Straussman's voice. Maybe the old hunk of deadwood had some sap in him, after all.

"Good," Besthoff said. "Then the matter is settled. Mr. Duchon will begin the investigation tomorrow evening."

Jules blinked rapidly three times as the reality of his situation sunk in. He had *taken on the job.* Finding the mutilator, dealing with him—this was his responsibility now.

What did he know about being a detective? He'd read hundreds of detective pulps in his youth. *Black Mask; The Shadow; The Spider.* He'd tracked down every single one of Dashiell Hammett's *Continental Op* stories, never missed a Philip Marlowe novel or movie. But what had he *really* done? There had been that nasty business with Baron von Kohenshrek, the German vampire, during World War Two, when Jules had been the Hooded Terror. And more recently, there was Jules's big war with Malice X . . . that had involved some detective work. Not much. But some.

Why had Besthoff insisted that Jules be the one to handle the investigation? Was it some secret plot to humiliate him, give him just enough rope to hang himself with? No, that didn't make any sense. In any case, now that he had taken the job, he sure as hell wasn't going to let that stuffed shirt suspect he had any qualms about his own competence. He would act like he knew exactly what he was doing. Who knows? Maybe if he acted that way long enough, he really *would* know what he was doing.

"Lemme see the bodies," Jules said. It was a start.

Besthoff nodded, and Straussman opened the lids of the two coffins. Jules had a pretty good idea of what to expect, based on what Doodlebug had told him. Still, what he saw hardly jibed with the pictures that had been floating in his brain, images of bloody dismemberments from the covers of 1950s EC horror comics; drooling maniacs leering above savaged female corpses, their axes dripping with gore.

"Geez," he muttered, "they look like they just turned in for the day. Except they're missin' body parts. What're their names?"

"This is Miss Victoria," Straussman said. "And this is Miss Alexandra."

"Attractive girls," Jules said, feeling he needed to say something. Well, they *were* attractive . . . way out of his league. Maureen had been at least this striking when he'd first met her; of course, back then, he'd been three hundred pounds slimmer, with way less mileage on his odometer.

Why would somebody want to do this? That was an obvious first question for a detective to ask. They were beautiful women. Beautiful women sometimes attracted homicidal maniacs; heck, even plain or ugly women did, sometimes. But this couldn't have been the work of your run-of-the-mill homicidal maniac. Either one of these women was as strong as seven or eight or your strongest homicidal maniacs put together. That meant that whoever had attacked them had either gotten extraordinarily lucky—or he'd known they were vampires and had figured out how to deal with them.

He leaned over Alexandra's coffin to take a closer look at her armless shoulder blades. Just like Doodlebug had said, it appeared as if she'd been born that way, a thalidomide baby, a genetic mistake. The skin was smooth, unscarred. He hadn't taken a mirror to himself (not that it would've shown him anything), but his crotch had felt exactly the same way to his fingers earlier that night—smooth as Teflon, as if he'd never had a dick in the first place.

"Hey, Doodlebug, come over here." Jules waited until his friend was standing next to him, then pointed to the long, smooth concavities beneath Alexandra's shoulder blades. "You think there's any chance maybe she's got some critter selves runnin' around? Where I'm missin', uh, what you know I'm missin', it's just the same as her there." Doodlebug appeared to mull the idea over, and Jules did some more mulling himself. "Naww . . . scratch that," he said. "Having one stray Jules-rat runnin' around hasn't left me in no coma."

"Don't be so quick to dismiss the idea out of hand," Doodlebug said. "Your experience is unique. Let's say these women were experimenting with multiple-body formation—how they would've even been familiar with the concept, I don't know, but for the sake of argument, we'll say they'd heard of it somehow. If they lacked an experienced guide, like you had when I was teaching you, things could've gone seriously awry. But what makes you think that might've been the case?"

Jules glanced at Besthoff, who was observing their conversation with keen interest. He didn't want to let anything slip that might make him sound like a ham-handed amateur. "It's just that, well, assumin' these gals got attacked don't make much sense. If there *was* an attacker, somebody who knew the gals were vampires . . . why would he have done *this*? If he had a real mad on, why didn't he just stake them or, y'know, knock them out and leave them in the open for the sun to kill them? Why cut off body parts? Even weirder, why go to the trouble of makin' sure they got rescued?"

"So how, then, would you explain the phone calls that Straussman received?" Besthoff asked.

Jules inwardly grinned. He didn't even have to break a sweat, coming up with a return volley. "Coulda been another one of your youngsters. If they were hanging out together in the city, playin' around with multiple transformations, and the gals screwed themselves up, the ones that were with them probably woulda wanted to cover their own asses. Throw you off the scent."

Besthoff turned to his servant. "Straussman, was the voice on the phone familiar to you in any way?"

"No, sir, it was not."

"So? That doesn't mean anything." The theory was his baby now. As proud papa, he didn't want to see anybody yank the milk bottle from its mouth. And showing off his deductive skills in front of Besthoff was a kick. "Them kids coulda easily hired somebody to make the calls. They get an allowance, don't they?"

"This line of inquiry is absurd," Besthoff said, a hint of anger breaking through his granite facade. "The members of my household are honorable. The children adore Victoria and Alexandra. None of them would ever dirty themselves that way. It is unthinkable."

And people call ME close-minded, Jules thought. "Okay, okay, it's just a theory, all right?" He massaged his left knee, which had begun throbbing. "Gimme a night or two, I'll come up with half a dozen more. Maybe you'll like one a them better."

"There is a dangerous savage somewhere in the city who is preying on my household," Besthoff said. He stepped closer to Jules. Radiating an aura of barely contained violence, he was a smoldering volcano wrapped in silk. "I expect you to find this person. I expect you to deliver this person to me. I expect that you will begin this work tomorrow night, by placing any young lord who leaves this compound under protective surveillance. Should any additional violence befall my household . . . rest assured that the consequences of such failure on your part will not fall upon Mr. Richelieu alone."

"Yeah, yeah," Jules muttered. *What are you gonna do—turn me into two hundred rats?* He wanted to say it. Badly. But out of respect for Doodlebug, he shut up.

"You must excuse me," Besthoff said. "I have my nightly duties with Katz and Krauss to attend to." His composure had reappeared as swiftly as if he'd pulled it out of a hat. "Straussman, assist them with anything else they may need. Good evening, gentlemen."

He left the room. The space immediately felt less claustrophobic and oppressive. Even Straussman seemed to relax slightly. Jules wished there were someplace to sit down. His knees were throbbing to beat the band. But he still had a few questions for Doodlebug before they called it a night.

"Hey, Doodlebug, you think these gals would still be breathing if their missin' parts had gotten destroyed? Like if the attacker dumped the parts in the river, say, and the sun ate 'em up?"

"I can't say for certain. That type of situation was not anything my monks had ever experimented with, for obvious reasons. It's a good question, though."

"Yeah." Maybe Doodlebug's Tibetan monks had never experimented with destroying a piece of a fragmented vampire, but Jules had. "When I had that death match with Malice X, the way I finally got him was to force him to change to a bat, and then I set his coffin on fire, burned up his spare proto-matter stuff. But I don't know if that woulda killed him, 'cause when he fell to the ground, the wolf-dogs tore him to bits. I'm just thinkin' out loud here, but maybe the fact that those gals are breathing means that their missin' pieces are still out there somewhere. Either as critters, if they was messin' around with multiple bodies, or as, y'know, arms and legs. You think if maybe we found the pieces, reunited them with who they belonged to, the gals might come out of their comas? Sort of like what you did with me?"

"That's very possible," Doodlebug said, enthusiasm lighting up his care-worn face. "If their missing body parts were placed in their coffins with them, Besthoff's powers of hypnotism might actually suffice to bring the girls out of their comas. Or they might spontaneously reintegrate."

Another idea occurred to Jules. "Hey, you think maybe when they lost their parts somehow, the parts changed to the goopy stuff and zapped themselves back to the gals' coffins? I'll never forget that time you made me sit next to my own coffin, change into a wolf, then watch my own proto-matter appear in the bottom of the box. Cripes, it looked like a cross between the Blob and spoiled grape jelly." He turned to the butler hovering behind him. "Straussman, where are the coffins these gals normally sleep in?"

"I am afraid you're looking at them," Straussman said. "Master Besthoff had their coffins removed from their bedrooms to this room as soon as their bodies were recovered."

Jules grumbled with disappointment. "Well, that whacks that idea." It would've made things so easy. The women could've been revived, and then they could've told him exactly what had happened. Tracking down whoever was responsible—assuming there even *was* some nefarious outside party—would've been made a whole lot simpler. But now he'd have to earn his Cadillac, and Doodlebug's Institute, the long and hard way. "I'm all outta bright ideas for the night. And I'm as beat as the bass drum at Preservation Hall. Let's all climb in our coffins and start again tomorrow."

"I'll escort you out, sirs," Straussman said, "once I have given Mr. Richelieu what he requires."

In the long dormitory hall adjoining the storage room, Straussman selected a spare blood-extraction unit and installed a sterile needle at the end of its plastic tubing. Then he rolled up his own sleeve, swabbed a portion of his forearm with alcohol, and punctured himself with the expert aim of a veteran phlebotomist. Jules winced, then quickly looked away before he got queasy. The sight of blood wasn't a problem for him—so long as it was normal people's blood. But watching blood exit a vampire's veins . . . that was a whole other story.

He leaned against a wall, rubbed his face, and tried to block out the gurglings of the retards and their unpleasant body odors. He still wished he could sit down. Damned knees. What was up with that, anyway? Hadn't Doodlebug proved to him months ago that all of Jules's age- and weight-related ailments—the arthritic knees, the aching back, the symptoms of creeping diabetes—were all in his head? That as a vampire, he was blessed with near-total control of his form? And all those aches and pains were the subconscious accretion of years of media "experts" telling him that's how fat people were *supposed* to feel? Right before his last battle with Malice X, he'd been able to switch it all off, all the nagging little agonies that had made him miserable for years.

He sort of remembered how he'd done it. It hadn't been hard, once he'd finally let himself believe it was possible. He closed his eyes and tried it again.

Nothing changed. His knees still felt as if he'd second-lined from Canal Street to the Arkansas state line. Even his back was starting to act up, just like the old days.

Whatever. Maybe it was just being around the damned High Krewe again. He'd feel better once all this was behind him. Once Daphne had found the missing rat.

Once Maureen was back with him again.

FIVE

Less than ninety minutes to sunrise, a cab dropped Jules off in front of Maureen's house. The linteled doorway, coated in shadow, waited for him at the top of three steps. Jules heard the cab drive off behind him. He suddenly missed Doodlebug's company enormously. Maybe he should've taken his friend up on the offer to sleep a night or two at the veterinary clinic?

"Just jitters," he told himself, staring up at that dark doorway. "Stupid jitters, that's all." He forced himself to climb the steps and place the key in the lock. Maureen's ghost wouldn't be waiting for him inside. And even if it were, it would be a friendly spirit, certainly. After all, hadn't he made plans to bring her back?

The air inside was musty, stale. The same dead air had been sitting in this house for the last eight months. He stepped haltingly into the foyer, then winced involuntarily. He expected something to hit him. Something plastic and hollow—the videotape that Malice X had left for him to find, that he'd hung on a length of twine from the ceiling so it would strike Jules in the face; the tape on which he'd documented and then boasted of his murder of Maureen.

Jules wiped the sweat from his forehead, then turned on his flashlight. Nothing was hanging from the ceiling. He waved the light beam around the parlor. No spirits waited for him there, either friendly or vengeful. At least none that he could see.

Still, it was both spooky and achingly sad to step into the rooms where he'd painstakingly swept up his lover's dust. Her magazines were right where he'd left them, piled on the end table by the sofa. *Good Housekeeping. Better Homes and Gardens. Martha Stewart Living.* Guidebooks to the respectable, ordinary, upper-middle-class life she'd dreamed of living, even though she'd been a blood-drinking stripper in a low-class French Quarter titty bar. Jules had sometimes poked gentle fun at her aspirations. Not much, though, because she would've leveled him for laughing at her. She, in turn, had mocked Jules for his contentment with his frayed working-class lifestyle, his refusal to even dream of rising above his station. It had been one of many minor irritants in their long, on-again, off-again relationship.

He started climbing the stairs to Maureen's bedroom, grasping the railing tightly, glad that she'd had a heavy-duty model installed. He wished her water were running. He'd pay serious money for a long, hot shower. His skin itched like crazy, probably the result of all that muck and garbage he'd been scurrying through during his months as a swarm of rats. But Straussman couldn't arrange to have water and electricity turned on again until tomorrow evening, at the earliest.

Jules thought about the butler, grunted, and slowly shook his head. Straussman and Maureen. *Who woulda thunk it?* But actually, the more he thought about it, the more he realized how much of Maureen's personality it explained. She'd always been so sensitive and secretive about her origins. In the long decades they'd spent together, all Jules had ever been able to pry out of her was that she'd been turned in 1902 and had lived with the High Krewe for the next twelve years. In 1914, she left them for unspecified reasons and moved into this house, which she'd inherited from a spinster aunt she'd never met. Jules didn't even know the year she was born, or whether she'd spent her childhood in New Orleans. He first met her in 1917, the year she took him on as her lover and made him one of the undead.

He hadn't been Mr. Most-Likely-to-Succeed when they met; the recipient of an eighth-grade education, he'd been working the docks to help support his mother, hanging out in Storyville gambling halls and brothels at night. He'd been debating whether to enlist in the Navy when Maureen's bite changed everything. She had the tragic, romantic air of a fallen angel, an exile from an ancient aristocracy. The biggest mystery for Jules during his first few years with Maureen hadn't been the existence of vampires in a rational world, a world with electricity and motor cars and radio—the big mystery was why she'd picked *him,* lowly Jules Duchon, to be her consort.

Well, maybe they'd had more in common than he ever realized. He'd always figured Maureen was an Anastasia, cut off from her world of wealth and privilege by some scandal or tragedy she wouldn't talk about. But Cinderella might be closer to the mark. If Straussman, the butler, turned her and brought her into the big house, Maureen would've been low gal on the totem pole. The other women, the blood-daughters of Besthoff, Katz, and Krauss, would've looked down their noses at Maureen something fierce. And Maureen had been nothing if not proud. No wonder she'd split. Knowing what he knew now, Jules was surprised she'd been able to last even twelve years with the High Krewe.

Jules paused in the doorway of Maureen's bedroom. The room he'd most dreaded entering. If her ghost was anywhere to be found, it would be here. Here, where she'd tended her plants and painted her toenails; here, where she and Jules had made love and fought and reconciled and made love again innumerable times over the past eighty-five years. He scanned the windowless room's four corners with his flashlight's beam. The beam illuminated falling clouds of dust, a stepping-stone path through the black earth surrounding her bed, and desiccated plants, brown as famine. In the middle of it all was her super-king-sized water bed, rumpled sheets undoubtedly untouched since the last night Maureen awoke, stretched, and rolled out of bed to ready herself for another shift dancing at Jezebel's Joy Room.

No ghosts. None that the light beam could touch. But really, Maureen's ghost was everywhere, because this whole house had been an extension of her, as much a part of her as the custom-made clothes she'd worn, her perfume, the little green breath mints she'd habitually popped in her mouth after draining a victim.

Jules set the flashlight on the floor, leaned on a chair, and stripped off his clothes. Then he walked to the edge of the bed, his bare feet crunching dry dead leaves. He pushed aside the covers and laid himself down in the bed he knew as well as his own skin. It was like being on an ocean liner in a gentle swell, the waves of the bed rocking him side to side. He pulled the sheet over him. Suddenly, she was there, all around him. Her scent. He lifted the sheet to his nose and breathed in deeply. White Shoulders. Her perfume. Even after eight months, the sheets were still suffused with it. He closed his eyes tightly and imagined her white shoulders, her big, broad, soft white shoulders, sinking his face into them, kissing them over and over.

Soon, babe. Soon we'll be lying here side by side again.

♠

Sewell Cadillac-Chevrolet was exactly where Jules thought a proper luxury dealership should be—downtown, in the heart of everything. The brightly polished cars sat behind huge glass-display windows like a line of monumental bowling trophies.

Jules frowned as he climbed out of the cab and looked around. This section of Baronne Street wasn't exactly the "heart of everything" anymore; the area sure had changed since the last time he'd set foot in the dealership, almost thirty years ago. The Civic Theater down the street, where Jules used to love going to see big Hollywood spectacles and the occasional live vaudeville show, was empty and dark; the building was now a sagging shell, although its dilapidated neon sign still had the power to impress. The long-closed furniture stores surrounding the theater building were in even worse shape. At least the area was looking a little less ratty than it had a couple of years ago. Signs had been posted across the boarded-up display windows, announcing the planned conversion of the old buildings to luxury condos. When it would happen was anyone's guess.

Peering through the window of a side showroom, Jules spied a convertible, and his heart took a flying leap. It didn't have tail fins (a disappointment), but it looked damn sporty. He eagerly walked into the dealership. Gleaming marble floor tiles and massive chandeliers immediately banished all thoughts of urban decay. And the cars! Being surrounded by so many brand-new gold and champagne Cadillacs made Jules feel like he was floating on a cloud, his equipment intact, and all was right with his world. Sure, there were a few hulking Chevy trucks lying around, too, but Jules ignored those affronts to good taste.

Straussman, whom Jules had arranged to meet, stood at the reception desk with a salesman. A lady salesman. Jules looked her over carefully, figuring it was always good to size up your opponent before entering battle. She looked like she should be driving a Cadillac, rather than selling them. In her midfifties, she wore a pink linen skirt suit with white lace collar, gold buttons big as Kennedy half-dollars, and shoulder pads that could put an eye out. Her bottle-blond coif looked stiff and sturdy enough to knock the wind out of an NFL lineman, should she ever decide to tackle one.

Her eyes brightened as Jules approached. "Mr. Doo-chon?" she said hopefully, emphasizing the first syllable of his name heavily. Jules nodded. He suddenly felt extremely self-conscious of his tight safari suit and stained trench coat. After he bought the car, he'd have to buy some new clothes to go with it. She smiled. Her teeth were big and square. She held out her hand, palm down. "Welcome to Sewell Cadillac-Chevrolet. My name is Mary-Ann—just like that cute little girl on *Gilligan's Island.*" She smiled again, flashing those teeth. "Mr. Straussman tells me youah interested in leasing one of our fine Cadillacs."

The accent hit him. She wasn't from around here. Mississippi, he guessed. He'd known a lady vampire from Jackson once. "Steel magnolia," hah. Steel battle-ax was more like it.

He shook her hand. "Yeah, that's right. And I know just what I want, too."

"And what would that be?" she asked chirpily.

"That Eldorado convertible in the side showroom."

"Eldorado convertible?" Her rodentlike smile faded. "Ah'm so sorry, but Cadillac hasn't made that car in many years."

"What're you talkin' about? I just looked through the window, and it's sittin' on the showroom floor."

"Oh! *That* car. But that's not a new car. And it isn't for sale."

Jules saw red. *Here it comes—the old bait and switch.* "This is a dealership, right? Not a museum? Why would you have something on the floor that's not for sale?"

"Well, that's the owner's son's project car. A 1993 Allante. A little two-seat sport model. He's been restoring it for years. We've been keeping it on the floor to draw in the walk-in crowd." She looked at her inventory clipboard, then flashed Jules an incandescent smile. "Actually, Mr. Doochon, I think we may be in luck. I believe that for the right price, the owner's son would be willing to part with this very collectible automobile. Would you lahk to see it?"

"Sure!"

Mary-Ann led Jules and Straussman through a side door into a smaller showroom. This showroom held only two cars, a new Corvette convertible and the Allante, surrounded by display cases filled with Chevrolet racing memorabilia and photos of historic Caddies and Chevies. Jules couldn't recall having seen an Allante before. Maybe

Cadillac hadn't made too many. This one was a beaut—candy-apple red, the color of passion, and although it didn't carry much chrome, the chrome it did carry was choice.

Jules walked around the back. The tail was higher than the nose, an aggressive, athletic stance, as if the car was ready to pounce on someone. Jules liked it. Overall, the car was small for a Cadillac, but it was bigger than the Corvette next to it, and it was bigger than the 1955 Thunderbird Jules had taken out for a test drive once. He'd fit in that okay; of course, he'd been a bit more svelte back then than now. He walked around to the front. The red hood was wide, long, and low, with a traditional Cadillac grille, a rectangular grid of chrome bars. And it had a hood ornament, the proud Cadillac shield and crest, a miniature metal flag that always made him feel like saluting.

He wanted the car.

"Now this car, the 1993 model," Mary-Ann said, glancing down at her clipboard, "this was the last Allante made. And the best one made. This was the only year to have the Northstar engine. Are you familiar with Cadillac's famous Northstar engines, Mr. Doochon? It's a very advanced V-8 engine, thirty-two valves, two hundred and ninety horsepower—"

"Can I sit in it?"

"Well, of course. By all means."

She opened the car's long door for him. Jules took his first glance at the interior. His heart sank. "No bench seat," he muttered. "And what's that big thing in the middle there?"

"That? That's a console. Just lahk in an airplane cockpit, Mr. Doochon. It has storage for all your little doodads, and it's also an armrest."

Jules squeezed himself into the driver's seat. The steering wheel poked six inches into his stomach. He found the tilt adjustment and moved the wheel to its uppermost position, which was better, but not much. Worse, with his right side squashed against the console, three-quarters of his left buttock hung over the seat's side bolster, making it impossible to slam the door shut.

"Oh, dear," Mary-Ann said. Her free hand fluttered to her blond helmet, as if she were afraid a bird might nest there. She patted herself on the cheek, then flipped rapidly through the pages on her clipboard. "I have another idea, Mr. Doochon. The Escalade sport utility is *extremely* popular right now. It has a heavy-duty suspension, and it's, uh, much more *commodious* inside. Why, lots of people of size, just lahk yourself, they absolutely *love* it, wouldn't drive anything else—"

"That's a truck, right?"

"Yes. Yes, it is. But it's very luxurious—"

"I ain't drivin' no goddamn truck."

The saleslady looked helplessly to Straussman, who had maintained his silence until now. The desperate appeal on her face must have affected him, because he stepped forward. "The vehicle she describes does sound far more practical, sir. This sports car, although handsome, does not have much storage. And since the intention is to lease you a work vehicle, not a pleasure vehicle—"

"Did I ask your advice?" Jules said. The wheel was making it difficult for him to breathe, but he'd never admit that. "You're a checkbook, Straussman. Not a goddamn issue of *Consumer Reports.*" Jules still wanted the car. Now that the saleslady and Straussman were trying to talk him out of it, he wanted it more than ever. At least with the open roof, his upper body had lots of room to spread out. He could hang his left arm over the door and steer with his right, if he didn't breathe too deeply. Assuming he could get the door closed, that is. The problem was that goddamn console. Without that in the way, he'd fit just fine.

"Hey." Jules gestured for the saleslady to come closer. "Can't you have your shop boys yank this thing out? It ain't important mechanically, is it? It's just storage, right?"

"Oh, dear," she said. "That—that would involve chopping through the plastic. It would leave a big, unsightly hole. And since the car would be leased . . ." She stared into Jules's determined face and blinked rapidly three times. "Well . . . I'll need to check with my managers on this. It might be possible. Of course, the down payment on the lease would need to be substantially larger, along with a capital-devaluation assessment. . . ."

"Yeah, yeah, whatever," Jules said eagerly. After all, *he* wasn't paying for it. "The High Krewe, they got money like I got hemorrhoids. Up the yazoo. Right, Straussman?"

The butler's thin lips moved about a millimeter. Jules decided it was a smile.

♠

Jules and Straussman sat together in the customer-courtesy area while Mary-Ann called in a technician (who charged double rates) to remove the offending central console. Jules absorbed free coffee like a sponge while Straussman genteelly but firmly negotiated the best short-term lease terms he could, given the unusual circumstances.

After Straussman and Jules signed the lease documents in triplicate, they heard the distant but piercing sound of a buzz saw coming from the body shop behind the showroom. Jules briefly wondered if he'd done the right thing; maybe that Escalade would've made more sense, after all. *Aww, what the hell,* he told himself. *Too late now.*

He glanced over at his silent companion. The two of them, Jules remembered with recurring surprise, were blood relations. In essence, Straussman was his blood-grandfather. Creepy, kind of. Still, Jules figured it was time he started cutting the butler some slack. Straussman couldn't be a cold, dead fish one hundred percent. Not if he'd picked out Maureen.

"Hey, Straussman? You want a cup of java? I'm gettin' another one for myself."

"No. But thank you."

Jules slowly pushed himself off the padded bench and walked over to the coffeepot, which was nearly empty. He struggled for some way to keep their nub of a conversation going. "I'll bet it's not that often that somebody asks *you* if you want something, huh?"

"That is quite true, Mr. Duchon. Thank you again."

Jules filled his Styrofoam cup about two-thirds of the way to the top, shaking out the last few muddy drops from the pot, then sat back down. "Well, thanks for workin' that deal for me. You like drivin' in open convertibles?"

"I can't say that I have ever done so. Although I must have, at some point, since most early motor cars were open in design, I recall. However, the masters did take many years to accept the replacement of horse power by horsepower."

Jules did a double take. If he'd heard correctly, Straussman had just made a joke. The guy was becoming more human by the minute. Jules thought back to the butler's emotional reaction to Maureen's death. For better or worse, it was something that tied him and Straussman together, even more so than their blood link. "Hey, there's somethin' I been wantin' to ask you. Did you sense anything eight months ago, when Maureen got murdered? See, she used to tell me that she could kinda feel it when I was around, like when she'd be upstairs at Jezebel's and I'd be down on the sidewalk, trying to decide whether or not to come up. She said it was because she was the one who made me. Do you feel it when one you made dies?"

Straussman was silent for a moment. "I did sense something, I believe now," he said, staring out the window into the dark street. "At the time, I did not know what this sensation was. But I have read of something similar. When a man loses a limb—a wounded soldier, for example—frequently that man complains to his doctors of pain from the leg that is no longer there. Phantom pain, I believe it is called. That is the closest analogy I can think of to the sensation I first experienced eight months ago."

"Huh." Since Maureen's death, Jules had been feeling like he was missing a part of himself, too.

Straussman turned to face him. "Mr. Duchon, if I may inquire, when do you plan to attempt Maureen's resurrection?"

"Later this week, I hope," Jules said. "As soon as they give me the car, I'm gonna go see my buddy Erato. He's been keepin' Maureen's ashes for me. Doodlebug's researchin' stuff. He's a fast study, that kid."

"Should you be successful—and I pray that you will be—would it be possible for you to bring Maureen to see me? It has been so many years."

"Uh, geez, there's no way I'd get her to go to your mansion. Not with how she feels about that place."

"Perhaps I could come visit her elsewhere, then?"

Hearing the muffled hope in Straussman's voice was painful. It echoed the fearful, halting hope in Jules's own heart. Doodlebug's resurrection spell had to work. It just had to. "Yeah. Bet I could arrange that." The butler smiled. Not much of a smile, but enough to make Jules feel a surge of warmth for him, almost as if he were a real grandfather. "Hey. I been wantin' to ask you this ever since I found out you were Maureen's blood-daddy. How'd the two of you hook up? Where'd you find her?"

Straussman's face seemed to soften. "I was granted special dispensation," he said, clearly savoring every word. "To find myself a companion. This was due to my hundred and fifty years of devoted service. I was carefully instructed that whoever I chose would need to be someone who would not be missed from the human community. My initial instinct was to seek my companion among the fallen women of the Storyville district."

Jules's eyes grew wide. "So Maureen was a hooker?"

"No," Straussman said. "The women whom I met there were too debased, too crushed in spirit or filled with hatred for the male gender to provide me with eternal companionship. I redirected my search one strata higher. I began attending dance-hall shows, performances by costumed comedians and singers of bawdy, popular songs. It was there that I met Maureen."

"She was a singer?"

"A singer, yes."

"What theater was it?"

"A small, rather grubby house called the Gaiety. It was just off Canal Street, I believe. The building was demolished long ago."

Jules tried remembering the place. It didn't register; he'd spent nights in so many cheap theaters around town. "Yeah, Maureen always had a good voice," he said. "She was always singin' around the house. Sometimes she'd talk management into lettin' her sing during her strip shows at Jezebel's." He remembered their first nights together, back in 1917. Especially that indelible night when she'd revealed to him what she was, and asked him to join her. "So, uh, how'd you do it? Did you, y'know, just take her? Or did you ask her first?"

Straussman grinned slightly. "Oh, I took a week to become acquainted with her. This followed many earlier evenings of coming to see her perform, and several times having flowers delivered to the stage. One cannot force another to be one's companion for all eternity. I wooed her."

Jules raised an eyebrow. "You sent her flowers? Heh. I'll bet she thought you were some slummin' big shot."

"Perhaps."

Jules drained the last drops from his cup, then tossed it into an ashtray. " 'Perhaps'? What, you mean you didn't tell her you were a butler before she let you fang her?"

Straussman's lips became a thin white line. "I was not entirely forthcoming regarding the nature of my employment."

Jules laughed, a loud bark that echoed off the display windows. "Hoo boy—I'll bet she sure was pissed when you brought her back to the compound, and she found out you weren't no Duke of Earl."

The butler sighed. "She was not pleased."

"So what happened between you guys? Maureen hung around the High Krewe for twelve years or so."

Straussman rubbed the smooth space between his nose and upper lip with his pinky, then folded his hands. "She was a strong woman. Strong, and strong-willed. She did her utmost to make the best of a difficult situation. She did not love me, but after the shock and disappointment had dissipated, I sensed affection from her. Given time, that affection might have blossomed into something more, if only . . ."

The butler's voice faded away. "What?" Jules asked eagerly. This was fascinating; in a weird way, it was almost like hearing details of his birth parents' long-ago (and brief) marriage. " 'If only' what?"

"The other women in the household. They were less than kind to Maureen."

"What? They made her do all the shitty jobs? Cracked wise behind her back? What?"

Straussman stiffened. He returned to being a wooden Indian in a penguin suit. "That was all a very long time ago, Mr. Duchon. And I have spoken out of turn. Gossip reflects very poorly on one of my station. I would appreciate if you would question me no further on this."

The lights in the dealership began blinking off one by one. The technician told Mary-Ann he was finished, and she handed Jules the keys to his new chariot.

Jules pocketed the keys, then took a closer look at his companion, the man with whom he'd begun feeling a sense of friendly kinship. *The other women in the household* . . . Straussman's words echoed in his head. Staring at the butler, he thought about Victoria and Alexandra lying in their coffins, beautiful puzzles each missing a piece. Had they been with the High Krewe a hundred years ago? Had they been among Maureen's tormentors?

Jules's stomach sank. If the missing and mutilated women had been evil bitches to Maureen, Straussman had a motive. Jules may have just met his first suspect. He wished Straussman a good night and forced a smile.

SIX

The night air felt great. Temperature in the midsixties, low humidity . . . If New Orleans weather were like this all year round, Jules thought, the city's population wouldn't be 480,000—it'd be ten million. And everyone would drive a convertible.

He turned onto Daneel Street, in a quiet residential neighborhood, and parked alongside the Neutral Ground Coffeehouse. Best known for its nightly folk-music performances, the Neutral Ground also had a computer that patrons could rent by the hour. Libraries didn't stay open past sundown; inconvenient for a vampire who needed to do some research. So the Neutral Ground would have to do, even though there was a good chance Jules would find the music obnoxious.

He reached behind him and grabbed the leading edge of the folded tan canvas convertible top, pulled it above his head, then latched it to the windshield. Then he wiggled himself out onto the sidewalk. He armed the car's alarm system by pressing a stud on his key fob (a gizmo he'd never had with any car before). The Neutral Ground was in a pretty decent neighborhood, right behind the exclusive Isidore Newman School. But a few blocks away, the neighborhood turned dicey, so there was no sense in taking chances.

His forebodings about the night's musical offerings were borne out as soon as he walked through the door. The joint's well-worn couches, easy chairs, and benches were crammed full of vampire wannabes—kids whose white-painted faces and black clothes made them look like a troupe of melancholy mimes. A trio who could've stepped straight out of one of Agatha Longrain's vampire potboilers performed acoustic covers of Courane L'Enfant's greatest hits. Terrific . . . hearing that asshole's Cajun-Goth-thrash "music," even in watered-down acoustic form, was sure to give Jules a headache, not to mention indigestion.

He almost turned back around and walked out. But then he saw that the computer wasn't being used. He might be able to find another coffeehouse somewhere that would rent him Internet access, but in tech-deprived New Orleans, always twenty years behind the times, that wasn't a sure bet. He squeezed his way through clumps of wannabes to the counter and signaled for the young hostess to come over. Thankfully, she wasn't wearing vampire regalia.

" 'Scuse me, miss, how much is it to rent that computer there?"

"Four dollars for thirty minutes."

"How about if I want to print stuff out?"

"Twenty-five cents per page."

He glanced quickly at the screen. Honestly, he didn't know much about computers and the Internet. Apart from looking at some porno stuff and buying a few old detective magazines using the machine Erato had set up for him at his old house, Jules hadn't messed with computers much. "I need to do some research, honey. You think maybe you could help me get started?"

The young woman stared at the pile of dirty dishes in the sink and the impatient customers lining the counter. "I'm sorry, mister, but this is a really busy night, and my backup called in sick—"

"There's a ten-buck tip in it for you if you do."

She bit her lip, but then followed him over to the computer. "What're you researching?" she asked, sitting down at the keyboard.

"Vampires in New Orleans."

She laughed. "Shit. You don't need a computer to research *that.* Just start talking with any of these jokers hanging out here tonight."

Jules didn't laugh. "Not them kinda vampires," he grumbled.

A few minutes later, coffee in hand, he started scrolling through descriptions of hundreds of articles featuring both NEW ORLEANS and VAMPIRES. Where to start? He wanted to find some clue as to what the High Krewe's youngsters had been up to while they'd been sneaking into the city. His interviews with them would be a lot more productive if he could go in armed with a little knowledge of their activities.

His index finger got tired from punching the mouse button. Vampire S and M sites. Courane L'Enfant fan sites. An offer for French Quarter tours conducted by a "genuine" vampire guide. Jules clicked on that last one, wondering whether the High Krewe youngsters might be earning some extra cash leading tourist tours, maybe nibbling a few necks on the side. But the site included a photo of the tour guide, which ruled out his being a vampire.

An article from *New Orleans Gambit Weekly* caught Jules's attention. It was entitled "Vampire Queen Versus Catfish King." Jules remembered the story well. Agatha Longrain and Van Goodfeller, founder of the Goodfeller's Famous Fried Catfish chain, had gotten into a pissing match over a piece of property on St. Charles Avenue. Four years ago, the fried-catfish king had scandalized the Uptown establishment by proposing to convert a surplus beaux arts school building on hoity-toity St. Charles Avenue to a flashy restaurant and hotel. Preservationists and patricians, Longrain and L'Enfant among them, kept him tied up in the courts and zoning-board meetings for months. But ultimately, Van Goodfeller's political connections won the day. From what Jules had read about him, Goodfeller had come up from nothing, a dirt-poor childhood in the projects, even though he was a white guy. Jules respected that.

He narrowed his search to *Times-Picayune* newspaper articles. Strangely enough, Van Goodfeller's name popped up again, still in conjunction with Courane L'Enfant. This article was much more recent, only two months old. The headline read, "Competing Plans for St. Thomas Redevelopment Spark Debates, Protests." Jules scrolled down and read the first paragraphs.

> Restaurateur Van Goodfeller and musician Courane L'Enfant again find themselves in opposition over a real-estate deal. However, this time the stakes are much higher than they were four years ago over the development of the La Strada Restaurant and Inn. The Housing Authority of New Orleans (HANO) has been utilizing Federal HOPE grants to demolish the sixty-year-old St. Thomas Housing Project. Now Goodfeller and L'Enfant are battling for the right to determine what kind of development will replace the long-blighted public-housing tract.
>
> Goodfeller, in partnership with the GoodiesMart Corporation, plans to build a mixed-income neighborhood anchored by a distribution facility and a large discount store and super-

market. Sixty-five percent of the housing to be built would be subsidized, with most of these units reserved for displaced project residents, and the remaining thirty-five percent would be sold at market rates. Costs not covered by the HOPE grants would be paid for through a thirty-five-year city tax abatement on property taxes and sales taxes.

L'Enfant, heading up a group of private investors, has a far different vision for the fifty-plus acres of prime land. He envisions a gated community that will duplicate the genteel, historic charm of the Garden District and provide a showcase neighborhood for the city. Despite utilizing Federal funds, far fewer units of subsidized housing would be provided than under the competing plan. Announced investors include famed vampire novelist and longtime Garden District resident Agatha Longrain . . .

Jules stopped reading. This was interesting, but it wasn't what he was looking for. Trying to narrow his search more, he typed in VAMPIRE ATTACK and NEW ORLEANS. Up popped references such as "*New Orleans vampire* fans verbally *attack*ed bookstore owners who failed to stock adequate supplies of the new Agatha Longrain novel," and "Financing for the planned film *Attack of the Vampires,* currently in preproduction in *New Orleans,* hit a snag . . ." This didn't seem to be getting him anywhere either. He impatiently paged down the list, wondering whether he was wasting his time. But then an article grabbed his attention. An article that described an actual attack, and a real death:

Body of Central City Pastor Found in Lagoon

Thomas Angelico, City Bureau

The body of Richard Hammond, pastor of Central City's Spirit Revival Full Gospel Church, was discovered at the bottom of a City Park lagoon Tuesday morning. Workers were using a backhoe to dredge the lagoon when the body was uncovered, partially buried in silt. The grim discovery confirmed the fears of many of Mr. Hammond's congregants, who believed he had fallen victim to an attack by neighborhood drug dealers or members of a "vampire" cult; he had denounced both groups from his pulpit. Police revealed the cause of death to have been a stab wound to the base of the skull, compounded by puncture wounds to the neck. Recently, Mr. Hammond had been one of the strongest proponents of the Goodfeller-GoodiesMart plan for the redevelopment of the St. Thomas Housing Project tract . . .

"Vampire" cult? Puncture wounds to the neck combined with a destruction of the brain stem? This sounded like a story that could have the High Krewe's youngsters' fingerprints on it. Jules printed the article. Now at least he'd have some idea where to steer his interviews once he got back to Besthoff's place.

But before he headed back to the High Krewe's compound, he had another errand he needed to attend to. A personal errand as close to his heart as the borrowed blood that flowed through it. He had to retrieve Maureen's ashes from Erato.

♠

Jules pulled into the parking lot behind the Trolley Stop Cafe. He maneuvered the Allante into a space at the corner of the lot, two spaces away from any of the police cruisers or taxicabs, so there'd be less chance of some careless idiot scratching his paint. He'd passed Erato's Town Car taxi parked on St. Charles Avenue, in front of the restaurant; it was 11:15 P.M., right around the time his friend habitually took his first break. Explaining to Erato where he'd been the past eight months wouldn't be easy. Especially not after the last conversation they'd had, when Jules had pretty much implied he'd be heading off on a suicide mission. He hated lying to Erato, and he avoided it whenever he could. But tonight, telling the truth wasn't an option.

He briefly considered pulling out of the parking lot. But then he reminded himself that his reunion with Erato was an unavoidable pit stop on the road to seeing Maureen again. The longer he procrastinated, the longer he'd be without her. So Jules steeled his nerves and turned his engine off.

The Trolley Stop's front facade still looked mostly the same as it had eight months ago; dark olive green, the color of the avenue's famous streetcars, with wooden cutouts of a streetcar conductor and Victorian-era passengers bolted to the weather boards. Jules noticed that the owners had added on a new room to the left side of the building. Good; that meant the joint was doing good business, and it would hang around for a while. One of the saddest aspects of being a vampire was watching beloved businesses go under as tastes changed or owners died and left behind no heirs willing to take up the burdens of retail. Whenever Jules got together with the crusty old vampires of the Deep South Lodge at one of their triennial conventions, he could count on hearing hours upon hours of sad groanings about the deaths of downtowns, how giant Goodies-Marts were turning Main Streets into ghost streets, how nobody knew how to make a decent chocolate phosphate or egg cream anymore.

He went inside, pushing past a group of black teens waiting impatiently for a table in the smoking section. Erato was sitting at the bar on his usual stool, next to the end stool where Jules had habitually perched himself. When Jules saw his old friend, his stomach lurched like it used to on that first big dip on the old Zephyr roller coaster at Pontchartrain Beach. This wasn't going to be easy. The best way to do it was to plunge right in and hope the ride would get easier after the first drop.

Jules slowly approached the stool where his friend sat. *Please, Erato—don't have a coronary. You and me, we're both carryin' around big spare tires, tough on the ol' ticker.* He stopped three feet to his friend's side and waited for Erato to swallow a sip of coffee, then put the mug back on the counter. "Hey, Erato," he said as gently as he could manage. "I'm back."

The black man's back stiffened, but not as radically as Jules feared it might. He didn't gasp in surprise. Instead, he grasped the edge of the counter tightly with his left hand and swiveled to his right. Both of his eyes, even the lazy one, focused warily on Jules's face. "So, Miss Doodlebug managed to root you out, huh?"

It was Jules's turn to be surprised. "How'd you know Doodlebug was lookin' for me?"

"I gave her a ride to Miss Maureen's house the other night. The house that been sittin' dark and empty these past eight months."

Jules felt the implied rebuke in his guts. He began unspooling his fabricated explanation. "I guess you been wonderin' where I've been, huh?"

"That be a decent guess, yeah."

"After Maureen died . . . I just about lost my mind." That much was true, at least; his mind had been subdivided into nearly two hundred bite-sized pieces. "I had to get away, leave behind everything and everybody who reminded me of her. This cousin of mine, he has this vacation house in the Bahamas. He let me stay there while I was gettin' my head back together. I wanted to let you know where I was, that I was doin' okay . . . but I just couldn't make myself talk to nobody who knew Maureen."

Erato's gaze hadn't wavered from his face. "And what about that dangerous business you tol' me you was headin' off to take care of eight months ago? What happened with that?"

Jules looked pained. "Aww, Erato, I can't go into any of that. I told you eight months ago I couldn't tell you nothin'. And I still can't."

"Then maybe we got nothin' to say to each other." Erato began twisting his body back to the counter and his unfinished dinner.

"All right," Jules said before his friend's back was completely turned to him. "I'll tell you this one thing. That guy who killed Maureen? He won't be hurtin' anybody anymore. Ever again. But that's all I can say."

Erato swiveled slowly back around, face flushed with anger. "I spent months worryin' 'bout you. Then I spent months mournin' you, figurin' you was dead. How much a postcard cost? One lousy postcard coulda saved me all that."

"But I told you—"

"I *heard* what you said. I just gotta decide whether I trust it. Here you are, bigger than life, wantin' to just take up from where we left off. But I got a choice, see? I can accept what you tell me, accept that you're gonna be a hoodoo man and disappear from the face o' the earth sometimes, and I just gotta trust that you'll pop up again and still be my pal. That's one choice. The other choice is, I put you out."

The odor of burning toast wafted from the nearby kitchen. Erato sat on his stool like a pensive bullfrog on its lily pad. Jules felt as rooted to the floor as a giant cypress in Honey Island Swamp. Until Erato said something more, he couldn't move a muscle, not even to avoid sunrise.

Somewhere behind Jules, a waitress banged into a table and dropped her tray. The clamor and resultant cursing broke the stillness between the two friends. Erato's lazy eye lost discipline and returned to its own eccentric orbit. Its owner furrowed his forehead and silently sighed. "Oh, what the hell," he said in a low tone. "Life's too short to be castin' away friends." He held out his thick right arm, inviting Jules back into the fold. Jules stepped into the awkward embrace. Erato's mug of coffee spilled onto the counter when Jules's elbow thumped it aside. His friend's grip around his shoulders was a strong one.

"Thanks, Erato. You're a real pal." Relief flooded over him like java from the upturned mug.

Erato released him, then stared sardonically at the brown puddle surrounding his plate. "Thank me by buyin' me another cup of coffee, okay?"

"Is it okay if we make that a 'go' cup? I was hopin' . . . well, I was meanin' to ask if maybe I could go back with you to your house. So I could get Maureen's ashes from you."

"Yeah, I was figurin' you was gonna ask that." He signaled for the waitress behind the counter to come over. "Honey, I'll take me a refill, but in a 'go' cup. And the check, too, okay? Thanks." He cut up his remaining piece of catfish with quick stabs of his knife and fork and stuffed the fried morsels in his mouth.

"No big rush," Jules said. "I don't want you gettin' no indigestion."

" 'Sokay," Erato mumbled between chews. "The less time I be hangin' around this joint, the more money I takes home."

After Erato paid the bill (Jules offered to pay, but then remembered he hadn't gotten his first expense payment from the High Krewe yet and sheepishly backed off his offer), they walked outside. "Hey," Jules said, recovering quickly from his embarrassment, "how about I drive us over to your place, then drop you back here?"

Erato grinned. "You still drivin' that ol' heap of a Cadillac?"

Jules nearly launched himself into an impassioned defense of his old Fleetwood, the faithful car he'd used as his taxi for nearly ten years, then decided to let it drop. "Naww. I got me another car now. Still a Caddy, but a newer one."

"Whoah! You mean to tell me you can't pay for a cup of coffee, but you got you a new Cadillac?"

Jules grabbed Erato's arm and guided him toward the back parking lot. "It's not *new* new. Just new*er.* It's sort of an advance on this job I'm doin'."

"You mean you ain't drivin' a hack no more?"

"Not right now I'm not." Jules remembered his own advice to Doodlebug about the folly of getting one's normal friends too involved in one's business. He knew he shouldn't even mention to Erato the kind of work he'd been dragooned into. But as much as he'd resented being forced into his new role, it was just too cool not to share with his best pal. "Wait'll you hear this, Erato. You wanna know the kind of work I'm doin' now?"

"I guess I gonna hear it whether I want to or not. Spill."

"I'll give you a hint. Sam Spade. Charlie Chan—"

"You runnin' a Chinese laundry?"

"No! I'm a private investigator."

Erato stopped walking. "No shit? I thought you hadda be an ex-cop to get that kinda gig."

"This is a special deal."

" 'Special deal,' huh? So what's this you investigatin'? The latest 'special deal' at the Dunkin' Donuts?"

Jules's sense of delight evaporated into wariness. "Uh, hey, it's kinda like that situation I got dragged into eight months ago. I can't say too much. . . ."

"Your secret life, huh? 'If I tells you, I's gonna hafta kill you'?"

Jules grunted with amusement, remembering the last time he and Erato had shared the same little joke. "Yeah. Or at least put sugar in the gas tank of that crappy Town Car you drive around."

Erato scanned the police cruisers and taxis crowding the rear lot. "So where's this new*er* Cadillac of yours?"

Jules walked a few steps further and pointed. "That one there."

"*That?* The convertible?"

"Yeah," Jules said, his chest inflating with pride. "The last convertible Caddy ever made. Ain't she a cream puff?"

"I'll say she *is,*" Erato said, circling the Allante. "But I always thought you liked bigger cars."

"Everybody's gotta have a convertible at least once in their life," Jules said, opening the door for his friend. *Or their undead life.*

♠

Jules gunned the big Northstar V-8, briefly flooring the accelerator. The Allante roared and leaped to fifty miles per hour, fifteen above the speed limit on St. Charles Avenue. A small crowd of Goth kids waiting for a streetcar at the edge of the neutral ground jumped out of the way as the red Cadillac hurtled past.

"Hey, no need to impress me!" Erato stammered. "I'm impressed enough."

Spotting a cop car approaching from downtown, Jules tapped the powerful brakes, slowing to a legal speed. "This is America," he said, smiling as he saw two of the tall, skinny kids, rapidly diminishing in his rearview mirror, shoot him the finger. "A man's got a right to play with his toys."

Compared with his old car, the Allante handled like a go-cart on rails. The grease monkeys had done a good job of taking out the offending portion of the console. They'd filled in the hole just behind the gearshift selector with a nice piece of polished walnut, and the bare space on the floor was disguised with a piece of carpet that blended imperceptibly with the rest. Even with the adjustments, the car still fit his lower half tight as a cocoon, particularly with Erato squeezed into the passenger seat. But that was okay; with the top down, his upper body had the entire sky, the whole universe to stretch out in.

They turned onto Jackson Avenue and drove toward the river. Jules had certainly seen some changes along this stretch during his hundred-plus years on earth. The neighborhood had originally combined grand antebellum mansions, a profusion of churches and synagogues, and closer to the river, cotton presses. Beyond Magazine Street, much of this had given way over the decades to various symptoms of blight: the St. Thomas housing project, dilapidated working-class shotgun doubles, and a shot-to-hell infrastructure that included a half-collapsed fire station, an abandoned hospital, and a public ferry landing that doubled as a drug market after dark. But none of the changes he'd seen prepared him for the visual shock that slapped him in the face when he and Erato reached St. Thomas Street.

"Holy *shit,*" Jules said, pulling over to the side so he could take a better look. "Where'd the housing project go?"

He stared across the four lanes of Jackson Avenue. The last time he'd looked, there'd been dozens of two- and three-story redbrick apartment houses, built by the Works Progress Administration during the Great Depression. They'd been lined with wrought-iron balconies and porches and mangled, sagging screen doors, surrounded by sixty-year-old live oaks and rusting playground equipment. A whole neighborhood; it'd been there so long, Jules could barely remember the older slum neighborhood the WPA had demolished and replaced with public housing.

Now it was gone. The newspaper articles he'd read at the Neutral Ground had mentioned that the project was being torn down, but they hadn't prepared him for a visual shock of this magnitude. Jules stared across the street at more than thirteen square blocks of dirt, weeds, and broken concrete. A few surviving oak trees tried valiantly to cover the emptiness. Near the back of the denuded tract, four of the brick project buildings, windows boarded over with plywood, huddled together like shivering, senile residents inexplicably left behind in a condemned nursing home.

"It's gone," Erato said, stating the obvious. "Torn down and hauled away."

"I remember them talkin' about this," Jules said. "Maybe a year or so before I went away. Tearin' down some of the crummier housing projects and building something else. But things move so slow in New Orleans . . . I never thought it'd actually happen." He couldn't stop looking at the huge emptiness across the street. It was like meeting an old acquaintance and finding she'd lost all four front teeth.

"The Housin' Authority's gotten pretty good at tearin' stuff down," Erato said. "What they ain't so good at yet is buildin' 'em back up. Me, I'm workin' with a group that means to make sure when they *do* build, they do the right thing. Both by the city at large, and by the folks what used to live over there."

"So where'd they go? The people who used to live there?"

"They been squeezed into other projects, doubled up in three-room apartments with other families. Or they's sleepin' on the couches of family or friends. Or they's sleepin' on the streets somewhere."

Jules started the car back up again. Erato's house was only a few blocks away, uptown on St. Thomas Street. "Well, whatever they end up doin' with all that land, you've gotta be happy they tore that project down. That place was a stinkin' armpit since the early seventies, at least. Fulla drugs and whorin' and crime. I always felt bad that you and your family worked so hard to keep your house nice, but because you were only a coupla blocks up from the project, your property values stayed in the crapper. Not to mention the burglar bars you had to put up, and the fence and alarm system, and all the trash you was always pickin' up from the kids that walked by and dumped it on your lawn. Maybe things'll get better now."

They drove slowly past a row of boarded-up shotgun doubles, houses that, with renovation, could potentially provide living space for a few of the displaced families. "You don't understand, Jules. Sure, some of them folks was trouble. But they was neighbors, part of the neighborhood. Them ladies from the St. Thomas I used to talk with at the corner store, most of them grew up there, raised their kids there. Lots of them was raisin' their grandkids there, too. It was home to them. Maybe not the nicest home in the world, but still home. They should have a stake in what gets built to replace the St. Thomas."

"And what's that gonna be? I hear lots of people got ideas about what gets built on that land."

Erato sighed. "Depends on whose plan gets pushed through. There's a lotta money floatin' around, see. Federal money. You heard of HOPE grants?"

"Read a little bit about them online. This has to do with that Van

Goodfeller versus Courane L'Enfant thing, right?" Jules pulled up to the grassy swale, neatly trimmed, in front of Erato's camelback house. The peach-colored house, single story in front, two stories in back, was much better maintained than its neighbors. It wouldn't look out of place, Jules thought, among the tonier neighborhoods of the University District uptown; except for the burglar bars, maybe.

"That's right," Erato said. "Thing is, HOPE grants give housing authorities flexibility. *Lots* of flexibility. Flexibility means choices. And you know who usually gets to make the choices around here. There used to be almost a thousand poor families lived in the St. Thomas. If the powers-that-be in this town get to choose between a development that's seventy percent poor folks or one that's ten percent poor folks, which do you think gonna get built?"

Jules closed the Allante's convertible top. "I don't see what you're gettin' at, Erato," he said. "City's got a black mayor. Most of the City Council's black. Heck, I'm pretty sure the head of the housing authority's black, too. They know where their votes're comin' from."

Erato frowned. "It's not a black-white thing I'm talkin' about here. It's a *green* thing. Who has the green. That's who makes the choices in New Orleans. Unless enough folks get together and make a big enough stink."

"So what're you sayin'? The St. Thomas is gonna get changed into Disneyland for the rich?"

"That's good land over there. *Good* land. Stuck right between that fancy Warehouse District, the Convention Center, and the Lower Garden District. There's a group of Uptowners who'd like nothin' better than to extend their Garden District downtown into the St. Thomas land, sprinkle in just enough subsidized apartments to be, y'know, 'politically correct.' "

Jules cut the ignition. "So let 'em! They'd be doin' you a favor! All these crummy joints up and down your street and Chippewa and Annunciation, they'd either get renovated or torn down and replaced by something nicer. The bums and pushers would be outta here. The value of your house would double, maybe triple, even. Let the Garden District come, Erato! It's the best damn thing that could happen to you."

Erato sighed. He looked away from Jules, stared out the window at his neighbors' sagging porches and rusting gutters. An old woman sitting on her porch across the street noticed him and waved. "It's not that simple. What's good for me . . . there's more to life than just what be good for *me,* the big payday for Johnny Erato. I done had my chances to leave. Leave this neighborhood. I coulda moved my family to the suburbs. Or out to the country, even, St. Rose or LaPlace. But I grew up here. I inherited this house. My pastor, he always said if the good ones leave the neighborhood, there won't be none left but the bad. I love this place with all my heart. There ain't nothin' I'd like to see more than for this neighborhood to come back. But it's gotta come back in the right way. A neighborhood ain't just buildings and streets. It's people, too. If the people get pushed out, then it ain't the same neighborhood no more."

Although he still favored the idea of the Garden District coming to Erato's street, Jules understood where his friend was coming from. He'd stayed in his mother's old house decades longer than he should've, given how the neighborhood had gone down. Heck, if Malice X hadn't burned it down, he'd still be living there, despite Montegut Street's crack dealers, abandoned lots, and derelict buildings. And he'd liked his neighbors, too. Lots of them had been downright tasty. "So who's side are you on? Van Goodfeller's?"

"Yeah," Erato said, brightening some. "Goodfeller and GoodiesMart, they're tied in with the Black Ministerial Alliance, ACORN, and the St. Thomas Consortium. Goodfeller wants to build a big distribution center where a buncha old, empty warehouses are now. GoodiesMart, they wanna build one of their giant discount stores. Tax abatements will let them corporations pay interest on federally backed construction loans for the subsidized housing. Plus, the St. Thomas residents who move back'll have jobs waitin' for them."

Jules was impressed by his friend's comprehension of the intricacies of local politics, not to mention his devotion to his neighbors. But he was getting impatient to reclaim Maureen's ashes. He opened his door, indicating with a jerk of his head that they should head inside.

"Sounds good, huh?" Erato said while they exited the car.

"Yeah, I guess it does," Jules said, carefully shutting his door, wincing when Erato slammed his. "So what's the catch? There's gotta be a catch."

Erato unlocked his black iron gate and ushered Jules inside. "The catch is, them old cotton warehouses, they're historic, supposedly. Couple of city agencies gotta give permission for Van Goodfeller to knock 'em down. Right now, the Zoning Board's leanin' in favor, but the Preservation Commission's definitely against. And them Uptown folks I mentioned? They hate the whole idea. And they *really* hate GoodiesMart. You should hear them bitch and moan at meetings"—he put on a falsetto, vaguely patrician voice—" '*it's so UGLY, with that big awful parking lot*' . . . course, they all got jobs and homes already, good ones. They just happy, most of 'em, to have the St. Thomas folks outta their area."

Erato unlocked his front door, opening the security grating first. Jules hadn't visited his pal at home that many times. As soon as he stepped into the foyer, he remembered why. The house was loaded with hanging crosses and framed pictures of Jesus—a black African Jesus, but Jesus, nonetheless. Jules immediately began sweating. If he stayed too long, his skin would begin to flake and smoke. Erato's house was almost as bad for him as a cathedral.

Erato started for the kitchen, then stopped when he realized that his friend wasn't following behind. "C'mon," he whispered. Jules remembered that the three kids were probably asleep by now. "Let's go into the kitchen. What's the matter?"

"I'm just . . . not feelin' too great," Jules muttered. "Gimme a second here."

"Stomach?" Erato asked. "I got some ice-cold Pepto in the fridge. Or Alka, if that work better for you."

"Naww." Jules grabbed his friend's shoulder and closed his eyes tightly. "Just a spot of vertigo. I get it sometimes. Lead me through to the kitchen. I'll be okay."

Not seeing the crosses and pictures made him feel incrementally better. Hanging on to Erato's arm, he shuffled blindly across his friend's living room. Once, he banged his thigh into something hard and sharp, probably the corner of a coffee table. Jules felt a pair of swinging doors brush his sides, which meant they were entering the kitchen.

"Johnny, that you? What you doin' home at this hour? And who's that you got with you?"

Hearing that gravelly female voice, so like a prison matron's, Jules remembered the other reason why he'd visited Erato's home so rarely. He reluctantly opened his eyes. "Hi, Caroline," he said.

"Hello, dear," Erato said to his wife. "I, uh, brought Jules home, just for a minute. You remember Jules?"

Caroline eyed Jules coldly. Jules met her gaze briefly, tried smiling, then was forced to look away by the large cross she wore around her neck. Not that there was much to look at. Some women had a Coke-bottle figure. Caroline had a figure like a thirty-two-ounce can of malt liquor. No breasts, no waist, and even less in the way of patience.

"Jules Duchon," she said slowly, spitting out the syllables like pits from sour grapes. "I thought you was dead."

"Now, honey, what kinda thing is that to say to a guest," Erato said cautiously. "Jules is feelin' a little under the weather. We got any soda water left in the fridge?"

"Oh, he's *always* feelin' 'under the weather' when he comes round here."

Jules grimaced, remembering the last time he'd visited, three years ago; he'd accidentally rolfed all over a four-foot-long diorama of the Last Supper. "Don't worry," he croaked, grabbing a chair to steady himself. He felt sweat gliding down his back. "I'm just here to pick up somethin' I left with your husband."

Caroline placed her meaty fists where her waist would be, if she had one. "If it's that money you gave Johnny for Lacrecia's schoolin', that's already been sent to Baton Rouge, over my objections. But if you want it back, I'm *sure* we'll find a way to get it to you."

"No, no," Jules stammered, "I don't want the money back, I wanted your family to have it—"

"Really, I'd be *happy* to return it," she said unsmilingly. "Lacrecia can go to community college for a year or two. That's blood money you gave Johnny, I'd swear on a Bible. Dirty, unholy money—"

"Caroline!" Erato looked half-panicked. His lazy eye circled in its socket like an out-of-control Tilt-a-Whirl ride. "Apologize to Jules! Where you be comin' up with allegations like that? You should thank him, honey! That money he gave us, it was money from the insurance settlement on his house. He wanted it to be a gift!" Another thought seemed to occur to Erato. He turned back to Jules. "*Do* you want the money back? Do you need it now?"

"Heck no, Erato. It's yours. It's Lacrecia's. I'm doin' fine with money now, just *fine.*" He mopped the sweat off his forehead with the back of his hand. *No good deed goes unpunished,* he thought darkly. Sure, he hadn't given Erato twelve thousand dollars for Lacrecia's college fund expecting that Caroline would love him for it. But he'd at least hoped maybe she wouldn't hate him anymore. So much for that. Somehow, she'd always seen right through him. Subconsciously or not, she knew him for what he was—a creature of the night, tainted, unholy. "Just give me Maureen's ashes, and I'll get outta your hair."

Jules's offer to promptly leave seemed to mollify Caroline. "I'll be headin' up to bed, Johnny," she said, not looking at her husband. "I'll see you in the morning."

She left the room. Erato went to the window above the sink and grabbed a green vase that sat on the window ledge. "Just like you wanted, she's been sittin' in the sunlight ever since you left her with me." He handed Jules the vase. "Here. I'm glad you takin' her. She belongs with you." He sighed and stared at the floor. "Look, about Caroline, I'm so sorry, man. . . ."

"Don't even mention it, Erato. Nothin' to apologize for." He experienced a bewildering mix of emotions as he held the vase in his hands—longing and sadness, fear and hope, the remembered horror of watching Maureen die on videotape. And what Elvis would call a hunka-hunka burning love. Vase and dust together weighed less than ten pounds. Amazing. "Thanks for watching over her, pal."

"Let's get me back to my cab," Erato said, warily glancing at the stairs. Jules kept his eyes open on this trip through the parlor, drawing strength from Maureen's closeness.

Out on the porch, Erato caught Jules's arm before he could walk down the steps. "I feel I gotta explain about Caroline," he said. "She didn't mean what she said. She's been on edge lately. Me, too. Our pastor . . . well, he was killed earlier this week. In the French Quarter."

Jules froze. "That was this week? I read about a pastor gettin' killed. But the paper said that was two weeks ago."

"Different man. That was Brother Hammond, from Spirit Revival Full Gospel Church over in Central City."

Two preachers in two weeks? "What happened to your guy?"

"Murder, it looks like. A shopkeeper found his body in an alleyway off Bienville, not far from North Rampart Street. The details got hushed up in the papers. But a buddy of mine on the force, a guy I hang with at Trolley Stop, he told me what done Pastor Johnson in. Bullet to the back of the head. But that wasn't all. He had wounds in his neck, like bite holes. And his body was almost all empty of blood."

"No shit," Jules muttered. He experienced a creepy sense of déjà vu. The description Erato had given him sounded exactly like one of his own kills; except that he'd normally been more careful in disposing of the corpse, either loading it on an outbound freight train, dumping it in the Mississippi, or carting it out to one of the swamps that surround the city. The description also matched what he'd read about the earlier murder.

They walked out to Jules's car. Jules closed the security gate behind him, shaking it to make sure it was tightly locked. He opened the Allante's door for Erato.

"You know anything about that Brother Hammond who got killed?" Jules asked, starting up the car.

"Yeah. Construction workers at City Park found his body in one of the lagoons, where they'd been dredgin'. The first story in the paper listed cause of death as a stab wound to the back of the head. And wounds on his neck, that crazy pagan-sacrifice shit, just like I heard with Pastor Johnson later. The follow-up stories, they still mentioned the stab wound, but the neck wounds, they was never mentioned again. And I never woulda known what killed Pastor Johnson if my buddy hadn'ta told me. Other black pastors around here and in Central City, most of them got police checkin' in on them now. Or they got private guards."

Jules turned onto Jackson Avenue, heading back to the Trolley Stop. They drove past the mostly demolished housing project. "So the cops think somebody's targeting black pastors?"

"Maybe not *all* black pastors. Maybe just pastors who's supportin' the Goodfeller-GoodiesMart plan for the St. Thomas. Pastor Johnson and Brother Hammond, they were two of the lead organizers of the St. Thomas for All of Us Coalition, headed up rallies in front of City Hall and the HANO offices. Pastor Johnson had his own Sunday-afternoon radio show, and the St. Thomas was all he talked about his last months on earth."

Erato kneaded his knuckles pink, a sign he was either embarrassed or reluctant to ask for something he desperately needed. "Jules . . . I know you can't tell me nothin' 'bout this thing you're investigatin'. But if you should chance across some information about these killin's . . . I'd sure be obliged if you'd share it. Bein' in the dark is drivin' me and the missus crazy."

"What about your cop buddy at the Trolley Stop? Can't he dig up some more information for you?"

"That spigot's been turned off. Nobody with the Coalition can get a word out of NOPD these last few days."

Jules was certain these killings had *vampire* written all over them. "Okay, Erato. I come across somethin', I'll let you know." One more lie to add to the night's pile. "But until this gets cleared up, stay away from them rallies for the St. Thomas plan, okay? Or at least don't make yourself noticed."

Erato scowled. "Maybe that's just what the killer and them that's behind him would want, don't you think? For men of conscience to take fright and stay away?"

In his own way, Erato was just as hardheaded and stubborn as his wife, Jules knew. He pulled over next to Erato's cab. "Well, just watch your ass, then," he said. Even as the words came out of his mouth, Jules realized that Maureen had told him exactly the same thing nine months ago.

"I will, my friend. I will. You watch *your* ass, too." Erato exited the car, then motioned for Jules to roll down his window. "God bless," he said.

Jules shivered. "Yeah. The same."

Jules didn't bother opening the convertible top back up before pulling away. He didn't want to be distracted by breezes and moonlight and neon on his way to the High Krewe's compound. He had too much thinking to do.

Victims left in French Quarter alleys or the shallow end of City Park lagoons. That meant either an extraordinarily sloppy and careless vampire, or a vampire who was sending a message. Given the risks inherent in verifying the existence of the undead, Jules leaned toward the latter theory.

But if someone *were* sending a message, who was sending a message to whom? And what kind of message? Jules knew of two groups of vampires who'd been active in the city. The High Krewe's youngsters, and the Malice X group. The latter comprised at least twelve black vampires, headquartered in an underground lair beneath the Canal Street casino. Eight months ago, he'd left them leaderless. Could these killings be part of a leadership struggle? Malice had flaunted his invention of a new drug, Horse-X, a mixture of heroin and his own blood that was intensely addictive. Maybe different factions of the surviving group were struggling for control of the market? Could they have corrupted local ghetto preachers into acting as conduits for drug sales, and the preachers who were killed were pawns caught in a cross fire?

It was possible. But it seemed to Jules there were too many *ifs* required to make this theory ring true. The black vampires had as much to lose as he did if the authorities ever became fully convinced of the existence of vampires in New Orleans. His black counterparts weren't dummies. Surely they could've come up with safer, more private ways to fight their internal wars.

The other possibility was the youngsters. Those pampered kids didn't know shit from shinola about the rough-and-tumble of the street vampire life, how careful one had to be. If any local vampires could've been sloppy enough to leave victims' bodies behind in the French Quarter and in City Park, it would be they. Or could they've been sending someone a message, as he'd first thought? What message, and to whom, he couldn't begin to conjecture at this point.

This whole line of thinking opened up another doorway, one that could have powerful bearing on the case he'd been assigned. If the High Krewe's delinquent escapees *had* killed the two black preachers, that was equivalent, in the eyes of the black vampires, to a declaration of hostilities. In the same way Jules had, they would've "poached" on the black vampires' turf. The mutilations? The disappearances? Those could very well have been early shots in a covert vampire-race war.

Jules grunted to himself as he headed toward Metairie Road. This theory had an upside and a downside. The upside was, he'd much rather discover that the black vampires were behind the dirty deeds than Straussman, a blood relation. The downside . . . well, the downside was, he'd have to tangle with Malice X's bunch again. And this time, do it dickless, maybe.

But he'd worry about that later. After he'd questioned the High Krewe's brats and big muckety-mucks. Depending on what they told him—or didn't tell him—his investigation might veer off in directions as unimaginable as his spending eternity without Maureen.

SEVEN

Heading out along Canal Street to the High Krewe's compound, Jules felt an urge to urinate. Spookily, he'd swear his dick was back, stiff with a desperate piss hard-on from the coffee he'd been drinking, pressing against his zipper for release. He actually took a hand off the wheel and felt himself down there, just in case. But no, it was still gone. Was this phantom pain, the same as a soldier sometimes felt after a leg amputation? Even worse was what he was feeling in the bottom of his guts. They felt like taffy being stretched and snapped on a taffy-pulling machine.

He glanced at the digital clock glowing on the dashboard. Twelve-seventeen A.M. The only places open this time of night would be bars. Up ahead, he spotted a neon-lit joint called the Tropical Paradise. Jules wasn't feeling especially tropical (unless Montezuma's revenge counted as such), and he sure didn't feel anywhere near paradise, but the bar was certain to have a bathroom.

One good thing about having a dick, he realized as he hastily pushed through the front door, was that at least you had something to squeeze with your fist in a situation like this. Now, he didn't know *what* to squeeze. He clamped his ass muscles tight, but he couldn't be sure that was the right thing to do. The bar was empty except for a group of college kids crowded around one table near the back. Despite a lack of dancers,, a large mirrored disco ball spun above the dance floor, and the bar shook with thumping techno dance beats. Spotting a dim sign indicating rest rooms, Jules half trotted across the deserted dance floor. The eyes of all six college kids followed him, undoubtedly hoping this apparently soused circus freak would provide them with a show. Well, if that men's room was locked, he'd give them more than they'd bargained for.

It wasn't locked. But the sole toilet stall was so narrow, it might as well have been locked. "Hell, this is gonna be a tight fit," Jules mumbled as he pulled open the stall door. With hardly any room to maneuver, he managed to get his pants down around his ankles. Hardly a second too soon, he blindly aimed his posterior at the seat. He heard a crack loud as a deer rifle—Jules wasn't sure whether it was the toilet seat breaking or his guts bursting like a stressed balloon.

Something slid out of him. It felt like a ball made of greased jello. It hit the water hard, showering Jules with an unwanted douche.

Cautiously, he stood up and peered over his shoulder into the bowl. What was floating there looked like a jumbo-sized egg that someone had cracked open, partially scrambled, and dumped into the toilet instead of a skillet—an obscene version of Chinese egg-drop soup. If ostriches could fly, this is exactly what they'd plop on cars.

Great. Now he was shitting like a giant bird. Sam Spade and Charlie Chan had never had to put up with *this.*

Jules was thankful that his stomach had settled down by the time he walked into Besthoff's office. Besthoff directed Jules to sit in one of the twin leather-clad chairs in front of his desk. "Now that Straussman has assisted you in acquiring the vehicle you desired," he said, "have you decided how you will begin your investigation?"

Jules squirmed in the chair. It was too small for him; he could fit only part of his rear on the seat, and he had to hold on to the overly confining armrests to keep from falling off. "Yeah. I've thought about it. Who were the first people to see the bodies?"

"Straussman took two of the other servants outside the gates to retrieve Victoria. Their names are Hecht and Otranto. Several days later, when we were alerted that Alexandra was lying in the cemetery, I took Straussman and my colleague, Krauss, to rescue her. My other colleague, Katz, was of course made aware of both situations."

"No one else has seen the two bodies?"

"Absolutely not. As far as the rest of the household are concerned, Victoria and Alexandra are missing, the same as Maxim and Jonathan."

"And they are—?"

"Two young male members of the household who left to go adventuring in the city, and whom no one has heard from for weeks. Maxim disappeared five weeks ago. My colleagues and I initially suspected that, unhappy with his junior status here, he had gone independent and feral in the city or had defected to a colony elsewhere. One with fewer senior members, perhaps. Jonathan vanished a few days before Victoria was savaged. That was nearly two weeks ago."

Jules leaned forward, trying to get more comfortable. "Doodlebug mentioned that someone phoned the house here twice, to tell y'all about the two women outside. Who took the calls?"

"Straussman took both calls."

"Is Straussman usually the one who answers the phone around here? Would you say it was any kinda weird coincidence that he should be the one to answer both times?"

Besthoff's smooth brow furrowed slightly. He leaned forward and folded his hands on the desk. "As head servant, Straussman is typically the one to answer the telephone or attend to visitors, so long as he is not detained by other tasks. We receive few calls. Do you have a reason for asking this?"

It was way too premature to call down any heat on Straussman. *The guy probably takes a year's worth of shit in a week around here,* Jules thought. "No. No reason. I'm just doin' my job, askin' about anything that seems out of the ordinary."

So he had five people to question tonight—minus Besthoff, whom he was questioning now—in addition to the wayward youngsters. Should he try to question everyone separately? In all the crime novels he'd read, the detective always made a big point of separating the witnesses and interviewing each by himself, so that conflicts between stories could be caught and analyzed. On the other hand, the English mysteries he'd read as a kid featured sleuths who questioned everybody together, usually in a big group around a dining table. That way, the detective could watch everyone's facial expressions while each suspect told his story, waiting for that decisive look of acid indigestion. It probably didn't make much difference—after almost two weeks, any guilty parties in the household would've had plenty of time to get their stories in line. So the precaution of questioning everyone separately might be moot.

"I wanna interview the five of you who saw the bodies or know what's been goin' on," Jules said. "And then I'll need to interview any of these youngsters you think been sneakin' out and cattin' around town."

"Interviewing the three servants is required, of course. But there is no need for you to speak with either Krauss or Katz. I know all that they know, and you have complete access to me."

"But they're witnesses—"

Besthoff dismissed the notion with a wave of his hand. "There is no need for you to disturb them. They do not speak with outsiders. Their duties and responsibilities occupy them most fully."

Jules rubbed his nose and sighed. Why did Besthoff pull shit like this—give him a job and then not let him do it? Another insult to remind him of his place? Surely he realized this would make Jules twice as anxious to get to his colleagues. Another possibility dawned on Jules: could that be part of Besthoff's game? Was this protective gesture a way of hinting to him that Krauss or Katz might have something to hide?

"Look," Jules said. "You gave me this job. I didn't want it, but it's my job now, and I'll do it—the right way or no way. Either let me interview my witnesses, or find yourself another private dick." Jules winced at that last comment; another instance when his internal editor had been too slow on the job.

Besthoff straightened his cuffs. Gold cuff links, studded with blood-red rubies. Then he carefully folded his hands on his desk. His stare fell on Jules like the weight of the ocean. "I will take your . . . professional opinion . . . under advisement. Interview the servants. I will consult with my colleagues."

♠

Jules decided to start with Straussman. Based on what Straussman told him, he'd know what to ask the other two servants.

He met the butler in Straussman's room. Straussman's living quarters were much tinier than Jules would've expected, given the gargantuanism of the rest of the house. There was barely enough room for a narrow day bed, a secretary's desk and chair, a bookshelf, and an unadorned, apparently ancient, black walnut coffin. A small window, now open, could be easily sealed against the light of the sun. The room looked like the quarters of a Capuchin monk; minus the crucifixes, of course.

"Why don't you sit at the desk," Straussman offered. "I imagine you may need to do some writing."

"Uh, thanks." The chair was plain and hard, without a cushion, but it looked sturdy.

Straussman sat on the day bed. "I apologize for the claustrophobic nature of this room. It's perfectly suitable for me when alone, but with a guest . . . if you would be more comfortable, I could see whether the library is unoccupied. Most of the young people prefer their cable television to reading."

"No. This is okay." Jules removed a small purple pad and purple pencil from the pocket of his safari vest; souvenirs of the defunct K&B Drug Store chain. He'd discovered them in one of Maureen's kitchen drawers. He took another look around the cramped room, hardly bigger than Maureen's bathroom. When Maureen and Straussman were together, did they live *here*? Or did Straussman have a bigger room back then? Maybe he got busted down to a smaller room when Maureen rejected him and hightailed it back to the city.

"Uh, tell me about that first phone call you got," Jules said. "The one where you learned about Victoria. Where were you when you took the call?"

"I was in the kitchen. Preparing evening cocktails for the masters, I believe."

"So, uh, what'd the caller sound like?"

"It was a man's voice. He failed to identify himself. After he gave his rather cryptic message, I requested his name and the name of his company, and he immediately hung up."

Jules hadn't needed to write notes this quickly since his final year of school—eighth grade, St. Leo's, middle-school class of 1908. He scribbled, in block letters:

VICTORIA CALL:
STRAUSSMAN—KITCHEN
MAN VOICE
HUNG UP

"Did his voice, uh, did it sound familiar at all?"

"No. It was not a voice I recognized."

"Do you remember kinda what it sounded like? High-pitched? A lisp, maybe? An accent?"

Straussman considered this. "It was a mature voice, rather low in tone. Perhaps a Bostonian accent. That peculiar elongation of the *ah* sounds. And the quality of the connection was quite poor, both times."

"Poor? Like he was using a cell phone, maybe?"

Straussman smiled faintly. "I'm afraid I'm unfamiliar with the more modern varieties of telephones. We receive so few calls at the compound."

"Okay. What did he say on the first call?" Jules was feeling more comfortable asking questions. You fell into a rhythm, taking turns speaking. It was like playing a game of Ping-Pong.

"His communication both times was quite succinct. I believe I can remember his first statement almost exactly. 'I've left a missing treasure outside your front gate. You'll want to retrieve it before sunrise.' "

"That was all?"

"That was all, yes."

"Was anybody around when you took the call?"

"Mr. Hecht, one of the other manservants, was nearby, preparing a sorbet. He saw the confused look on my face and asked me about the caller. He was the first person I revealed the disturbing message to."

Jules felt relieved. So long as the other servant corroborated his account, the likelihood of Straussman's being the culprit receded considerably. "So what did you do next?"

"Mr. Hecht and I gathered Mr. Otranto, another servant, and we went to look outside."

"Why didn't you go immediately to Besthoff or one of the other bosses to let them know what was going on?"

Straussman's expression didn't change; it remained alert but unworried. "Apart from the reference to 'sunrise,' which I noted at the time was unusual and could be significant, there seemed every chance that this was a trivial matter. Possibly a prank phone call. Victoria had not been absent long enough to cause major concern. The masters had long suspected that some of the youngsters had established auxiliary coffins in town. And we have a long-standing policy that matters of lesser importance should be handled autonomously by the staff."

"Okay. So the three of you went outside. Did you see anything unusual?"

"Apart from Miss Victoria lying on the forest floor without her legs?"

"Right."

"No. We did not see anyone 'fleeing the scene,' as you might put it."

Jules caught up on his note-taking before asking the next question. Later, he'd need to ask Straussman to show him the places where they'd found the two women. "How about the second phone call?"

"That I remember quite well. After Miss Victoria was recovered, I made a habit of having one of the other servants also pick up the line whenever I did. So that in case that mysterious gentleman should ever call again, we would have a second witness." *Smart,* Jules thought. "During that second call, Mr. Otranto also picked up. The caller, of necessity, was slightly more loquacious this time." Straussman put on a passable Bostonian accent. " 'Another missing treasure. I've left it in Metairie Cemetery. By the tomb of Lieutenant Micah Micholson, Washington Artillery. Collect your treasure before sunrise, or lose it.' And then he terminated the call."

Jules shook out his hand to avoid a cramp. "So Otranto heard that whole conversation, too, huh?"

"Yes. Although he may have missed the first word or two, since he picked up just after I did."

So at least Straussman hadn't invented the outside calls. He was looking cleaner. Unless . . . unless he was working with a second man, a partner either inside or outside the compound. Then Straussman would've known the calls were coming, could've made sure he had witnesses ready when the phone rang.

Jules rubbed the space between his eyes with his knuckle. He was getting ahead of himself. Just because Straussman was the first person he'd met who might have a motive to commit the crimes—and he wasn't even sure of *that* yet; he couldn't be until he found out whether the victims had all been members of the household when Maureen had been with the Krewe—that was no reason to construct a big conspiracy theory with Straussman in the middle. Not yet. He hadn't even gotten around to poking into the affairs of Malice X's old gang.

"And that's when you went to alert one of the bosses?" Jules said.

"Master Besthoff, yes."

"And you, Besthoff, and Krauss went over to the cemetery."

"Yes."

Okay. He'd get the rest of that story from Besthoff and Krauss, assuming that Besthoff backed off his refusal to let Jules speak with his reclusive colleagues. And he could follow up with Straussman when the two of them visited the sites where the victims had been found.

Jules stuck his pad and pencil back in his pocket. "That's it for now," he said. "I'll check back with you later, after I talk with some of the others. I'll wanna pick up my cash advance before I leave. Thanks for answering my questions."

They both stood. Straussman shook his hand. "You're very welcome, sir. Your payment will be waiting for you when you leave, and something else you may find useful."

♠

Jules interviewed Hecht and Otranto separately. Apart from their fangs, they were mostly colorless little men, the type Jules would look straight through passing on the sidewalk or in a grocery store. They both backed up Straussman's accounts of the two telephone calls and retrieving Victoria.

One new bit of information he collected was the approximate dates when the four victims had joined the High Krewe's household. Alexandra had come over from Europe with Besthoff, Katz, Krauss, and a few of the others. Maxim was brought in sometime during the 1890s; Hecht and Otranto disagreed on the exact year. They did agree, however, on when Victoria joined the Krewe—1912, the year President Woodrow Wilson was elected. Right around when Maureen would've left. Jonathan wasn't brought in until later, in 1923. So only two, maybe three of the victims could potentially have been among Maureen's tormentors. Neither of the servants recalled any bad blood between Maureen and either Alexandra or Maxim, and Otranto thought Victoria arrived after Maureen had left, although Hecht wasn't sure of this. All in all, the scales weren't tipped heavily toward a theory of Straussman settling old scores.

Jules finished up with Hecht. When Jules climbed the damp steps from the wine cellar where he'd conducted that interview, he found Straussman waiting for him.

"The three masters will see you now," Straussman said. "In the chapel." His tone and manner conveyed a new undercurrent of respect. Maybe getting to see Krauss and Katz was a bigger deal than Jules had thought.

Jules had never seen the High Krewe's chapel before. Straussman paused before opening the large double doors. "Sir," he said, "I must request that you remove your shoes before entering."

"Huh?" Jules checked the bottoms of his sandals. They looked relatively clean. He then noticed that Straussman had removed his own shoes and placed them outside the door. "It is a custom in our household," Straussman said. "A show of respect for the ancient ways."

"Okay. Sure." Jules wiggled out of his sandals and placed them near Straussman's highly polished shoes.

The butler opened the doors and stepped inside. "Sirs. Mr. Duchon is here to speak with you."

The chapel was narrow, tall, and windowless. Apart from its lack of windows, it was set up much like Jules remembered the chapel at St. Leo's School, with a small raised altar and pulpit at the front and pews that could seat the whole High Krewe, about two dozen persons. The chapel had no electric lighting. All illumination came from four chandeliers, each of which held dozens of burning candles. Looking around, Jules felt immediately peaceful, almost sleepy. He realized why. Given the brass fittings on the altar and pews and the dark tapestries and tufted red velvet that lined the walls, the chapel resembled nothing so much as a spacious and supremely luxurious coffin.

"Please join us in the front, Mr. Duchon."

It was Besthoff's voice. Jules blinked. His eyes slowly adjusted to the dim candlelight. He could roughly make out Besthoff and two other figures sitting on the raised dais, behind a wooden table. The table was supported by carved winged figures; angels or devils, Jules couldn't tell.

He walked down the central aisle. The stone floor felt cold against his bare feet. He didn't see another chair up there on the dais. Would they make him stand?

"You may sit in one of the front pews, Mr. Duchon." This was a new voice; one of the others, either Katz or Krauss. It sounded like a prepubescent boy's voice. Weird. It was like listening to Doodlebug before he'd learned how to "adjust" his form and take on the voice of an adult woman.

"We ain't been introduced," Jules said. He didn't sit. Sitting would just make the three of them on the dais loom taller. Although the figure who'd just spoken, the one in the middle, looked like he could use all the help he could get. Besthoff towered over him; unless he had very long legs, the little guy couldn't be taller than five-foot-two.

"I am Gregory Krauss," the diminutive man said. Now that Jules's eyes were adjusting, he could see the man's face. It was smooth, unlined, an altar boy's face. His long sideburns and the hair above his slightly pointed ears were flecked with silver, but it looked unnatural, like stage makeup for a high-school production of *Our Town.* "You already know Georges Besthoff. My colleague to the left is Nikolas Katz."

The other man was even more in shadow. His head wasn't any higher than Krauss's, but this was because he was hunched over, cradling his long, eggplant-shaped chin on interlocked fingers. He appeared much older than Besthoff; certainly more so than Kid Dracula. Flickering candlelight reflected off the liver-spotted sheen of his hairless pate. His head jiggled incessantly, like the bobbling hips of a dashboard hula dancer. The candlelight glinted, too, off something liquid dribbling down his chin. Drool?

Holy moley, Jules thought. *No wonder Besthoff's the public face around here.* "Nice to meet you guys," he said.

"Please sit," Krauss said. Despite his small stature and squeaky voice, his command had centuries of authority backing it up. Jules sat.

The elderly figure wagged a long, bony finger in Jules's direction. "De chul-drun . . . tell him, Gregory . . . vhat ve spoke of . . . de chul-drun . . ." If Jules closed his eyes, he could swear he was listening to Bela Lugosi on a sterno bender, circa *Bride of the Monster.*

"We understand that you intend to question a number of the youngsters," Krauss said.

"Well, sure," Jules said. "Isn't that what you guys hired me to do?"

The childlike man's gaze was every bit as stony as Besthoff's had ever been. "We have hired you to locate a criminal for us, Mr. Duchon. Locate him and deliver him to us. We understand that a certain amount of interaction with the youngsters may be necessary for you to accomplish this task. However, you are under strict instruction not to reveal to any of them what has happened to Victoria or Alexandra."

"Wait a minute." Jules shifted uncomfortably in the pew. "You guys are sawin' the legs out from under me. How can I find out anything useful from the kids if I can't talk about the victims? Besides, what's the difference if I do? They all know *something's* happened to those two gals. Maybe them knowing the real deal would be a good thing. Put the fear of the bogeyman in 'em, keep 'em from sneakin' out at night."

Besthoff cleared his throat. "You misjudge the character of our younger members. They are young lions, proud of their position at the top of the food chain. Any inkling that one of their own has been victimized—particularly in the monstrous way Victoria and Alexandra have been—would send them immediately into the streets of the city, seeking bloody vengeance."

"We cannot allow this to happen," Krauss said.

"De chul-drun . . . dey are *precious* to us." Tiny flecks of spittle flew from Katz's mouth.

"So why don't you lock them down here at the compound?" This "interview" wasn't going anything like what he'd intended—it was just more of Besthoff's bossing him around, times three. "If it's so damn dangerous for them out there, why haven't they all been, I dunno, grounded or somethin'? Take away the car keys. Don't let them have no cash for a cab. If they break the rules, bust down their blood rations. Or yank their goddamn cable TV."

Krauss smiled. The expression on his childlike face was devoid of innocence. "Have you ever tried caging a vampire, Mr. Duchon? Ten vampires? Wolves are swift and can leap high walls. Bats blend into the night. Mist can slip the hold of any shackles or chains."

"Penalties or harsh restrictions would only breed resentment and revolt," Besthoff said. "Even before the assaults and disappearances, the mood of the youngsters was tending toward rebelliousness. Their discovering that they have been targeted by an outside enemy would only serve to turn a combustible situation explosive. But these explanations are unnecessary. You have been told not to reveal what you know. And you are far too astute a man to risk our displeasure."

Besthoff's and Krauss's silent glares blasted Jules like the high beams of a pair of oncoming eighteen-wheelers. Jules couldn't tell whether the old fart was glaring at him, too; his eyes were sunk too deeply into his wrinkled face. This wasn't worth arguing about. So he wouldn't warn the kids about what was waiting out there for them. So the three bosses didn't have the balls to enforce their own rules. So what? What did it matter to him if a few more High Krewe brats got whacked before he pegged the culprit? He was seeing Besthoff and company for what they were—*wimps.* Parents scared of their own kids, more afraid of putting their own authority on the line than the consequences of letting the youngsters run wild.

Still, he'd taken the job. He had Doodlebug's interests to look after. He'd read that lots of the best police detectives didn't give a rat's ass about their cases' victims; they just wanted to prove they were smarter than the criminals were. All Jules wanted to prove was that he could do this job right.

"Do any of you have any idea what they *do* while they're out there?" he asked.

"We can make certain assumptions," Krauss said. "But the youngsters are extremely tight-lipped. And they protect one another's privacy."

"The only way to know what they are doing in the city is to follow them," Besthoff said. "And that is your job, not ours."

"I *meeese* zhem," Katz said, "when zey are gone."

Well, *that* was informative. He decided to try another tack. "Y'all had any trouble lately from the black vampires? The ones that live downtown, underneath the big casino? If your kids are out and about, pickin' off victims in certain neighborhoods, it could be pissin' them off something fierce. Believe me, *I* know."

Jules watched their expressions closely. He didn't really expect a straight answer. But their physical reactions might tell him a lot.

Krauss raised a delicate eyebrow, then turned to Besthoff. " 'Black' vampires? I was under the assumption he had cleared away that unfortunate aberration some months ago."

Besthoff shook his head. "No. Mr. Duchon killed their leader. But he failed to clean out the nest." He turned back to Jules. "We have heard nothing from your colored vampires. Our youngsters know better than to consort with such persons. Had any aggressive acts emerged from that quarter, we would have been immediately informed."

Yeah, right, Jules thought to himself. He glanced over at Katz. The old man had made a sour face and was swatting at something in front of his nose; tiny gnats, maybe.

"How about Federal agents?" Jules asked. "Anybody from the government been snoopin' around the compound? You guys up to date on your taxes?" It was a long shot, bringing that up. Cutting the limbs off vampires . . . that didn't seem like Veronika's style. Still, he couldn't completely write the thought off, not when Veronika had made it perfectly clear eight months ago that her covert agency was dead set on cleansing New Orleans of its bloodsuckers.

"Taxes?" Besthoff asked, clearly nonplussed. "I fail to see the relevance of your question."

"There was this dame, see, and she worked for this agency, the Strategic Helium Reserve . . ." Jules realized he could easily spend the rest of the evening trying to explain his semipassionate, semideadly encounter with Veronika. "Aww, ferget it," he muttered.

"If that is all"—Krauss began to say; he was suddenly interrupted by fierce pounding on the table to his left.

"He *smell*!" Katz pointed a trembling finger at Jules, then resumed waving his hands in front of his nose. "He smell *bad*! I am *tired.* Make heem go ah-*way.*"

Besthoff coughed into his fist. "This interview is concluded," Krauss announced quickly. "You may arrange through Straussman to speak with other members of our household. But remember our injunction regarding revealing information to the youngsters."

Jules stood up. He discreetly sniffed his armpits; they weren't too bad. Could it be his feet?

One more question occurred to him. A real Hail-Mary pass, unlikely to score him a touchdown. But never say *never,* he told himself. "None of you guys would happen to have a stake in the redevelopment of the St. Thomas Housing Project, would you?"

Stony silence, mixed with what seemed to be genuine puzzlement—Besthoff and Krauss stared at him as though he'd just sung a Norwegian lullaby while hopping on one foot. "St. Thomas . . ." Krauss said at last. "That is an island in the Caribbean, is it not?"

"Izz he a Cath-o-lic saint?" Katz asked, pausing from waving away fumes. "Eef he izz, we haf a stake in heem—we *puut* a stake through heem! Through hees heart!" The old man cackled loudly at his own joke. At least he wasn't complaining about Jules's odor anymore.

"All right," Jules muttered. "Ferget about it. Have a nice night, gents." He turned and walked back up the aisle before Besthoff could make an equally ridiculous remark. Marble statues of various vampire saints stared down at him from raised alcoves. Varney; Udolfo; others he didn't recognize. One of the statue's faces seemed more reptilian than human. Looking up at this statue's coldly slanting eyes and wide, grinning mouth, Jules felt a twinge of anxiety puncture his newfound sense of superiority toward the masters of the High Krewe. They'd gotten him completely offtrack; he hadn't asked any of the questions he'd intended to.

Serpents . . . ever since the days of the Bible, they'd always been the embodiment of deceit.

EIGHT

"The youngsters have been informed by the masters that they must talk with you and answer your questions," Straussman informed Jules. "These are Miss Pearl's quarters. Please ring for me when you are done."

Straussman left him standing in the hallway before the ornately carved door. Jules knocked.

"Come," a woman's voice replied from inside. Not the most inviting invitation he'd ever heard.

Jules opened the door. The bedroom was vast, its ceiling easily fifteen feet high. The furniture looked as if it'd been carted away from one of the antebellum plantation museums upriver. Pieces his dear, departed mother would've killed for—including a canopy bed big enough to hide a troop of Confederate cavalry (their horses, too).

The bedroom's occupant was just as impressive. Pearl was nearly as tall as comatose Alexandra, with a figure that would get a rise out of even senile old Katz (where did the High Krewe *find* these women?). Wavy auburn hair framed her heart-shaped face. Initially, her features seemed softer, more open than the feral Alexandra's; but then the cruel twitch of her mouth when she saw him dispelled that notion. She was curled up on a green silk sofa, dressed in an emerald gown that didn't leave much to the imagination.

"So," she said, eyeing him as though he were a spoiled piece of fish, "you're this 'detective' I was told to expect."

"Yeah. Jules Duchon. Pleasure to meet you."

She shifted slightly, rearranging her pure cream bare feet more comfortably on a sunset orange pillow. "You're even more repulsive than rumors said."

Jules let his outstretched hand fall to his side. "I don't need to win no beauty contest to do my job."

Her perfect eyebrows arched ever so slightly. "And just what is your 'job'?"

"Keepin' you from"—he was about to say, *from gettin' carved up like a Thanksgiving turkey,* but then he remembered Besthoff's and Krauss's admonishments—"from, uh, from somethin' bad happening to you."

"Really?" She smiled. Her show of teeth was as dazzling as a *Playboy* centerfold's, and just as sincere. "How sweet." She stretched a long, ivory limb to a goblet on a side table and took a slow sip. Her lovely, insolent gaze never left his face. When she removed the goblet from her lips, a thin red mustache remained. She removed it with the tip of her tongue. "Please pardon me if I don't invite you to sit. I'm afraid none of my furniture would hold you."

Lovely, Jules thought. *A wolverine wrapped in a mink's coat.* He squelched his rising anger. Engaging her in a battle of insults would play right into her hands. Besides, she'd win.

"Where do you go," he asked, "when you sneak outta here?" He leaned against one of her bed's lofty posts and was gratified to hear the old wood groan.

"Who says I 'sneak out' anywhere?"

"This log." Jules removed a manila envelope from the clipboard Straussman had supplied him with, then slipped a lined notepad from the envelope. "Straussman's been doin' a nightly check of the house and grounds, just before sunup. According to this, you were nowhere to be found on February fourteenth, February twenty-first, February twenty-sixth, and March third."

Her smile faded like mildew sprayed with ammonia. "Straussman is a liar."

It was Jules's turn to smile. "You got any theories on why the butler would lie about you?"

She sipped from her goblet again, more quickly. Her cocktail left no mustache this time. "I'm not in the habit of guessing the motivations of the hired help."

"Okay. If you didn't sneak out, then how about tellin' me where you were those nights I listed?"

She sat up and hugged her knees to her ample chest. "This is a very grand estate. Do you have any idea how many rooms the main house alone has? I *sincerely* doubt Straussman checked all the rooms in all the buildings, plus thoroughly walked the grounds. Why, he'd have no time for anything else if he did that every night."

"So what were the places Straussman didn't look the nights he didn't see you?"

A grin slowly grew on her face. "The three lords, they're always after us to practice our transformations. Most of the other women prefer their wolf forms. They think bats are icky. Not me. There's this huge old live oak tree near the southwest corner of the estate. It's infested. With termites. They've eaten a hole the size of a tangerine into the trunk, maybe about twelve feet from the ground. Just big enough for a dainty little bat to crawl inside. That's where I was the four or five nights you mentioned, Mr. Duchon. Those termites . . ." She grinned more broadly. "They're simply *delicious.*"

This was getting him nowhere fast. He decided to sit on the bed. It creaked ominously. His posterior formed a crevice in the mattress, causing a small mountain of pillows to tumble toward the middle.

Pearl's expression turned hard. "Don't do that. Get up."

"Were you pals with Victoria or Alexandra?"

"Get up."

"How about Maxim and Jonathan?" He bounced up and down on the bed a couple of times. The old iron springs squealed and thudded against their support slats. "Nice bed you've got. Comfy. Maybe I'll lie down—"

"No!" She nearly rose from her sofa, a murderous look on her face. Jules had little doubt she could bench-press him if he ticked her off enough. But then she composed herself. "I've never been close with Victoria. Alexandra and I are friends. Maxim and Jonathan? If they're truly gone, I say good riddance. They're like little boys, younger brothers who never grow up and give up their stupid boy games. I never had any time for them. Randolph is my consort. A *real* man."

Randolph? Jules made a mental note to question him next. He got up from the bed. "So do you have any idea what happened to the four of them?"

"No."

"No idea at all? They just, like, turned to mist and got sucked up by some big flyin' vacuum cleaner from Mars? Poof—gone?"

She smiled again. "Sure. That's as good an explanation as any."

"Don't feed me a nest of termites, honey." He sat back down on the bed again. Hard. Something cracked this time. "We both know you've been sneakin' out nights. You, and most of the others, too—you've all got spare coffins hidden somewhere in town. You're into somethin' bad, and somethin' bad's pickin' you off, one by one. How about clueing me in on what that bad somethin' is? Don't you wanna spend all eternity makin' goo-goo eyes with Randolph? Won't happen if you both get sucked up by that big vacuum cleaner from Mars."

Pearl bit her lip. Her teeth furrowed her thick lipstick. "I—I can't tell you anything."

" 'Can't'? Or won't?"

She remained silent.

"I guess things get kinda dull around here," Jules said. "Lots more excitement in the city, huh? Dance joints. The casino. Even other vampires. You been gettin' a little tired of the pickings around here? Real-man Randolph not crankin' your ignition so good anymore? Maybe you've developed a taste for us 'free-range' vampires. Some of them black dudes with the fangs, they're pretty good-lookin', huh?"

Some of the anger drained from her face, replaced by contempt. "From what I've heard, I'd say *you're* the one with a nasty fixation on black vampires. Not very politically correct."

He pulled the newspaper article he'd printed out at the Neutral Ground from his pocket, the one about the discovery of Brother Hammond's body. He shoved it under her nose. "How about black preachers? They more to your taste?"

He watched her eyes scan the article. They didn't widen with any surprise he could detect. She handed the sheet of paper back to him. "I'm into health food," she said with practiced nonchalance. "Unlike you, I care about what I eat. If I had to guess, I'd say it was you who dumped this man in the lagoon."

Jules decided to toss the same football he'd thrown for the three bosses. "Y'know, I hear those black preachers in Central City have got the inside track on redeveloping the St. Thomas project. They're bringin' in a GoodiesMart, subsidized duplexes for poor folks, the whole shebang."

"Current events bore me," she said. "The only part of the newspaper I bother with is the gossip column."

She was good. She almost hid it. But Jules caught a tiny jerk of the left side of her mouth when he mentioned the St. Thomas housing project.

He got up off the bed, pushing the mound of cushions aside. "Thanks for the pillow talk. Be seein' you around." As he opened the door to leave, he heard one corner of the box spring hit the floor. The crash of splintering wood was as satisfying as a goblet of blood.

Jules found Randolph in the billiards room. He was alone, leaning over one of three pool tables, stick in hand, standing on a small step stool. He was dressed like James Cagney in *Public Enemy*—vested gray suit with stripes as wide as the stripes on old whitewall tires; starched white shirt, open at the collar, loosely knotted necktie sagging from his vest; and a gray felt fedora pushed back on his head. He even looked like Cagney, down to his diminutive height. Jules pegged him at about five feet tall.

Jules stood in the back of the room and watched Randolph make his shots. He was sharp. Better than sharp—he was one of the best players Jules had ever seen, and Jules had hung around some real sharpies in his years. He made each shot in seconds, with no show of concentration, and he didn't take the easy shots, either. Following each play, he nudged the step stool to where he needed it next, climbed up, and made his next shot, paying as much attention to a wall-sized flat-panel television at the opposite end of the room as he did to the table. Jules glanced over to see what he was watching. It was some MTV reality show about college girls pledging a sorority in Hawaii, standing around the rim of a smoking volcano in thong bikinis and platform heels.

Randolph tapped the pocket to his left with his stick. His last ball was only inches away from that pocket. Rather than sinking the easy shot, he bounced the ball off three walls before it obediently disappeared where he'd said it would. Only then did he turn his head toward Jules. "Want to play a game?"

Jules walked over to the table. "Naww. I'm a decent player, but unless I won the break, I wouldn't get a shot off before you'd cleared the table."

Randolph snickered. "Smart man. You know not to start a game you can't win." He collected the balls from the leather pockets and racked them up, coldly appraising Jules. "You're not what I was expecting. Are you sure you're the same man who walked into Malice X's compound and snuffed him in front of his whole gang?"

Actually, Jules ruefully reflected, he *wasn't* the same man. But he certainly wasn't going to explain that to this punk. "That was me."

Randolph broke the triangle of balls with a thundering crack. Two striped balls zoomed into separate pockets. "Really? You don't look like you could knock over a kid's lemonade stand. Unless you leaned on it."

Jules'd had some recent practice ignoring insults. It was easier now. "I just talked with your girlfriend."

"And?" Another striped ball vanished.

"I asked her where she's been sneakin' out nights. She says she's been stayin' put, that she and the rest of you mooks are innocent as little lambs. Even though I know better. I got her to admit to something, though. You and your buddies are stickin' your noses into the St. Thomas project."

Randolph didn't look up from his game. "The St. Thomas project? That's a housing project for blacks, right?"

"That's right. At least that's what it used to be."

"That where you buy your clothes?" He moved his stool to the far side of the table. "Pearl didn't say anything to you about a housing project. Unless it's featured on *Lifestyles of the Rich and Famous,* it's not worth her attention."

"You weren't there when I was talkin' with her."

"Didn't have to be. What'd you do, bribe her with a gaudy piece of costume jewelry to get her to support your favorite theory? Pearl's a silly cunt."

"You want me to tell her you said that?"

He paused a second before making his shot, then followed through. "Be my fucking guest."

Jules leaned on the side of the table opposite Randolph. Five of the remaining balls rolled a few inches in Jules's direction. Randolph eyed him with cold hatred, or a pretty good imitation of it. "Look," Jules said, "I don't know why you squirts are stonewallin' me. It's not *my* buddies that're disappearin', one by one, somewhere out there in the city."

His game ruined, Randolph reracked the balls. Even standing on his stool, he was forced to look up into Jules's eyes. "We can take care of our own."

"Yeah? You're doin' a real good job of it. At this rate, another six months, the only billiards partner you'll have left'll be old man Katz."

Randolph froze, his mouth a thin line. Jules's offhand remark had unexpectedly hit pay dirt. "What do you know?" Randolph asked slowly. "What do you know about Alexandra?"

"I can't tell you that."

"Where has she gone? Has someone hurt her?"

"I'm the one askin' questions here. Not you." Jules took a closer look at the younger vampire's stricken expression. Maybe Alexandra ranked a little higher in his esteem than Pearl, the "silly cunt." "Hey. You start givin' me some cooperation here, and maybe I'll have a chance to help your missing friends. How about it?"

"How about this?" Randolph set his stick down on the table. "How about, when you find out anything useful, you come to me instead of Besthoff? He can't be paying you much. He's a fucking skinflint when it comes to outsiders. Me? I'll make it worth your while."

"What? You'll give me billiards lessons?"

Randolph smiled slightly. Jules noticed he could use a few sessions in an orthodontist's chair. "I've got outside resources. Contacts, people with money, who'd be willing to spread some around. How about it? You'd like to dick over Besthoff, wouldn't you?"

Was the kid serious? Or was this something Besthoff had set up—some kind of loyalty test? It wouldn't be out of character for the suave snake. On the other hand, all of Randolph's reactions since Jules's crack about old man Katz had seemed genuine, unrehearsed. Maybe if he could play along with the kid, find a way to do it without alerting Besthoff (or let Besthoff know what he was up to?—another option), he could pull the coffin lid off this case. "I'll think about it," Jules said. "But in the meantime, how about givin' me a straight answer or two, so that I can go out there and find out stuff you'll want to pay for?"

Randolph wandered toward the couches facing the wall-screen TV. "No freebies, fat man. You agree to work for me, let one of my lieutenants tag along with you, and I'll be straight as a razor."

He slid onto a couch, grabbed for the remote, hoisted one leg onto an ottoman. Jules stood in front of the screen. Static electricity made his back and neck tingle. "I'm not done with you yet. Have you or any of your buddies developed a taste for black preachers recently?"

Randolph looked past him, at the edges of the TV. "Preachers? We have our own chapel here. I think you saw it earlier. We never invite guest preachers. Although that might spice up services some. I'll put a note in the suggestion box."

"Cute. The cops found a dead preacher in an alley off Bienville Street in the Quarter. They dredged another out of a City Park lagoon. Both of them had little holes in their necks. They were both short a few quarts of blood."

Randolph's expression remained bored. "Maybe you should ask your friends in Malice X's shop about that. We don't need to sup on black preachers. Who knows what they get into when they take off their collars? Hepatitis, HIV . . . supposedly our stomachs burn away all the nasty viruses, but why take a chance? Especially when we've got the healthiest blood in Louisiana right here, waiting to be drained?"

"You took the question right out of my mouth, pal."

Randolph checked his watch. "The big finale to *Bachelorettes on the International Space Station* is coming on. I've been waiting weeks for this. Show me some loyalty, I'll show you some answers. Otherwise, show yourself out."

Jules interviewed six other junior vampires, four women and two men. When he was through, he didn't know any more than he had when he left Randolph in the billiards room. They were all as obstinate and closemouthed as Pearl had been. Apart from Randolph, none dangled any form of cooperation in front of him, strings attached or not. Jules figured that made the little billiards champ their leader.

Should he take Randolph up on his offer? Doing it without informing Besthoff beforehand was too risky . . . too risky for Doodlebug, who'd bear the brunt of Besthoff's fury at Jules's "betrayal." So what were the risks of letting Besthoff know? How would he react? He might applaud Jules's initiative, give his complete blessings. Or he might decide to squash Randolph like a bug. Would that be a bad thing? If Besthoff took down the apparent ringleader and disrupted the youngsters' plans, whatever they were, that might get them to confine their activities to the compound. Which would presumably keep them out of danger, which was one of the things Jules was hired to do. But this might also make it impossible for him to track down their attacker. Without all the balls in play, the attacker might pack up his cue stick and go to bed. Which wouldn't be such a bad thing, either, unless it resulted in the High Krewe keeping Jules on their leash for months, tracking a perp who'd lost interest and faded away.

Jules would have to wait and see. If something didn't break his way soon, maybe within a week or so, he might have no choice but to take Randolph up on his offer. But even if he crawled into bed with Randolph, who's to say the Cagney wannabe would feed him the straight dope even then?

The heroes in the hanging tapestries, the marble busts of the High Krewe's honored ancestors, all leered at Jules as he walked the halls toward his rendezvous with Straussman in the entrance foyer. Every single one of them, if he glanced at them from the corner of his eye, wore the serpent's features of the unnamed saint in the chapel.

Straussman was waiting for him near the front door. He handed Jules a thick sealed envelope. "Here is your advance payment, sir," he said. "And I have something else for you as well. Something that may prove handy during your investigation."

He handed Jules what looked like a small, square leather wallet. Jules opened it. It held a gold badge embossed with a pelican and a five-pointed star, and a laminated ID card that identified Jules as a private investigator officially licensed by the State of Louisiana.

"I was told you shouldn't try to use this to gain advantage with a police officer," Straussman said. "However, it should prove adequate for impressing an average citizen."

"Hey, thanks," Jules said. He looked at the badge again. Even though it was counterfeit, it still looked nifty. And it probably would come in handy. He could hardly wait to show it off to Erato. He slipped the badge and the money into a zippered pocket in his vest. "That's really great. And forget that 'sir' business, okay? Call me Jules."

"Of course, sir. Would you like for me to show you where we recovered Victoria and Alexandra now?"

"Sure. The night's not gettin' any younger, and neither am I."

Jules felt his shoulders loosen up as soon as they walked outside. He hadn't realized how tense he'd gotten inside the big house, questioning the big bosses and their obnoxious, secretive offspring. Now, with the moon overhead and a cool breeze ruffling his hair, he felt as if he could breathe again. Straussman led him through the front gate to the four acres of woods between the compound's walls and Bamboo Road. Acorns and dry leaves crackled beneath Jules's sandals as they walked toward the tallest oldest oak tree in the grove. A leaf got wedged between the big and second toe on his left foot; one of his first errands would have to be buying some decent shoes and clothes.

They stopped beneath the crooked branches of the big live oak.

"This is where we found Miss Victoria," Straussman said. He pointed to a leaf-covered spot between gnarled eruptions of the tree's roots.

Jules stared up at the security cameras that lined the ramparts of the compound's wall. They were installed about fifty feet apart and were trained on the surrounding woods, along with floodlights. "How long have those been up there?"

"We had them installed the night after we recovered her. They swivel to follow any detected motion. And they record both the visual and infrared spectrums."

"Infrared? That's body heat, right?"

"That is correct, yes."

Body heat. Fine for picking out humans in the dark. But it wouldn't pick up diddly if an intruder were a bloodsucker. Still, with the floodlights on, the cameras should catch anyone or anything emerging from the woods—short of a buck-naked vampire. "Where does the feed from the cameras go?"

"We installed a watching station in a corner of the kitchen, where at least one of us will normally be present during nighttime hours. Of course, it is impossible to have the station manned twenty-four hours per day. One of Mr. Otranto's new duties is to watch the speeded-up digital recordings from the previous day, and to alert me should any unfamiliar visitors appear on tape."

"Have any?"

"No. You and Mr. Richelieu have been our only visitors."

Jules took a last look around the base of the tree and the surrounding ground. Almost two weeks had passed since Victoria had been left here. Any impermanent physical evidence—footprints, say—would've been obliterated by rain and wind, not to mention Straussman's, Otranto's, and Hecht's efforts in moving the body. And the attacker hadn't been kind enough to drop a wallet with his picture ID.

"Let's go take a look at where you found Alexandra," Jules said.

"Shall I drive?"

"Naww. It's not that far. Let's walk."

Jules stayed off the walking path and Bamboo Road. Instead, he led Straussman through the patch of woods that separated the compound from Metairie Road, a four-lane thoroughfare that bordered Metairie Cemetery. The illuminating power of the High Krewe's floodlights ended just a few yards inside the tree line. He scanned the forest floor with his flashlight, searching for anything the attacker might've dropped.

Jules's beam looked especially puny on the forest floor, a droplet of light in a sea of darkness. After he saw where Alexandra had been found, maybe he'd come back here in his wolf form, nose around some, see if he could smell anything suspicious. He heard an unpleasant, breathy sound, then realized it was he himself, wheezing. He was carting around more weight than he'd been used to, thanks to eight months of rodent feasting.

Jules turned to Straussman. "Hey, y'know what I been wondering? What's the story with old man Katz? I thought vampires lived forever. I ain't never heard of a senile vampire before. Was he eighty years old when he got bit?"

"I am not familiar with most of Master Katz's personal history," Straussman said. "I do know that he is far older than either Master Besthoff or Master Krauss. Regarding his apparent . . . frailty . . . This is a state of affairs that did not frequently erupt before we moved to Louisiana. Since then, he has found it increasingly necessary to rejuvenate himself with the . . . close presence of the young masters. You did not see him at anywhere near his best. Once he has been, oh, rejuvenated, I daresay he strikes an even more formidable figure than Master Besthoff does. You would hardly believe it, but at those times, Masters Besthoff and Krauss defer to him quite readily."

Jules rubbed his forehead with his flashlight. It didn't take too prurient an imagination to figure out what form this "rejuvenation" process might take. No wonder Katz had prattled on about his precious *chuldrun.* He tried picturing Pearl, or even Randolph, in bed with the shriveled old vampire, his papery skin dry as a cracked river bottom. Jules shivered. *Yuck.* No wonder the kids wanted to stay away from the compound as much as possible. At least that made more sense now.

What still didn't make sense was why Katz had fallen into decrepitude at all. Was it the great distance from his birthplace—the wide ocean that separated New Orleans from Romania or Transylvania? Or was it the result of subconscious expectations, his body taking on changes it thought it *should*? Doodlebug had explained eight months ago that Jules's symptoms of creeping diabetes and arthritis resulted, not from actual illnesses, but from his own belief that these were ailments obese people were automatically nailed with. Once he'd convinced himself otherwise, the symptoms had disappeared. Although now, for some reason, they seemed to be creeping back.

Maybe Besthoff and company kept Doodlebug on a short leash because they recognized his special skills would be vital to them someday?

Besthoff and Krauss both must realize they were staring down the barrel of what was happening to Katz; maybe centuries down the road, but it was coming. And maybe they wouldn't be able to hang on to a harem of young "rejuvenators" until then. Doodlebug's incredible discipline over his own form, if they could learn it, might save them from an eternity drooling on the porch of some vampire rest home.

Jules and Straussman reached the edge of Metairie Road. Traffic was light. In less than a minute, they were able to cross two lanes to the grassy neutral ground in the center, then cross another two lanes to the cemetery side. Straussman led Jules to a wrought-iron gate and removed his ring of keys from his pocket.

"What's up with the key?" Jules asked. "The High Krewe got folks buried in here?"

"I don't believe so," Straussman said. "But the masters make an annual donation to the cemetery's directors for upkeep and restoration of the older tombs. Many of our young people enjoy coming here for picnics on pleasant evenings."

The gate squealed like an annoyed pig as Straussman pushed it open. Access. That was a possible clue. Who else had a key to the cemetery? Was Straussman the only possessor of one? On the other hand, Metairie Cemetery was practically a small city, covering dozens of acres. The fence and gates that surrounded it were at least a century old. There could be several easy entry points along the long perimeter, places where locks had disintegrated or where gates had been stolen from their hinges.

"Lieutenant Micholson's monument is this way," Straussman said.

They walked between rows of tombs. The causeway between rows was wide enough that Jules was able to avoid uncomfortable proximity to the crosses that topped many monuments. Jules stared at the crypts, many of them taller than houses. He passed replicas of famous cathedrals, Greek temples, plantation homes, Roman halls of government. Lots of them looked big enough to live in, if you lived alone and didn't have much furniture. Probably cost as much as a house would, if not more. The cathedrals had stained-glass windows, which would be pretty to see in the sunlight. Jules had been inside this cemetery only once before, as a little boy with his mother. He tried to recall if he'd noticed the stained-glass windows then, if he'd seen what they looked like with sunlight streaming through them. He couldn't remember.

They came to a tomb set several rows back from the street. This one was different. It looked like a small, grassy hill, shaped like half an egg, with a Civil War cannon on top. The cannon's muzzle pointed north. The little hill had a marble doorway built into one face. It was just big enough for a moderately tall man to walk through without stooping.

"This is where we found Miss Alexandra," Straussman said, pointing to the doorway. "She was wrapped in a blanket, propped up against that doorpost, as though she'd sat there to rest and had fallen asleep."

Jules stared up at the cannon. "This Micah Micholson, he have any connection to the High Krewe?"

"Not that I'm aware of, no."

"You have any idea why the attacker might've chosen this particular tomb to leave his victim at?"

"I really wouldn't know, sir. The only notion that comes to mind is that this is a particularly prominent tomb, somewhat of a landmark. Obviously, the criminal meant for us to find Miss Alexandra. Perhaps he was merely making it easy for us to do so."

Jules clicked his flashlight back on and walked slowly around the monument, playing his beam up and down the steep grassy slope. That cannon . . . it had to *mean* something. There were plenty of other prominent tombs in Metairie Cemetery. Why this one? Jules thought back to his conversation with Erato about the bloodless bodies recovered in a French Quarter alley and the shallow end of a City Park lagoon. Somebody had been sending a message by leaving those bodies there; Jules was sure of it. And he was almost as positive someone had been sending a message here, too. Cannon. War. Had someone declared war on the High Krewe? A Civil War, maybe?

Jules walked back to the front of the tomb. He shined his flashlight beam into the doorway, searching its corners. Above the doorway's marble lintel, a portion of earth and grass had eroded away, leaving a slotlike concavity. If he stood on his tiptoes, he could just about see in. He lifted his flashlight over his head to banish the shadows. There was something in there. Something dark and round, about the size of a blackened baseball.

Jules reached up and retrieved the object from the hole. It was lighter than he'd expected it to be, less than half a pound. It was damp and partly covered with something fuzzy or stringy. He aimed his flashlight at it. The pit of his stomach went instantly sour.

It was a coconut. But not just any coconut. Jules had seen one like this before. It had a face painted on it, eyes, nose, and mouth outlined in white. A black minstrel face, just like the faces painted on coconuts handed out by the mainly black Zulu carnival krewe at their parade on Mardi Gras Day. Only this minstrel face had white fangs.

The last and only time Jules had seen a coconut like this was eight months ago, when Malice X had begun slaughtering Jules's friends. Jules had found his onetime boss and mentor, Doc Landrieu, retired city coroner, dead and bloodless in his basement laboratory, bloodstained glass-tube "straws" poking from veins all over his body. A small coconut painted just like this one had been lodged in his mouth.

Jules stuck the coconut in his vest pocket. Straussman looked at him with curious eyes. "Is that something important, sir?"

"Yeah. Maybe." Jules rubbed his temples, trying to stave off a headache before it got rolling. But he couldn't rub away the bad memories. Lots of them. He took one more glance up at the cannon.

Bang. The headache hit him between the eyes.

Shit, Jules thought. *Message delivered.*

NINE

The black vampires . . . Jules wasn't eager to lock horns with them again. But if a fresh confrontation was unavoidable, he didn't want to return to their underground lair looking like a Jackson Square bum. As soon as the sun set the following evening, Jules emerged from Maureen's bedroom, determined to spend some of his advance money on decent clothes.

He drove to one of his old haunts, Trader Ray's Discount Salvage on Airline Drive, out in Jefferson Parish; it was one of the few area haberdasheries that stayed open until ten. Just blocks from the Texas Motel, where televangelist Jimmy Swaggart's reputation had met its demise in the arms of a lady of questionable virtue, Trader Ray's usually offered a decent line of big-and-tall men's wear, along with its other specialties of beanbag chairs, velvet paintings, and reconditioned hunting rifles. Selection was entirely dependent upon the number of disasters, natural or manmade, that had recently struck stores and warehouses around the country. Luckily for Jules, flooding had been rampant in the upper Midwest that past spring, so Trader Ray's was well stocked with clothing in his size. His prize find was a seersucker suit, which, once dry-cleaned of mud streaks, would be perfectly presentable. He slipped on the pants, which were pleasingly commodious around the waist, emptied the pockets of silt, and paid the man at the register.

Jules's hovering cloud of foreboding was temporarily dispelled by the thought that, thanks to his new purchases, he'd at least look sharp when

Maureen reappeared on the scene. He hoped Doodlebug had been making progress with his research. Carrying his bags of clothes out to his car, he spotted a pay phone near Trader Ray's entrance. He should check in with his friend.

The phone's receiver smelled like cheap, strong cologne, and its push buttons were grimy as a janitor's fingernails. Jules dialed the bed-and-breakfast where Doodlebug was staying. The desk clerk said that Miss Richelieu was out. Maybe Doodlebug had left him a message on Maureen's answering machine? Jules remembered there was a way to access messages if he punched in a code after the machine picked up. He dialed Maureen's number, trying to recall what her code had been. B-L-O-O-D?

He was startled when someone picked up the phone. "Hello?" It was Doodlebug's voice.

"Doodlebug? That you?"

"Jules?"

"Yeah, it's me. What're you doin' over at Maureen's?"

"I came looking for you. I'm so glad you called." Doodlebug sounded almost giddy. "I've got exciting news. Thanks to a friend in Ukraine, I believe we have a way to bring Maureen back. Are you in the middle of something urgent? We can start the procedure as soon as you're able to get here."

"I'll be there in two shakes of a rat's tail," Jules said, heart surging.

His reunion with the black vampires would have to wait.

♠

Jules found a parking spot two houses down from Maureen's. A lucky find; spots in the Quarter weren't easy to come by, not even this close to North Rampart Street. A rusty Pontiac Catalina honked impatiently as Jules hurriedly backed into the tight space. He winced as he heard his right rear alloy rim scrape against the curb. The car's first blemish. Oh, well; he had more important things to be concerned about right now than a dinged-up alloy rim.

The parlor lights were on, and the door was unlocked. Jules found Doodlebug waiting for him in the parlor, dust whisk and lint tray in rubber-gloved hands. "What're you cleanin' up for?" Jules asked. "Place wasn't *that* messy."

Doodlebug pulled off his gloves, smartly snapping them. "I was trying to make sure we've collected every last particle of Maureen we can," he said.

"But I was superthorough nine months ago, when she got turned to dust—"

"I'm sure you were," Doodlebug said. Jules couldn't help but notice the worry lines surrounding his friend's eyes. "But one can't be too careful with a procedure like the one we're about to embark upon."

Jules chose to ignore the note of caution in Doodlebug's voice. His friend had said Maureen would be coming back. That was all Jules wanted to hear. "What'd you find out? How're we gonna do it? How long'll it take?"

"One question at a time! With the help of my friend in Kiev, a vampire antiquarian, I was able to locate the proper incantation. I learned part of it through e-mail. But to get all the vocalizations right, I had to spend several hours with him on the phone."

"The long-distance bill must've been a killer."

"No matter," Doodlebug said, smiling nervously. He tipped what was in the lint tray into a glass jar that was already partly filled. "I'll list it as a business expense on my taxes. Were you able to retrieve Maureen's ashes from Erato?"

"They're sittin' in a vase in the kitchen."

"Good. I have Mr. Straussman's blood donation. The only other things we need are blood from you and blood from me."

"How come?"

"Apart from Mr. Straussman and the not-so-dearly-departed Malik Raddeaux, you and I are Maureen's closest blood relatives. Mixing the three strains of blood together will give the incantation greater potency. It'll make it more likely that Maureen is returned to us as . . . healthy as possible."

Jules winced when he heard Doodlebug's pregnant pause before the word *healthy.* "You think—you think there's a chance she ain't gonna come back to us all . . . right?"

"There's always an element of danger involved when one invokes an incantation of this power," Doodlebug said, seeming to weigh his words carefully. "Reincarnations are tricky things. The ideal is always to do it as soon after disincorporation as possible, when all physical remains have been confined to the deceased vampire's coffin. The great unknown in Maureen's situation is how much of her remains were lost."

"I did the best I could," Jules said plaintively. "I swept everywhere. But that sonuvabitch Malice left the windows open after he shafted her—"

"I know," Doodlebug said kindly. He patted his friend's thick arm, but his smile had a forced hopefulness. "You did everything you could. And somewhere, I'm sure Maureen knows it, too. Even if we're still missing part of her, it's possible that mixing blood from three of her closest relations with the dust we have will allow the incantation to fill in what's missing. We'll just have to pray for the best and see what happens."

Jules squashed the spurt of panic in his gut. He couldn't let any doubts stop him now. "Let's get on with it. Where are you gonna set up?"

"The bathtub would be best, I think."

Doodlebug retrieved two small boxes from the dining-room table, and they climbed the stairs to the second-story bathroom. Jules clutched the vase to his breast like an infant he was trying to shield from a thunderstorm. How would Maureen react to his changed, reduced state? Until now, he hadn't given that much thought. What if he or Daphne couldn't find the rat? What if it had skipped town or, worse, been eaten by a cat? In that case, Doodlebug could probably teach him how to make a spare penis from his excess blubber. Hell, if the kid could form a pair of C-cup hooters for himself, maybe sacrificing a half inch of height in the process, surely he could teach Jules how to make a measly ol' penis. It had to be easier than forming almost two hundred separate rat bodies.

They entered the bathroom. Its most prominent feature was a tremendous claw-footed bathtub. An oversized model originally crafted to allow a couple to comfortably bathe side by side, it had permitted Maureen to take the long, luxuriant soaks she'd loved.

Doodlebug inserted the tub's rubber stopper into the drain. "Spread her dust along the bottom of the tub," he said. "Try not to clump it anywhere. And, of course, make sure that it's all out of that vase."

Jules removed the tin foil from the top of the vase and followed Doodlebug's instructions, sprinkling the dust in a rough approximation of a voluptuous female shape. Then he scraped the vase's insides with a toothbrush, shaking out any remaining dust in the vicinity of the two-dimensional golem's chest area. Doodlebug sprinkled the contents of his glass jar, lint balls and all, over Jules's creation. "What's next?" Jules asked anxiously.

"Next comes Mr. Straussman's donation to our cause," Doodlebug said. He opened up one of the two boxes and took out a plastic vial containing about a half pint of blood. He poured the blood over the dust, taking care to spread it as evenly as he could. The dust became a reddish paste. The musty air within the bathroom took on a pungent metallic tinge. Jules involuntarily licked his lips. He'd never tasted another vampire's blood before. Speaking of blood, the High Krewe had better cough up the blood supply it had promised him, and soon. He was getting hungry.

"Okay. Now it's our turn," Doodlebug said. He put back on one of the rubber gloves, then opened the second box and removed an antique carving knife. "I bought this earlier tonight on Royal Street. Pure silver. Any other cutting element wouldn't do the trick—our bodies' automatic healing properties would seal the wound before we'd lose much blood. They'll still counteract wounds produced by a silver cutting edge, but it'll take much longer. Unfortunately, it'll also hurt a good deal more than an ordinary cut."

"Doesn't matter," Jules said. He'd let his head be chopped off if it would bring Maureen back.

"Here we go then," Doodlebug said. Knife in gloved hand, he sliced diagonally across the veins of his opposite wrist. He hissed with pain. "It . . . burns a little," he said, his voice wavering, forcing a smile. He bent the wrist of his wounded hand back so that the blood would flow freely and aimed the steady drip over the red paste hourglass shape at the bottom of the bathtub. After fifteen seconds, he held his wounded left wrist above his heart to staunch the flow, and he squeezed the edges of the wound together. As Jules watched, the torn edges of Doodlebug's skin, aided by forced compression, gradually knitted themselves back together, although at a much slower pace than if the cut had been caused by steel.

Doodlebug dabbed away tears with a tissue, trying to spare his mascara. "Your turn, Mr. Duchon."

Jules held his left arm over the bathtub. He wasn't going to be a pussy about this, no matter how it might sting. Doodlebug took hold of Jules's wrist. Before Jules could see it coming, his friend had sliced a slanting gash across his white flesh.

"Hey, you gotta cut me so *deep*—?"

A thousand burning fire ants bit into his forearm at once. "*Shit* that *stings*!"

"Keep it over the tub, Jules, you're dripping on the floor—"

"Yeah, yeah. Thanks for the advice, Jack the Ripper. Remind me never to get you mad at me. Cripes."

Jules imitated his friend and bent his wrist back so that his blood would flow more freely. Dizzy, he leaned against the tiled wall. A growing whirlpool of weakness swirled in his guts. He watched droplets of his strength and vitality splash into the muddy puddle that would soon become Maureen. She couldn't belittle him or sass him again, not after this. Not when his own blood, freely given, would be a part of her.

Jules didn't know how many seconds had gone by when he heard Doodlebug say, "All right, that's enough, Jules. Hold your arm above your chest and squeeze the wound closed." He slumped onto the edge of the tub and followed his friend's instructions. He pressed the sides of the wound together and waited for the itchy sensation of his skin knitting itself back together. It didn't come. Blood spurted out between his fingers. Then it began flowing freely down his arm.

"Jules, you aren't pinching it tight enough—"

"I couldn't pinch it any tighter with a goddamn hydraulic *press,* okay?"

Doodlebug grabbed Jules's arm and examined the profusely bleeding wound. "This shouldn't be happening. It should heal. I don't understand . . ."

What could he do? Drink his own blood as it leaked from his wrist? It'd be like a snake swallowing its own tail. His heart pounded in his ears. He was bleeding to death. He couldn't believe it. "Do something, dammit! Or you'll have to say a fuckin' resurrection spell over me, too!"

Doodlebug snatched a towel and wrapped it around Jules's forearm, just below the wrist. He tied it so tightly that Jules felt the twin bones of his forearm scrape together. The alarmed look on his friend's normally placid face was more frightening than the blood loss. Jules's body had never betrayed him this way, at least not since he'd been a vampire; the last time he'd bled like this, he'd been ten years old, and another boy had accidentally whacked him in the forehead with a baseball bat.

The bleeding slowed. "Thank Varney," Doodlebug said. He took a face towel and pressed it over the gash. "Apply pressure with this, and keep it elevated for a good while yet. You should be all right now. If I'd known something like this could happen . . . I still don't understand it."

"Thanks, Dr. Kildare," Jules muttered, swimming against the undertow of shock. He'd wanted to say *Dr. Kevorkian,* but that would've sounded petty.

"Do you want to go lie down for a while?"

He felt like sleeping for a week. But he didn't want to delay Maureen's resurrection another second. "Naww. I'll be okay. Lemme just sit over there on the commode for a while, and the room'll stop spinnin'.

Get on with the rest of it. I don't want that blood to dry up, and then I gotta give more."

Doodlebug helped Jules over to the toilet. The dizzy vampire plopped on the closed lid, and the air-cushion inner seat hissed angrily. He propped his wounded arm up on the sink, continuing to apply pressure to his wrist. "So what you gotta do next?" he asked. His voice sounded like it was echoing from the end of a long tunnel.

"Believe it or not, now comes the tricky part. At least for me." Doodlebug took a piece of paper from his pocket and unfolded it.

"What's that?"

"My cheat sheet. I memorized the chant, but if I get even one of the intonations wrong, the incantation will be worthless. This is actually a little musical score. The transliterations are more memory aides than actual pronunciation guides, however, since the language of the incantation is prehuman. Pre–Homo sapiens, anyway."

"What? You mean Neanderthal-Man language? I didn't know they could talk."

"I don't believe these particular ancestors of ours were Neanderthals. To the best of my knowledge, no fossil records of these prehumans have ever been excavated. All I know for certain is that, whoever they were, they had vampires among them—whatever it was that created the first vampire had already left its mark, eons ago. My Tibetan teachers have preserved elements of their ancient language and religion. The truly challenging aspect of re-creating their chantings is that, physiologically, they were very different from us. Their heads were flatter, their jaws and noses more elongated. And most unusually, their tongues were bifurcated."

"Bi- what?"

"They had forked tongues. That, combined with their more expansive nasal passages, produced vocalizations impossible for modern Homo sapiens to duplicate."

"So what are you sayin' here? You gotta take that silver knife and cut your tongue in half before chantin' this spell?" The image made him feel queasy all over again. "And how do you know all this stuff about what these weird cave men looked like, anyway?"

"The monks preserved their cave paintings, in addition to their chantings. One of the skills the monks practice is the ability to alter their cranial-facial structures so that they can voice the chants."

"And they taught you that?"

Doodlebug blushed. "No. I, uh, I never advanced to that point.

There was a more lofty hierarchy of monks I never was allowed to meet. I heard a rumor that at least one member of that higher stratum is actually one of those prehumans himself. Which would make him several *millions* of years old." Doodlebug was silent for a moment. "My friend in Kiev, however, was able to advance further than I did. Before he was asked to leave, he made reproductions of the cave paintings, and he shared them with me. Also, he was kind enough to give me a crash course in the facial transformation."

"Over the phone?"

"He could tell how right or wrong I was by how I sounded. The trickiest part was hitting on the correct shapes of the nasal cavities and palate. But according to him, I've come close enough."

Doodlebug didn't say anything more. He closed his eyes tightly and puckered his small, delicate face. If Jules didn't know any better, he'd swear his friend was struggling with a stubborn bowel movement. The shape of Doodlebug's head began changing. Like a wax mannequin head subjected to heat and invisible pressure, his cranium became flatter and wider. His eyes, still closed, grew wider apart and took on an almost reptilian slant. At the same time, his jaws and nose expanded outward, his nostrils elongating until they were wide enough to stuff Kennedy half-dollars inside.

When Doodlebug opened his eyes, Jules was staring at a face unlike any he'd ever seen before. A face that no eyes on earth, outside of those of a few hidden monks, had seen for millions of years. An amalgamation of proto-human, wolf, and serpent; yet still vaguely recognizable as Doodlebug.

Doodlebug opened his new mouth, flexed his jaw experimentally. Jules could see the long forked tongue flicker inside. *"Whaassshk k'uuu aeiiiye r'uuuuk raeiiiyek?"* he asked.

"Can't understand a word you're sayin'," Jules said. He didn't ask Doodlebug to repeat the question. Hearing it the first time had sent shivers up his spine.

Doodlebug turned over his cheat sheet, took a pen from his pocket, and wrote out the question: WHAT DO I LOOK LIKE?

"Like that Bald Mountain devil guy at the end of *Fantasia,* crossed with *An American Werewolf in London,* maybe. Creepy as green leprechaun turds on your front lawn. Hell, I can't describe it. I'll give it another crack later, after you bring Maureen back."

Doodlebug nodded, understanding the impatience in Jules's voice.

He took his sheet and turned toward the bathtub. As he leaned over the damp shape at the bottom of the tub, he sang syllables unlike any sounds Jules had ever heard. Hollywood's sound-effects technicians had never come close to *this.* Jules's skin tingled as if it were infested with tiny crawling mites. The hairs on the insides of his ears flattened against his auditory canals, as if they were trying to retreat inside his head and escape the hypnotically rhythmic, inhuman vibrations.

Just when Jules thought he'd have to retreat from the bathroom, unable to take the auditory assault anymore, something began happening. Jules leaned around his friend to see better. Grayish smoke began obscuring the bottom of the tub—smoke that looked miraculously similar to the smoke that heralded a vampiric transformation. She was coming back. The incantation was working. Maureen was coming back!

The smoke swirled like octopus ink inside an aquarium. Between the wisps, Jules could briefly glimpse the shape at the bottom of the tub. It wasn't flat anymore. It was slowly taking on rounded contours, becoming more human with each passing second. Jules's nostrils widened. He detected a familiar scent—Maureen's scent after she'd come home from a long, sweaty night of dancing beneath the stage lights at Jezebel's Joy Room, before she had a chance to wash and change into her nightgown. He *loved* that smell. Once she'd returned to dancing at Jezebel's, he'd never let her bathe again.

Doodlebug stopped chanting. The sudden silence felt like a crash into a brick wall. Jules held his breath. He leaned over the tub, holding on to the rim so tightly that his fingers went numb. The still-swirling gray smoke began to subside. A new sound began filling the room. Both guttural and high pitched, it came from beneath the smoke. It grew louder and louder, until the medicine cabinet's glass doors began shaking.

The smoke settled like a gossamer nightgown on a voluptuous form, then disappeared, revealing everything. It was Maureen, all right. He'd recognize those breasts anywhere. And that face. Even though it was twisted into a ghastly mask of unimaginable anger and pain.

That increasingly loud sound was a wail issuing from her lips. Jules reached for her, then pulled back in shock as he saw more than her face. Not all of Maureen was in the bathtub. Her right wrist ended in a fleshy nub. Her right leg ended at what was once her knee, now a mess of exposed cartilage and bone. Most of her left leg wasn't there at all. Portions of the creamy white flesh that was supposed to cover her lower torso were gone; her intestines rubbed the side of the tub like pulsing purple eels.

Her eyes suddenly popped open. Her wail died on quivering lips. She unclenched her teeth to catapult a single word at the massive figure looming over her.

"JULES!!!"

He forced himself to look only at her face, the face he'd longed to see again. "Baby, oh baby, oh my gawd I've missed you so much, I'll make it all better, baby, I promise—"

"JULES!!! You fucking son of a bitch!!! Put me *back*! Put me BAAACK!!!"

Jules felt his heart shrivel to the size of a raisin. The night, once so full of promise, had descended into a hell even the devil wasn't cruel enough to have designed. He reached for her, feeling numb, outside himself. Maybe if he caressed her cheeks, lovingly smoothed her long, blond hair, he could calm her down? But strong hands pulled him away, guided him into the hallway outside the bathroom.

"I was afraid this might happen," Doodlebug said in a low voice. Jules dimly registered that his friend's face had returned to normal.

"I'm a *freak*!" Maureen's voice echoed through all the drafty rooms of her house. "A pathetic, crippled *freak*!"

"You can fix her, can't you?" Jules asked, sounding like a scared little boy. "You can say another spell, right? *Abracadabra*, she's good as new? Right? Just tell me that's right."

Doodlebug stared at the floor and shook his head. "No. I don't know any incantation that can fix this. I wish . . . I wish with all my soul that I did."

Jules glanced back at the bathroom, where Maureen was shrieking again, this time more from fury than pain, if her tone was any indication. "We can't—we can't just *leave* her like that. We've gotta do something." He scoured his memory for tidbits of medical knowledge, all learned from old episodes of *M*A*S*H* and *Marcus Welby, M.D.* "Skin grafts? Artificial limbs? *What?*"

Images flashed through his mind at herky-jerky speed. He saw himself in wolf form, staring over the lip of his coffin at his own pulsing proto-matter, the first time he'd ever realized such a thing existed. Doodlebug taught him to manipulate that mass, how to shape it, claylike, into undreamed-of new forms. That was his special blessing, Doodlebug had told him—that he had so *much* mass to manipulate, more than virtually any other vampire . . .

"I've *got* it!" Jules shouted. He pinched one of his belly's floppy folds in his fist. "Look at this. Look!" He shook the roll until his entire belly undulated. "Spare mass, right? Can't I donate some to Maureen? I mean, I'm the guy who turned into two hundred rats, right? Can't I will part of this belly and these big fat thighs to turn into proto-matter, then become new legs for Maureen? A new hand? Tell me I can do it!"

Doodlebug rubbed his face, then massaged his temples with small fists. "I don't know. I don't know. It's never been done before. Theoretically . . . theoretically, it's possible. If you'd always remain in close proximity; if you'd mentally discipline yourself, concentrate on the grafts retaining their forms, so they wouldn't devolve back into proto-matter and return to you. Maybe then. But I can't—I can't know for sure." He stared at his friend with plaintive eyes. "Jules, we shouldn't experiment more. Not with Maureen. We've already screwed up too much—"

But all Jules had heard were the words *maybe* and *possible.* "Thanks, pal! I can always count on you to believe in me!" He hugged Doodlebug, then strode back into the echoing bathroom.

Maureen's shrieking came to a halt when she saw the incongruous smile on his face. "Jules. My entire *fucking* body—what's left of it—feels like an abscessed tooth under a dentist's drill. But I'm going to . . . *try* . . . to appeal to you rationally. Let me die again, Jules. Let me go back into the dark. Because if you don't . . . if you *don't* . . . I'm gonna take these loose intestines, wrap them around your throat, and *strangle* you."

"Don't sweat it, honey," Jules said, making his voice as soothing as he could. "Everything's under control. Ol' Jules has it all figured out. Just gimme a minute here, and you'll be all patched up, good as new."

He closed his eyes. It was best to do this as a two-part process. First, wish part of his substance away, returning it to his resting place as proto-matter. It wouldn't go far; he didn't have his own coffin anymore, and since the last place he'd slept was Maureen's bed, just yards away, it'd reappear there. Then, the dicier part: fashioning it into new body parts for Maureen.

He thought about this some more. Actually, even Step One wasn't that simple. He'd never just "wished away" part of his mass before. The only way he'd ever made that happen was to transform himself into a smaller creature, a bat or a wolf. So maybe the best thing to do would be to change to a bat, then fashion new parts for Maureen, *then* concentrate on transforming back into a somewhat more svelte Jules, minus seventy pounds or so. That seemed to make the best sense. He figured he could count on his innate, subconscious sense of anatomy and physiology to form proper spare parts for Maureen. If he were being called upon to provide any of her *female* parts, *then* he'd worry; but, thank heavens, she seemed to have returned with all of those intact.

So bat it was. No problem. Just concentrate on wings, leathery wings; big hairy ears; long snout . . . no problem. *C'mon, wings. Flap, flap, flap.*

Nothing.

Don't panic. He was out of practice, that was all. Bats were hard. They were weird, alien, barely mammalian at all. Wolves were easier. He got down on all fours, to help get himself in the right frame of mind. He sniffed at the air, even howled a couple of times, not that his pathetic facsimile would've fooled any child older than the age of three. *Paws, not hands. Color eyesight goes black-and-white, remember? Long, hairy snout. Wet nose. Bushy tail. Full-moon HOWLING, goddamn it . . .*

He gave up and leaned dejectedly against the toilet. Even his wrist was bleeding again. "Shit. What the hell's *wrong* with me?"

Maureen, who'd been holding it all in, exploded. "AAAHHHHH!!! JULES, my PATIENCE is at an END!!! Send me back to the darkness, Jules. SEND ME BAAAACK!!!"

Again, Doodlebug dragged Jules out into the hallway. He made sure to close the doorway this time. "I've figured it out," he said.

"How to fix her?" Jules said, his chest reinflating.

"I wish. No, I've figured out what's going on with *you.* I should've realized it as soon as I saw you wouldn't stop bleeding. Your body's in stasis. It's stuck in one form. Until you recombine with that missing rat, you can't change into anything else. And your accelerated healing powers are gone, too."

"But . . . but that didn't happen to me before, when you had me practicin' multiple bodies, when I changed into a bat and a wolf at the same time. Remember? That can't be right. It's gotta be somethin' else wrong with me. This whole situation, maybe it's got my head all outta whack—"

"No. I'm right, Jules. You remember when you turned yourself into three identical midgets during your fight with Malice X?"

"Sure."

"Your mind occupied all three heads, didn't it? Your consciousness was split among all three of them?"

"That's right. It was like I had three pairs of eyeballs, three sets of ears. Whenever one of them little guys got hurt, I felt it in all three bodies at once."

"Right now, do you see anything out of that missing rat's eyes? Hear anything through his ears?"

Jules started catching his friend's drift. "No," he admitted.

"You've drifted into two separate consciousnesses, you and that rat. You've spent too much time apart. Until you voluntarily recombine—and it *has* to be voluntary, on *both* your parts—both of you are trapped in your current forms. And neither of you will have access to special vampiric abilities, although you're each stuck with all the usual vampiric vulnerabilities."

It was too much bad news, with too little time to digest it. "Ain't that a blue plate special," Jules murmured. His head was pounding.

Doodlebug's eyes were terribly sad. "About Maureen . . ."

Her voice cut through the door like a buzz saw. "JULES!!! Put me back RIGHT NOW, or I swear I'll KILL you, and then I'll bring you back to life so I can KILL YOU AGAIN!!!"

"Right now . . . there's nothing we can do for her, Jules. We can't make her better. The only thing we *can* do for her . . . the only humane thing to do . . . is follow her wishes."

Jules ran his friend's words through his mind a second time, trying to find some way they could mean something other than what he dreaded. "You . . . you can't be serious?"

"I've never been more serious, I'm afraid."

"I can't lose her again, Doodlebug. I just can't."

Doodlebug put his arm around Jules's shoulders. "It doesn't have to be forever. I'll do all I can. I promise. I'll return to California, scour my library for an answer. I'll get my friend in Kiev working on it. If need be, I'll go back to Tibet to consult with the monks, if they'll grant me an audience. And we'll do our best to convince Daphne to keep searching for that rat. But right now . . . it's cruel to leave her the way she is."

Maureen's wailing began again. Jules's eyes clouded over. His throat became so thick he couldn't swallow. "Is there a . . . y'know, a spell to undo what we did? To make her go back to—to dust? Nice and easy, like?"

Doodlebug looked away. "No. There's only, well, the traditional method."

Now Jules could hardly see at all. The hallway looked like it'd been inundated by a biblical flood, and he was being swept away by a cold, murky tide. "Ohhh . . . you're gonna hate me for this, buddy. But I can't . . . I can't . . . I just *can't*—"

"I understand. It's okay—"

"You gotta do it for me." The words came out in a garbled rush. "I just can't do it, Doodlebug. My *hands,* they won't do it."

"I understand. *I'll* do it."

Jules leaned against the wall and tried to breathe. He rubbed his eyes with both hands. His left eye stung, and he realized that he'd gotten blood in it, blood mixed with tears. He heard Doodlebug descending the steps to the first floor. A few seconds later, he heard a sharp crack—the sound of his friend breaking off the wooden leg of a chair or a table.

He couldn't stay here and witness it. Where could he hide? His car was downstairs. But he couldn't leave Doodlebug here by himself. Jules would never forgive himself for running out on him.

He heard Doodlebug climbing the stairs. *Where?* Jules stumbled into Maureen's bedroom. Her closet was a walk-in, and it had a door. He pulled the door shut behind him and sat on the floor in the dark, against the wall farthest away from the bathroom. Her dresses and nightgowns surrounded him like shrouds. Their silken folds touched his neck, his arms, cruelly reminding him that their mistress was less than a hundred feet away. Her shoes crowded his thighs, poked him, reproached him with their lingering odors of Maureen, supplicated him to stop what was about to happen. But he couldn't.

Maureen's angry screaming stopped. Doodlebug must've entered the bathroom. Jules put his hands over his ears and pressed as hard as he could.

He might as well have tried holding back a hurricane. When it came, Maureen's death wail shook the walls of her two-hundred-year-old house. It lasted a terribly long time. But just before it faded, her wail became a song.

TEN

Jules let Doodlebug drive him back to the bed-and-breakfast. Seeing Maureen in such agony had been like sawing off his own leg. Now that she was gone again, nothing mattered anymore. For the first time since she'd bitten him and infected him with the virus of eighty-five years of a sometimes quixotic love, he truly felt like one of the walking dead.

Doodlebug led him into his cottage by the hand, as though Jules were a sleepwalker. Then he headed for the refrigerator. "I'm going to get you some blood."

Jules slumped into a chair at the dinette table. "Not hungry," he mumbled.

Doodlebug filled two large tumblers full of thick red liquid. "I don't care if you're not hungry. You're going to drink every drop." He set a glass in front of Jules, then sat down and drank deeply from his own glass. He didn't look so good, Jules realized; worry lines had etched themselves into his forehead, and he had bags under his eyes. If Jules looked half as bad as his friend did, he was in trouble. He lifted his glass and took a sip. It was like drinking life itself. Thirst seized him. He downed the entire glass. Doodlebug poured him another. Drinking it down, Jules began feeling almost human again.

Doodlebug pulled his chair closer and took one of Jules's hands, the one with the bandaged wrist. "Jules, I can't apologize enough for what happened. I *swear* to you, I'll do everything I can to make things right."

"Yeah. I know you will." Jules's reassurance did nothing to erase the pained, guilt-stricken expression from his friend's face. "Look. Don't beat yourself up too much over what happened. You did the best you knew how. And I was pushin' you into it, even after you told me there was risks involved. So if there's any blame, we split it, fifty-fifty. Hell, I'll take the lion's share, okay?"

Doodlebug rested his forehead on his fists. "Jules, I'm torn. I can do my best work for Maureen back at my institute in California. All my books and research materials are there. I've got the names of other experts I can contact. Honestly, the more time that goes by, the more estranged Maureen's spirit will become from this physical plane, especially now that we've attempted a resurrection and failed. The longer we wait, the less chance we have of success. But I don't want to leave you alone like this. Not now."

Jules forced himself to sit up straight. "First thing tomorrow night, you book yourself a flight back to California. No ifs, ands, or buts."

"But you must feel like you're going out of your mind—"

"I'll be *fine,*" Jules lied. "Go back to California. I got plenty goin' on to help take my mind off Maureen. Like this investigation you got me dragooned into."

Doodlebug looked stricken. Jules was immediately sorry he'd phrased it that way. "I should help you," Doodlebug said. "You're without your transformative powers, without your healing abilities—"

"No." Jules grabbed hold of his sole responsibility for the investigation like a drowning man clutching the rim of a lifeboat. "It's my job now, whether I originally wanted it or not. And I'm gonna see it through to the end. I already got started. Last night, I spent almost six hours at the High Krewe's compound."

"What did you find out?"

"I found out those 'youngsters' are a bunch of pricks. Not that that was any big surprise. I wouldn't lay a thousand bucks on it yet, but I'm gettin' a pretty strong feeling that the kids offed two black preachers. And this might tie in somehow with what's gonna be happening with the old St. Thomas housing project. I also found out our little rebels without a cause might *have* a cause, after all. You ever met Katz, one of the three big bosses?"

"No. I've only dealt with Besthoff."

Jules grunted. "Figures. Neither of them other two bosses are what you'd expect. Katz is this decrepit old codger, drool drippin' down his chin. I was shocked to see it. I thought that, y'know, vampires live forever, and they don't really change that much."

"*You've* changed since you've become a vampire, and it's only been eighty-five years."

Jules frowned. "Some of that's been in my head, like you told me. The diabetes and arthritis and stuff—I expected it to happen, so it did. How about your monks over in Tibet? I'll bet some of them are way older than Katz. They got drool rollin' down their chins?"

"Attitudes toward aging are much different in the East than in the West. The old are objects of veneration there. It's helped keep them young, relatively speaking."

"Yeah? Well, I think Katz's got his own special formula for a fountain of youth. Straussman tells me Katz gets temporary face-lifts from the kids. And I'll bet dollars to donuts it involves squeakin' bed springs, if you know what I mean. You ever hear of anything like that?"

Doodlebug rubbed his chin. "Temporary transference of vitality through sexual relations; a kind of psychosexual 'leeching' . . . some of the texts I've read have made veiled allusions to it. I've picked up some dirty gossip over the years, but none of it's ever been substantiated. It's one of the more outré legends of the vampire world."

"Well, this ain't like alligators livin' in the sewer pipes. I'm pretty sure 'leeching,' or lechery, is what's going on in that Vincent Price castle of theirs."

"And you think this could be behind the youngsters' insistence on leaving the safety of their compound, despite the recent attacks and disappearances?"

Jules smirked, glad to be thinking of something other than Maureen. "Hey, if you had some horny old fuck climbin' into your bed every night and tryin' to ram it up your ass, don't you think you'd look real hard for someplace else to sleep?"

"Good point."

"Damn right it is."

Doodlebug's expression brightened slightly, responding to the upswing in Jules's mood. "It sounds like you've made some progress. Where do you plan to go from here?"

Jules fingered the coconut hidden in his vest pocket. If he even mentioned the words *black vampires,* Doodlebug would glue himself to Jules's side until the investigation was over. Jules had to admit his ex-partner had been a huge help the last go-round; Jules would've ended up a bunch of soggy ashes at the bottom of a French Quarter urinal if the kid hadn't shown him the ropes. But as much as Jules could use Doodlebug's help here in New Orleans, he needed his friend working toward rescuing Maureen more. Much more.

"I'm thinkin' about tailin' one of them kids when they sneak outta the compound," Jules said, "see where it is they get themselves to." He had another idea, too. "I also want to ask around and see if maybe some of them antivampire Federal agents aren't still in town. Starting with that hotel where I dumped Veronika." He'd love to discover that Veronika was behind the mutilations. After the way she'd betrayed Maureen to Malice X, handing that bitch over to the High Krewe's tender mercies would feel like winning the Powerball lottery.

"There's one thing you could help me with here," Jules said. "Have you made any progress talkin' Daphne into sticking with the rat patrol? I get my dick back, maybe I can help make parts for Maureen."

Doodlebug looked embarrassed. "Daphne . . . she, uh, she won't speak with me. I can't say I blame her much. The only time she's opened her mouth recently is to ask a few questions about you."

"Huh. What's she been askin'?"

"She asked whether you're rats that became a man or a man who'd become rats. I told her the latter, but I don't think she believed me."

"What else?"

"She asked whether you were good or bad."

"Oh? And what'd you tell her?"

"I said that, like almost everyone, you're a mixture. Although I think you tend more toward good, thanks to that strong Catholic upbringing."

Sarcasm? Jules couldn't be sure. The kid was usually so earnest. "So it sounds like I'm the one who's gotta do the heavy lifting with her."

"At least she hasn't fled the city. That's a good sign. I get the impression she's been waiting for you to ask for her help."

♠

The lights were still on in Daphne's cottage. Jules figured she hadn't been able to switch back to a normal sleep schedule yet. He knocked lightly on her door.

"Who's there?"

"It's Jules. The rat guy."

He heard a bolt being slid back. The door opened three inches, and she peered out at him briefly before opening it all the way. Jules stepped inside. Daphne was dressed in a pink cotton nightgown with a blue and white bunny embroidered on its front. The television was on. It was tuned to the Cartoon Network. Pepé Le Pew was engaged in his eternal, hopelessly amorous pursuit of the she-cat with the accidental white stripe. Love never worked out in the cartoons.

"Let me turn off the TV," she said. She clicked it off. Jules noticed that her bed and the floor next to it were littered with empty corn-chips bags, Snapple bottles, and fruit-pie wrappers.

"You been eatin' anything decent the last few days?" Jules asked.

Daphne sat on the bed. A cellophane wrapper crackled beneath her. Her hair was a disaster, even more so than usual. "I don't know where any restaurants are. There're snack machines in the laundry room. And a change machine."

"Doodlebug hasn't taken you out somewhere? Hasn't brought you any food?"

"She tried getting me to go out to eat. I didn't want to. So she brought me some takeout, left it outside my door. Chinese. I left the bag outside. I think the cleaning lady took it away."

Cleaning lady ain't been inside here in a while, Jules thought. "You want me to take you out for some chow? I know lots of places that stay open all night."

She fished a broken potato chip from one of the open bags on her bed. "I'm not hungry." Her quick, nervous bites seemed to belie this. Jules remembered he'd said the same thing a half hour ago, then gulped down a quart of blood. "You want a soda?" she asked. Her eyes suddenly grew wide. "Uh, do you . . . do you *drink* sodas?"

"Only when I'm a rat. I'll eat and drink just about anything then. But when I'm like this, I only drink, y'know, blood. And coffee, sometimes."

She scooted a little closer to him. "Can you—can you change into a rat? Right now? There's an ice-cube tray in the little fridge. I could pour some of the soda in it for you. And I've got Chex Mix. Rats like Chex Mix. They sit up on their hind legs and eat it like a squirrel would."

Jules ambled over to the couch next to the bed and sat down. "I got this problem, see? I can't change back into no rats."

She looked up at him with distressed eyes. "Why not?"

"It's the one that got away. See, I'm like a puzzle that's missin' a piece. Until that last rat and me join back together, I can't do any of my usual tricks. Can't change into a bat, or a wolf. Or a bunch of rats. I'm stuck just like I am."

She inched a little closer to him. "That's horrible. All those beautiful rats, trapped inside you."

"Uh, yeah. A real shame. All those poor rats, trapped in here." He patted his stomach; it sloshed like a slow-motion ocean. "So, uh, what I was thinkin' of askin', if it wouldn't be too big an imposition and all—"

"You want me to find that rat for you. So you can change again."

"That sure would be a big help. You bein' the rat expert, and all." Jules smiled inside. *Women—whenever you need them to do somethin', it's always a good idea to let them think they came up with the idea themselves.*

She seemed on the verge of agreeing to help. But then her resolve melted away. She scurried back to the top of her bed and hid beneath the rumpled bedspread.

"Hey, what's the matter?" Jules asked.

"How do I know you're *you*? The one I trust? How do I know you're not Miss Richelieu trying to trick me, or an evil clone, or you really *are* you but you're really, really *bad*?" Her voice was fast and jagged beneath the covers. "I don't know what's *real* anymore. This could all be a nightmare. The whole last two years. I could wake up any second and find myself back in Los Angeles with Mr. Busby. Vampires. Rats who change into big fat men. Doesn't it sound like a nightmare? Maybe I'm sick. Maybe I'm running a high fever. You think you could maybe call a doctor?"

She was sliding into the deep end, sinking to the bottom of the pool, and fast. If he didn't think of something fast, he was going to lose Daphne. The men with the butterfly nets would come, and the dick-rat would remain footloose and fancy-free in Bourbon Street's storm drains. Jules felt himself starting to sweat. That gave him an idea. He stuck his right hand under his left armpit and rubbed it around until it was thoroughly damp. Then he cautiously approached the bed, trying not to spook her.

"Daphne? I'm gonna prove it's me, okay? Really, really *me,* the same lovable guy you warmed up to back in that pet hospital. I'm gonna stick my hand under the covers, real slow like. I'm not gonna grab you or nothin'. I just want you to take your time, honey. I won't make you come out until you feel safe. Okay?"

He didn't hear any protest. "Okay," he continued. "I'm lifting the covers now. Just enough to put my hand in. Here it comes. It's not gonna do anything scary." He watched the covers move as she moved her head closer to his hand. He was pretty sure he heard her inhale deeply a couple of times. In the trapped air under the blankets, his scent must be pretty strong.

Her hands emerged from beneath the covers. Slowly, they pushed the blankets away from her face. Her eyes were still big. "Are you going to bite me?"

"Did any of your rats ever bite you?"

"Sometimes."

"It hurt?"

"A little."

"Well, I won't even do that. I promise."

"Swear?"

"Yeah. I swear. On my mother's grave." Considering that Jules had been flat broke when his mother died and had buried her in a paupers' cemetery, it wasn't much of a promise. But it was the best one he could come up with.

"If I agree to help you . . . will you promise me something else?"

"Depends."

"If I help you find that last rat, and you guys join up again, will you turn into two hundred rats again?" She was eager as a five-year-old approaching the gates of Disneyland. "I could help take care of you. My rats were always fat and healthy. I mean, you wouldn't have to stay rats all the time—if you didn't want to. We could talk sometimes, maybe, uh, go out for a cup of coffee or something. Would you do that for me?"

A little lie right about now wouldn't be hard. But Jules thought about it. What if things continued going in the crapper? What if getting Maureen back turned out to be hopeless? Would he want to stay a four-hundred-and-fifty-pound (or heavier) vampire? Even without a cute young caretaker, life as 187 rats had been pretty darn good.

"Sure thing," he said.

♠

Daphne insisted that she didn't want to stay at the bed-and-breakfast anymore. If she'd be helping him, she wanted to be staying where he'd be staying, in the French Quarter, close to where the missing rat would be found. Her things fit in a single suitcase, and the suitcase fit in the Allante's small trunk with room to spare.

Before going back to Maureen's, Jules took her to the Trolley Stop. Sure, there were all-night places in the Quarter, but none of them made omelettes as big as the Trolley Stop's (and none of them were as cheap, either). Service was quick, and a good thing, too. A swarm of army ants couldn't have devoured a potato-and-onion omelette any quicker than Daphne did.

Jules unlocked the door to Maureen's house with queasy trepidation. It was a much better base for rat hunting than the bed-and-breakfast; and besides, Jules didn't want to sponge off Doodlebug. But until they successfully resurrected Maureen, this would remain haunted territory. And Jules couldn't help but wonder what Maureen's ghost would think of his bringing Daphne here. This was strictly business, of course, pure and simple. But an observer couldn't be blamed for thinking otherwise, not with Daphne hanging on his arm and smiling dreamily through a series of girlish burps.

At the top of the stairs, he showed her the bathroom (which he avoided looking at) and the guest room. "Can't I stay in the same room as you?" Daphne asked.

Uh-oh. Jules hadn't seen this coming. "What would you want to do that for? Don't you want your privacy?"

She grinned up at him. "Not really. I don't sleep well when I'm by myself. Usually I've got my rats in the room with me, keeping me company."

"Yeah? Well, that's too bad. You might not have a thing for privacy, but I do. Vampires get used to sleepin' by themselves."

She put on a pathetic face straight out of a big-eyed clown painting. "Don't you want me to be well rested when I go out looking for your rat? I won't bother you. That bed in the guest room's just a light little cot. I'll pull it into your room and stick it in the corner. I don't snore."

Jules shook his head and pointed firmly at the door of the guest room. "I don't care if you're quiet as a church mouse. Jules Duchon sleeps alone. Ain't nobody ever told you it's unhealthy to sleep with a vampire?"

"Can you at least leave your door open?"

"No. Sunlight might get in." She silently implored him and made no move toward the guest room. He had an idea. He went to the closet at the end of the hall. It was still there on the top shelf—the big pink stuffed teddy bear he'd won for Maureen one night at the Pontchartrain Beach amusement park. It smelled a little musty, but it didn't seem infested with bugs. He handed it to her. "Here. Try sleepin' with this."

"Okay . . ." She didn't look much happier, but at least she shuffled off toward the guest room.

Jules went into Maureen's bedroom and shut the door. Before turning out the lights, he jammed a desk chair beneath the door knob. *If Maureen's ghost is hangin' around,* he thought, *she'll know I'm bein' a good boy.*

A ringing phone in the hallway woke Jules before his internal alarm clock could. He checked the digital clock on Maureen's nightstand before opening the door. Seven-twelve P.M. After sunset—safe. Walking out of the bedroom, he nearly fell over Daphne's cot. She'd pulled it right next to his door. Apart from the teddy bear, it was empty; a strip of light shone from beneath the bathroom door, and he heard water running in the shower. Shaking his head, he walked to the phone mounted on the wall near the stairs and answered it.

It was Doodlebug. "Daphne isn't in her cottage, and her things are gone. Have you seen her?"

"Yeah. She's in the shower over here right now."

A pause on the other end. "She stayed the night at Maureen's?"

"Yeah. On a cot. In the guest room." It was mostly true.

"So she's agreed to help you?"

"She's on board. Maybe a little *too* on board."

"What do you mean?"

"Nothing. Ferget it." The water stopped running in the bathroom. Jules heard Daphne whistling. It sounded like "Some Enchanted Evening" from *South Pacific.*

"Jules, I have a plane reservation lined up for nine-thirty tonight. Are you *sure* you don't need my help here?"

Actually, Jules hated for his friend and partner to leave. But the fact that they were working against a deadline regarding Maureen settled matters. "I'm absolutely sure. Get your tail back to California and your books. I'll hold down the fort on this end."

"All right then. But remember, the minute you need me back here, I'll get on the earliest red-eye flight I can. Oh, I'll leave a pair of cell phones at the B&B for you and Daphne, so you two can easily stay in touch."

"Thanks, buddy. I appreciate it. That, and everything. Have a good flight home."

He hung up the phone, then heard the bathroom door open. Daphne had wrapped herself in a towel, with a second towel wound around her head like a turban. "Hi," she said.

" 'Lo," Jules said. He was suddenly acutely aware of the fact that he was wearing only a pair of boxers, and even those were barely visible from the front. He wished he had a towel of his own.

"Who was that? On the phone?"

"Doodlebug."

Her expression turned wary. "She doesn't want me to go back to the bed-and-breakfast, does she?"

"Naww. She's headin' back to California tonight. Guess she trusts me to look after you."

"I trust *you* a lot more than I trust her."

"Well, that makes one of us. Is there anything you'll be needin' for tonight? For, y'know, rat patrol?"

She came closer to him and sat on the edge of the cot. "What is your favorite food of all time?"

Aside from the blood of a big, fat New Orleans mama? "Oh, I dunno . . . it's been years since I been able to eat much of anything. See, after you've been drinkin' blood for a bunch of decades, your system gets used to that, and you can't tolerate normal food no more. Unless you change into something that ain't been drinkin' blood for decades, like a rat. But let's see . . . I guess if I had to pick a single favorite food, it'd have to be the breaded veal from Mandina's on Canal Street."

"Then let's go there. I'll use their veal for bait."

On their way out the door, something caught Jules's eye. A package poked out of Maureen's mailbox. It hadn't been there last night. He lifted the lid of the box and pulled it out. His heart jumped.

"What's wrong?" Daphne asked.

"Nuh-nothing," Jules muttered. Maureen's name wasn't on the package. *His* name was. Just his first name, written with a laundry marker and underlined with a flourish. Who knew he was staying here? Just Doodlebug and Straussman. The handwriting looked vaguely familiar, but it wasn't Doodlebug's.

Jules tore open the brown wrapping paper. Inside was a thick magazine or large paperback book in a plastic sleeve. Jules stepped to the edge of the porch so he could look at it in the light of a street lamp.

It was an issue of *The Shadow Magazine,* cover dated April 1943. Staring at it, he felt as though dozens of tiny, icy legs climbed up his back. He'd owned this fat old pulp magazine before. It had been part of his tremendous collection of vintage pulps and comics, destroyed when Malice X had burned down Jules's house.

"Someone leave you a present?" Daphne asked, glancing at the pulp in Jules's unsteady hands.

"Guess so. But I'll be damned if I know who."

They walked down to the Allante. Jules carefully placed the pulp on the floor between the two seats. Driving away from the Quarter, his mind traveled back to his lost library at the rickety old house on Montegut Street, the home he'd shared for so many years with his mother. He'd had six shelves lined with mystery and adventure pulps. His mother used to buy them for him, inexpensive gifts that they both enjoyed. Sometimes she'd been cute and hidden them in places where he'd find them, inside his underwear drawer or next to his pitchers of blood in the refrigerator.

But his mother hadn't left him this one. He'd laid her in her grave more than forty years ago.

♠

They stopped by the B&B to retrieve the two cell phones Doodlebug had left. Daphne promised she'd keep Jules informed of her progress. Then he drove her to Mandina's on Canal Street, a modest restaurant in an old wood-frame house surrounded by oaks whose roots were tearing up the sidewalks. Jules hadn't eaten there since just after World War Two, but the place hadn't changed much, thankfully. The same Mid-City types as always hung out at the bar—small-time horse gamblers celebrating winning a few bucks at the Fairgrounds; lawyers from the DA's office wetting their whistles after a late-breaking case at the Criminal Courthouse—and the same kind of creaky, middle-aged waiters patrolled the dining rooms in their shiny mustard jackets. Best of all, the food still smelled the same. They waited at the edge of the bar until a waiter brought Daphne a "to go" plate of breaded veal. Then Jules put her and the food in a cab heading for the French Quarter.

His first stop of the night, before he'd start chasing after Veronika and her agents or the black vampires, was the home of his old boss, the deceased Doc Landrieu. During their quarter century working together, Landrieu had made studying Jules's unique "condition" one of his priorities. He'd wanted to discover everything that could be scientifically known about the phenomenon of vampirism; toward that end, he'd analyzed decades' worth of cell and fluid samples drawn from his nocturnal subordinate. The last time Jules had ever seen him alive, Landrieu's basement had held three filing cabinets full of research notes. It was a long shot—who knew what had happened to the house and its contents in the months since Landrieu's murder?—but if Jules could retrieve those notes, they might provide exactly the clues he and Doodlebug needed to successfully resurrect Maureen.

Doc Landrieu didn't live far from Mandina's—just a mile or so west on Canal Street, toward the cemeteries. Canal Street was torn up with massive construction. Driving slowly around safety cones and barricades, Jules read a sign that said the Regional Transit Authority was building a streetcar line. There hadn't been streetcars on Canal Street since 1964, when they'd been replaced by buses. *Maybe "progress" ain't so irreversible after all,* Jules thought.

He spotted the marble crypts of Greenwood Cemetery up ahead. He was close. The last time he'd been at Doc Landrieu's house wasn't a good memory. Not even close. Everything had happened so fast after Jules found his old boss murdered at the hands of Malice X and his cronies. As soon as he'd seen the body, he'd realized with horrible prescience that Maureen might be next, and he'd rushed to the Quarter. He never had a chance to alert the authorities to the killing and the blood-drained corpse Malice X had left tied to a chair. What the cops would've made of the painted coconut jammed into the corpse's mouth was anybody's guess.

How long had it taken before someone discovered the body? Doc Landrieu had lived by himself in a big, quiet house surrounded by a cemetery on two sides and a funeral home on a third. He'd been a solitary man, with few friends, and a lifelong bachelor. Jules hated the idea that his body might've sat in the basement for days, or even weeks, before someone made the ghastly discovery.

He turned onto the narrow side street next to the Hebrew Rest Cemetery and pulled up alongside his old boss's house. The lights weren't on. The big two-story colonial was dark, with no car in the driveway. A "For Sale" sign stood in the middle of the carefully trimmed lawn.

Who was selling the house? Enough time had passed for Doc Landrieu's will to go through probate; Jules remembered the process from the year his own mother had passed. Landrieu must've had relatives or heirs Jules hadn't known about. Jules copied down the Realtor's name and phone number. If the house hadn't been sold, maybe those filing cabinets were still down in the basement.

A good plan would be to take a tour of the property with the Realtor, make sure the cabinets were still there, then break in later. It wasn't too late to call the Realtor for an appointment. The cell phone was a frustration—its tiny buttons made it impossible for his sausagelike fingers to accurately dial the number (who did they make these things for—the midgets from *The Wizard of Oz*?). After three tries, he pulled a pencil from his pocket and used the eraser end to dial. The Realtor didn't answer. He left a message asking her to call him, leaving the cell phone's number.

What next? He fingered the coconut in his pocket—one of the black vampires' nasty forget-me-nots, or a pretty damn good replica. The obvious thing to do would be to hang around the Central City ghetto until he spotted one of Malice X's old cronies, then tail him and try to corner him alone. But Jules wasn't especially eager to tango with the black vampires right now. And, appearances aside, he didn't have proof that they had been the ones who'd left the coconut at Lieutenant Micholson's grave site for him to find.

Who else might know about the coconuts and what they meant? Who would have an interest in trying to ignite a war between different vampire clans?

Those *Man from U.N.C.L.E.* wannabes from the Office of Strategic Helium Reserve, that's who. Them and Veronika. It'd be just like that sneaky bitch to try to get Jules, the High Krewe, and the black vampires to do her dirty work for her . . . go to war and kill each other off so she wouldn't have to muss her hair. Besides, she had to be way pissed at him for the way he'd left her in that French Quarter hotel—three-quarters drained of blood, but kept from attaining her goal of vampirehood by just a smidgen. Screw going after the black vampires. For right now, at least. If Veronika had her tricky fingers in this, Jules wanted to slam the door on them hard.

So Jules would be doing some rat hunting of his own. His next stop would be the Château LeMoyne Hotel in the Quarter. The last place he'd seen Veronika, the rat who'd ratted out Maureen.

♠

Jules replaced his vest with his new suit jacket before leaving the car. The hotel lobby was deserted. White lilies sat in a vase on a table, giving the place the feel and aroma of a mortuary. A single clerk sat behind the desk, a young man reading a copy of the *Houston Chronicle. Lookin' through the want ads, probably,* Jules thought.

"Hey. How ya doin' tonight?"

The clerk put down his newspaper. "Oh, hi! What can I do for you this evening, sir?"

"Were you working the night desk last summer? Say, late last June? I stayed here a night back then."

"No, sir. I've only been here since the beginning of January. But my supervisor, Carlos, he's been here for at least a couple of years."

"Working nights?"

"I think so."

"He around?"

"He's on break right now, sir. Would you like me to ring for him?"

Jules shrugged. "I hate to drag a man away from his cup of coffee. How about you point me to the break room. I'll only need to talk with him a minute or two."

"Second door down the hallway, on the left."

The break room was a converted men's room. Although the stalls and toilets had been removed, a urinal still hung from the wall. Someone had put a potted fern in it; Jules supposed this made watering the plant exceptionally convenient. A short man, his slicked-down black hair glistening like polished vinyl, sat on a small couch that faced away from the door, shoeless feet up on a coffee table. A soccer match played on a small TV.

The man didn't look back when Jules walked through the door. "Juan Chavier! Did I not tell you I am *not* to be disturbed during the big game?"

"I'm not Juan Chavier. I'm Jules Duchon."

Now the man turned around. "Oh! I am very sorry, sir. This is not a place for the public. If you are looking for the men's room—"

Jules pulled his phony investigator's badge from his pocket and flashed the shiny emblem. "I'm an insurance inspector from Big Southern Casualty and Life. I'm investigatin' a claim from an incident that dates back to last summer. It might involve the management of this hotel."

"Oh!" The supervisor quickly stood and extended his hand. "I am Carlos Fernandez, night manager. I will be happy to assist you in any way

I can." He looked less than happy turning off the soccer match, then struggling into his shoes. "Shall we go to my office?"

"Don't think that'll be necessary. I only need to ask you a few questions."

"Would you like me to get you a chair?"

"Naww. I'm fine standing. You can sit, though." Carlos sat. "This involves a woman named Veronika—" Jules realized she'd never told him a last name. "Uh, Veronika Nobles. She may've checked in here using a different last name. She would've been staying here the fourth week of June last year."

Carlos shifted uneasily on the couch. "Mr. Duchon, I am sorry, but if she was registered here using a different last name, I am likely unable to provide you with any helpful information—"

"You'll remember this one," Jules said. "You ever look at that men's magazine, *Big Cheeks Pictorial*?"

The head clerk blushed. He shook his head sharply. "No, no, that is not a magazine I am familiar with at all."

Jules wished he still had his copy from last summer to show the man. "Well, she was a cover model. Amazing woman. Every part of her defied gravity, like she was standing on the moon. Her figure—it was like *this.*" He made a violin shape in the air with his hands, but with much more exaggerated curves. "I'm not kiddin' you. Blond, like Mamie Van Doren in her prime, but younger and bigger and better lookin'. According to my report, she got badly hurt in her room on the second floor. She was attacked, like by an animal. She lost a lot of blood—"

"Oh!" Carlos turned white, as though he'd lost a quart of blood himself. "Yes, yes, I remember it! A terrible thing! The paramedics came for her. I saw them roll her out on a stretcher. She looked barely alive—so pale!—and her clothing was all in shreds. Terrible!"

"So it was paramedics who took her away, not guys in black suits?" Not that it necessarily made any difference; if she'd contacted her agency handlers, they easily could've disguised themselves as paramedics to avoid complications.

"No, the ambulance men came. A guest in the next room heard her screams and called the front desk. My assistant went upstairs to find the disturbance. It was he who called 911."

"Do you know where they took her? Did they mention the name of a hospital?"

"Charity Hospital. I believe that is where they took her. They have the finest emergency room in the city, the doctors who know how to fix the stabbings and shootings."

Jules took a pad and pencil from his pocket and pretended to take notes. "Any cops come by afterward to interview you or your staff?"

"Yes. A detective came by later that evening. He spoke with both me and my assistant."

"You remember what he asked?"

"Ahh . . . he, uh . . ." The clerk slumped into the couch, looking suddenly sick to his stomach. "He asked whether we had a rodent problem, whether we have regular visits from the pest-control man."

"And do you?"

"Oh yes, yes! Weekly, ever since that night!"

Jules put away his pad and pencil. "Thanks, Mr. Fernandez. That'll be all for now. Enjoy your match."

Charity Hospital was a short drive from the French Quarter. Jules parked on Tulane Avenue and stared up at the soot-stained art deco monolith across the street. He remembered when it had been built, during Huey P. Long's administration in the late 1930s. Back then, the new hospital, with its sleek granite towers and its up-to-the-minute electric equipment, had been at the cutting edge of modern technology. Now it was at the trailing edge of urban decay. Most of the building was dark; the majority of its medical services had been moved to a newer hospital complex a few blocks west. Only the emergency room remained, kept vital by a constant infusion of fresh medical residents.

Jules walked around the block to the emergency room's entrance. If the concrete ramp leading to the sliding doors was jammed with ambulances, red lights flashing, he was screwed; nobody inside would be able or willing to give him the time of day. Thankfully, the ramp was empty. He wheezed slightly as he climbed the ramp, holding on to a guardrail; if any nurse spotted him now, she'd have a bunch of aides hustle him off to a cardiac emergency unit.

He stepped into the intake room. Despite the late hour, the room's folding chairs were all occupied. A colicky baby cried in its mother's lap in a corner. Jules breathed in the odor of a room crowded with poor people; a mix of sweat, soured laundry, rotting teeth, shitty diapers, and dime-store perfume. The emergency room served as family doctor for about a hundred thousand New Orleanians, Jules figured. If he were a normal man, he was sure he'd be regularly sitting here among them; cab drivers' benefits, such as they were, didn't include health insurance.

Being in the room brought back memories. How many nights during the past twenty years had he sat in his cab near the bottom of the ramp, waiting for discharged patients too weary to stand inside a bus shelter? People looking forward to whatever meager comforts awaited them at home . . . instead ending up, stiff and bloodless, at the bottom of a swamp or on the wooden floor of a freight car leaving town. After years of doing it, the guilt had gotten to him—all those pained, weary eyes staring at him from the backseat, so grateful he was taking them home—and he'd switched to collecting victims from the lines outside soup kitchens and homeless shelters. At least those people hadn't had homes to look forward to.

He walked up to the intake window. A tired-looking young woman in a white uniform asked him what he needed to see a doctor for. "I'm not sick," he said. He pulled out his badge and briefly held it up to the window. "I'm a detective from the Lake Charles Police Department. I'm investigatin' a disappearance. It involves a young woman who was admitted here last June. I need to take a look at her medical record, talk with someone who'd remember her."

"Let me get a nurse," the woman said wearily.

A few minutes later, a middle-aged woman in blue scrubs opened the door to the emergency room and gestured for Jules to come. The emergency room was partitioned into numerous curtained cubicles and examining areas with big windows. Patients on gurneys talked anxiously with a doctor or stared up at the ceiling. Nothing too urgent seemed to be going on beneath the harsh fluorescent lights, although an old black man, his hair a stiff wreath of gray, stared at Jules with mournful eyes from a bed; his swollen, bandaged left leg ended at his ankle.

The nurse motioned Jules into an empty curtained cubicle. "Where did you say you're from?" she asked.

"Lake Charles Police Department. I'm investigatin' the disappearance of a young woman named Veronika Nobles. Attractive young blond woman, early twenties, full-figured; nearly as big as me. She was admitted here June twenty-seventh of last year. Neck wound. Major loss of blood. I need to see her discharge record. Hopefully talk with somebody who'd remember treatin' her."

The nurse pushed her spectacles higher on her nose. "She was here last June twenty-seventh? You guys certainly take your time with your investigations."

"She only disappeared last week. We got reasons to suspect her disappearance is connected with the attack on her here in New Orleans. I need to find out where she was discharged to, who picked her up when she left here. That person or persons could be a suspect. That's why I need to see her discharge papers."

"You've got a court order?"

"Huh?"

"I'll need to see a court order in order to show you her medical records. And the records office won't open until seven-thirty tomorrow morning, although I can write up a request for you tonight."

Jules frowned. "Don't tell me my paperwork hasn't arrived yet. My city attorney promised me he'd get that request mailed here days before I'd drive to New Orleans. I'm sure it's just sittin' on some administrator's desk here. How about writin' up that request for me so I can come see the records tomorrow night?"

The nurse shook her head. "I'm sorry. I can't do anything for you until I actually see the court order."

Jules put on the sweetest smile he could manage without showing his fangs. "Ma'am, it's a long drive back to Lake Charles."

She didn't smile back. "I know. I'm from Port Arthur, Texas. Come back with a court order, and I'll be happy to help you then."

She walked back to her nursing station. Jules scowled as he left the cubicle. What a pain. Maybe Straussman could get some phony documents made up for him?

Jules felt a tap on his shoulder. "Hey, mister?"

He turned around. A short, stooped, black woman orderly stood next to him with a mop. She'd been cleaning the floor outside the cubicle. "Yeah?"

"I heard what you was sayin'." She looked around, then continued in a lower voice when she saw no one was standing nearby. "And I know who it was you was talkin' about. I got this friend who works here, he's been goin' on about her all the time since last summer. You wanna meet him?"

Jules checked to make sure the nurse wasn't watching him anymore. "Sure. Where's he at?"

"He be over in the ICU, straightenin' up." She looked up at him with expectant eyes and held out her calloused palm. "You wanna make the trip, you gotta pay the fare."

Jules dug a ten out of his wallet. The woman smiled. She folded it carefully and inserted it in a small plastic change purse. Then she led him out of the emergency room, deeper into the dimly lit maze of the old hospital. Jules was glad to leave the emergency room behind; the aroma of blood had nearly gotten saliva rolling down his chins.

Several dingy corridors later, she pushed open a door that led to a small ward of six beds. The ward's only occupant was a black male aide, whom Jules guessed was in his early fifties. The aide dumped his collection of dirty linens in a cart when Jules and his informant walked in. "Hey, Lanelle," he said.

"Hey, Shannon. I got somebody here who wants to talk with you. He wants to know about this hoodoo lady you been runnin' your mouth about. The big white gal."

She explained who Jules was and what he'd said to the nurse. Shannon stared at Jules with undisguised skepticism. "You sure don't look like no police detective I ever seen," he said.

"I'm from Lake Charles," Jules said. "Not too many murders there. Leaves me lots of time on my shifts for eatin' donuts."

"Bull*shit* you's from Lake Charles. I *know* what folks from Lake Charles sound like. You's from the Ninth Ward, just like half my family is."

Damn. He was pegged. Pulling out the badge now would be useless, Jules realized; it was only good for flashing in the faces of people with no reason to be suspicious of his identity. "All right," he said, shrugging his shoulders slightly. "Guess I can't fool a man sharp as you. I'm no cop; you're right about that. I'm Veronika's brother."

Shannon smiled broadly and slapped his side. "I *knew* it! You two coulda been twins, only I doubt your mama coulda carried you both at once."

"I'm older," Jules said.

The man's face suddenly turned serious. "Not now, you ain't."

"Whadda you mean by that?"

"When's the last time you saw your sister?"

"Almost a year ago. Before she came to New Orleans and got hurt."

"She's changed," Shannon said. "I saw it happenin' with my own eyes. She came in here a pretty young thing; aside from the blood and scratches and all. I don't get to see too many gals, 'specially not white ones, as big as her but with a figure and face so nice. So, y'know, I kinda kept my eye on her the few days she spent in the ICU. Thought maybe I could hear what had happened to her. She was like in a coma the first coupla days, never opened her eyes. But somethin' bad was happenin' to her, even while she slept."

"What?" Jules said.

"She was turning *old.*" Shannon hunched his shoulders and puckered in his cheeks, acting out his tale even as he told it. "She didn't turn into a crone overnight, oh no, nothin' like that. But being in her room a few times a night, I done watched the years creepin' in on her. Her skin was so firm the first time I seen her, like the skin on a ripe peach. But then these lines start spreadin' on her face, like some spider was layin' down webs on her forehead and 'round her eyes. Her hair—you remember how blond and full it was, almost gold?"

"Sure, sure."

"It got thin and dull, like old dry straw. Started fallin' out in clumps on her pillow. I had to sweep it up off the floor."

This wasn't like anything Jules'd ever heard of. Then again, he'd never drained somebody within an ounce of their mortal life before, then stopped himself. "So what happened to her? She get transferred to another hospital? A buncha guys with government IDs come and cart her off?"

"Two nights after she got here, she opened her eyes. The docs wanted to transfer her to some research hospital, but she wouldn't have none of that. She spent a lot of time on the phone. Then, the next night, this white dude with long hair came by to pick her up. Looked like a junkie cowboy outta some weirdo Western movie. The docs said she was nuts to be leavin', but this dude, he musta had some weight to throw around, or cash, 'cause he yanked her outta here without any problem. She walked out hangin' on his arm, lookin' like somebody who coulda been his mother, when just two days before, she coulda been his *daughter.*"

Jules took his cash roll from his pocket and peeled off a twenty. "Any idea who this 'junkie cowboy' was?" Certainly didn't sound like anyone from the Strategic Helium Reserve.

Shannon barely glanced at the twenty. "Nope. Was nobody I ever seen. Word around the wards was that he was somebody big, somebody known. There was this gal used to work here, white gal, a dietetic intern, she told me who the dude was, but it was nobody I ever heard of . . ." He slapped the side of his head as if this would dislodge the stubbornly elusive name. "*Damn!* I wish I could remember that name!"

Jules fingered his cash roll again. "That intern, any chance of introducin' us?"

Shannon frowned. "Sorry, man. She done graduated the end of last summer. I can't even tell you what school she was at."

Jules wrote his name and cell phone number on a slip of paper, then wrapped it around the twenty. He slid the small bundle into Shannon's shirt pocket. "Whenever you remember that name, you give me a call, okay?"

Jules followed Lanelle back to the emergency room, then walked down the ramp to Gravier Street. Rapid aging. Something else to ask Doodlebug about. He found it hard to muster any sympathy for Veronika. Maybe she'd end up like Katz—increasingly feeble and senile, but never quite crossing existence's finish line. Couldn't happen to a nicer Fed.

Jules was bummed. The Veronika trail had come to a dead end; at least for now. He'd been really looking forward to nailing her and tossing her treacherous carcass to the High Krewe. Now the only trail left for him to pursue immediately was the one that started with the coconut. And messing with the black vampires again could end up being like shoving his hand into a seething nest of wasps.

How should he do it? He mulled over his earlier notion of hanging out in Central City until he spotted one of their operatives running drugs or stalking a victim. That could take nights of watching and waiting . . . nights when he'd have nothing to do but think about Maureen. The best thing to do would be to go straight to the source—their lair beneath the Canal Street casino. That's where he'd find the bigwigs, like Preston and Elisha. People who would know useful information, whether or not they'd be of a mind to share it with him.

How could he get in to see them? Sneaking in wasn't an option. Changing into a bat or mist wasn't in his repertoire anymore; and in human guise, he wasn't exactly built for stealth.

Going in through the front door was the only way. Which would take balls of steel . . . balls he didn't have, steel or otherwise.

He crossed Tulane Avenue and climbed into his car. He fiddled with the ignition key, twirling it. Three ambulances . . . he'd wait until three ambulances passed him on their way to Charity, and then he'd drive to the casino. Three was a lucky number. And he needed all the luck he could get tonight. He'd just put down the top, turn on the radio, lean back, and relax while waiting for three ambulances to pass.

While he was folding the top down, Jules heard a siren echoing off the elevated expressway, speeding toward him. He listened more keenly. Not *siren. Sirens.*

He watched them fly by him in the opposite lanes and careen around the corner. One, two—four ambulances. So much for the joys of procrastination. Jules cursed under his breath and shoved his key in the ignition.

ELEVEN

The big casino was busier than the last time Jules'd been here. The electronic bleatings of hundreds of slots and video-poker machines piled onto his eardrums, obtrusive enough to give a deaf man a headache. Cigarette smoke formed a noxious haze that floated just below the sparkling lights in the ceiling, overwhelming the efforts of a battery of fans and smoke eaters.

Jules scoped out the crowd. There wasn't a tuxedo or even a decent sports coat in sight. This was an American casino crowd all the way. Texas tourists straining the seams of green cotton-poly golf pants; boisterous homies draped in sports paraphernalia, stacking empty plastic beer cups on their favored slot machines; grannies in low-cut tees, cigarettes dangling from their mouths as they stared at their screens, hypnotized by the spinning symbols—all in all, the most racially integrated crowd to be found in the entire town, except maybe at a Saints game. Jules figured the casino's ad campaign had finally begun to work, helped, undoubtedly, by the funds freed up when the legislature had cut the casino's tax bill in half. He wondered whether the place would ever get so busy that the black vampires would no longer feel comfortable using its secret underground level as their base.

Jules ran over his game plan again. It had the virtue of simplicity: he'd walk in their front door and start asking questions, then keep asking them until instinct told him whether they were involved in the mutilations. Once he'd figured the black vampires out, he'd head for the exits, then call in backup from the High Krewe if the situation seemed to warrant it. He didn't want to involve them before he was pretty darn sure of the black vampires' complicity; Besthoff and the youngsters were hungry for vengeance, and Jules didn't want them flying off the handle prematurely and starting a needless war.

If I walk in lookin' confident, he told himself for the tenth time, *they'll think I got a reason to BE confident, and they won't wanna mess with me.* Every vampire in that underground compound would remember the pack of vicious vampire wolf-dogs that burst through the courtyard's glass ceiling at the climax of Jules's death match with Malice X. For all they knew, this time he'd have a pack of vampire *elephants* waiting at his beck and call.

He approached the private elevator he'd used once before. The same two beefy white guys still guarded it, ex-linebackers in extra-wide tuxes. Jules decided he'd be extremely hurt if they didn't remember him.

They remembered him. He could tell by the way their eyes got big, the way they both instinctively reached for the bulges beneath their jackets. They let their hands drop to their sides, though. Guns weren't much good to threaten vampires with. At least not vampires in possession of all parts and powers.

The taller one spoke up when Jules was ten feet away from the elevator. "Sir, do you have an appointment?"

"Nope. No appointment. That a problem?"

"No one goes downstairs without an appointment."

Jules did his best to channel the ghost of Robert Mitchum. "Listen. You know as well as me that I coulda gotten into that underground playpen a dozen different ways, none of them involvin' making small talk with you. I'm not here to cause trouble." Jules pointed his thumb at the walkie-talkie hanging from the guard's belt. "Ring Preston up. Tell him Jules Duchon is here. He'll want to talk with me. That's the best bet going in this whole joint."

The guard stepped off to the side and spoke quietly into his radio while his partner eyed Jules nervously. After a moment, the first guard returned. "You're cleared to go down," he said. He inserted a key into the elevator's control pad and pressed the down button.

Jules stepped inside. The elevator, much like the High Krewe's chapel, was decorated like a robber baron's coffin, polished teak paneling alternating with tufted red velvet. No mirrors. Jules hoped he wasn't visibly sweating. He dabbed his forehead; it felt dry. Maybe this wouldn't go too badly. Despite Preston's braggadocio and threats, he'd actually struck Jules as semireasonable during their last encounter, a man driven more by rational self-interest than vendettas. In that whole crowd, the only one who'd really given him the willies was Elisha Raddeaux, Malice's sister. However, the last time he'd seen her, she'd been a shattered husk of a woman, clinging to Preston's knees and wailing inconsolably over the death of her brother. Despite the fact that she'd tried ramming a stake through Jules's chest, he hoped Preston had taken decent care of her.

The doors opened. Jules immediately noticed the warmer air down here, heated especially for a vampire's comfort; a welcome contrast to the overly air-conditioned atmosphere up in the casino. The ceiling of the formerly abandoned highway tunnel was still artificially lit to simulate a night sky full of stars and streaking comets. Maybe the smartest thing Malice had ever done was to sink his drug profits into the casino, allying its management to his own interests; then he'd been able to build this underground, sun-proof compound, whose construction had been masked by the construction of the gambling palace above it.

Two black vampires approached him. They were dressed identically in black leather pants and tight black tank tops, which showed off Olympian upper torsos. Jules vaguely remembered their faces from the big fight in Central City he and Doodlebug had gotten suckered into. They remained mute while escorting him toward the Southern colonial mansion that sat in the middle of the tunnel, flanked by glassed-in, heated gardens and courtyards. Jules was gratified to see them covertly glancing back over their shoulders as they walked alongside him, as though their nerves were primed for Jules's invisible confederates to leap out of the shadows. He hoped all dozen black vampires would feel equally on edge.

As they approached the entrance to the main courtyard, Jules saw the gate at the opposite end of the tunnel open, near where the vampires parked their SUVs and tricked-out pickup trucks. A van pulled in. A vampire dressed the same as Jules's escorts got out and opened the van's sliding side door. A group of black men and women slowly stepped down, assisted by the vampire. As best Jules could tell, the eight of them ranged in age from their teens to their sixties. Led by the vampire, they shuffled toward the courtyard, a team of sleepwalkers.

Jules entered the arena of his hard-fought victory over Malice X. The square of grass where they'd struggled had been replaced by beds of tropical flowers, lush with startling pink, yellow, and purple blossoms. His escorts motioned him toward a set of sliding doors that led into the main house. Near the patio wall, he noticed a group of cots laid out in a row, interspersed with medical equipment that looked startlingly similar to what he'd seen at the High Krewe's compound. Behind him, the first of the sleepwalkers stepped into the courtyard. Her face was slack, her eyes glazed, their pupils shrunken to the size of pencil tips. It was a look Jules remembered having seen before, that night eight months ago when he and Doodlebug staked out Malice X's Central City drug trade.

Jules nudged one of his escorts. "You guys setting up a charity blood drive?"

The man refused to meet Jules's eyes. He slid open the glass door. "None of your business," he muttered.

The empty den they entered contained the sort of high-end home-entertainment equipment Jules would've expected. What was less expected was the room's color scheme—couches, chairs, fixtures, and walls all in varying shades of mauve and pink. Either a woman was wearing the pants around this house, or Preston was gay. Jules'd never picked up that kind of vibration from Malice's number-one lieutenant, but there had been that whole shtick with the buckskin jacket and cowboy hat—so who knew?

They walked down a long hallway toward a pair of marble doors with large brass doorknobs cast in the shape of bats. "So this is where I get to meet with the big boss man, huh?" Jules said.

His escorts opened the doors. "Make that 'big boss *lady,*' " a familiar feminine voice commanded.

On an elevated platform at the far end of a long onyx conference table, Preston sat in a high-backed leather chair, still wearing the fringed jacket and black Stetson that Jules remembered. But the chair he sat in was subsidiary to another seat. That throne was occupied by a steely-eyed Elisha Raddeaux, coiled tight as a maddened electric eel.

This wasn't good.

"Jules Duchon," she said from behind barely unclenched teeth. The room's recessed lights shimmered off the metallic emerald silk dress that snugly wrapped her curves, so that her seething bosom and hips appeared to be emitting sparks. "I should be grateful. You saved us the trouble of comin' to look for you."

Jules silently counted the men and women sitting around the table.

Adding in his two escorts, now behind him, that made eight black vampires, plus at least one more outside in the courtyard. "Lots of folks have come lookin' for me lately," he said. "I'm a popular guy."

Her elegant fingers, nails painted a brilliant green, tightened on the arms of her throne as she leaned forward. "You regain your appetite for black blood lately?"

"Whadda you mean by that?"

She smiled a tight, bitter smile. "Don't play dumb with me, fat man. Pastor Nicholas Johnson. Brother Richard 'Hardball' Hammond. Two black preachers from Central City. Both their churches located within a half mile of the New Orleans Mission, your old happy huntin' ground, I do believe. Both found dead, brain stems destroyed. Drained of blood, too. And it just so happens both men were on the portly side. I bet their blood was downright finger-lickin' good, wasn't it?"

Idiot, he silently reprimanded himself. *Should've seen this coming.* "It wasn't me," he said, wincing as he said it, realizing how lame his denial must sound.

She continued her accusation as if he hadn't spoken a word. "Now, it would've been one thing if you'd stuck to your homeless cuties and welfare mamas. That we coulda overlooked, so long as you didn't get too greedy. But to go and fang our community's *leaders*—have you lost your pea-brained *mind*? Did you really think we'd just lay back and spread our legs for you, O Great White Hunter?"

Jules tried to look on the bright side. They outnumbered him at least eight to one, but no one had jumped him. Evidently, Elisha was every bit as interested in information as he was. "I told you, it wasn't me who done it. I been layin' low since the last time you saw me. The Feds have been after my ass. I haven't fanged a single victim in New Orleans in over eight months. Aside from your own group's victims and those two preachers, what other blood-drainin' murders have you heard about since last summer? That should be proof enough I ain't been around."

"That don't prove a thing," she said contemptuously. "Even if you did go away, so what? You're here now, and who's to say you didn't come back three weeks ago and restart your local blood-drinkin' career by chuggin' down some Christian Brothers wine?"

Jules grunted sourly. He couldn't very well tell her that, up until three nights ago, he'd been living as 187 rats in the French Quarter. Well, he *could,* but he didn't want to—not so long as any chance existed that he might use that same escape route again. "Listen—if it *was* me who'd killed those two preachers, and was so sloppy about it that everybody knows how they died, why would I be walkin' in here through the front door, wantin' to talk?"

She leaned back in her chair and thought about this for a moment. "Maybe you're wantin' to throw suspicion off yourself, huh?" Her face was more pensive than angry now, however; maybe his words had done some good. "Well, why *are* you here?"

Jules reached into his jacket pocket for the coconut. His two escorts jumped to restrain his arms, trying to make up for their failure to frisk him earlier. "Hey, relax, okay?" he said, shaking them off. "It's nothin' nasty. In fact, this is nothin' nobody here ain't seen before. I should start hummin' 'Return to Sender.' " He held up the grinning coconut so that its eyes and fangs faced the vampires around the table. "Take a gander."

Elisha stared at it for several seconds. "Where did you get that?"

"I found it sittin' on the tomb of Lieutenant Micholson of the Washington Artillery, over in Metairie Cemetery." He watched her expression, and Preston's, carefully. "Next to where leaders of the High Krewe of Vlad Tepes found one of their members laid out."

"Dead?"

Elisha's question sounded genuine. "Uh-uh. Not dead. But pretty damn close." *Unable to personally ID whoever attacked her,* Jules thought.

Elisha put her hand on her companion's shoulder. "Preston, go take a closer look at that thing."

Preston rose slowly, centered his Stetson on his head, and approached Jules, who handed him the coconut. The black vampire then surprised him by sliding a pair of glasses out of his jacket pocket, scowling as he put them on. A vampire with reading glasses; that was something Jules didn't see every night. Preston examined the coconut carefully, turning it over in his hands, peering for a long time at its gnarled bottom. Then he walked over to one of the male vampires sitting at the table. He handed it to the man. "Leon, this one of yours?"

Leon immediately looked at the bottom of the coconut. "Those're my carvings, my mark, yeah." He turned the coconut right side up again and stared at its stylized minstrel face, black paint on top of white paint. "Only thing is, this is *old.* I stopped paintin' 'em this way almost a year back. Changed to a new series end of last summer. Added more colors, made it look more Haitian voodoo–like. Figured if, y'know, Jazz Fest has themselves a new poster every year, we should have us a new coconut every now and then." He handed the coconut back to Preston.

Elisha gestured for Preston to bring the coconut to her. "When's the last time any of us would've put one like this into circulation?"

"Would've been when your brother was still around," Preston said. "When we was harassin' *him.*" He gestured with his elbow toward Jules, as though he might sully himself using his index finger to point at the white vampire. "Knockin' off his friends to rattle him. I left one at that autopsy doctor's place. Pretty sure Malice left another one at the stripper's."

The stripper. Jules brain went crimson, hearing Maureen referred to that way. In his mind's eye, he leaped at Preston, transforming into a five-hundred-pound swordfish in midflight and running the bastard through. But this wasn't Fantasy Island, so he'd better keep his temper well in check. He wasn't going to be changing into a swordfish anytime soon.

"So let me get this straight," Elisha said. "You're tellin' me the last two times we used that kind of coconut, on either occasion our visitor here could've pocketed one, right?" She turned to Jules, the hard, bitter smile back on her face. "What's this shit you're pullin' now, fat man? You tryin' to start a war between us and the High Krewe? Next thing I know, you'll be tellin' me it was the High Krewe fanged those two preachers. Right? You show any of those Euro vampires that coconut you *claim* you found on that grave?"

"No . . . not yet," Jules admitted. Boy, this dame sure knew the best defense was a good offense! Had Elisha just pulled a judo flip on him? Her indignation at his supposed ignominy hadn't sounded rehearsed. But she was smart, sharp as barbed wire, and just as tough. He simply wasn't sure. "Look, I *swear* I found that coconut on Micholson's grave. I didn't palm it off the body of one of my friends—although the more I think about it, the more I wish I woulda *been* so smart, y'know? Shit, if I were smart enough to plan out the kinda conspiracy you're pinnin' on me, I'd start my own fuckin' Internet company and get rich off some stock scam. So I'm not tryin' to pull anything on you guys, okay?"

Elisha dropped her smile. "If you're not, then who is?"

"I dunno. It's not me. But I think somebody's tryin' to pull somethin'. Maybe it's those Feds I was talkin' about. They meant to wipe out all the vampires in New Orleans, black *and* white. I was tryin' to track down one of their agents earlier tonight, but the trail went cold."

"That woman," Elisha said. "The one you claim the High Krewe found in front of the tomb. What was done to her?"

"What's it to you?"

She shook her head and sighed, scolding him for his obtuseness. "Think! If someone's attacked a High Krewe vampire, put her outta commission and got away with it clean, who's to say they won't come after *my* clan next? I need to know what was done to her so we can work us out a defense."

Should he tell her? He tried thinking like a detective, not like an amateur rapidly getting in over his head. Hearing her or one of her cronies accidentally blurt out a detail only he, the High Krewe bigwigs, or the perp should know would give him definite proof of her involvement. Spilling the beans to her now would wipe out that possibility. Later, if he felt like he trusted her, he could always tell her what he knew. "That's confidential information," he said a little reluctantly.

She sighed impatiently. "All right . . . what's your stake in this? This woman that got hurt, were you involved with her? You defendin' white vampires in general, on principle? Or did the High Krewe hire you as their private dick?"

Jules winced. There was that word again. "The latter," he said. "I'm here representin' the High Krewe's interests."

"Well, then it sounds like our interests might be runnin' in tandem. *I* want these killin's of preachers to stop, and I think maybe *you're* behind them. You say you ain't. High Krewe wants attacks on their own stopped. *You* say I'm behind it, but *I* say it ain't me, babe. You know what I think? I think somebody's fuckin' with us *both*. And if we wanna avoid a war, we's gonna have to work together here, start pullin' on the same set of oars at the same time. I coulda had you killed a dozen ways to Sunday soon as you waddled in here, but I wanted to hear what you had to say. Now that I have, you done bought yourself a reprieve." She turned to Preston, standing beside her. "Pres. As of tonight, you're off the Seventh Ward project. Turn it over to Leon. Sunset tomorrow, you and Mr. Duchon is partners."

Shock bloomed on Preston's normally impassive face. "What'd I hear you just say?"

"You. And the fat dude. You're the Mod Squad, but without the blond chick."

"*Whoa.* Baby baby *baby,* you got you a mean sense a humor—"

Elisha failed to smile. "This is no joke, Preston. Do it, or I'll find me a man who will. And you *know* what I mean."

Jules broke in. "Hey! Nobody here's asked *my* opinion. The High

Krewe are payin' me to do a job, and that job ain't got nothin' to do with teaming up with Midnight Cowboy here. I mean, this guy was in on the killin' of my old boss, one of the best friends I ever had. He nearly killed *me* once. You can't *expect—*"

"Oh, but I *do* expect. I expect both of you half-wits to suck it up and put your heads together, so you'll have a whole wit between you." She stepped down from her platform and strode toward Jules, dark and threatening as a storm front. "War was my brother's thing. I prefer buildin' up to tearin' down. But that don't mean war and me can't be on a first-name basis. Until I get some answers to what's goin' on, Preston's gonna be on you like white on rice, and you're gonna *like* it. And if that don't suit you, I'm declarin' war on your big ass. And on the High Krewe, too, if I have to.

"Have I made myself perfectly clear?"

Staring into her eyes, Jules thought he could see the ancient, reptilian ancestor of all vampires buried in her black pupils, coldly laughing at him. "Yes, ma'am," he muttered.

Good thing he was sans balls. Or she would've handed them to him, impaled on cocktail toothpicks.

TWELVE

The next night, driving back to the casino to pick up his unwilling partner, Jules couldn't get a certain old movie out of his head. *The Defiant Ones.* Hadn't seen it in years. In fact the first time he'd seen it, on its initial run in 1958, he had to go catch it at the Carver, a crummy little black movie house with no air-conditioning; the big mainline houses on Canal Street wouldn't show it, because there were scenes of Tony Curtis and Sidney Poitier sharing a cigarette. But he'd liked Tony Curtis, so he'd gone. Those old black-and-white images of the two escaped convicts, driven apart by reciprocal race hatred but tied together by a three-foot length of steel chain, played over and over on the movie screen of his mind. They hadn't come to a good end, those two.

Jules pulled over to the curb on Poydras Street, across from the casino's rear entrance. Preston was waiting for him, leaning against the corner of a neon-lit parking garage. Jules waved but didn't smile. Preston ambled over to the Cadillac, his legs slightly bowed, as if he'd been riding a cattle drive for the past month. Looked like John Wayne's walk. Jules hadn't noticed it before; he wondered whether Preston was strutting the walk especially for tonight, or whether it was just his walk.

Jules put the passenger window down. He didn't unlock the door, not yet. Preston eyed the car, a momentary glint of appreciation in his dark eyes, tried the locked door, then leaned on the windowsill. "Whassup?" he grunted.

"Before you get in here," Jules said, "we gotta hammer out some ground rules. Rule number one: no eatin' or drinkin' in the car."

Preston sneered. "Now *what* you suppose I be wantin' to eat or drink in your car?"

"I dunno. You drink coffee?"

"Sometimes."

"Well, cup-holders or no cup-holders, no coffee in the car."

Preston shrugged. "No big deal."

"Rule number two: driver controls the radio dial."

Now Preston looked more concerned. "Get this—I don't listen to no Perry Como and no Garth Brooks, understand?"

"Me neither."

Preston tilted his black Stetson back on his head. "So what *do* you listen to?"

"WWOZ. I don't bother with no other stations."

Preston thought about this a minute. "New Orleans old school, right? Frogman Henry? Fats Domino?"

"Yeah, mostly. Little bit of zydeco and Cajun mixed in."

"Well, okay, that'll do. What else?"

The movie relooped through his mind again, the opening scene on the prison truck. "Rule number three: no singin' spirituals about cornbread and washing machines."

Preston's eyebrows shot up. Then he stuck his head through the open window. He sniffed loudly. "What kinda weed you been smokin' lately? You still got some?"

Jules ruefully shook his head. *Kids under sixty—no appreciation for decent culture.* "You don't know what that's from?"

"Hell, no. Maybe your headshrinker knows."

"It's from *The Defiant Ones.* Black convict who's chained to a white convict in the back of a prison truck, he's singin' this spiritual to piss off the guards in front." Jules grinned smugly. "Ferget about it. It's before your time, junior."

Preston leaned further into the car, far enough to reach the electric-lock switch. "Like *hell* it is. One thing I remember is Sidney Poitier laid one hell of an ass-whuppin' on Tony Curtis. And you ain't no Tony Curtis."

Jules considered raising the window. But Preston's neck was so stiff, the glass would likely bust. "Yeah? Well, you ain't no Sidney Poitier, either. At least he knew how to dress."

Preston snorted. "You one to talk, man. Thrift store shopliftah." He leaned back out of the car and spit on the sidewalk. "You gonna let me in the fuckin' car or what? I don't wanna do this. You don't wanna do this. But if we *don't* do this, we both get cut with razors and dunked in the shark tank. Dig?"

Jules unlocked the door. Preston got in. "Nice wheels," he said, buckling himself up. "Least I won't be embarrassed drivin' 'round with you."

"Thanks."

"So how we gonna do this? You got your questionin' to do, and I got mine."

"I figure we can alternate," Jules said. "One night we do my stuff, the next night yours." He pulled a quarter out of his jacket pocket. "I say we flip for first night."

"Got no problem with that."

Jules spun the quarter in the air, barely missing the headliner. "Call it."

"Heads."

Jules caught it in his left palm, then immediately covered it with his right. He stuck his hands toward Preston and uncovered the coin. The street light glinted off George Washington's big nose.

"Huh," Preston grunted, satisfied. "Ol' slave owner's payin' me back some."

♠

Following Preston's directions, Jules drove to the home of Pastor Nicholas Johnson on Dryades Street. Preston wanted to find out what he could from the pastor's widow. The pastor's two-story home was an oasis of order and cleanliness on an otherwise run-down, even derelict stretch, just as Erato's house was. Jules started to park directly in front of the house, but Preston told him to pull up two lots beyond. "How come?" Jules asked.

"Gotta do somethin' first." Preston pulled a flat, round plastic container from his jacket pocket. "Help me out with this damn makeup, will you?" He unscrewed the container and stuck two fingers into what looked like dark brown greasepaint, then began slathering it on his face.

"What? You want me to paint you?" Jules had gotten so used to seeing the black vampire's grayish-brown skin tone, it looked perfectly natural to him. But then he realized it wouldn't look natural at all to most people. His own appliance-white complexion wasn't exactly natural, either; but somehow, at least in his own mind, it didn't look as ghoulish as Preston's skin. "I ain't no good at applyin' makeup . . ."

Preston grimaced. "Just help smooth it out some. Can't rightly use a mirror, can I?" He pulled a packet of tissues out of his pocket. "Here. Use these, if you want."

Jules ripped open the packet, nervously eyeing Preston's fingers to make sure they didn't land on his upholstery. "How come you didn't do this at home?"

"Damn shit makeup wears off if I wear it too long. C'mon. I won't bite."

"Hold your damn horses, okay?" The notion of touching his enemy/coinvestigator's face felt wrong, as flinch-inducing as kissing a sea slug. *Or Tony Curtis sharin' a cigarette with Sidney Poitier, maybe.* Jules tried smoothing out the makeup on Preston's cheeks with the edge of a tissue, but tissue fibers got stuck in it. He briefly considered leaving Preston like this, perhaps spreading more lint all over his murky brown forehead, but then figured he had as much of an interest in Preston's appearing normal as Preston did. Instead, he used his fingers, gingerly at first, then more aggressively, smoothing a clump out of an eyebrow, spreading the makeup down Preston's neck below the collar line with his thumbs. It was like finger painting; almost fun. When they were done, Jules checked their handiwork. It was passable, if you didn't look too closely too long.

"It okay?" Preston asked, pulling on a pair of black leather gloves.

Jules wiped his fingers thoroughly with the remaining tissues, then deposited them in the glove compartment. "You're gorgeous, a regular Michael Jackson."

Preston grunted, then turned his attention to a figure standing across the street. "Hey, that's one of my men over there," he said as he opened the door. He quickly got out of the car and walked toward the man. "Rawls, what you doin' here?"

The man waved and walked over. His uniform of shiny black leather pants and tank top was toned down somewhat by a long black trench coat. "Hey, Preston. You come lookin' for me?"

"No. Come to see Mrs. Johnson. Why aren't you guardin' Reverend Tonqelle's house like you supposed to?"

"Reverend Tonqelle come over here. He wanted to visit with Pastor Johnson's widow before goin' over to that forum tonight." Rawls jutted his thumb at the pastel blue Victorian house. "You goin' in there?"

"Yeah. Why?"

"Watch out for all them crosses, that's all."

Preston rejoined Jules and rang the buzzer on the white-iron gate that surrounded the house. "You know this lady?" Jules asked.

"Not personally, no."

"Then how d'you know she'll wanna talk with you?"

"I don't."

A bank of floodlights mounted on the balcony burst into life. The front door opened, and an attractive, middle-aged black woman stepped out onto the porch. "Yes? Can I help you with something?"

Preston removed his hat. "Mrs. Johnson? My name's Preston Conklin. I'm with the Central City Citizen's Defense League. I'm terribly sorry 'bout your husband's murder, ma'am. My group 'n' me, we're tryin' to make sure nothin' like that happens again."

A tall, younger black man, in his midthirties, Jules estimated, joined Mrs. Johnson on the porch. Dressed in a tightly tailored, double-breasted plum suit, he put a protective arm around her shoulders. "It's all right, Annelle. I'm familiar with this man's organization. He's all right."

"Ma'am," Preston continued, "we don't feel the police are movin' fast enough on these killin's of our preachers. Would I be imposin' too much to come in and ask you some questions?"

Mrs. Johnson looked to her companion, who nodded. "All right . . . just for a few minutes," she said. She reached inside her front door and pressed a button, which released the lock on the gate.

Preston led Jules between neatly trimmed hedges and up the steps to the porch. He took Mrs. Johnson's hands between his. "Ma'am, I can't say I was ever lucky enough to know your husband, but I know his good works. Community lost a good man when we lost him. My condolences."

"Thank you very much."

Preston turned to her companion. "Rev'rend. Good to see you." They shook hands. "Rawls been lookin' after you good?"

"Yes. Thank you. His presence at night has made my family and me feel much safer. I just wish he felt more comfortable joining us inside the house. With him outside all the time, I think my missus worries about him more than he worries about us."

Preston smiled. "Aww, Rawls, he be all right. He likes it outside."

Outside. Jules often felt on the outside, but not often as acutely as he did now. Talk about a fish out of water . . . he was a great white *whale* out of water. Apart from the fact that he'd never blend in with the Full

Gospel crowd, here was a woman who'd just lost her husband, almost certainly to a vampire. What could he say to her that wouldn't have hypocrisy and falseness woven in through and through? Jules couldn't be sure, but there was a good chance Preston thought he'd done the killing, and he'd be listening intently to Jules's expressions of sympathy for any wrong notes.

Mrs. Johnson turned to the corner of the porch where Jules was standing. "Mr. Conklin, you haven't introduced me to your friend."

Preston looked slightly surprised that Jules was still there. "Oh! Yeah. This is, uh, Jules."

Jules walked a couple of steps toward the trio. "Jules Duchon, Mrs. Johnson. I, uh, run a taxi service that does a lot of business in Central City. That's how come I'm involved with Preston's group." He walked closer to shake her hand. Her touch was much warmer than he'd expected. Fighting off embarrassment, he looked at her face. She tried to force a smile. But in its slight trembling and her sunken, haunted eyes, he saw a woman who'd had her whole world yanked away from her in an instant. "I, uh, I lost somebody, too. Not real long ago." He hadn't meant to say it, but something in her face had made the words come out. She looked at him more closely now. "This sounds silly, I guess, 'cause she wasn't my wife, but . . . but I think maybe I kinda know what you're feelin'. Just a little." He sensed his eyes filling up, and his chest was full of swelling cork. He felt ridiculous, but he couldn't stop. "And nobody should hafta feel that way . . . *nobody* . . . not that I'm sayin' I know what you feel, 'cause I don't—I mean, nobody *can*—but, but I guess what I wanna say is . . . hell, I don't know what to say."

She smiled then, a real smile, and took his hand in both of hers. "Thank you for coming, Mr. Duchon. Oh, your hand is *cold*! Please come inside. I've got some hot coffee in the kitchen, warm you up."

Mrs. Johnson and Reverend Tonqelle headed back into the house. Jules started to follow, but Preston caught his sleeve.

"Man, that was one fuckin' *performance,*" he whispered. "I'm *impressed.*"

"Wasn't no performance," Jules muttered. "C'mon."

As soon as they entered the front parlor, Jules realized why Rawls had warned Preston. The room was full of elaborate floral arrangements, many of them in the shape of crosses. Wreaths surrounded cardboard portraits of Jesus, both Northern European and black African versions. Jules felt himself begin to sweat, and a tropical storm swirled in his stomach. Before he stared down at the floor, he glanced over at Preston, who looked equally uncomfortable. Hopefully, the kitchen would be relatively free of religious sympathy gifts. Otherwise, Jules and Preston would be having their coffee on the back porch.

"Gentlemen, we're back here."

Jules followed Mrs. Johnson's voice back to the kitchen. Apart from a plain wooden cross mounted on her stove's exhaust fan, which Jules was able to avoid, the room was thankfully empty of Christian symbolism. Jules noticed Preston patting his forehead, where sweat had turned the makeup murky. He hoped his companion wouldn't rub it off.

Reverend Tonqelle had seated himself at the kitchen table. Mrs. Johnson stood by her counter. "Mr. Duchon, how do you take your coffee?"

"Black. Thank you."

"And Mr. Conklin?"

"The same. 'Preciate it."

The three of them joined the reverend at the table. The aroma of freshly brewed coffee mingled with the sweet vegetable scent of cut flowers. It wasn't unpleasant. Jules waited for Preston to speak. This was his play. "Mrs. Johnson," Preston said, "the night your husband got killed, was he on his way to meet someone? Do you know why he went down to the Quarter?"

Mrs. Johnson's face turned tight. Not dramatically so, but enough for Jules to notice. "Nicholas told me he had an Economic Opportunity Council meeting to go to downtown. An emergency meeting. I know he liked going out for a glass of wine at some of the nicer restaurants in the Quarter. It was one of the few ways he knew how to unwind. He'd been working so hard, especially on the St. Thomas issue. I suppose he decided to relax some after his meeting, before coming home."

"Did he call you after his meetin'? Tell you he'd be runnin' late?"

Mrs. Johnson shook her head. "No. But that wasn't unusual." She smiled ruefully, Jules thought. "Nicholas liked his independence. He loved going to his church conventions in other cities, without me along. And pastor retreats where the men would go off to some cabin in the woods without their families, 'huntin' and prayin'.' He wasn't the kind of man who'd cede authority to a woman, allow a wife to try and rein him in. I learned to accept that."

"Were there any friends he might've gone and had that glass of wine with? Fellow members from that council, maybe?"

Her ironic smile faded. "I gave the police the names of the other members, Mr. Conklin. They interviewed them. There wasn't a meeting of the Economic Opportunity Council that night, emergency or otherwise."

Reverend Tonqelle laid his hand on top of hers. Jules's heart sank. Losing her husband was hard enough. Losing him and catching him in a lie at the same time . . . he remembered how he felt when he'd learned about Maureen's affair with Malik Raddeaux, later Malice X. His reactions hadn't been printable in a family newspaper.

How Preston was digesting this, Jules couldn't be sure. The man's face didn't reveal much. "Mrs. Johnson," Preston said, "did anybody ever threaten your husband? Leave him notes or phone messages, maybe, tellin' him to lay off on the St. Thomas issue?"

Mrs. Johnson shook her head. "Not that I was aware of, no."

"Would he have shared that kinda thing with you?" Jules asked. Preston shot him a pissed-off look, warning him against butting in.

"Probably not. He wouldn't have wanted to worry me. The police asked me if they could search through papers on his desk. I don't think they found anything."

Jules knew where the cop's investigation, and Preston's, might eventually lead. Questioning Pearl, he'd gotten a strong gut feeling that the High Krewe's youngsters had been the ones who'd knocked off the two preachers, even though he had no idea what their motivation could've been—apart from hunger. If his and Preston's investigation led back to the High Krewe, what would Jules do then? What level of loyalty did he owe them? How hard should he work to avoid a war that might be inevitable? Would it matter to him who came out on top?

Another question popped into his head. If the black vampires were, in fact, the ones who'd carried out the mutilations, that'd mean they already knew the High Krewe's youngsters had fanged the preachers and were taking their revenge. So what was all this business about forcing Jules to work with Preston? A ruse on Elisha Raddeaux's part to throw Jules off the scent?

Mrs. Johnson broke the silence. "Would anyone like another cup of coffee?"

"Sure," Jules said, taking his last sip before handing her his cup. The coffee's warmth, flowing down his throat into his belly, felt reassuring, somehow, a small comfort he could cling to. He decided something. It was better for him to know, one way or the other, whether the High

Krewe's youngsters had done in the preachers, even if his finding out meant Preston's finding out at the same time. None of the youngsters were experienced hunters. But several of them were exceptionally attractive women; cover models, if a camera existed that could photograph them. Given what Mrs. Johnson had let slip about her husband's habits, it sounded like he would've been susceptible to the feminine brand of enticement.

Mrs. Johnson handed him his refilled cup. "Thanks," he said. This wouldn't be easy to ask. But she'd already hinted at it, and he needed to know. "Uh, Mrs. Johnson, there's, y'know, no real tactful way for me to ask this . . . but sometimes a wife hears, well, *things* about her husband. Things her friends tell her, stuff they've heard or picked up around town . . ."

Mrs. Johnson sat down across the table and looked at him intently. "What kind of 'things' are you asking about, Mr. Duchon?"

Jules felt himself redden. He wished he hadn't started the question, but he couldn't drop it now. "Uh, did you hear about any, well, girlfriends? Women not from his church who he might've been hangin' out with, maybe down in the Quarter?"

Mrs. Johnson flinched, as if Jules had just tossed his hot coffee in her face. Reverend Tonqelle stiffened. "That's completely uncalled for," he said, his diction rich with indignation. "This is a house of mourning."

Mrs. Johnson shut her eyes tightly, but the tears still escaped. "I don't . . . I don't want to talk about—*why* did you have to ask that question?"

Jules's ears were hot enough to burst. "Look, I'm sorry, I wasn't thinkin' right—"

"I think you men should leave now," Reverend Tonqelle said.

Preston shot a disgusted look at Jules before turning to the reverend. "Please 'scuse my partner, sometimes he stick his foot in his mouth. He didn't mean nothin' bad by it."

Reverend Tonqelle lightly squeezed Mrs. Johnson's shoulders, then checked his jeweled wristwatch. "Annelle, I'm sorry, but I need to be heading out. That forum over at the elementary school is supposed to get started soon. Do you want me to call Patricia to come stay with you?"

Mrs. Johnson dabbed her eyes with a napkin and shook her head. "No, Albert, I feel like I've been leanin' on your family too much. I've got other friends to call. Don't worry about me. I don't want you late for that forum. Nicholas would've wanted to be there himself." She turned to

Jules and managed a weak smile. "Mr. Duchon, I don't want you feelin' bad, you hear? I'm glad you're trying to help. It makes things seem a little less horrible."

Jules cautiously met her gaze. "Thanks, Mrs. Johnson," he said softly. He picked up the empty coffee cups from the table and put them in the sink.

Reverend Tonqelle said his goodbyes, then led the two men outside. "You two want to do some real good?" he asked. "Don't be pestering grieving widows." Preston started to protest, but the reverend cut him off with a gesture. "Look, I know your hearts are in the right place, and I appreciate the guard you sent to watch over me and my family. But if you want to find out who's behind these killings—follow the money."

"What do you mean?" Jules asked.

"Who stands to benefit if the GoodiesMart-Goodfeller plan for the St. Thomas gets derailed? Who yells 'throw me somethin', mister!' and gets beamed with a sack of cash? Ask yourselves that. Here's a rumor for you. I haven't been able to substantiate it, but maybe you can flesh out the bones. You know who's supposedly been buying up options on properties all around the St. Thomas tract? Who already owns a huge home in the area? None other than our local musical priest of Satanism, Courane L'Enfant."

"Who?" Preston asked. "Courane the infant?"

"I'll tell you about it later," Jules said. "If you thought Perry Como was the worst Caucasian music has to offer . . ." He shivered.

"He'll be speaking at this forum at Laurel Elementary," the reverend said, checking his watch again. "Which I'm gonna be late for in six minutes. Need to run." He pressed the buzzer to open the gate. Before getting into his car, he turned back to them. "Remember. Follow the money. And if you dig something up, don't bother with the *Picayune.* L'Enfant and others have spent tens of thousands on ads. Go to the black press." He climbed into his silver Infiniti sedan and drove off, followed fifteen seconds later by Rawls in a black Dodge Durango.

"How about we go check out this forum?" Preston said.

"It's your night," Jules said. They walked to the Allante. "I'll see if maybe I can find a Courane L'Enfant song playin' on the radio."

"Thanks."

"Don't thank me 'til you've *heard* it . . ."

Spinning the radio dial, they didn't come across one of Courane L'Enfant's compositions on the short drive over to Laurel Elementary School, near where the St. Thomas Housing Project once stood. The forum must've attracted a crowd. Jules wasn't able to find a legal parking spot anywhere close. He circled the poorly lit residential blocks that surrounded the school until he found a spot on Chippewa Street, in front of a boarded-up double shotgun.

"You gonna leave your top up?" Preston asked as they were getting out of the Allante.

"Well, sure," Jules said. "Don't want nobody messin' with my radio and stuff."

Preston smirked and shook his head. "How much you suppose that convertible top of yours cost?"

"I dunno. Eight hundred bucks? A grand?"

"More than that. More than that there stereo costs, anyway. Not that some dude with a scissors gonna care."

"Well, what if it rains?" Jules shut his door and pressed his key fob until his horn politely chirped. "I got an alarm."

"*Ev'ry*body's got an alarm. Go off all the damn time. Nobody listens. So they ain't worth shit."

Jules shrugged. "It'll be fine. Let's just go."

Preston pushed his hat back on his head and lifted his eyebrows to the stars. "Hohhh-*kay.*"

The small auditorium was crowded. Jules estimated that the place held a hundred and twenty seats, and they were all filled. Larger members of the audience, of whom there were more than a few, stood along the walls or in the aisles, since the wooden theater seats looked sized for grade-school kids. The crowd was about three-quarters black, with most of the white attendees bunched together in the front rows; Jules figured they'd come together and arrived early. Jules and Preston pushed past a coterie of smokers defiantly puffing away in the back of the auditorium. A dozen cops lined the walls, but they didn't appear to be concerned with this violation of the fire code.

Jules and Preston found an empty standing space in back of a battered upright piano not far from the stage. Six participants sat behind a long table on stage. They were divided by a portable lectern into two groups of three, each group sharing a microphone. Jules figured one trio supported the GoodiesMart-Goodfeller plan, and the other trio opposed it. Interestingly, both trios were racially mixed. On one side sat Reverend

Tonqelle; an attractive, light-skinned black woman whom Jules didn't recognize; and a tall white man whose tanned, muscular neck and tufts of dark chest hair protruded from a silk peach-colored shirt and an expensive blazer. Jules was almost positive this was Van Goodfeller, the fried catfish king himself.

The other side of the table held a more heterogeneous trio. Sitting closest to the lectern was a middle-aged black man in an ill-fitting brown suit, his Afro splitting the difference between the shaved heads of the early nineties and the towering hairstyles of the late sixties. He kept mopping his forehead with a handkerchief, even though it wasn't particularly hot in the room. Next to him, and currently speaking, was a short blond woman in a navy blue business suit, her black horn-rimmed glasses too large for her narrow face. All the way to the right was the man Jules and Preston had come to see—although, given the long, braided hair that fell below his waist, an observer couldn't be faulted for mistaking him for a woman. *Or maybe a vampire,* Jules thought. Courane L'Enfant looked like a sunken-eyed cadaver wrapped in a leopard-spotted burial sheet; Jules wondered whether the leopard spots on his robes were an attempted sop to the primarily African American audience. Black calfskin gloves stretched to his elbows. He rested his long, pointed chin on tented fingertips, observing his companion with eyes like those of a sentient monitor lizard.

He tried focusing on what she was saying. Whatever it was, the majority of the crowd didn't look into it.

". . . historically, this tract was part of the Lower Garden District and what later became known as the Irish Channel. Look at architects' plans of the homes and businesses that got torn down in 1938 to build the housing project, and you'll see a mirror image of the early nineteenth-century buildings that still stand in the Lower Garden District. All that's gone, of course. But what's still standing is of immense cultural and historical significance to this city. The three brick warehouses that line Tchoupitoulas Street—the ones Mr. Goodfeller wants to tear down so he can build his distribution facility—they were a central element of the cotton processing and shipping industry that made New Orleans America's second richest city prior to the Civil War—"

A woman stood suddenly in the back of the auditorium. "That's cotton my great-great-granddaddies was *enslaved* to pick! We oughta burn those piece-of-shit old warehouses *down*!"

Several audience members near her began aggressively clapping.

Jules noticed a few white attendees close to him look nervously around for the closest police officer. The moderator, a local newscaster with light brown skin and perfect makeup, stood and spoke forcefully into the microphone. "I need to ask members of the audience to save their comments for the question-and-answer period. Anyone who persists in speaking out of turn, or who makes threatening comments, will be escorted outside." She turned to the opposite side of the table. "Ms. Bookers, had you wanted to give the rebuttal?" Jules wasn't sure that the historian lady was finished yet; she certainly didn't look finished. But Ms. Bookers stood, picked up the microphone with the ease of a talk-show host, and shut the door on further commentary about the historic value of cotton warehouses.

"I have a question for Ms. Hirschoff and the others on that side of the table," she said. "Not to imply any disrespect for her or the value of the work she does at Tulane University. But when it comes right down to it, what's more important—buildings, or *people*?" The back of the room erupted into cheers. "Who was that land set aside for over sixty years ago? People who can't afford a decent home for their families if left to the 'tender mercies' of the market. Why do you think the Federal government calls the grants meant to rebuild our public housing 'HOPE' grants? With almost a third of the citizens of our city living below the poverty line, we can't afford to be quibbling about a few dusty old warehouses. Our people need *jobs*! They need *decent* places to live! The GoodiesMart-Goodfeller plan provides both." She walked to the front of the stage and spoke directly to the back two-thirds of the auditorium. "If you want good-paying jobs, if you want dignity and a fair share of the good life New Orleans has to offer, I urge you to call your city councilperson—call the mayor, too!—and give them the courage to do the *right thing*!"

Ms. Bookers floated back to her seat on a cloud of cheers and applause. Jules started wondering about the caliber of the advocates the other side had brought. The black man in the cheap brown suit looked like he was about to deposit the contents of his dinner all over the table. Jules felt sorry for him—his handkerchief was so saturated that all it was doing was smearing his sweat from one side of his forehead to the other. The moderator turned to him next. "Mr. Branford, you have three minutes."

Mr. Branford started to stand, then thought better of it and sat back down. He pulled a set of notecards out of his jacket pocket and quickly rearranged them. The microphone squealed as he pulled it closer. "Uh, lots of you out there know me. I've got the B&S Food Store, just two blocks from here. Some of you been buyin' groceries from me goin' on fifteen years. Well, I got to tell you, that GoodiesMart Superstore come in less than a mile from me, it gonna put me right outta business. Me, and lots of other small businessmen on Magazine Street, and Oretha Castle Haley, and even over on Claiborne Avenue. And don't be fooled, thinkin' all them GoodiesMart jobs gonna replace the jobs that get lost"—he looked down at his notecards—" 'cause only one outta five jobs they gonna give you be full-time. The rest be part-time, with no benefits. And they sell all that stuff what's made by prison laborers in China. The jobs in my store, they may not pay bankers' wages, but at least they full-time. And the profits stay here, in New Orleans—"

"He's a *front*!" the same woman who'd interrupted the historian earlier bellowed. "He don't own that store! He's a front for the Arabs, so they can say they's a minority-owned business! Don't pay him no mind and no dollar for them overpriced groceries!"

This time two cops shoved their way into her aisle and began maneuvering her toward the exit. "Get your *hands* offa me!" she shrieked. Several audience members began booing the police. "I'm *goin'*! But you can't keep me outta here forever!"

The moderator turned back to Mr. Branford, whose forehead glistened like a disco ball. "I apologize for that interruption. You still have a minute left. Would you like to continue?"

"No, ma'am." He sighed, glancing out at the audience like a cat treed by a pack of baying hounds. "I done said my piece."

Van Goodfeller raised his hand. "I'd like to be the one to do the rebuttal, Ms. Dupre," he said, his charming, "aww-shucks" demeanor reminding Jules of a slick Li'l Abner. He stood, as impressively at ease as Mr. Branford had been ill at ease. "I really wish we'd been able to get one of my friends from GoodiesMart to come here tonight and defend that fine company. Not that they need much of a defense. I mean, we're talking about a company that's consistently at the top of the Fortune 500, a company more people choose than any other when they go shopping for all the little things that make a home a home. Hey, why should only folks in the suburbs get all the benefits of a nearby GoodiesMart? Why shouldn't the residents of Central City and the Irish Channel and Pigeon Town?"

"Amen!" a man shouted from the back.

Goodfeller allowed himself a brief, grateful smile. "I'm not the best qualified person to defend GoodiesMart. What I *am* qualified to defend is the integrity of my own company. Lots of you here tonight know that I grew up in the Lafitte Housing Project, built at the same time the St. Thomas was. There's no way I'd advocate for something against the best interests of working people, people struggling just to break even and keep a roof over their heads. I mean, I've *been* there. Sure, I might live in a big mansion today, but you know what? You come visit me at my office, and on my desk you'll see a photo of my mom and me standing in front of our three-room apartment in the Lafitte. I've never forgotten where I come from, and I never want to. Those two hundred jobs my distribution center will create? Those're gonna be *good* jobs, jobs that'll support a family. You've got my word on that. And that's a promise you can take to the bank."

He waved to the crowd before putting the microphone down, and the rear two-thirds of the auditorium answered with Saints-in-the-play-offs enthusiasm. *If nothin' else,* Jules thought, *he just sold a few thousand more boxes of fried catfish.* Jules glanced over at Courane L'Enfant, who was left with the unenviable task of batting cleanup for his team, down by at least seven runs in the bottom of the ninth. Strangely, he didn't look too concerned. In fact, with his vapid grin and hooded, distant eyes, he seemed to be watching the whole debate on satellite television in his bedroom.

L'Enfant pushed a few stray braids away from his face with a gloved hand, then blew into the microphone to make sure it was still on. The resulting feedback made him smile. "Mr. Goodfeller just asked why the heart of New Orleans shouldn't have its own GoodiesMart," he said. His voice was more melodious than Jules would've expected, given his raucous recordings. "One might as well ask why we can't have some of the other defining features of suburbia, as well—the sprawl, the homogeneity, the lack of character and soul. It's a package deal, my friends. Ms. Hirschoff told you that, a hundred and fifty years ago, New Orleans was America's second richest city. That was a very long time ago. All that keeps this city alive today, and all that provides hope for a better future, is the happy fact that New Orleans is not like other American places. The very things that called me back to my ancestral home—the Franco-Spanish heritage that stubbornly refuses to fade away; streets of antebellum mansions and humble shotguns that lie together beneath sheets of swirling fog—these are the same things that call artists, musicians, and creative people of all kinds here. And keep them here. Unlike the plan proposed by the good people on the far side of the lectern, the Lower Garden District Reclamation Plan does not despoil our heritage or the character of our city . . ."

Preston nudged Jules. "I wish we could figure out how to get near this guy, interview him. Guy like that's got a posse thick as a brick wall, though."

"Shame we don't have press passes," Jules said, glancing over at the section of seats occupied by TV and print journalists. One of them, a young black man with a camera slung around his neck, sidestepped his way out of the aisle, then walked quickly toward the rear exit, holding himself in a way Jules recognized from countless nights of too much coffee drinking. "Hey," Jules said, pointing at the exiting journalist. "I'll bet that guy's heading out to take a leak. Why don't you follow him, see if you can get him alone, then hypnotize him and borrow his press badge and camera?"

Preston scowled. "How come *you* don't go out to the john and hypnotize him?"

Jules wasn't about to tell him that his hypnosis powers, like so much else, were saddled with an "Out of Order" sign. "Who d'ya think's gonna be less intimidating to that guy—you or me?"

Preston thought this over. "Yeah . . . you go try and talk him up in the john, he's gonna think you a fruit fly. Good luck hypnotizin' him then. *I'll* go."

Not the thought process Jules'd hoped to encourage, but he'd gotten the result he'd wanted. He turned his attention back to the stage. ". . . an opportunity to redevelop such a large and central piece of the city only comes along once in a generation," L'Enfant was saying, his weighty tone belied by his amused, superior expression. "Surely, given our famous creativity and joie de vivre, we can do better than a catfish warehouse, a GoodiesMart, and a parking lot bigger than the Superdome. I love this city, and I know we can do better—"

Reverend Tonqelle jumped from his chair and grabbed the microphone. "If you claim to love this city so much, why do you poison the minds of her young people with your satanic music? Why do you celebrate blood rituals and blood-drinking?"

The moderator rushed back to the podium. "Reverend, please, you're speaking out of turn. You'll have your chance to make a rebuttal—"

"Let 'im talk!" a man shouted from the back.

"Yeah, let the rev talk!"

L'Enfant smiled, as though he were observing mischievous children at a playground. "That's all right, Ms. Dupre." He turned to face his accuser. "Reverend, you're an intelligent man. Surely you know the difference between reality and performance. I know you do. You're performing right now."

Tonqelle was unfazed. "It's your 'concern' for this city that's the performance. Where does all this 'public spiritedness' suddenly come from? I'll tell you where. There's talk all over my neighborhood about the real-estate transactions you're involved in, the purchase options you've been snatching up—dilapidated, depressed rental properties all around the edges of the St. Thomas tract. When your housing project for the rich gets built, you evict those poor tenants out onto the streets, flip those properties at inflated value, and your dirty millions get multiplied."

Angry mutterings filled the auditorium. Jules felt the small hairs on the back of his neck stiffen. The crowd was turning ugly, as ugly as a Bourbon Street gutter on Mardi Gras night. Strangely, L'Enfant seemed unconcerned; maybe his years of safely performing for arenas packed with drunken, screaming fans had inured him to the violent potential of aroused mobs. "Rumormongering is beneath you, Reverend," he said. "I invest in properties all over New Orleans. I'm bullish on the future of this town. Real estate is a sound investment. And historic properties need someone who loves them and who has the resources to restore them. Someone like me, Reverend. But while we're on the subject of profit, maybe you'd like to explain the generous donations the GoodiesMart Corporation has been making to your church?"

Reverend Tonqelle looked like he'd just sucked down an entire bottle of Tabasco. "That—that's an outrageous *slander*!"

"Oh, come, come, Reverend. Didn't your church just finish building a new educational wing two months ago? Aren't you and your deacons all driving new luxury cars? Have weekly collections risen *that* much?" L'Enfant turned to the assembled journalists with a flourish of his gloved arms. "There's a story for you, gentlemen and ladies. It's not just Reverend Tonqelle's church swimming in GoodiesMart money, either. What kind of support have those donations been buying—"

"*Stone* him!" The expelled lady was back. "Somebody stone that debbil wushipper!"

The first missile, a can of Big Shot orange soda, missed Jules's head by inches. It clattered off the upright piano and sprayed him with orange fizz. The next bombardier had a better arm, reaching the stage with a bottle of malt liquor that shattered with a noise like a gunshot. Suddenly, the stage was swarming with bodyguards—Van Goodfeller's and Courane L'Enfant's, who formed human shields around their employers. Jules saw Rawls dart out to retrieve Reverend Tonqelle, but the other speakers had to fend for themselves, rushing into the shelter of the wings.

A few more bottles flew, and some of the smokers began a chant of "No justice, no peace." But the cops swiftly yanked the rabble-rousers out of their seats and cuffed them. The half dozen police were fortunate that more of the crowd didn't have a taste for blood. Rather, the cops' show of force inspired a dash for the exits. Things got messy. The doors had been built for fifth-graders, not a stampede of Oprah-sized adults. Bodies careened off one another. Elbows mashed breasts, breasts butted stomachs, and noses grew intimate with walls.

Luckily for Jules, one of the emergency exits was next to the piano, so he wasn't required to add his five hundred pounds of flesh to the human pressure cooker. Outside in the breezeway, he saw Preston coming back from the men's room with a camera and a set of badges. He waved at him, then pushed through the growing swarm to reach him.

"Hey! What the fuck's goin' on?" Preston said, glancing around at the people emerging scuffed and tousled from the auditorium. "What'd I miss?"

"Democracy in action," Jules said. "Some assholes decided to cast votes with bottles."

"*What?!?* You mean I went to the trouble of gettin' us this stuff and swipin' an extra badge for you, and now we ain't gonna be able to get near that L'Enfant guy?"

"Maybe. Maybe not." Jules scanned the open-air hallways, trying to remember which direction the school's parking lot was. "C'mon," he said, grabbing Preston's sleeve and pulling him toward a mostly deserted breezeway. "I'm pretty sure this is a back way to the parking lot. We'll look for the biggest limo there. It'll either be Van Goodfeller's or L'Enfant's."

Their quick footsteps echoed off the windows of dark classrooms, covered with children's drawings. Following the noise of engines sputtering to life and the stench of burning motor oil, they found the parking lot. Sure enough, an extra-long black Lincoln limousine idled near a fence surrounding the athletics field. Jules spotted L'Enfant in the middle of a circle of hired muscle, heading for the limo.

"There he is," Jules said. He clipped on his press badge, noticing it was from the *Louisiana Weekly,* a black newspaper.

"How we gonna do this?" Preston asked, pressing his hat more securely on his head. "Just walk up and ask for an interview? Man's prob'ly not feelin' real sociable right 'bout now."

Jules glanced at the limo. A man with a trim goatee and a sharp midnight blue suit stood by the front of the car with a clipboard. "Let's go talk with that guy. Bet he's a handler or a manager."

Preston handed him the camera. "Here. *You* be the photographer. I'll be the reporter. Since we supposed to be from the *Louisiana Weekly,* let me do the talkin', okay?"

They reached the limo ten seconds ahead of L'Enfant and his phalanx. Preston approached the man with the clipboard, who looked at him with brief concern until he saw the press badge. Preston offered his hand. "Howdy. I'm Preston Conklin, *Louisiana Weekly.* This here's Jules, my pho-tog. You with the Courane L'Enfant outfit? 'Cause I'd sure like to set up an interview with him."

The man shook Preston's hand. "I'm Mike Bronson, Courane's executive facilitator. You were at the forum?"

"Sure was. Shame Mr. L'Enfant didn't get a chance to finish his remarks. I'm sure my readers would like the chance to read what he has to say."

Jules glanced behind him as the entourage reached the limo. A bodyguard opened one of the rear doors for his employer, but L'Enfant didn't slip inside. He leaned on the door frame and stared intently at Jules, as if he were trying to place him. Jules had no idea why the musician was eyeballing him. It made him uncomfortable. He turned back to Preston and the manager. "Mr. L'Enfant's got a really hectic few weeks ahead of him," Bronson was saying. "He's got a mega event coming up four nights from now, and then he heads out for a fifteen-city tour. Doesn't look like we'll be able to squeeze you in until late May."

Jules put his face closer to Bronson's. "Maybe you weren't payin' attention at that forum. Your guy's got a PR disaster on his hands. With the black community especially. We're from the state's biggest black newspaper. Take a closer look at that schedule."

Bronson compressed his lips tightly. Then he pulled a Palm Pilot from a holster on his belt, flipped it open, and tapped its screen several times with a stylus. "Really, I'm not seeing even an open hour. Can you give me your business card? I'll need to talk with Courane about this—"

"No you won't, Michael." Jules and Preston turned around. L'Enfant stood behind them, flanked by his two burliest bodyguards. "I've made up my mind to give these gentlemen their interview." He turned to Jules. "Would eleven o'clock tomorrow morning be soon enough?"

Bronson quickly tapped on his Palm Pilot. "But that's when you've got your aromatherapy session—"

L'Enfant waved his gloved hand dismissively. "Cancel it."

Jules still didn't like how the musician was staring at him. He felt like the choicest rump roast on the Sav-A-Center meat rack. "That's, uh, real good of you, Mr. L'Enfant. But daytime hours, they don't work for us. We both got day jobs. Reporting's a night gig only."

"No daytime appointments . . ." L'Enfant's eyes grew wider as his smile expanded. Jules noticed that his teeth had a phosphorescent glow in the dim light, like the antennae of deep-sea fish. "How absolutely wonderful. Well, we will have to accommodate your special needs." L'Enfant sounded strangely pleased. "Tonight. We will speak an hour from now. Michael, give them a card with the address for the Saulet Orphanage. That's where I'll be spending the evening." He smiled at Jules again. "This evening will be doable for you?"

Jules glanced at Preston. His companion didn't protest. "Uh, yeah, sure."

"Wonderful. A good interview will be most . . . relaxing. An hour, then." L'Enfant grinned a phosphorescent smile, then disappeared into his limousine.

THIRTEEN

They watched L'Enfant's limo glide out of the parking lot. Neon lamps beneath its frame made it seem to float on a cushion of alien moonlight.

"Shee-yit." Preston spat into the weeds near their feet. "Dude wanted to eat you up like pumpkin pie. You in the market for a new boyfriend?"

"You in the market for a busted mouth?"

Preston's eyes flashed. "Heh. You wanna find out, fat man?" But the fierceness that had animated his face quickly tapered to a low simmer. "Forget it. Shouldn't be bustin' your chops. You got us the interview."

"Damn right I did."

Jules stared at the card L'Enfant's assistant had given him. He recognized the old orphanage complex whose picture was embossed on the card. Located not far from Magazine Street in the Lower Garden District, it had been empty for years, its masonry and plaster crumbling, creeper vines winding around its cracked columns. Vagrants often bedded down on the grounds, in the outbuildings; Jules had sometimes found easy meals there. Now it was one of L'Enfant's collection of homes.

"Jules, is that *you*? Hey, Jules!" A familiar, friendly voice called out from behind him. Jules turned and saw Erato, waving and walking toward them from the other end of the parking lot. His friend eagerly clapped his arm in greeting. "I *thought* it was you in there! Just couldn't figure out why you'd be at the forum, though. Thought you were busy with that private-eye business."

"Who's this?" Preston asked.

Glad as he was to see Erato, Jules was wary. He wanted to keep his friend as far removed from vampire business as possible. "This is John," he said reluctantly. "A cab-driver buddy of mine."

Erato grinned and poked him where his ribs should be. "Your *best* buddy, you mean!" He turned to Preston and stuck out his hand. "Johnny Erato. You another friend of Jules's?"

Preston chuckled and shook his hand. "Wouldn't go so far as to say that."

"Erato, this is Preston. He's, uh, an associate of mine."

Erato eyed the black vampire with new interest. "Another investigator?"

"Yeah, another investigator," Jules said.

"So what'd you guys come to the forum for?"

"Long story," Jules said. "Preston's upset about those preacher murders, too. Him and me, we got some . . . interests in common. So I figured I'd do some pokin' around into this preacher business, like I told you I might."

"Man, you are the *best.*" Erato looked at him with eyes that were almost worshipful. "I'm not gonna forget this, Jules. My wife, she's got you all wrong. And I'm gonna tell her that, too." He glanced at his watch, then grimaced. "Hell, it's gettin' late. Gotta get my ass back in the saddle, y'know?"

"Yeah," Jules said. "Every minute you spend jawin' with me's a minute you're not chargin' on your meter."

"Ain't that the sad truth." Erato turned to Preston. "Good meetin' you, man. Best of luck. Those were good men got killed. And watch after Jules, okay?"

Preston just smiled a crooked smile.

"So long, Erato," Jules said.

"So long, Jules. God bless."

Preston waited until Erato was out of earshot, then said, "So that's your 'best buddy,' huh?" He threw his head back and laughed. "Yeah, right. Rabbi be eatin' a ham po'-boy next." He stared at Jules with an exaggerated arch of his eyebrows. "This a put-on for me, right?"

Jules scowled. "Right. You got it. While you was in the john, I slipped that guy a twenty to act like my pal. 'Cause all my real friends wear white sheets and hoods, right?" He started walking toward the exit. "Believe whatever you fuckin' want."

"What you gettin' all touchy about?"

"Let's just get back to the car, okay?" he mumbled. The strength of Jules's feelings surprised him. He hadn't realized it until now, but one of the things about the whole Malice X business that'd really stuck in his craw was the implied accusation that he'd been fanging black victims because of race prejudice, rather than the fact that they were flavorful and convenient. His whole life, he'd always given people a fair shake, white *or* black, long before the end of Jim Crow. Why *couldn't* he have a black friend? Why should somebody presume that Jules Duchon couldn't judge a person based, as the man said, on "the content of their character"? Or the taste of their blood?

Preston caught up to him on the sidewalk in front of the school. "Hey. Was just kiddin' around with you, all right? Don't go all sensitive on me."

"Just drop it, okay?"

"Whatever. Sure."

They walked along Jackson Avenue toward the river, beneath street lamps that filled the night with sizzles and pops. Yellowed sheets of crumpled newspaper bounded down the asphalt, chasing each other like stray dogs in heat. The looming Greek Revival houses, homes that'd already been fifty years old when Jules was a boy and were now broken up into cheap, decrepit apartments, cast shadows murky as the depths of the Mississippi. Near the back of one sagging porch, Jules saw tiny flashes of light. Looking closer, he saw that it was light reflecting off something shiny and thin, like . . . a needle. He saw the hands then, just visible beneath the glow of a cigarette, as they made part of the needle disappear into the dark flesh of a forearm.

It made Jules think of the people he'd seen last night at the underground compound, the men and women with glassy eyes who'd shuffled out of the van like a chain gang of zombies. Who'd presumably offered their veins to the blood-extraction equipment without a syllable of protest. "Hey, Preston?" Jules said. "Why is it you and Elisha are so bent outta shape over those preachers gettin' killed?"

"She done told you." Preston cleared his throat and spat. The gob landed on the sidewalk ahead of Jules's feet. It had a faint reddish tinge;

he'd probably imbibed just before Jules had picked him up. "They's leaders of the community. They support the best plan for the St. Thomas. Don't want them gettin' messed with."

"And why does it matter to you? It's not like you guys're plannin' on livin' in whatever replaces the St. Thomas."

Preston kicked at a sheet of newspaper that tried wrapping itself around his leg. "No. But it's a black place. And we want it to stay that way."

Jules decided to cut to the chase. "You guys are still dealin' Horse-X, ain't you? Even though Malice X is dead. You're usin' somebody else's blood—maybe his sister's blood—and mixin' it with regular heroin, then sellin' it so Elisha can mentally turn the users into zombies any time she wants." He tried reading Preston's expression. But the black vampire's face was hidden in the shadow cast by his hat. "I saw the blood-bank equipment back at your house. I saw the faces of the people who climbed outta your van. Addicts, every one of them.

"You don't wanna lose a good territory. That's it, ain't it?"

Preston was quiet for several long seconds. "Yeah? And what if we don't?" Preston pushed his hat back off his forehead. Jules could see his expression now. It was determined, defiant, maybe even a little defensive. "Look. I'm not gonna try bullshittin' you. Sure, we sell the junk. So what? Business model can't be beat. We come out ahead two ways—first, when they pay cash; second, when Elisha puts a brain-whammy on 'em and they come and donate blood." He looked Jules straight in the eye and smirked. "Shee-yit. Bet you wish *you* had it so good."

So that was the basis of the black vampires' economy. Heroin adulterated with vampire blood, a mixture which, according to what Malice X had boasted, gave triple the high of standard heroin, was twice as addictive, and which rendered the user increasingly susceptible to the donor-vampire's long-range hypnotic control.

"Like *hell* I do," Jules muttered.

Preston rolled his eyes. "Oh, come on," he scowled. "Don't be gettin' all 'holier-than-thou' with me. What, sellin' them drugs is worse than *killin'* them? What've *you* been doin' for sixty, seventy years? Sellin' *Bibles*?"

"Least I haven't been turnin' them into, y'know, *slaves.*" His choice of analogy appeared to bite Preston on the nose. Good. He pressed his advantage. "I mean, when I catch somebody, it's luck of the draw. They could've been hit by a bus or somethin'. It's all over before they know it. But what you do . . . it never ends. You're ruinin' their lives with drugs, and then you're feedin' off them whenever you damn well feel like it."

Preston's hands tightened into fists. "Look. Don't be givin' me none of that 'slavery' crap. Not *you.* Nobody forces nobody to buy our smack the first time. It's *their* choice. They don't buy from us, they'd buy from the dealer down the block. Hell, I know math ain't your specialty, but you got any idea how many killin's it'd take to feed thirteen vampires, if we do like you? It'd be like the fuckin' Vietnam War, man. Body bags all over the place. Ain't no *way* we could cover that up."

Jules had no answer to that. It made sense, what Preston had said. Jules should even be grateful. By keeping blood-draining murders to a minimum, Preston's crew were helping keep the heat off all the Crescent City's vampires. But it still didn't sit right with him. It still smelled dirty.

Preston's hard expression loosened into a grin. "I see how you lookin' at me. You think I'm a bad guy, huh? A monster?" He draped his fangs over his lower lip and posed like John Carradine in *Billy the Kid vs. Dracula.* "Well lemme tell you a secret that's not so secret. *Ev'ry*body's a monster." He watched a boy, maybe eleven or twelve, walking down the other side of Jackson Avenue. "Look at that kid. You see them tennis on his feet? Nikes? Adidas? You got any idea how much them shoes cost? Near two C notes, most of 'em. But every kid's gotta have 'em, man. How many mothers in this neighborhood can cough up two C notes for a pair of tennis? Kids *kill* for them shoes. Shoot some dude dead and take 'em off his feet. Guys that own the shoe companies, they know this goes on. But they keep payin' Michael Jordan ten mil a year to make black kids dream about them shoes, then say that's why the price so high. But you know what? They pay some dudes over in Thailand fifty cent a day to stitch them tennis together. So they could sell 'em for twenty bucks, and no kids be killin' other kids for shoes.

"So who's the worse monster? Me? Or the guys makin' billions off them shoes?"

"Now wait a minute, just wait . . ." Jules really hated the smug look on his companion's face. "First off, sellin' sneakers is legal, even for two hundred bucks a pair. Sellin' heroin, with or without vampire blood mixed in, ain't. Another thing—it's not like them kids are stealin' them fancy sneakers 'cause they ain't got no other shoes to wear. Me, I went through the Great Depression. People were *really* poor then. And I didn't see nobody killin' anybody for a pair of shoes. Back then, folks knew what a life was worth. They were raised knowin' that."

"Bingo." Preston smiled again. "You just made my point, man. These days, *ev'ry*body's a monster, absentee daddies included."

"Yeah? Well, not everybody's gotta stay that way. And it don't excuse you. Or me."

They started walking again. Jules was happy to have gotten in the last word, even temporarily. He knew that state of affairs wouldn't last, though. When they reached the corner of Chippewa Street, across from the edge of the huge empty lot that was once the St. Thomas Housing Project, Preston stopped walking.

"Hey," he said. His voice sounded less cocky, almost wistful. "That business about Horse-X, markets, blood . . . that ain't the only reason I want the GoodiesMart-Goodfeller plan to go through. I spent part of my growin' up there, in the St. Thomas. My mom and me, we moved in when I was fifteen. It was a good place then, the late sixties. People knew each other, watched out for each other. It got bad later, sure. But when I was there . . . it was decent. A decent place to be poor and black and have kids. I'd like to see it be that kinda place again."

"We almost moved into the St. Thomas ourselves, my mom and me," Jules said after a few seconds had passed. He found himself wanting to stake a bit of a claim to this land himself. "My mom went to look at it the first day they opened it to the public, in 1939. The apartments were nice, she said, with good iceboxes. But she decided she didn't want people livin' all on top of her, not with me sleepin' in my coffin. Y'know, the St. Thomas, it was originally built as a white project," Jules added, wanting to see what kind of reaction he'd get. Actually, the low-income neighborhood that had gotten torn down and replaced had been shared almost fifty-fifty between whites and blacks. But Jules wasn't going to mention that.

"Maybe it was," Preston said. "But you can be sure it was black backs got broke clearin' the land in the first place."

"Coulda been Irish backs," Jules said. "They were the ones who dug all the canals."

Preston grinned, enjoying their little cutting contest. "Yeah, and before they got here, and before the French and the Spanish and the Africans, I s'pose all this was Indian land. We could make this a reservation for Choctaw Indians, let 'em run a casino and sell cheap cigarettes right here."

"And before *they* were here, what was it? Alligators? Birds?"

"Dinosaurs and shit. Could make it a nature preserve, maybe."

"Yeah," Jules said. "Let's make it a fuckin' bird sanctuary." He turned the corner onto Chippewa Street. "C'mon. We got us an interview to make."

Despite Preston's dire warnings, they found Jules's car in the same shape they'd left it, a fact that inspired several minutes of silent gloating on Jules's part. At a stoplight, the bright red glare reflected off his plastic-coated press badge. He looked down and checked the name printed on it. Ferdinand Melton. He'd have to remember that.

"What's the name on your badge?" Jules asked. They were stopped on Camp Street, just off Coliseum Square, a few minutes drive from the former Saulet Orphanage, now Chez L'Enfant.

Preston glanced down at his badge. "Arthur Anderson. Why?"

"Didn't you tell that manager guy your real name?"

Preston shrugged. "I dunno. Maybe. So what if I did?"

"What if he checked the name you told him against the name on your badge? What if he's told L'Enfant we're phonies?"

Preston snorted. "You're bein' paranoid, man. Parking lot was dark. Guy couldn't even *see* the names on our badges. Besides, L'Enfant wasn't around when I said my name. Don't worry about it."

"So we go with the names on the badges?"

"Sure. Whatever. Fine by me."

Ferdinand Melton. Ferdinand Melton. Ferdinand Melton.

Jules turned toward the river on Race Street, driving past a row of restored antebellum homes. Their gas lamps cast a flickering, Halloween glow on freshly painted white columns and subtropical gardens so abundant they hid adjacent sidewalks beneath canopies of green and pink. He crossed Magazine Street, remembering when, not so many years ago, this neighborhood had been a district of decaying flophouses, dotted with bars so rough even he would've thought twice about walking through their blood-spattered doors. That coffeehouse on the corner had been the pioneer. Some brave entrepreneur had believed in the neighborhood, dug in his heels, and kept a decent business afloat, giving people courage to move into the area and fix up the grand old houses. Certain blocks of the neighborhood were still dicey. But depending on what got built on the nearby St. Thomas tract, longtime residents could wake up one morning to find their familiar old skid row transformed into Savile Row.

A block past the coffeehouse, modern asphalt gave way to centuries-old cobblestones beneath the Allante's tires. Jules pulled over to the curb. The Saulet Orphanage towered above its neighbors, overshadowing them with both its mass of brick and stone and the dark solemnity of its architecture. Its grounds were surrounded by an eight-foot-high wall of weathered red bricks, which threatened to tumble onto passersby any time a vehicle heavier than a mail truck might rumble past. The main building, three stories tall, was a facsimile of a French monastery from the time of King Clovis. Its Romanesque arches were surrounded by twin bell towers shaped like upthrust daggers, their points sharp enough to puncture the bloated moon.

Guess the city had a lotta orphans a hundred and fifty years ago, Jules thought. He eyed the rest of the complex while getting out of the car. Two wings, their open-air galleries with railings of wrought iron shaped into wild grape vines, projected into the rear courtyard, which also held several outbuildings. *And now just one guy lives here, and this ain't even his main house.*

Jules and Preston walked along a moss-coated brick sidewalk to the orphanage's main gate, sidestepping places where tree roots made the bricks erupt like crooked teeth. Jules was surprised to find the gate had been left unlocked; maybe the neighborhood was gentrifying, but this was still New Orleans. They climbed five steps to a broad porch that ran the entire front width of the building. The air felt damp and smelled of mold. Jules nearly slipped as he went to knock on the door—the porch's uneven wooden floor was slick with dewy condensation.

The door unnerved him by opening before he touched it. Bronson, the manager, ushered them inside. "Thanks for being prompt," he said. "Mr. L'Enfant's got an incredibly tight schedule. Try and make it short, okay?" He glanced past the entrance foyer to a grand curving staircase at the far end of what might once have been an assembly hall. "Mr. L'Enfant's making himself comfortable. He'll be down in a minute or two. In the meantime, can I get you guys something? Beer? Lemonade? Mrs. L'Enfant loves lemonade. Gotta always have the fresh-squeezed stuff on hand."

"We'll pass," Preston said.

"Suit yourselves," Bronson said. "If you need me, I'll be in the office. Third door on the right."

Preston waited until Bronson was out of earshot. "There's a *Missus* L'Enfant?" he whispered.

"Sounds that way," Jules said. He wandered over to a wall in the big room that held a display of framed gold and platinum records and their corresponding album covers. The first record, *The Courane L'Enfant Experience,* looked to Jules like it'd been made in the late 1970s or early 1980s. Something about it said "disco." Maybe it was the garish, Day-Glo graphics, or maybe it was the photo of L'Enfant sweating above an electric keyboard, poufy hairstyle rivaling Diana Ross's grandest Afro, gold medallions swinging from his neck, cartoon lightning bolts shooting from his fingertips.

The next album even Jules had heard of, although he wished he hadn't. This was probably the musician's biggest record ever, the multiple-platinum *L'Enfant Terrible,* on which he'd first conjured his unique Goth-thrash-Cajun sound. He'd abandoned his synthesizers and horn section for Acadian-style squeeze-box, fiddle, and washboard—pumped up to brain-withering levels and backed up by industrial-strength guitars and percussion.

"Oh, God, look at this one," Jules muttered, staring at the next gold record. L'Enfant, in full Goth regalia, was doubled over backward, impaled by a gigantic stake longer than he was tall, blood streaming from his open, presumably screaming, mouth. Jules gestured for Preston to come over. "You ever had the displeasure of listening to this shit?"

Preston appraised the framed CD cover artwork. He read the name of the album aloud—"*Spare the Rod, Spoil L'Enfant.* Nope. Don't think I was payin' much attention when this came out. Pretty sure this was right around when Malice turned me, so I had other stuff on my mind." He took a closer look at the gory image. "Hey, wasn't that when L'Enfant started bitin' the heads off puppy dogs?"

"Rats," Jules said. One more reason to dislike the guy. "Right after that record came out, the AC in my cab went on the fritz. So I was stuck drivin' up and down Decatur Street with my windows down, and every goddamn Goth bar in the Quarter is blarin' this goddamn record. That Halloween, a buncha bar owners got L'Enfant to give a free street concert in the Lower Quarter. Musta been a billion vampire wannabes turned out for that. Since then, the Quarter's had more wannabes crawlin' around than flying roaches."

"Kids nowadays," Preston said, shaking his head and clucking his tongue.

From somewhere above them, a bell chimed three times, its clear tones echoing down the staircase. L'Enfant descended the stairs. His braids were held aloft by a superstructure of lacquer combs. His full-length black silk kimono swished against the marble stairs with each step. He looked like Dr. Fu Manchu, channeled by Norma Desmond of *Sunset Boulevard.*

"Gentlemen, welcome to my home," he said, smiling. "One of my homes. I'm so glad you could come." He approached Jules, his eyes lively with interest. "I'm so sorry, but we weren't introduced before. Please tell me your name?"

Shit. "Uh, Frederic Melon," he said, praying his memory hadn't just screwed him.

L'Enfant's catlike eyes (was he wearing contact lenses?) darted to the badge hanging from Jules's jacket. "Is that Melon? Or Mel*ton*?"

Jules forced a chuckle. "Melton, sure. Guess I must have melons on my mind. Hungry or something."

"Really?" L'Enfant's smile broadened. "I just so happen to have a marvelous melon in my refrigerator. Would you like some? It's quite . . . plump. And juicy."

Jules squirmed. "Uh, thanks, but no thanks. Fruits aren't really my favorite."

Jules heard Preston squelch a laugh, but their host seemed not to notice. L'Enfant extended his hand, which barely projected beyond his silk sleeve. "Good to meet you, Mr. Melton." Jules shook his hand. L'Enfant held Jules's hand long enough to make Jules uneasy. "Cold hands, warm heart, hmm?" His eyes flashed with self-satisfied amusement. He finally released Jules's hand and turned to Preston. "And this member of the Fourth Estate would be . . . ?"

"Arthur Anderson," Preston said. He shook L'Enfant's hand. L'Enfant didn't retain his grip as long this time, Jules noticed, but longer than was customary for a casual handshake.

"You two are a matched pair," L'Enfant said. "I'd almost think I'm back in Ontario in mid-January. Come. Let's go sit and talk in the parlor. I'll be happy to answer any and all questions."

The parlor, long and narrow, with exposed wooden beams, looked like it might've been the old dining hall. Red leather sofas extended along the walls. In the middle of the room was a large display table, about five feet square. It was covered with a black cloth attached to a silk rope that extended to the ceiling. A pulley system had been rigged up so that someone could pull on the rope by the rear wall and lift the cloth.

"What's on the table?" Jules asked. Given L'Enfant's tastes, it could be either a display of the Marquis de Sade's signed first editions or a glass-encased nest of tarantulas.

"Oh, that?" L'Enfant said with a backward flip of his hand. "I'm afraid I can't show you that quite yet. Its big debut is coming up three nights from now, at my Vampyres and Live Wires Soiree. Normally, it'd be scheduled for the weekend before Halloween. But this year, outside events have overridden my self-centered calendar . . ." He approached the table and slowly caressed it, the silk of his sleeve rasping against the rougher black fabric. "I can't show it to you, but would you like to know what it is?"

Jules nodded.

"It's a model, quite a lovely piece of work. A scale model of the Lower Garden District Reclamation Project."

"Any reason why we can't take a look at it now?" Preston asked. "You got nothin' to hide, right? You're proud of it?"

"Of course I'm proud of it," L'Enfant responded, unfazed by the aggressiveness of Preston's questioning. "But it would be so very unfair of me to show it to you before your fellow reporters. If I were to give you a scoop, the good people at the *Times-Picayune* might never grant me a positive review ever again. Come. Let's sit, and you can tell me what the readers of *Louisiana Weekly* would most like to know about Courane L'Enfant."

The three of them sat on the long red sofa nearest the covered display table, L'Enfant between the two vampires. Preston removed a yellow legal pad and pen from the shoulder bag he'd "borrowed" from the reporter in the men's room. "Okay. The first thing my readers wanna know is, how come a millionaire musician like Courane L'Enfant is so interested in the St. Thomas? What's your dog in this fight?"

"Nothing complicated or nefarious, Mr. Anderson. I'm a resident of Uptown New Orleans. I've lived here since my return to the city more than twenty years ago. My family farmed this land in the decades prior to President Jefferson's purchase of Louisiana from Emperor Napoleon. I own a considerable amount of property in New Orleans, and much of it is in the Uptown area. The redevelopment of the St. Thomas tract is key to the health and vitality of the entire lower portion of Uptown, just as the health of Uptown is key to the prosperity of New Orleans as a whole. I have economic interests in this project, but my greater interests are public-spirited ones. Heritage is the life's blood of this city. It's why I chose to rescue this orphanage from decay and demolition."

Preston looked up from his pad. "How about those rumors that you own a bunch of properties surrounding the redevelopment site, that you stand to make a killin' if the fancier project gets built?"

Jules didn't see L'Enfant flinch from the question at all. Not even the tiniest involuntary tic marred the placidity of his Kabuki mask of a face. "As I've already told you, I own considerable property in the Uptown area. I saw the potential for this particular neighborhood's development years ago, when I purchased this orphanage. So I bought quite heavily on the surrounding blocks, some of which also border the St. Thomas tract. No one else believed so strongly in this area's possibilities, so prices were quite cheap. I'll give you a little inside tip, Mr. Anderson. No matter which project gets built, the value of my properties will increase substantially. Economically, I'm in a win-win situation."

"But you make out a whole lot *better* if the deluxe project gets built, right?"

"Perhaps. Perhaps not. Should the GoodiesMart-Goodfeller plan be selected and some of my properties are rezoned from residential to commercial, I could profit quite handily selling out to gas stations and fast-food chains. And as you said before, Mr. Anderson, I already have more money than I know what to do with. The difference between five-million-dollars profit and ten-million-dollars profit is immaterial to me. Rather than maximizing my personal gains, I'd much prefer midwifing the kind of development that will raise New Orleans's profile nationally and attract higher strata of human capital, which hopefully will spawn investment in the kinds of new-generation industries we currently sadly lack. Modernizing New Orleans's economy will benefit all of her citizens, much more so than the few dozen additional part-time jobs a GoodiesMart will generate. In order to attract today's entrepreneurs, we have to be able to offer something that Atlanta, Houston, and Miami can't—our heritage, the beauty and grandeur of our historic neighborhoods."

"But this project you wanna build," Jules interjected, "it won't *be* a historic neighborhood. The historic neighborhood on that site got flattened over sixty years ago. You wanna build a brand-new neighborhood."

"But it will look just like a historic neighborhood," L'Enfant said. "Part of the plan is to rescue architecturally significant homes from decaying neighborhoods and move them to this site, where they will be restored in a harmonious ensemble and occupied by owners who can afford to care for them."

"Disney World," Preston said sourly.

The comment chipped L'Enfant's smooth mask. "What?"

"You wanna build Disney World for rich folks."

L'Enfant's painted mouth twitched. "I reject that completely. Disney World is ersatz. Cotton candy. A plaster facade built on a filled-in swamp for tourists with impoverished imaginations. What we will build will re-create an urban landscape and a way of life with roots that extend back more than two centuries."

"And what *else* do you wanna bring back from two centuries ago?" Preston said in a tone almost sure to summon the resident body-guards. "You gonna have costumed employees in that theme park of yours? Maybe some of the ex-residents of the St. Thomas can get good jobs pluckin' banjos and pickin' fake cotton?"

L'Enfant's eyes turned hard, but then he forced a smile and turned to Jules. "Your friend is trying very hard to bait me, Mr. Melton. Rather uncouth for someone I've invited into my own home, wouldn't you say?" Before Jules could answer, L'Enfant turned back to Preston. "I don't need to justify myself to you, Mr. Anderson. But please be aware of this. I pump more money into the African American community in one month than you will in a natural lifetime. Ask your editor at the *Louisiana Weekly* about that. He'll verify it. Now, before I ask you to leave, do you have any final questions?"

"Yeah. I do." Preston barely tamped down his hostility. "There's been two preachers killed. Two 'African American' preachers who been out front of the movement to build what you say you don't want. Kinda convenient, huh? Those preachers not able to mouth off anymore, just a month or two before everything gets decided. *Mighty* convenient, wouldn't you say?"

L'Enfant threw his head back and laughed. Laughed hard enough to dislodge his lacquer combs and scatter his braids like Medusa's swirling snakes. When he opened his eyes again, tears had made his black eyeliner fuzzy. "Oh . . . oh, goodness . . . my reputation is more fearsome than I could've ever dreamed! You should be my publicist! Quit your job at that threadbare newspaper and I'll give you a job in my organization. I'm a *performer,* Mr. Anderson. The satanic rituals, the torturing of small furry animals—it's all *pretend.* Print anything like what you just implied, and I'll happily sue you and your paper for libel. Besides, haven't you heard the rumor that they were killed by some kind of a blood-drinker? A vampire? Is that what you think I am, Mr. Anderson?" Preston said nothing, just radiated heat like a manhole cover on a hundred-degree day. "Well, some of my favorite people are vampires, I admit. My favorite *fictional* people. Because we all know there's no such thing as vampires. Don't we, gentlemen?"

Jules was ninety-eight percent certain his leg was being pulled, hard enough to tear it from its socket. L'Enfant turned back in his direction, relaxed now that he was fully in control of the conversation again. "Mr. Melton, you've been so quiet. I'd say you're the good cop of this good cop/bad cop duo, but you've really been the silent cop. Do you have a last question for me?"

"I'd like to see what's under that curtain, on that table," Jules said.

"Well, I believe I can arrange that," L'Enfant said. He reached into his kimono and pulled out a pair of gilt-edged black tickets, embossed with shiny red lettering. He handed them to Jules. "Those are a pair of tickets to my Vampyres and Live Wires Soiree. Come, and you'll be one of the first people in town to see what's under the curtain. Bring your sweetheart, or, if he promises to behave, Mr. Anderson. Costume is de rigueur. Although if the two of you show up exactly as you are, I'm sure you won't be turned away."

Two of the bodyguards Jules recognized from the school parking lot walked into the room. Their time was up, Jules realized; he and Preston stood and followed the men to the front door. Before he could step back out into the damp evening, he felt a tap on his shoulder.

"Mr. Melton," L'Enfant said, "I do hope to see you again three nights from now. I have a friend I'd very much like you to meet. I believe you two might share a very special connection."

Jules walked toward his car in a kind of fog. The meeting with L'Enfant had creeped him out. What he'd just said about "a very special connection" . . . Either he wrote scripts for *Touched by an Angel* on the side, or he was being deliberately mysterious, counting on the tease to lure Jules back to the orphanage for the big party. Well, it had worked. Jules stared at the invitations in his hand. He knew where he'd be spending at least a couple of hours three nights hence.

"What a goddamn prick," Preston muttered as they reached the car. "You think he's mixed up in the murders?"

"My gut says he's mixed up in *something*," Jules said. L'Enfant and the St. Thomas . . . the St. Thomas and the High Krewe kids, he was almost positive there was a connection there, too. Now, if he could just find a link between L'Enfant and the junior vampire league, he'd be a giant step closer to solving both his own mystery and Preston's. The party—just from its name, he was sure it'd be swarming with vampire groupies and wannabes. Maybe real vampires, too. L'Enfant had been a little too cute near the end of their conversation. If real vampires *did* show up, especially ones sneaking out past curfew, Jules would be ready with a fistful of questions they couldn't sidestep.

He started to unlock the car with his key fob, then changed his mind. He needed a cup of joe. "Hey, Preston, you mind if we take a break? There's a coffeehouse a block and a half away, at the corner of Magazine. I'll buy."

"If you're buyin', I'm drinkin'."

The Rue de la Course Coffeehouse, occupying what had once been a small corner grocery store, exuded a pleasant atmosphere of genteel decay. Its pressed-tin ceiling, covered in flaking tan paint, supported six drooping fans, only half of which worked. Rather than cool the room, they helped spread the nutty aroma of freshly brewed coffee. It wasn't a big place. By himself, Jules took up a fifth of the available floor space. Still, that didn't seem to perturb the tattooed, pierced young woman who took his order; she filled two cups with the requested chicory coffee, affecting a studied boredom, although Jules could've sworn her shoulder tattoo of Horton the Elephant winked at him as she carried the cups and saucers to the counter.

Horton wasn't the only character in the joint giving Jules the eye. While he was digging in his pocket for four bucks and change, he noticed an older man staring at him and Preston from behind a copy of *Mother Jones.* As Jules and Preston walked past with their coffees, the man laid his magazine down on his table. "Hey," he half whispered at them in a gravelly voice, "didn't I see you two at the forum on rebuilding St. Thomas?" He stared at their badges, and his eyes widened slightly. His tongue darted out to dampen chapped lips. "You're journalists, aren't you?"

Jules stared around the room. The only clean, unoccupied table was next to the table where this man sat. Conversation seemed unavoidable. "Yeah, we were there," Jules said, setting his coffee down.

"That slick iguana, L'Enfant, he was something, huh? Sparked a riot without even half trying."

"Yeah, he's slick all right," Preston said, sitting down. "We just got a whiff o' his snake oil up close and personal."

The man's cratered face lit up like a full moon. "You were just over at the orphanage? You interviewed him?"

"Yeah. What's it to you?"

The man leaned closer. Jules noticed that his long, gray hair was gathered in a filthy ponytail, and he was missing several of his front teeth. His voice dropped back to its conspiratorial half whisper. "Fifty bucks buys you front-page dirt on Courane L'Enfant. You interested?"

Jules stared at Preston. "Whadda you think?"

Preston shrugged, trying to look nonchalant, but Jules could tell he was more interested than he let on. "I'll pony up half if you will."

They both dug twenty-five dollars from their wallets and handed it to the older man. He counted it carefully, smiling so broadly that drool nearly spilled out onto the money from the wide spaces between his surviving teeth. "I was Courane L'Enfant's folk-dancing instructor back in 1980," he said once the bills were counted.

"What?!" Preston grabbed the money back. "We didn't pay no fifty dollars to find out L'Enfant's some goddamn *folk dancer*!"

The man snatched the money in turn, surprising Preston so much that the vampire didn't flatten him. "Hold up! Let me finish! See, he wasn't 'Courane L'Enfant' back then. And he wasn't from Louisiana, either. His real name was Corey Lawrence, and he was a fucked-up nobody from Ontario, Canada. He's always bragging about his 'ancestors' from colonial New Orleans. Shit, he doesn't have any relations from New Orleans. He's not even French Canadian! He started hanging out with my group back in 1980, taking the free, introductory lesson over and over again, trying to score with the lonely middle-aged widows. Couldn't decide whether he wanted to be a writer, a dancer, or a painter. Shoulda been a house painter, maybe. He idolized Sammy Davis, Jr., he said, so he talked with a rabbi who danced with us about converting to Judaism. Three weeks later, he was buddying up with this Sikh guy I knew. Every other day it was something different."

Preston shot Jules a dubious look. He seemed ready to grab his money back again. But Jules wanted to hear more. "If what you're sayin' is true," he said, "how come the *Times-Picayune* or some music magazine ain't broke the story that L'Enfant's not who he says he is?"

"That's the beauty part," the man said. "After he decided he wanted to be Courane L'Enfant, the first thing he did as soon as he started pulling in the music bucks was to cover his tracks. He had a new birth certificate forged. He got somebody to destroy his records back in

Canada. He paid some phony researcher to 'discover' these prominent L'Enfant ancestors in the Tulane University archives. It was just like what Elvis's manager did. Colonel Tom Parker. Everybody figured Parker was some carny from Oklahoma or Arkansas. But the man was from Holland. Fucking *Holland*!"

Jules warmed his hands against his coffee cup. "And how come you're so eager to spill the goods on your old dance student?"

"Bastard never paid me for the last two months of lessons," the man said, his face hard. "Idiot that I was, I let him slide on credit. Twenty years, I've been trying to square that debt."

Preston scowled. "Can you back any of this up, or are you all lip?"

The man smiled his jack-o'-lantern smile again. "I got documents. A cool thousand and they're yours, boys."

Preston smacked the table, splitting the wood and jarring the coffee cups to the floor. "That's a crock of *shit* if I ever smelled one—"

Jules's breast pocket began buzzing. It took him a second to realize it was his cell phone. No one had ever called him on it before. He removed it from his pocket, not sure he knew how to answer it. He looked helplessly at Preston, but his partner's attention was fiercely riveted on the old man.

Jules didn't want to embarrass himself with the phone in front of Preston. "Uh, 'scuse me, I gotta go take this outside," he mumbled. He pushed through the door, walked quickly under a street lamp so he could see the phone better, and managed to flip it open. Gambling, he pressed the button marked Talk and pressed the phone to his ear.

"Mr. Duchon?" a distant, static-marred voice said. Jules thought it was female, but it didn't sound like Daphne.

"Yeah, this is him."

"I apologize to be calling so late, but I was out of town and just got your message, and you said I could return your call any time in the evening hours. This is Fannie Yishinsky. I'm the realtor for the house on Cleveland Avenue."

Jules remembered the message he'd left the previous night. "Oh! You mean Doc Landrieu's old house in Mid-City."

"Yes. Are you interested in looking at the property?"

"Actually, I wanted to find out who's selling it. I didn't know Doc Landrieu had family. I wanna express my condolences."

"Who's selling it?" Even with the cell phone's abysmal fidelity, Jules could tell the realtor sounded confused. "But . . . but I thought you said you know the owner. Dr. Amos Landrieu, the owner, is the seller. Is there a specific time that's good for you to look at the house? I could speak with Dr. Landrieu and get back to you—"

"But—but that's impossible. Doc Landrieu is—" Jules stopped himself before he said the word *dead.* A chill knifed down his back. Just how positive had he been, when he stumbled onto the body, that his old boss had been well and truly *dead*? He'd certainly *looked* dead—Jules had found Doc Landrieu trussed up like a pincushion, a dozen or more glass laboratory tubes sticking out of his veins, his eyes glazed over, his limbs stiff. But then again, Jules hadn't spent more than thirty seconds in the basement with Doc Landrieu's body, and his mind had been clouded with shock and grief. He hadn't thought to check for a bullet wound in the back of Landrieu's head. Had Malice X and crew delivered the customary coup de grâce, destroying their victim's brain stem before he could rise again? Had it even been necessary? Maybe the black vampires had killed him first, *then* sucked him dry. Or maybe they'd forgotten the bullet, or been interrupted before they could finish . . .

"Mr. Duchon? I'm having difficulty hearing you. Could you please repeat what you just said?"

Electronic bleatings shattered the night's silence, adding to his confusion. "Hang on," Jules said, "let me try to get away from this noise, I can't hear you—"

He walked quickly away from Magazine Street, but the noise, which sounded like synthesized Indian war whoops, only got louder. It was a car alarm, Jules realized. On the next block, a distant car's headlights flashed on and off. Jules saw the hindquarters of two dark figures, silhouetted by the strobing lights, protruding from the car's open doors.

He'd started walking toward the stricken car as soon as he saw the flashing headlights. Now he began running. It was his Allante.

"Hey!" he shouted, the cell phone in his hand forgotten. *"Hey!!"* In his human form, *running* was pretty much a misnomer—he race-waddled toward the thieves, slapping his thighs together with a sound like gelatinous thunder. He pushed his circulatory system to the max, until Horton the Elephant sat on his chest and threatened to smother his heart. But adrenaline kept him shuffling forward, his arms reaching for the despoilers now less than half a block away.

"Hey—you—mother—fuckers—get away from—my goddamn—Cadillac . . ."

One of the figures, a black kid no older than sixteen, emerged from the Allante's driver's-side door with the car's stereo-head unit. The other boy, even younger, crawled out of the passenger side, saw Jules laboriously advancing, and shot him the finger. Then, to make his point more explicit, he thrust his knife through the Allante's convertible top, already holed, and performed a backward moonwalk while slicing the roof from windshield to backlight, not turning to run until Jules was less than ten feet away.

Jules leaned on the Cadillac's hood, still vibrating with the raging alarm, while he waited for his heart rate to slow to sublight velocity. Then, breath returning, he looked at his car. His convertible top was in tatters. The interior looked like a miniature Hurricane Betsy had blown through. They'd even slashed his leather seats.

He yanked the key fob from his pocket and silenced the alarm. It didn't improve things. His head was throbbing with the alarm's vicious rhythm. Could the night get any worse?

Thirty seconds later, he'd receive a call on his cell phone that would make the night's events to that point seem like a riverboat pleasure cruise.

FOURTEEN

The rat was having fun.

His oddly attractive playmate was back. The rat's tail twitched with happiness. She waited for him near the food alley, waiting to see what he would do. Oh, he couldn't see her, not from this particular ledge, at least. She hid behind the screen door that led into the wonderful-smelling room where his food came from. But he knew she was still there. He'd seen her leave the plate of brisket inside the little house with see-through walls on the floor of the food alley. Then she'd gone inside the wonderful-smelling room and hidden herself behind the screen door. Even with all the tantalizing odors coming from the wonderful-smelling room (*kitchen*—that word floated into his head, then burst like a soap bubble) and from the big, green, yummy box (*Dumpster?*), he could still pick up her distinctive scent. His nose twitched as he smelled it—nervous sweat, both fresh and dried on her clothes, and foot sweat (very strong, and very exciting, too), and another odor, not pleasant, an odor that made his eyes water if he got too close to it (*Right Guard*?).

The rat's brain had been much busier lately. Ever since the woman and the man and the other person who was both a man *and* a woman (and was also his friend, the rat was sure of this) had taken away all of his brothers in the little houses with the see-through walls, the rat had felt his thinking begin to change. Even that notion—*thinking,* that *thinking* was something he did, like *eating* or *sleeping*—was new to him. Lately, when he'd been listening to the people chopping food in the wonderful-smelling room, listening to the sounds they made when they were with one another, he'd begun to realize that these sounds often weren't just sounds. They were *words,* sounds that had meanings attached to them. He couldn't always understand the meanings, but with every night that passed, the rat found himself understanding more and more.

He crawled from the ledge onto the sloping roof, and from there onto a sagging rain gutter. From this improved vantage point, he could see the young woman. She was sitting on a stool near the screen door. Her gaze was fixed on the little house in the food alley that held the brisket. Even though she undoubtedly wanted to take him away to wherever she'd taken his brothers, the rat was not angry at her. He liked her. He liked that she showed him so much attention. He even thought she was pretty, although this concept confused him, particularly since he was a rat and she was a woman. And the words *too skinny* kept surfacing whenever he looked at her . . . what could that mean?

Still, he liked her. In fact, if he didn't value his independence so much, he'd be happy to descend the wall, saunter into the food alley, and wait there for her to catch him. But he *did* value his independence. Even though he couldn't explain to himself why this passion for freedom could make him forgo mouth-watering brisket, the companionship of his brothers, and the touch of this pleasing young woman.

Someone approached her. It was the man the rat recognized from several nights ago, the man who'd helped the young woman take away the rat's brothers. He leaned over her and put his arm around her shoulders. The rat didn't like this. The hairs all along his back bristled. He hissed, although some part of him told him this was senseless, and his lips pulled back in a feral snarl.

". . . sure you don't want . . ."

The rat perked up his ears so that he could better hear what the man, the interloper, was saying. ". . . be happy to open up the Dumpster again and toss in some food garbage. If he jumps in there, I'm sure I could run out in time to slam the lid shut and trap him."

The young woman turned toward the man. The rat was thrilled to see her squirm out from beneath his arm. "No, Hank, I don't think that'll work. This rat, he's too smart for that. And besides, he's too fast. If he's not coming out for his favorite food, I'm not sure *anything*'ll bring him out. You think, maybe since we took all the other rats away, he's found another colony to join in some other part of the Quarter? Maybe I'm wasting my time waiting here?"

"Why is this *particular* rat so important, anyway? Didn't I just help you catch, what, about two hundred other ones? Big fat white rat, hell, we could probably find one in a pet store, no problem." He dug into his pocket and pulled out green paper. "Here, I'll even spring for it—"

"Hank, I told you, I can't explain why this rat is so important. He just *is.* And if he doesn't show up here in the next couple of hours, then I'll need to go look for him somewhere else. At least with him being so big, his scat's unusually big, too. I'll have that to look for."

The rat's chest expanded with pride. Clearly, he was very, very important to the young woman. But pride wouldn't fill his belly. Two nights now, that brisket had rested inside the little house with the revolving door. He was pretty sure, having watched many of his brothers go through the doors of similar little houses, that there was a way for him to go inside and still be able to get out. If he poked only the front half of his body through the door and reached as far as he could with his paws, he might be able to grab some slices of brisket, pull them toward him, and wiggle his way back out with his prize. Of course, he couldn't do this while the young woman and this abhorrent Hank were watching. Surely they couldn't watch the alley forever?

After another few minutes of watching and waiting, the rat became restless. He began pacing in the rain gutter. Even the gutter's collapsing beneath him, spilling him onto the cobblestones, would be better than the big nothing that was going on. Apparently the rat wasn't the only restless one. The Hank person returned after a few minutes of welcome absence and attempted to drape himself over the young woman again. "Hey, Daphne, I'm getting off in forty-five minutes. How about letting me take you out to the Clover Grill for a burger—"

Daphne!

The young woman had a name! And the interloper was using it!

This was almost more than the rat could bear. He wanted to bite those filthy fingers that were beginning to creep slowly down Daphne's bare arm.

He had to do something. Anything.

If he showed himself, if he walked out into the alley just long enough for Daphne to see him, maybe he could get her to chase him. Maybe she would leave the interloper behind and follow him through the streets and alleyways of the Quarter. It would be fun, being chased by her. Much more fun than waiting up here on this rain gutter. He could lead her around the neighborhood, sharing with her his favorite music and most wonderfully smelly green boxes. And if the rat were really, really lucky, he might lose her for a few minutes by the time he got back to the food alley. And then he could work on getting at that plate of brisket.

He crept along the gutter until he came to a rain chute, then wriggled inside. It was a tight fit, and dark, but at least the corroded aluminum gave his claws some purchase as he headed straight down. The blood rushed to his head, making him slightly dizzy. Sounds of cockroaches scurrying out of his way echoed through the chute, making it sound as if he were surrounded by a million little tapping feet.

He came to a slick patch. *Whoa!* Assisted by gravity, the rat skidded into a ninety-degree bend and found himself deposited, snout first, on the damp cobblestones of the food alley, surrounded by a half dozen disoriented roaches. He shook his head, trying to return all the parts of his face to their proper alignment. Then he heard Daphne say in an excited whisper: "That's *him*! He just popped out of that gutter drain!"

Still groggy, the rat rolled off his back onto his paws. He gathered his strength to dash out of the alley, although not so fast that Daphne couldn't follow.

"Hand me my net," Daphne whispered.

"D'you want me to go out there and catch him?"

"No, no, I'll do it."

"What if he bites you?"

"He won't *bite* me. I've been handling rats since I was eight years old. Just give me the net."

The screen door slowly opened. Daphne emerged, holding the door so that it wouldn't slam, and softly descended the steps to the cobblestones. She held the net, attached to a pole as long as her arm, making no effort to hide the tool. She smiled a big, appealing smile as she stepped closer, but he could hear her heart accelerate.

"Hey there, big guy," she said in tones as sticky and creamy as caramel. "I'm not going to hurt you. I just want to take you back to Jules. That's where you need to be, back with Mr. Jules. Do you remember him?"

Jules. That name did seem *awfully* familiar. Where did he know it from?

Step by tiny step, she came closer. "He's a very nice man. You two belong together, you know. All I'm going to do is, I'm going to scoop you up, and I'm going to pet you some, and I'm going to feed you some of your favorite food—baked brisket, and maybe some chicory coffee from an eyedropper. How's that? And then I'm going to take you to see Mr. Jules. And you two will have a big, happy reunion. That doesn't sound so bad, does it?"

Actually, it didn't sound bad at all. Although he couldn't be sure about this Jules character. Daphne was inexplicably willing to subject herself to the slimy attentions of Hank, so this Jules could turn out to be nasty as an alley cat.

In any case, he wasn't ready to be caught. Not yet.

She was only three steps away from him now. Close enough to use the net. He watched her net hand, ready to sprint away the second he saw it make a threatening move. She extended her free hand for him to sniff. "Steady, boy," she said in a sweet whisper. "Take a little smell, all right? I'm not going to hurt you, sweetie . . ."

Obligingly, he sniffed the glove. It smelled a lot like his brothers, but it smelled more like her. The rat felt himself stiffening all over in a most delicious way. His vision went fuzzy with pleasure. So fuzzy that he almost didn't see Daphne carefully place the net on the ground and reach for him with her other hand.

But he did see it. The touch of her fingers on his fur threw him out of his reverie, reignited his wariness. He leaped out of her grasp, then hit the cobblestones running.

"Oh, *poopy-doo*!" he heard her mutter. He heard the net's handle scrape against the ground as she scooped it up, followed swiftly by the bang-clatter of the net's rim hitting the spot where he'd been just a half second ago. He zigzagged up the alleyway, scurrying for the sidewalks and garbage-choked storm drains he knew so well. But he kept one ear open for Daphne's footfalls, making sure he didn't get too far ahead of her.

He led her out onto Bourbon Street, figuring the crush of people would slow her down and he could enjoy the game more. Most people didn't notice him running between their feet. They were too preoccupied with bar doors that swung open to show naked woman flesh, or people on balconies who threw rings of colored beads to the ground. One little girl in a stroller did see him, however. She squealed with delight, pointed at him scurrying only inches from her stroller's wheels, and shouted, "Look, Mommy! Little white doggie!"

He paused beneath the tires of a Lucky Dog wiener cart, waiting to see how far behind him Daphne had fallen. While he was scanning the street for her, he licked blobs of spilled ketchup and mustard from the sidewalk. A man with a hanging gut and a rubbery face who'd just bought a hot dog noticed the little loiterer beneath the wiener-shaped cart. He grinned at the rat conspiratorially, leaned over, and motioned for him to come closer to his dirty sneaker. "Don't feed th' pigeons, they sez," he sputtered, swaying dangerously. "Well, *you* ain't no *pigeon.*" He tore off a piece of his hot dog and bun and dropped it next to his shoe. "Here, buddy. Bone appetitty!" The rat ate the piece of hot dog. It was much more satisfying than the condiment smears had been.

As soon as the pink meat by-products vanished down his gullet, the rat resumed looking for Daphne. He didn't have to look long. She was crouching near a curb thirty feet away, shining a flashlight into a storm drain. The drunk who'd shared his weiner stumbled over to her. The rat emerged from beneath the cart, afraid the man might fall on her or otherwise inadvertently hurt her. "You an in*shpectur*?" the drunk asked Daphne. "I didn't feed no pigeons. Not me, no ma'am. But I made this rat's day, see? Fed him a *shteak* dinner."

Daphne looked up at the man. "You fed a rat? Where? What'd he look like?"

"Cute. White." He held his hands, one of them still holding the hot dog, three feet apart. "*This* big. Back there, under that big weenie—"

Daphne's eyes met the rat's. For a split second, they were both frozen with excitement. The rat unfroze first, dashing into the street, and the chase was on again.

The rat led her past a corner jazz club he hazily remembered having spent time in. He leaped over shuffling human feet and dropped daiquiri cups to the syncopated melodies of a cornet and clarinet. The music made his tiny, hammering heart yearn for a time when he'd been younger, when he'd loved a woman much different from Daphne. That woman—her house hadn't been very far from here. He turned in the direction he thought he remembered, away from the Bourbon Street crowds and their blind, dangerous feet.

Half a block off Bourbon, something else distracted him. A familiar scent, astringent, musty, and pungent. The scent brought many pictures into the rat's head, confusing pictures, images of people who slept on strange, flat beds that slid out of a wall, people who obviously didn't want to wake up because they'd pulled the sheets over their faces. For some reason he didn't understand, his mouth filled with saliva, even though the chunk of hot dog had taken the edge off his hunger.

The rat ducked beneath a raised house. He needed to sort these thoughts out. The memories were from a long time ago. How long? He had no idea. But that scent, he'd smelled it much more recently, too. When his brothers had still been with him. What had happened then? He sat up on his haunches and rubbed his nose with his paws, trying to force the elusive memories to coalesce. Hadn't he followed two people out of the food alley? Had the scent come from one of them?

He peeked out. Daphne was coming closer, shining her flashlight beam into the dark spaces beneath the old houses. One thought knifed its way through the swirling fog of the rat's memories. The scent, strange and unappealing as it might be, belonged to a friend. Yes, he was sure of that. This certainty made him very happy. His tail twitched with excitement. A friend was nearby. And Daphne was nearby, too. Two friends, so close! His friends should meet each other. If he could find this mystery friend, he could lead Daphne to this person. He could watch them and listen to what they would say. It would make the night more fun.

He crawled out from beneath the house and chittered as loudly as he could. As soon as he was certain Daphne had seen him, he dashed half a block to the nearest intersection, following his nose toward his mystery friend.

He rounded the corner. The street he turned onto seemed a world away from helter-skelter Bourbon Street. Devoid of neon, it was lit by gas lamps whose dim, wavering light cast shadows as sinuous as jellyfish. The rat searched for his mystery friend. The scent was much stronger here, but he saw no one on the street or sidewalks or wooden stoops.

Two houses down the block, a door opened. The rat saw a young woman emerge onto a small gated porch, followed by a man who hovered in the open doorway. He didn't recognize either of them. But something about the young woman roused his curiosity and made him creep closer. He'd seen another like her not too long ago—the same pale skin, the same hungry leanness, the same aroma of rusting iron and ancient dried flowers.

"So there's no possibility the zoning commission won't rule our way?" the woman said to the man standing in the doorway.

"It's a slam dunk," the man said. He had a thick black mustache; its tips formed curlicues like the wrought iron of his house's balcony. "Three of the members were leaning your way before y'all did a thing. And now three of the other six have ten thousand reasons to zone upscale." He laughed. "Me, I've got more reasons than that."

"More and better reasons, yes." The woman leaned closer to the man, put her arms around his shoulders, and pressed her lips against his. The rat felt his spine stiffen. He wondered whether the tips of the man's mustache might poke her in the eye. Their words didn't mean anything to him, but they were very interesting to watch.

Behind him, the rat heard someone crossing the street. He turned around. It was Daphne, passing up the street the rat had turned onto. As soon as he located his mystery friend, he'd have to go corral her. In the meantime, he wanted to see what else would happen between the pale dried-flower woman and the man with the mustache.

She pulled away from him, even though he tried to hang on. "Let's save some of this for later," she said. "After the vote."

"You're not going to make me wait *that* long, are you?" the man said. "I'll see you before then at the party, right? You going to wear something special?"

The rat saw her smile. The gas light flickered off her teeth. They looked very white, even whiter than the rest of her. "I always wear something special," she said. "My invitation—did I leave it on your coffee table?"

"Let me go get it for you." He disappeared back into the house, then reappeared a few seconds later and handed her an envelope. "Hang on to this, okay? It'd be a real bummer if the ball was minus its belle."

"Of course," she said. "Good night." They pressed their lips together again, briefly, before the woman pushed him back inside his house and pulled the door closed.

She descended to the sidewalk, then began walking toward the rat, who backed into a crevice beneath a stoop. He heard a second set of footsteps, coming from the opposite direction. It was Daphne, who had circled back around and was peering under houses with her flashlight. Crouching on the sidewalk about fifteen paces from where the rat was hiding, she didn't seem to notice the pale woman. But the pale woman noticed her. And the pale woman smiled. Suddenly, the rat didn't like that smile.

The pale woman approached Daphne. "Have you lost something, dear?" she said. "Perhaps I can help you find it."

Daphne looked up and trained her flashlight on the woman. "Oh! Hi! I'm searching for a big white rat . . ." Daphne's voice died in her throat as she stared up at the other woman's face. From his low vantage point, the rat couldn't see what Daphne saw. But he could see Daphne's expression—one of quickly dawning horror.

Something terrible was about to happen, the rat sensed. He readied himself to jump on the pale woman's back, to give Daphne time to run away. But before he could move from his crevice, the rat heard a loud creak from the balcony above him. He felt his fur pinned back as a large falling object displaced the air around the stoop. A man wearing a long gray coat, hat, and muffler landed, catlike, on the sidewalk. The medicinal odor the rat had been following was suddenly very strong.

The pale woman turned toward the newcomer. She bared her fangs, and her face was not nearly so beautiful as it had been only moments before. But the man in the long coat moved faster than anyone the rat had ever seen. He plunged something into the woman's neck, something shiny and sharp, the size of a human index finger. And the rat suddenly remembered where he'd last seen this strange figure—in a nearby alleyway, doing almost exactly the same thing to another pale woman.

The dried-flower woman slumped to the sidewalk as soon as the man withdrew the object from her neck. Daphne hadn't moved. Frozen in her half crouch, she stared up at the strange man. "This creature won't hurt you," the man said. "She won't harm anyone ever again." *That voice,* the rat thought—it was even more familiar than the acrid scents swirling out of his clothing.

Daphne still didn't say anything. She stared up at the man with eyes as terrified as they'd been before his sudden arrival. Maybe more so. "You have nothing to fear from me, miss," the man said. He offered her his black-gloved hand. In response, Daphne dropped her flashlight. Her eyes rolled up in her head, her eyelids drooped and flickered, and her body went slack. She crumpled onto the sidewalk next to the pale woman. Was this some kind of game humans played, the rat wondered? A copying game? It didn't look fun, or comfortable.

He waited to see what the man would do. The rat had no fear that the man would harm Daphne, unlike the woman. The man glanced up and down the street. His gaze came to rest on the crevice where the rat hid, as if his eyes were magnets and the rat were a big lump of iron. The rat couldn't see those eyes, because they were covered by dark glasses, yet he felt the force of that stare. The rat wondered whether the man would come closer. Perhaps then the rat would remember why the man was so familiar. But the man didn't come any closer. He leaned down and picked up the pale woman as if she weighed less than a feather pillow. Then he vanished around the corner, his legs moving so swiftly they were little more than a blur.

The rat wanted to follow the man. Hungry as he was for brisket, he was hungrier for clear memories, for knowledge of his past life. But he didn't want to leave Daphne asleep on the sidewalk, all alone. There might be other pale women in the French Quarter, eager to do frightful things to a young woman who couldn't run away.

The rat climbed onto Daphne's chest, rising and falling with shallow breathing, and gently crawled forward until his muzzle was near her face. Then he licked her cheek and chin with his sandpapery tongue until she murmured and moved her head from side to side.

He jumped off her shoulder when she made an effort to sit up, then hid behind a parked car's tire. "Oh God . . ." were the first words that spilled from her trembling lips. Eyes large and damp, she looked around her, jerking her head with the nervousness of a bird surrounded by unseen but hissing snakes. She grabbed her flashlight from the ground. Her hand hesitated an instant above the envelope the pale woman had dropped, but then she grabbed that, too.

"Oh God, oh God, oh God—"

She ran toward the nearest well-lit, open business, a bar a block and a half down.

The rat followed.

FIFTEEN

The phone. Lying open on his car's hood, where he'd let it slip from his sweating fist, Jules's cell phone buzzed, tapping against the metal like a tiny Bojangles. He was breathing so hard from running after the car thieves that he almost hadn't heard it.

Was it the realtor lady calling back? Jules realized he hadn't finished their conversation. He wasn't in any mood to speak with her now, even though he realized that her assertion that Doc Landrieu was still alive meant he'd have to talk with her, sooner rather than later. Might as well get it over with. He wiped the sickly sweat from his forehead, slowed his breathing to a moderate pant, and pressed the Talk button.

"Hello? Doosh—Duchon here."

"Jules? Oh thank God I've reached you! You've got to come get me!"

It wasn't the realtor. "Daphne?" He slumped against the Cadillac's bumper. "This—this better be real important, sweetheart. Like, 'I caught the rat' important. You're callin' at one helluvah time."

"Jules, I'm so scared. I've never been so scared my whole life."

She *did* sound scared. Even with the phone's lousy reception and what sounded like a boisterous crowd in the background, her fear was unmistakable. "What's the matter? What happened?"

"I was chasing the rat through the Quarter, and this horrible woman—she—she was one of you!"

"Whadda you mean, 'one of me'?" Daphne had just done the impossible. She'd taken his mind completely off his car. "She was a vampire?"

"She looked beautiful at first. But then she smiled, and her smile got wider and wider and *wider,* until she didn't look like anything human anymore, and then I saw those *teeth*—"

"Did she hurt you? Bite you?"

"No. This man, he leaped from somewhere high, and he stuck this thing, I think it was a hypodermic, in her neck. It happened so fast—he moved so fast, and then he said something, and then I fainted . . ."

The vampire mutilator. It had to be. Daphne had seen the vampire mutilator. "Where are you?"

"I'm at this bar. The Good Friends Bar. It's on Dauphine Street, I think. Wait a second, I'll ask for the address—"

"It's okay. I know where it is. Stay there, okay? Assumin' my car still starts, I'll be there in fifteen minutes. Otherwise, I'll get a cab and maybe be there in a half hour. Don't go outside."

"I won't. I promise. Just be fast, okay?"

"I'll do my best, sweetheart. Hang in there."

He snapped the phone shut and stuck it in his pocket. The night had a different quality now. The city had begun feeling comfortable again; he'd almost been feeling like his old self, the master of his own small, personal domain, even though hardly anything was the same as a year ago. But now, in two very different ways, the night had pimp-slapped him with its invisible tentacles, reminding him that blows could land unseen from any direction. The fact that both a vampiress and the vampire mutilator had gotten so close to Daphne . . . He shivered. Suddenly the whole case had a more visceral, more personal edge.

He slid into the Allante. The steering column's plastic casing was cracked, but no loose wires protruded. Maybe he'd interrupted the thieves before they'd done any serious mechanical damage. He inserted his key in the ignition, crossed his fingers, and turned the key. The powerful Northstar V-8 throbbed to life without a second's hesitation. Thank Varney for that, at least. He leaned across the cabin and pulled the open passenger door shut.

Passenger . . . Preston was still in the coffeehouse. Jules could easily pull away without him. He still wasn't comfortable involving the black vampire in his business, not with the chance that Elisha's crew might be responsible for the mutilation attacks. But dumping Preston now would abrogate Jules's truce with the black vampires, and he couldn't afford that. Besides, so far, Preston hadn't given Jules any reason not to trust him.

He pulled up in front of the coffeehouse and honked. Preston came out, then did a double take worthy of Danny Thomas. "What the hell happened to your car?" he asked through the holes in the roof.

"Had a visit from the Lower Garden District Welcome Committee," Jules said. "Doesn't matter. Get in."

"Doesn't *matter*?" Preston's eyebrows arched as he entered the car and saw the flayed leather upholstery. "Somebody fucked you over, man. You see who did it?"

"Yeah. A pair of punk kids. But we don't have time for that now."

"Why the hell not? We should chase 'em down, drain 'em dry real slow. Show 'em *nobody* fucks with a blood-suckah."

Jules crossed Magazine Street, heading for Camp Street, downtown, and the Quarter. "Forget hunting those punks. We got a bigger fish on our plate. Right now, we're hunting the vampire hunter."

At the Good Friends Bar, they found Daphne huddled on the bar stool farthest from the door. Her shaking fingers clutched a sweating bottle of Barq's root beer. She looked like she'd break it over the head of the first patron who made a move in her direction.

Her small face flooded with relief when she saw Jules squeeze through the front door. "You're here!"

"You okay?"

"Yeah," she said, bravely forcing a smile. But the tiny whimper that escaped her lips betrayed her.

Jules tilted his head toward an empty booth in back. "Let's go talk back there."

Daphne grabbed Jules and buried her face in his padded chest. "It was *horrible,*" she said, her voice muffled. "I was beginning to think all vampires were nice, until I met *her.*"

Jules winced and looked quickly around him. Had anyone overheard? The other patrons appeared well lubricated, and none were close. "*Ixnay* on the *ampirevay* talk," he said in a low voice, "until we're in the booth." He patted her awkwardly on the back, trying to soothe her.

Daphne loosened her grip. She stared warily at Preston, who stood a few feet behind Jules, arms crossed, looking on with no little amusement. "Who's that?"

"That's Preston. He's a friend."

Daphne's eyes grew a little wider. "Is he a vam—a you-know-what?"

"Yeah. The town's crawlin' with us lately." He maneuvered her toward the booth. "Let's go sit."

The semicircular booth near the rest rooms looked like it had been lifted from a defunct Denny's. Dirty white foam puffed from fissures in the red vinyl upholstery like the mashed-potato remnants of some ancient home-style dinner special. The air stank of cheap cigarettes and cheaper beer. Daphne slid in first, keeping the bulk of the table between her and Preston. The table, bolted to the floor, kept Jules from sliding in more than halfway, even though Daphne clearly would've preferred him closer.

"Tell us what you saw," Jules said. "Try not to leave anything out, okay?"

Daphne took a long swig from her Barq's, then wiped her lips with the back of her hand. "I was chasing your special rat. I was *so close*! I almost had him in the service alley by Arnaud's, but then he slipped by me and led me onto Bourbon Street, through the Quarter—"

"Rat?" Preston's eyes squinted with perplexity. "What's she talkin' about?"

Jules waved him off. "It's nothing. Too complicated to go into." He turned back to Daphne. "Forget the rat for now, sweetheart. Where'd you see this, uh, vampire?"

She pointed to the door. "Just up the street. About two blocks from here, on Dauphine. I was crouching down, looking with my flashlight under houses for the, y'know, the rat. I kind of heard somebody walking toward me, and then I heard this woman's voice, asking me if she could help me find whatever I'd lost. I looked up—it sounded like a nice, friendly voice. And she was really pretty—"

"You got a good look at her?" Jules asked. "What'd she look like?"

"White woman?" Preston asked.

"*Very* white," Daphne said. "As white as Jules. And she was wearing a white dress, very short, very low cut."

"You remember her hair color?" Jules asked. "Anything unusual about her face? How tall was she?"

Jules saw Daphne stiffen. He was asking questions too fast. But he felt time slipping away. If the scenario was what he feared, there could be another special delivery of body parts to the High Krewe before dawn.

"She was tall, I think," Daphne said, frowning. "It's hard for me to remember, because I was crouching. But she seemed tall. Hair color? Kind of dirty blond. Her eyebrows were thick. That I remember."

Jules searched his memory. He'd interviewed at least a couple of young women at the High Krewe's complex who'd had dirty-blond hair. Bushy eyebrows? That didn't ring any chimes. But maybe he'd been staring at some other part of her anatomy when he'd been conducting that interview. "You remember what her figure was like? Thin? Busty? Any birthmarks?"

Daphne's lower lip began trembling. "When she opened her mouth . . . so wide . . . all I could look at . . . all I could see—those *teeth*—" She clenched her eyes shut, and when she opened them, they glistened damply. "I'm suh-sorry. I don't know. I think she was skinny, maybe."

Jules patted her hand. The poor kid had been through hell. "How about this guy who attacked her? Where'd he come from?"

"I saw him land behind her. He leaped from up above, a balcony, I guess. He moved so fast. Faster than any normal person could."

Jules noted that remark, and he saw that Preston had, too. "Can you describe him, honey?"

"He—he was tall. Taller than the woman. He wore a long coat and a hat. And his face was covered up by some kind of cloth. Like a scarf or something."

Vampires are always looking to conserve body heat, Jules thought. Or maybe this was just the best disguise this guy could come up with. But a leap from a balcony? Not too many normal humans could manage that without injuring themselves. Preston leaned across the table. "Was this a white guy or a black guy?"

"I—I couldn't tell." She looked at Preston, then back at Jules. "He was all covered up. I think he wore gloves, too. Yes—I'm sure he did."

"You see any of his hair under that hat?" Preston asked. He removed his own hat. "Was it kinky? Processed, like mine? Or straight?"

Daphne's face tightened. "I just—it happened so fast. I wasn't looking at his hair. I was looking at what he did to the woman."

"Tell us about that," Jules suggested.

"He stuck her in the neck with something. It wasn't a knife. I think it was some kind of hypodermic needle."

"So he injected her with something?"

"I think so. It had to be that, because she collapsed so suddenly. She didn't scream or make a sound. I wanted to scream, but I couldn't. It was like there was a gag over my mouth. And then he told me he wouldn't hurt me. And he said something else, too—"

"He talked to you?" Jules asked. "You remember anything about his voice?" He thought about Straussman. Straussman was tall. "Did he have any kinda accent?"

"Did he sound black or white?" Preston asked.

Daphne stared at Preston blankly. "What do you mean?" She looked from him to Jules. "Both of you sound the same to me. Like somebody from New Orleans."

Preston didn't look pleased with this observation. Jules wasn't all that pleased himself. "Well, did he sound like either of us?" Jules asked.

"I—I don't think so. He was wearing that cloth around his face. I couldn't really tell what he sounded like."

"Try your best, sweetheart. This is important. Did he have a foreign accent? German? European?"

"I didn't hear an accent. He sounded . . . plain."

"Plain?"

"Yeah. Like somebody from California, maybe. His voice was kind of deep. He only talked to me a little. Wait"—her face brightened—"I remember what else he said. Something about the woman, the vampire, not being able to hurt anybody ever again."

Preston grunted, smoothed his hair, and placed his Stetson back on his head. "Huh. Think that rules out my posse, Jules. Ain't none of them sound anything like they's from California. You know that as well as I do."

"Guy had a scarf around his mouth," Jules said. "I'm not rulin' out anything or anybody just yet—"

Daphne dug into her jeans pocket. "Here." She handed Jules a bent envelope. "The woman—the vampire—she dropped this. She had it in her hand when she was talking with me. I found it on the sidewalk after I woke up."

Jules opened the envelope. He pulled out a familiar-looking black card with gilt edges and red-embossed lettering. An invitation to Courane L'Enfant's Vampyres and Live Wires Soiree. He handed the card to Preston. "Check this out."

Preston looked at it and smirked. "So he wants some *real* vampires at his party, and not just us. I *knew* this guy was a lot less innocent than he was lettin' on." He stared at the envelope still in Jules's hand. "Hey. There's a name on that."

Jules flipped the envelope over. Printed in red letters that dripped blood was the name Flora Ann Mallory. *Flora.* Jules was certain he'd interviewed a girl named Flora at the High Krewe's compound. And she'd been a dirty blonde. He had a hectic night ahead—the festering red pimple this case represented could come to a head before dawn. And Jules had to get himself in position to squeeze it until it popped.

Jules looked into Preston's eyes. "I know what this guy's gonna do," he said. "I know exactly what he's gonna do, and about when he's gonna do it. I've gotta make a call. We're gonna have to move fast."

He stood up and pulled his phone from his pocket. He punched in the High Krewe's number while pacing in the narrow dark space between the booth and the men's room.

On the fourth ring, someone picked up. "Good evening. This is the Tepes residence." Straussman's voice. Jules checked his watch. Eight minutes past one A.M. At most, forty minutes had passed since Daphne had called him. Enough time for Straussman to have returned home?

"Straussman, it's Jules. We've got us an emergency."

"An emergency, sir?"

Forty minutes since Daphne called. How long before that had she encountered the vampire hunter—five minutes? Ten? Could Straussman have made it from the French Quarter, victim in tow, back to the Jefferson Parish line, stashed his victim somewhere, and returned to his duty station in three-quarters of an hour? Possible, but not likely. He hoped that someone at the house would verify that Straussman had been busy there the past hour. Jules realized how relieved he'd be when he heard that alibi.

"Flora Ann Mallory," Jules said. "She's not there tonight, is she?"

Straussman hesitated before replying. "I have not seen Miss Flora so far this evening, no."

"You'll be seeing her soon. Missing something she shouldn't be missing. Chances are, it'll be later tonight."

"I take it . . . you've learned something, then. For Miss Flora's sake, I hope you're mistaken." The phone was silent for a second. "Let me have you speak to Master Besthoff."

Thirty seconds later, Besthoff came on the line. "Mr. Duchon? I'm told we may have a dire situation developing. Enlighten me."

Jules explained what Daphne had seen, stressing her physical description of Flora Ann. He didn't mention the invitation to L'Enfant's gathering with Flora's name on it. The L'Enfant connection was a rich vein still to be mined. Jules didn't want the High Krewe's elders storming the musician's various mansions before Jules had a chance to dig.

"My child is in terrible danger," Besthoff said, his voice choked with more emotion than Jules was accustomed to hearing from him. "What do you intend to do about it?"

"I've got no way to track him," Jules admitted, scratching the back of his neck. The tension was making his head itch. "No way to prevent . . . what he might be doing to her. But we got an advantage. He doesn't know that we know that he just abducted Flora Ann. We also know that he delivers his, uh, leftovers near your compound, then calls to tell you where to find them. We don't know how long he hangs on to the bodies before he dumps them. But chances are, he's planning to pay your neighborhood a visit sometime tonight. And if we've got people waiting in the places he might go—"

"We will catch this devil. And we will exterminate him so thoroughly, it will be as if none of his ancestors ever drew breath."

Jules winced, picturing what this might entail. "Yeah, that's kinda what I had in mind, too. But before he gets all exterminated and all, you'd better let me interrogate him and find out where he's got all those parts stashed that he removed. Assuming they're still around someplace. So's we can put your young ladies back together again."

"Agreed. You must come here immediately. Is Mr. Richelieu with you?"

"No. Rory went back to California. I've got another associate workin' with me now."

"That is . . . unexpected." Jules could hear the displeasure in Besthoff's voice. "This person is trustworthy?"

Jules looked at Preston and swallowed hard. "Uh, yeah. Of course."

"When will you be here?"

"About a half hour. Forty minutes on the outside. You're gonna station your people in the woods and over in the graveyard?"

"We will speak about that when you arrive. Do not tarry." Besthoff severed the connection.

Jules stuffed the phone back in his pocket. "We gotta motor," he said to Preston. "Out to the High Krewe's mansion." He turned to Daphne. "Sweetheart, we can't take you along with us. I'm gonna have to drop you home, back at Maureen's place."

Daphne's eyes flared like terrified novas. "But, but—you *can't* leave me *alone*!"

"Honey, I don't have time to argue." Jules laid a hand on her shoulder before she could spring from the booth and grab hold of his leg. "You ain't comin' with us. It's too dangerous. Is there anybody you can get hold of who'd come stay with you at the house?"

Daphne's face lost some of its desperation. "Well . . . well, there *might* be Hank. If he hasn't gotten off work at Arnaud's yet . . ."

"You got his phone number?"

Her face tightened to the point of tears again. "No—he tried giving it to me, but he's been coming on to me, and I—I threw it away!"

Shit, Jules thought; *I really don't have time for this* Days of Our Lives *crap right now.* "Look. Arnaud's is just a few blocks away. We'll drive over there. If he's gone, maybe somebody else'll have his number. Okay? Let's move."

Daphne sat awkwardly on Preston's lap during the short ride to Arnaud's. She looked distinctly uncomfortable, her most recent run-in with an unfamiliar vampire having been less than pleasant; but Preston didn't appear to mind. When they reached the restaurant, its windows were already dark. But a block away, Jules spotted his old white Cadillac Fleetwood. Someone was getting in the car. It had to be Hank.

Jules pulled up alongside the Fleetwood. His old car looked pretty darn good, especially now that the Allante had been mauled. He leaned out the window. "Hey, kid. You got a few hours to take care of Daphne here?"

Hank turned around, then did a double take when he saw Jules. "Hey, you're . . . you're that Jules guy. The guy that gave me my car. You come to take it back?"

"Nope. Got another Cadillac, as you can see." Although the notion of taking back his old car wasn't as ludicrous now as it would've been at the beginning of the night. At least the Fleetwood had a hardtop.

"What's this about Daphne?"

Jules leaned back in his seat so Hank could see her. "She had a bad scare a little while ago. Doesn't want to be alone. My partner and I need to go do some business, and we can't take her along. Thought you might sit with her a while. She's got the key to my house."

Hank smiled as though he'd just won the Publisher's Clearing House Sweepstakes. "Well, yeah. I mean, yeah, sure!" Hank stared through the Allante's window at Daphne, his eyes brimming with hopeful expectation. "Daphne, that okay with you? You wanna hang out with me awhile? Take a break from rat chasing?"

Daphne frowned and looked at Jules. But Jules refused to soften. "Yeah, I—I guess," she said. Preston opened the door, and Daphne reluctantly climbed out.

"Take care of her," Jules said, "or—"

"Or you'll come back and haunt my ass. Yeah, I know." Hank waved him off, then turned to Daphne. "Am I glad to see you! You had me scared shitless, y'know, when you didn't come back to the restaurant. I was just about to drive around the Quarter looking for you. . . ."

Jules pulled away. He looked in the rearview mirror and saw Hank slip his arm around Daphne's shoulders, her looking as miserable as a kid whose red balloon had just floated away. Preston chuckled. "Young love," he said. "Gotta love it, man."

Jules picked up speed as soon as he left the Quarter's narrow, car-clogged streets. Besthoff would have a conniption when he saw who Jules had brought along with him. Jules didn't feel so comfortable himself, bringing Preston to the High Krewe's doorstep. But for better or worse, he and Preston had that metaphorical three-foot length of steel chain binding them together. "So you and me, we go back to being Curtis and Poitier," Jules said.

"Yeah," Preston said, reclining his ripped seat and resting his elbow on the open windowsill. "Only difference is, Curtis and Poitier, they spent the whole movie runnin' *away* from trouble. You and me, we runnin' in the opposite direction."

♠

Besthoff eyed Preston coldly, as though Jules had wheeled a cart loaded with decaying sides of beef into his office. "Mr. Duchon," he said with quiet, controlled intensity, "have you taken leave of your senses?"

Jules saw Preston, who radiated defensive hostility, start to respond, but he motioned for him to keep quiet. "Mr. Besthoff, Preston's here to help. I can vouch for that."

Besthoff shook his head slightly, apparently incredulous of the pair standing in front of his desk. "Why have you chosen to associate with this person? Why have you involved him in our affairs? I believed you and the *shvartze nosferatus* to be bitter enemies."

Jules swallowed. "We, uh, well, we *are.* Sorta. But we've got this truce thing going. You remember during World War Two, when the

United States had to work with the Soviet Union against Hitler, and all of a sudden Stalin became sweet ol' Uncle Joe? This is kinda like that, see. I had reasons to go talk with them at their compound, about this investigation—"

"What reasons?" Besthoff said.

Jules squirmed. "Can we go into that later, maybe? We don't have much time. Anyway, I told them about this mutilator. And they realized he could be as much a threat to them as to you guys. That's why Preston's workin' with me." He'd left out big chunks of the story. But there was no way he could spell it all out right now—nor did he want to.

"What I was told," Preston said slowly, making an obvious effort to stay calm, "is to help Jules any way I can catchin' this evil punk and makin' sure he don't cut up any more pretty young ladies. In return, Jules is helpin' me look into some crimes my people be concerned about."

"I do not like this," Besthoff said, having pinned his merciless stare on Jules throughout the exchange. "I do not like this at all. But I concede the fact that we have more urgent issues to deal with. What plans have you formulated for tonight?"

"How many people've you got in the household?" Jules asked.

Besthoff compressed his aristocratic mouth into a thin line. "Originally, there were thirty-two of us, servants included. Now, there are twenty-seven."

Enough to blanket most of the surrounding area with eyes, Jules figured, even if everyone worked in pairs. Which would be essential, given what Daphne had told them about their opponent. "This guy we're after, he's fast, and he's smart. He knocks out his victims with some kinda injection before they can even begin to fight back. There's a good chance, given what we know, that he's a vampire himself. Your people, for safety's sake, they gotta work in pairs. With me and Preston, that's, let's see, fourteen pairs, assumin' somebody stays behind to man the phone. In case, y'know, we miss him somehow, and he calls. We need to have people throughout Metairie Cemetery. That's a big place, maybe six or seven pairs spread out over there. At least one pair to watch your patch of woods. A couple more to keep an eye on the woods linin' the Seventeenth Street Canal outside your property. Then there's all that commercial property nearby on Metairie Road—"

Besthoff shook his head. "I will not expose my youngsters to more danger. I have already alerted the appropriate persons in my household to be ready for your and my instructions."

"How many?" Jules said.

"Fourteen, including myself, Master Krauss, and Master Katz. Master Katz has been . . . rejuvenated since you saw him several nights ago."

Jules ran the numbers in his head. "It's not enough," he said, hating the prospect of another war of wills with Besthoff. Did the High Krewe's leader *want* Jules's investigation to fail? "Look, this could be the best shot we'll ever have at cornering this sucker. You gotta use everything you've got. Have you ever hired a squad of rent-a-cops you'd trust for something like this?"

"Day people?" Besthoff looked dubious. "No. We make every effort to keep the involvement of ordinary humans in our affairs at a bare minimum. You are the first mercenary we have seen fit to hire in almost fifty years."

Guess I should feel honored, Jules thought. *It's like winning the prize, "World's Smartest Moron."* "Look," he said, steeling himself for an argument. If he didn't fight now, he might as well throw in the towel and quit. "I can understand keepin' the girls locked up in the mansion. Aside from those two young men who disappeared almost a month ago—and that might not even be the same guy's work, 'cause they don't fit his pattern—it's the women this mutilator's interested in. But your younger men? Mr. Besthoff, you've *got* to put them out there. Chances are, we won't get this lucky again—"

"I would *not* consider Miss Flora's being brutally abducted as *luck*—"

"You know what I mean. Do any of your people have cell phones? Two-way radios?"

"Straussman may have some radios to help him keep in touch with his staff."

"Then give the radios to your younger men, the ones you're worried about, and you keep one. So the second they see something, they raise you on the line and bring you runnin'."

"There is still too much risk involved—"

Jules slammed his fist down on Besthoff's desk. If he had his normal strength, it would've cracked in two. "The goddamn *risk* is that we let this guy slip through our fingers!" He pictured Daphne, terrified into unconsciousness on a filthy French Quarter sidewalk. "Besthoff, either you gamble all your chips, or I fold my cards and go home. I'll quit this case, and you can find some way to lock the Junior League in their rooms for the next century or two."

Besthoff locked eyes with Jules for several long seconds. Then he did something Jules had never seen him do before. He broke eye contact, staring down at his hands. The elder vampire sighed, so quietly that Jules would've missed it if he hadn't been listening for it. "Very well. I bow to your wisdom in this. I will summon Straussman and tell him to gather all the male members of the household. And I will tell him to bring every radio we have."

SIXTEEN

The marble crypt Jules leaned against was cold and wet. A light rain had fallen while Jules and Preston were in the High Krewe's mansion. A late-season cold front moved through, turning the air clammy, particularly unpleasant for a vampire. Jules wanted to sit down, rest his knees, but the swampy state of the strips of grass between the tombs dictated against that. Instead, he continued crouching low, keeping out of sight as best he was able. He was the same color as the marble crypt, he mused. If he took off all his clothes, he'd probably be invisible. He'd also be one gigantic goose bump.

Jules reran his recent activities through his head. He and Besthoff had given the ten observation teams their instructions. Straussman had gathered six two-way radios to hand out; Jules carried one of them. Jules had managed, as discreetly as possible, to ascertain that Straussman had been busy with Otranto in the blood-farm dormitory during the hour preceding Jules's call to the High Krewe earlier tonight. That was one worry off his mind.

The biggest surprise of the night so far had been seeing Katz. The drooling, senile antique Jules remembered had been replaced by a still-aged but powerful figure, a vampire who looked like he had demolished half the Turkish army back in his prime. Whatever vitamins (or sexual pick-me-ups) Katz was taking, Jules hoped they'd still be available when he reached the ripe old age of eight hundred himself. The rejuvenated Katz had insisted on watching the swath of woods in the front of the High Krewe's property alone, with no partner. Besthoff, not to be upstaged, then took on the responsibility of patrolling the neighboring canal banks on his own. The remaining elder, Krauss, the permanently pubescent one, evidently felt no compulsion for macho competition; he'd willingly partnered with Randolph, his match in stature, if not seniority. Randolph had sneered condescendingly at Jules as he and Krauss drove past on their way to the monied neighborhood that bordered the cemetery. Jules hadn't taken him up on his request to switch loyalties. He wondered what the punk thought about the night's agenda.

Jules and Besthoff had assigned four teams to the cemetery, three staking out the main entrances, and Jules and Preston watching the area near Lieutenant Micholson's tomb, where Alexandra had been left. Preston was hiding behind a church-shaped crypt about fifty yards away. Both he and Jules had a good view of the grassy mound of Micholson's tomb, and they were also in visual contact with each other. Jules glanced over at the church-shaped crypt. Preston wasn't there.

"Hey."

The voice was behind him. Jules jumped almost high enough to impale himself on the closest crypt's spire.

It was Preston. "Whoah—little jumpy, huh?" He grinned.

Jules stifled an urge to explode with profanity. They were on a stakeout; cursing out Preston was a luxury he couldn't afford. As soon as his heart descended from his throat, Jules managed to croak, "What's up?"

Preston wrapped his arms tightly around himself. "It's cold as fuckin' Antarctica, man." Preston's fringed buckskin jacket didn't look very thick, and its collar was wide open. "Cold as Elisha's titties after you offed her brother. Can't say I really miss ol' Malice, though. Dude was a pain in my ass big time, even if he did bring me in the life. Who brought you in?"

"Maureen," Jules said. "She made Malice, too."

Preston's grin faded. "Oh. Well, like I said before, I'm sorry 'bout that whole mess. I wasn't in on that hit. That was a Malice thing." After a few seconds, though, his grin took on new life. "Y'know what, though? That makes Maureen, like, my 'grandmother,' right? And you . . . holy shit, man. You's my *uncle.* Ain't *that* a fuckin' kick in the head?"

Jules thought about it. Sure. Preston was absolutely right. When Maureen had crossed the racial divide, in a certain way she'd dragged Jules right along with her. And assuming that Malice had made all the other black vampires in New Orleans, either directly or second generation, Jules was a blood relation to all of them, too, just as he was to Straussman.

Jules laughed. Fate could sure throw some mighty wicked curve balls. "Yeah, well, just don't call me 'Uncle Tom,' okay?"

"Don't worry. You don't qualify."

"Hey, thanks for not goin' ballistic on Besthoff before. Not that he didn't have it comin'."

Preston pulled his jacket more tightly around him. Jules wished he would've thought to order coffees to go at the Rue de la Course. Better yet, filled a thermos. Doodlebug would've thought of that. " 'Sallright," Preston said. "Rich dudes like that, I expect the attitude. Dude's from where? Bulgaria? Prob'ly never saw a black man in his life before he came over here."

"Yeah, but he's been over here since before the Civil War."

Preston smirked. "Yeah? Well that explains the attitude, don't it?" He rubbed his hands together briskly, then looked around him at the long rows of crypts glowing whitely in the moonlight. "Hey, 'Unc,' whadda you think the chances are this mutilator dude's a vampire?"

"Pretty good chance, I think." Jules wished he could still turn into a bat; a high vantage point would make watching their section of the cemetery much more efficient. He could ask Preston to do it, but he hardly had the heart to ask his shivering companion to strip off his clothes. In this one instance, his insulating layers of fat gave him an advantage. "The way he's been able to overpower three vampires, even if they were all women who'd never done anything more strenuous than paint their toenails . . . he can't be just a normal guy."

"So whadda you think's his motivation?"

"I dunno. Could be a psycho, maybe. Or if he's a vampire, he's new to town, and he's tryin' to wipe out some of the competition."

"If that's the case, though, wouldn't he be goin' after us black vampires, instead? Them High Krewe women, they get all the blood they need from them retards, like you told me."

"Yeah. Good point." *Huh.* Preston had just shot down a theory that would've steered suspicion away from him and his gang. More evidence that Preston wasn't scheming. Jules realized that ever since he and Preston had responded to Daphne's distress call, his feelings toward the black vampire had subtly shifted. He hadn't noticed until this instant, but he no longer harbored any gut suspicion that Preston was connected with the mutilations. He was beginning to trust him.

"You up to fightin' another vampire?" Preston asked. "You handled yourself pretty decent when you fought Malice. That body-splittin' trick was pretty slick. Just try not to do midgets this time. Hey, you think I should look for some stakes for us, just in case?"

Actually, Jules wasn't up to battling a fellow vampire. But he wasn't about to reveal this to Preston. He was starting to trust the black vampire a little, but he sure didn't want word of his disability getting back to Preston's clan. "I'll do just fine," Jules said, forcing as much false heartiness as he could manage. "Look, I hate to ask this, you practically freezin' your pecker off and all, but would you mind changin' into a bat and doin' some recon? I could hunt up some wood for stakes while you're flyin' around."

Preston's eyebrows arched. He slapped his arms, trying to get his blood flowing faster. "How 'bout *you* do the bat thing and *I* go look for wood? You look a whole lot less frigid than me, man."

"Yeah, but with this belly of mine, flyin' ain't exactly my specialty—"

Jules stopped talking. He'd heard something. A crunching sound. He gestured for Preston to be quiet. He heard it again. From his expression, Preston heard it, too. Footsteps on gravel.

Jules and Preston crouched low. They crept around opposite sides of the tomb to where they could both look down the corridor of grave monuments.

Jules saw a figure walking toward them, about two hundred feet away. He was tall, and he was carrying something almost as big as himself. After a few seconds, Jules could see the figure was a man dressed in a cloak or cape. The object he was carrying was a woman. Her long hair billowed in the breeze, whipping against his cloak in mute protest.

The figure approached the grassy knoll of Micholson's tomb. Jules gestured to Preston that he should circle around the tomb's left side. Jules would circle around from the right. His chest felt hollow. He took three deep breaths, but still felt starved of oxygen. At least Preston was here. But Jules found himself wishing for Doodlebug.

He heard a rough crinkling sound, like a tarpaulin being unfurled.

Then he heard a voice. Not a deep voice like Daphne had described, but definitely male. "Count to five, baby," the voice said, "and Count Shlongula's gonna give rigor mortis a good name . . ."

Jules heard another sound. A zipper, very clearly being unzipped. *The sicko. The sick fuck.* Anger and revulsion overwhelmed the butterflies in his stomach. Jules abandoned stealth and began running around the mound. From the staccato footsteps on the other side, Preston was doing the same.

He saw the woman. She was lying on a plastic sheet on the grass. The man was on his knees between her legs, his slacks down, his cape shielding the backs of his legs. His hands clutched the sides of his red boxer shorts. They froze as soon as he saw Jules and Preston on either side of him.

The woman's eyes snapped open. They darted from Preston to Jules. "Nick! Fuck! *Fuck!* You fucker! You *swore* to me all the caretakers were gone after midnight!"

Jules stared down at them. He saw familiar pressed white powder, eyeliner, black lipstick, and the pewter Egyptian ankhs purchased in some trendy French Quarter Goth market. Wannabes. Teenage vampire wannabes, about to screw each other in a graveyard.

The kid in the cape looked paralyzed. He tried to say something but could only manage little high-pitched croaks. Jules was suddenly grateful he hadn't located a stake for Preston—the black vampire looked like he'd happily run the kid through.

Jules glared down at them. "Why aren't you two at the lakefront, fuckin' in the back of an SUV like all the other kids? Get outta here before my partner and me show you what a *real* vampire can do—"

The two-way radio stuffed into Jules's jacket pocket squawked. The two kids took advantage of the interruption to bolt, leaving their tarp on the grass, the boy stumbling as he pulled his pants back up around his waist.

Jules ignored them. He removed the radio from his pocket and pressed the Receive button. "Duchon. Your plan failed." Besthoff. Even through the static, Jules could hear—and feel—his fury. "The demon called the house. He's left us something in the grassy field behind Charvet's Tree Nursery, on Metairie Road. Get over there."

Jules's heart sank. The tree nursery was a third of a mile from their closest sentries, just four blocks from the Seventeenth Street Canal. If only he'd had more people . . . He pressed the button that would let him talk. "We'll be right there" was all he could think to say.

They hustled to Jules's car. He'd parked it by the side of the cemetery, in a dark spot beneath low-hanging tree branches. Jules felt water soak through the bottom of his pants after he sat down. He'd forgotten all about the tears in his roof. Damn rain. Damn, damn rain.

Less than three minutes later, they drove onto the dirt road that led to the field behind the tree nursery. Two late model Mercedes sedans were already parked at the end of the road. Jules got out of the Allante. The field, bordered by a barrier of pine trees, had recently been mowed. The air was fragrant with the scent of damp, freshly cut grass.

Besthoff, Krauss, and Katz were there. Along with Straussman and Otranto, they stood in a semicircle around a large, square object near the edge of the field, close to the trees. Jules and Preston walked across the field. Pieces of wet grass stuck to Jules's shoes and the hems of his trousers. He wished he were somewhere else. Anywhere else.

The large, square object was a wooden crate. Jules didn't like the looks of it. A lot of unpleasant things could be stored in a crate that size.

"Open it," Besthoff said.

Jules halted in front of the crate. He and Preston completed the circle. "Have you looked . . . ?"

"Open it," Besthoff repeated.

The crate was about three feet square. Its lid was nailed shut. Jules wondered whether his fingers had strength enough to dig into the wood and yank the lid open. As if he could read Jules's thoughts, Straussman handed him a tire iron, probably from the trunk of one of the Mercedes. Jules worked the iron's thin edge into the gap at the top of the crate and leaned his weight on the lever. The lid burst from the crate, one nail snapping like a firecracker.

Jules looked inside. Time seemed to bend and drag, as if he were caught in a nightmare. The top of the crate was filled with wads of bubble wrap. Jules pulled it up and let it fall onto the grass. Beneath the bubble wrap, sitting on a cushion of more bubble wrap, were two long white legs, folded at the knees, and two slender white arms. They cradled a head with closed eyes and flowing dirty-blond hair.

Jules heard someone retching. He looked up. It was Otranto. Blood-retch was much nastier than food-retch; the servant looked as if he was expelling his own lungs. But the change that overcame Katz was far worse. The vampire elder's sharply chiseled features began to dissolve into formless chaos. He leaned over the crate, squeezing the wood until it burst to powder, then continued to squeeze until his fingernails drew rivulets of blood from his own palms. He shrieked, his eyes transfixed on the torsoless limbs and head, still suffused with a frozen, undead life. The louder he screamed, the faster his youth and vitality melted away. Until he devolved again into the hunched, frail fossil Jules had met two nights earlier.

"De chul-drun," he sobbed. "De chul-drun . . ."

Krauss and Straussman helped him to one of the Mercedes. As soon as Otranto stopped retching, he refastened the lid on the crate, picked it up, and carried it to the trunk of the other car.

Jules was left standing in the field with Preston and Besthoff. The vampire elder had not uttered a sound since ordering Jules to open the crate.

"Give me four more nights," Jules said. "Four more nights to find out what's going on and nail this guy."

After a few seconds of explosive silence, Besthoff said, "Give me one reason why I should."

"I got a lead I need to follow. In four nights, there's gonna be a big party in the city. More than just an ordinary party. I think some of your youngsters are plannin' on being there. I think there's more to their constant sneakin' out than just boredom. I think if I can find out what's drivin' them, what's behind their activities in town, I can figure out who benefits from choppin' them up. And if I can figure that out, then we can take the fight to him."

Besthoff's stony expression remained unmoved. "You do not offer me much fresh meat, Mr. Duchon. Your behavior thus far has been less than satisfactory. You have neglected to provide me with regular reports of your progress, or with evidence of any progress whatsoever. You have involved yourself in matters outside the assignment, distracting yourself, perhaps making tonight's debacle more likely. You have shown an appalling lack of judgment in choosing to involve certain outsiders in our affairs—"

"Hey, man, why don't you cut him some slack," Preston said. "Jules had the right idea tonight. If you hadn't of shorted him on people, maybe it woulda worked—"

Besthoff whirled on Preston, eyes livid. "Be *silent*! You have no standing in this, less than the black mud beneath my shoe!"

"Euro-trash, you can suck my muddy black dick—"

Jules came between them, an immense fleshy wall. "Preston, zip it up. Please." Keeping the black vampire behind him, Jules turned to Besthoff. "Okay. So maybe I ain't been producin' like you want. I'm man enough to admit I ain't no expert detective. But what's your alternative? Cannin' me, screwin' me over, and then screwin' over Doodlebug to top things off? What does that do for you? Make you feel good? Make you feel in control of somethin', maybe. 'Cause right now, you don't feel in control of much of anything. But after makin' yourself feel good, you'll still be stuck with the same problem you got right now. You dragged me into this. But now I got reasons of my own for wantin' to see this thing through. So what do you lose, givin' me four more nights?"

Clouds drifted over the moon, leaving Besthoff's face masked in shadow. "Four more nights, then," he said. "Show me results, Mr. Duchon. Or I will show you results that you will not like." He walked past them to the remaining Mercedes, the one whose trunk held portions of Flora Ann's body. Otranto opened the rear door for him, and they drove off without a backward glance.

"Muthuh-fuckuh," Preston muttered, watching the sedan go.

"Can't disagree." Of course, under the vampiric definition of the term, Jules had been one, himself. And he prayed to be one again real soon. "Hey, Preston. Not that it was a good idea, you gettin' all huffy with Besthoff just now. But I wanna let you know, I appreciated the sentiment."

"No problem. Sorry things didn't fall your way tonight."

"Yeah. Me, too. Good thing there's a tomorrow night."

They started walking back to the Allante. Jules heard a twig snap behind him. "Regretting your decision?" a familiar voice said.

Jules turned around. Randolph emerged from the darkness of the pine trees. He wore the same fedora and archaic pinstripe suit Jules had seen him sporting two nights ago in the billiards room. He tossed two broken halves of a tree branch onto the grass and smiled.

How long was he standin' there? Jules asked himself. *Long enough to see the body? Long enough to hear me tell Besthoff about my headin' for L'Enfant's party four nights from now?* "Yeah. Maybe I am regrettin' not takin' you up on your offer." Just as Besthoff had nothing to lose by giving Jules more rope, Jules had nothing to lose by seeming to throw in with Randolph now. Everything hinged on his discovering the youngsters' motives. Jules would have no trouble justifying to Besthoff a temporary alliance with the arrogant young vampire. "The offer still open? I'm sick as hell of eatin' Besthoff's shit. I'm willin' to bet whatever you serve up'll taste better."

Randolph smirked. "Sorry. Café's closed to you. It's been rented out. Private party. Proper attire required."

Jules stepped closer. He towered over the younger man. "You're makin' a big mistake, Randolph. You can't handle this mutilator on your own. He'll slice you up as easy as he did Flora Ann. And Alexandra."

Randolph flinched at the mention of Alexandra's name. But he quickly recovered his composure. "Obviously, you're the expert on this bastard. You proved it tonight." He laughed. "Actually, what you proved is you're a gone pecan. Yesterday's news, ink I can rub off my fingers."

"What's that supposed to mean, you sawed-off little punk?"

Randolph held his ground. "Don't flatter yourself by thinking you can get involved in my business, fat man. It's beyond you. *I'm* beyond you. I'll take care of this mutilator in my own good time. And if he picks off a few more High Krewe floozies before I get him—so what? Besthoff and Katz, they made the mistake of getting emotionally involved. What they forget, and what I *never* forget, is when it comes to vampires, you can always make more. And when you make 'em yourself, you get to be the boss. So long as you've got the smarts. 'Fraid that leaves you out, Duchon."

Preston grunted, visibly impressed by the diminutive vampire's chutzpah. "Jules, I say I take an arm and a leg, and you take an arm and a leg. And we pull until this little dude's wishbone snaps."

"Let him go," Jules said.

"First smart thing you've done tonight," Randolph said, not looking the least bit concerned by Preston's glowering. "Remember. Stay out of my way." He turned and vanished back into the patch of woods, whistling the "Baby Elephants' March."

"So that's the high-an'-mighty High Krewe," Preston mumbled. "Nervy buncha fucks. Got a mind to find me a big knife and start carvin' 'em up myself."

Jules let the comment go. He didn't want Preston to realize just how much he shared the sentiment. Something bothered him, something more than Besthoff's high-handedness and Randolph's infuriating efforts at being superior and mysterious. Had the mutilator just gotten lucky tonight, picking a place to dump his crate where no sentries happened to be posted? Or had someone in the mansion tipped him off?

Pictures of body parts floated in Jules's mind like pieces of a child's puzzle. They twisted and twirled until their matched edges locked together. Legs. Arms. Torso. Was the mutilator a collector of some kind? A puzzle builder? If so, all he was missing now was a head.

SEVENTEEN

The following night was about five degrees warmer, and drier, too. Considering that Jules might be standing out in the woods for hours, and Preston had to expose himself buck naked at least twice without a protective layer of fur, this was definitely a good thing.

They'd taken up a surveillance position about fifty yards from the northeast corner of the High Krewe's walled compound, where they could see both the front gate and two sides of the complex. Jules had decided their best plan of action would be to tail whichever of the young vampires left the compound, and then hopefully learn what was drawing them to the city. The possibility existed, too, that whoever left the mansion for the city would attract unwelcome attention—and Jules and Preston would make every effort to be in position to intercept the interceptor.

Jules shifted against the trunk of an oak tree and tried to get more comfortable. He fiddled with the night-vision binoculars Preston had brought (Malice had loved military toys, Preston explained, and the black vampires' compound was home to an extensive collection of exotic military-surplus items). They worked amazingly well. Jules scanned the forest floor, coming across a pair of squirrels working on the next generation of forest rodents. He estimated he was able to see things in the dark about as well as he had in his wolf form.

A few yards above him, Jules heard the leathery fluttering of bat wings. Preston must be thirsty again. Jules hadn't forgotten the coffee tonight. Their first stop on the way over here had been at a CC's Coffeehouse. He'd purchased a Krups thermos to keep the java hot. Jules unscrewed the stainless-steel thermos and removed a wide-mouthed plastic cup from Preston's duffel bag. He put the cup on the ground and filled it about half full with steaming coffee.

He heard Preston land. Just for fun, Jules trained the night-vision binoculars on his partner. He got a certain amount of twisted enjoyment from seeing Preston so much smaller and further down on the evolutionary ladder. The bat partially folded his wings and half shuffled, half waddled to the cup, using the tips of his wings as balancing struts. He looked like a little old man wearing a black cape and using two canes. Now came the money shot—no matter how many times he watched this, Jules would never get tired of seeing it. The bat didn't drink like a dog or a cat would; bats lived most of their lives hanging upside down in caves, Jules reasoned, where water condensed on the ceiling near their feet and ran down their bodies to their waiting mouths. Preston plunged his head into the coffee cup, tilting the cup and spilling most of the dark liquid on his wings and fur. Then he stuck out his incredibly long, dexterous tongue and licked the coffee off himself. It was one way to keep warm, Jules figured.

As soon as the bat was dry of the last drop, he flew off again. Although Jules couldn't follow Preston's entire flight pattern with the binoculars, he knew his partner was circling the walls of the High Krewe's compound, searching for any signs of persons (or animals) exiting on the sly. Jules was curious how the youngsters managed their escapes. Ever since the first mutilation attack, the compound's ramparts had been lined with cameras. These cameras wouldn't pick up a vampire, but they would register a vampire's clothes. And Jules was pretty sure the youngsters weren't going into the city naked.

Jules checked his watch. It was 10:37 P.M.; they'd been watching the compound just over two hours. If someone from inside were planning to make a break for it, they'd probably do so soon, before too much of the night was lost.

Jules began unscrewing the thermos to serve himself. But just then, he heard a loud rustling in the tree branches high overhead. Acorns and bits of broken branches bounced off his Vitalis-stiffened hair. Preston was signaling him. Something was happening inside the compound.

Jules scanned the tops of the walls with his binoculars. He hoped this wasn't a false alarm. Even if tonight was a little warmer than last night, a chill had begun creeping into his century-old bones. Something flew above the ramparts, traveling so fast it might've been shot out of a cannon. A few seconds later, he heard it land well behind him, crashing through the canopy of branches and landing with a muffled thud.

Jules took the glasses away from his face. The moon was bright enough for him to spot anything else like that heading his way. Sure enough, he heard a distant grunt from behind the walls, and then a second package soared above the ramparts in a high, long arc. As best Jules could see, it was roughly cubical, about the size of a stuffed backpack. It traveled almost the same path as the other package. Then Jules heard other sounds—high-pitched beeps, coming from about where the objects would've landed. Beacons to help the tosser find his belongings?

More acorns fell on Jules's head. Preston was signaling him to pay attention to the compound again. Jules heard, very faintly, the sounds of multiple wings flapping rapidly, desperately. Bats wouldn't be very visible even in good moonlight, so Jules resorted to his binoculars again. His expectations were borne out when two large bats rose from behind the ramparts. Their ascent looked erratic, and Jules soon saw why—they shared the weight of a package in their claws, and it forced them to fly too close together, their wing beats brushing against each other.

Why hadn't they just tossed whatever was in this package with the other stuff? Maybe this thing was fragile, whereas the other stuff had been crushable—clothing, maybe? Sure—they couldn't fly with their clothes on, and tossing their clothing deep into the woods was one way to evade the cameras.

The bats were almost overhead now. Jules figured they'd be looking for the packages that had landed behind him. He didn't want to be cut off from his car, so he quickly scooped up Preston's duffel bag and the thermos and headed as quietly as he could toward Metairie Road, where he'd parked. He hoped the two bats' attentions were riveted on staying aloft with their burden, and they wouldn't notice him below.

The beeping grew louder as Jules hurried toward the road. He almost tripped over one of the backpacks. He was tempted to look inside, see if it held an old-fashioned pinstripe suit, but he figured he'd see who the bats were soon enough. Jules moved as quickly as he could, trying not to break too many branches in his rush to his car. When he paused for a second to get his bearings in the dark, he heard the faint rustling of wings above and behind him. They were still looking for a break in the tree canopy to descend through. Jules would lose sight of them once he reached the Allante, but he wasn't too concerned; if they were heading into the city, Metairie Road was the only way to go. He'd latch onto them. And if he somehow lost them, Preston would provide a second set of eyes overhead.

The Allante was parked in a shadowy clearing fifty feet off the access driveway that led into the High Krewe's property. Jules might've scratched up the Cadillac's paint backing into the clearing, but considering what the rest of the car currently looked like, he wasn't too bummed out about that. He wasn't sure whether the youngsters would risk taking one of the compound's vehicles or whether they'd have a cab pick them up, so he'd positioned his car to be able to follow them whatever they did.

The inside of his car smelled faintly nasty. Some of the carpet had gotten soaked with last night's rain, Jules figured, and a hint of mildew was beginning to overpower the scent of tufted leather. He glanced over at the big silver roll of duct tape that Preston had brought. Later, whenever they'd find themselves with a few spare minutes, Jules would need to patch up his convertible top.

Headlights flashed on Metairie Road. Jules noticed a Town Car limousine, long, black, and sleek, heading out from the city. It coasted to a crawl, then made a U-turn onto the tree-shaded swale that fronted the High Krewe's acreage. Jules cranked his own ignition but didn't turn on his headlights, not yet.

Two figures emerged from the woods. Both carried a backpack. One figure, the one wearing a hat, also carried a second package. The hat was the tip-off—it had to be Randolph. A car passed, and its headlights briefly illuminated the other figure's pale skin and long amber hair. This was most likely Pearl, Randolph's "silly cunt," tagging along. Randolph opened the limousine's door. Jules waited to see whether he'd let his female companion get in first. He didn't; he handed her his backpack and the other package and climbed in himself. No big surprise—Jules hadn't expected the runt to be a gentleman.

As soon as the woman closed the door, Jules pulled out of the clearing. He didn't turn on his headlights until he reached Metairie Road. The limousine was already two blocks ahead, moving at a good clip, heading toward Canal Street.

Jules heard an ominous buzz coming from his dashboard. His digital gauge display flickered briefly, then returned to its full brightness. Some water must've gotten into the dashboard, probably through the big gaping hole the punks had left when they'd ripped out his stereo. A bigger concern than his strobing speedometer was how well Preston was keeping up. Jules and the limousine were zipping along at close to forty miles per hour. How fast could a bat fly?

Jules caught up to the limousine at a stoplight at the Canal Street intersection. A small crowd of commuters huddled close together beneath the bus shelter at the corner. When the light changed and Jules turned the corner, he glanced quickly at their faces. Puffy, tired, mainly black; most were trying to get home from jobs cleaning downtown hotel rooms or slapping together take-out orders of Goodfeller's Fried Catfish. This had been a profitable corner for Jules, back in his cab-driving nights, back when he'd go trolling for workers too tired or frustrated to wait for the bus anymore.

Traffic was thicker on Canal Street than it had been on Metairie Road. The limo slowed to thirty. Jules slowed to twenty-five and let a car get between him and the big Lincoln. Hopefully Preston could catch his breath now.

Jules passed Doc Landrieu's street. So his old boss might still be around and kicking . . . Jules made himself a mental note not to let that appointment with the realtor dangle much longer. Memories of his ex-employer's patrician face mingled in his mind with the faces of those bus passengers waiting at the corner. Those had been the kind of people Doc Landrieu spent his whole career worrying about, the people he'd hated seeing wheeled into his morgue on a police stretcher. Doc Landrieu had worked for decades trying to find a permanent solution to Jules's hunger for blood. He never found it. That failure, and his being voted out of office, negating his ability to satisfy Jules with the blood of fresh corpses, had been the biggest disappointments of Amos Landrieu's life.

Traffic slowed even further. Three river-bound lanes narrowed to two, then one, as construction on the soon-to-be-resurrected Canal Street streetcar line gobbled up more of the roadway. Maybe after they brought back the old streetcar line, Jules mused, they'd bring back all the big stores that had abandoned Canal Street in the last twenty years—D. H. Holmes, Krauss's, Maison Blanche, Godchaux's. *Sure they will—when pigs fly.* Maybe when he got his powers back, he'd try changing himself into a winged pig, just for the hell of it.

They passed beneath the I-10 overpass, the unofficial gateway to downtown. Jules slowed again to let himself fall two cars behind the stretch Lincoln. The limo turned onto Chartres Street, heading into the Quarter. There wasn't much chance Jules could lose the huge vehicle in the Quarter's grid of narrow one-way streets. The hairiest situation facing him, if the two young vampires were dropped off here, would be finding a parking spot before they disappeared.

Out of the corner of his eye, Jules saw the red-neon sign that beckoned horny visitors to Jezebel's Joy Room. He tried not to think about Maureen, but he couldn't help it. How was the beer-stained old dive holding up now that its star attraction was gone? He wasn't doing so hot without her. If Jezebel's business was off as much as his spirits were, the place was in sorry shape.

The Lincoln turned onto St. Louis Street, just beyond the old Wildlife and Fisheries building, now surrounded by construction scaffolding. Jules followed. At the next corner, the limo turned again, this time onto Royal Street. Halfway up the block, in front of Brennan's restaurant, it pulled up to the curb in a no-parking zone.

Jules slowed to a crawl and searched frantically for a parking spot. The sidewalk in front of the Wildlife and Fisheries building was blocked off by a construction fence. All the legal spots on the block were occupied, and the temporary access space the limo had pulled into was zealously guarded by a maitre d' standing just inside the restaurant's etched-crystal doors.

Pearl and Randolph climbed out of the Lincoln; Jules could clearly see it was them. He drove past the limo at normal speed, counting on its tinted windows to shield him from being noticed. What now? He couldn't turn the corner without losing sight of them. And there was nowhere to park on this next block, either. Antique stores, a photography museum, the Eighth District police station . . . He checked his rearview mirror for the two young vampires. They hadn't gone into the restaurant. They'd walked to the corner and were crossing the street, coming toward him. He couldn't see their faces in the mirror, but he could see their clothes. And that damn Jimmy Cagney hat.

He'd have to park illegally. His heart sagged—even that looked impossible. The sidewalks were blocked with cast-iron hitching posts. The only places the sidewalks weren't blocked were directly in front of and just beyond the police station, where the cops usually stashed their patrol cars. One cop space was empty. This was going to be a hundred-buck parking ticket for sure. He'd be lucky to avoid getting towed. But there was no way around it, unless he could manage to fold the Allante up and stick it in his pocket. He maneuvered partway onto the sidewalk, leaving just enough space in the road for a Caprice taxicab to creep by.

Randolph and Pearl stood directly across Royal Street, staring in the window of an antiques emporium. Damned good thing there was so much in that display window to draw their attention. Jules crouched down in his seat as low as he could, which wasn't very low. The pair walked an additional half block, then stopped in front of a narrow storefront. Its dimly lit window was crammed with cuckoo clocks and paintings of plump, demure nudes in gilded frames. Jules read the store's sign. J. Wiltz & Sons, Antiques & Fine Art. Randolph, still holding the wrapped package beneath his arm, pressed a buzzer next to the door. A light came on in the back. A diminutive elderly man, even shorter than Randolph, let the two vampires come inside, then took a moment to relock the door behind him.

Something landed on the roof of Jules's car, causing the damaged canvas top to bulge inward. Judging from the sound of tiny feet scurrying for purchase, it was probably Preston. Jules was relieved his partner hadn't gotten left behind. He grabbed Preston's duffel bag and got out of the car, taking care not to slam the door too loudly.

Sure enough, there was a bat sitting on the Allante's roof. The bat looked expectantly at Jules, then chittered and hopped up and down. Jules found himself wishing for the kind of telepathic communication he'd shared with Doodlebug when they'd both become bats together. But until Preston returned to his human form, Jules would have to guess his partner's wishes. He laid his forearm on the roof to see what Preston would do. The bat quickly hopped onto his arm and climbed his jacket sleeve to Jules's shoulder. *Good thing this is the Quarter,* Jules thought. *Nobody'll blink twice at a man using a bat for his parrot.*

Carrying the duffel bag, Jules backed into a darkened doorway alcove. From here, he could watch the entrance of the antiques emporium, hopefully without being seen. "They went inside J. Wiltz and Sons," Jules whispered to the bat. "But I guess you saw that on your way down. It's definitely Randolph and Pearl we're dealin' with here." He leaned down and slid the duffel bag between his legs, behind him, into the dark alcove made even darker by Jules's shadow. "I wanna see what they're doin' in there, but I can't go up to the window and look myself. Change back and get dressed."

Jules felt the bat climb off his shoulder and down his pants leg. As soon as the bat was behind him, Jules spread open the sides of his jacket like a cape, completely blocking the back of the alcove from any passers-by. He felt a quick frigid sensation and sucking in of air, as if a doorway into a dimension of subzero vacuum had opened for a millisecond. A brief blast of heat followed (friction from the accumulation of mass?), along with the squishy *shglorp!* noise Jules had come to know so well while practicing his own shape changes. Then Jules sensed a man-sized presence close behind him. "Welcome back," he muttered.

"Feel like I just ran a goddamn marathon," Preston complained, unzipping his bag. "*Flapped* a marathon, more like it. You had to drive so damn fast?"

"Couldn't help it. Maybe next time we'll tail a mule-drawn cart, and you can take it easy."

"Hell with that. Next time, *you* be the bat."

Thirty seconds later, Preston pushed his way past Jules's shielding jacket. Jules grabbed his hat. Preston swirled around, looking ready to bite. "Hey! That's my *hat*!"

"Right," Jules said, sticking it behind him so Preston couldn't grab it back. "And if there's one thing Randolph would remember about you from last night, it's the ten-gallon hat. Without it, you're just some black dude stickin' his nose up against the window. Got it?"

Preston grumbled, but evidently he recognized Jules's logic. He rubbed his hands together, smoothed back his hair as best he could, and strode across the street. Jules noticed he was wearing a black buckskin jacket, instead of his usual deer brown. A gesture toward stealth, maybe? The black vampire stared in the antiques emporium's window for several minutes, pretending to look at the cuckoo clocks and other bric-a-brac. Then he came back across the street.

"Could you see what they're doin' in there?" Jules asked.

"Looks like the old man, the owner, he's appraisin' what they brought in. Couldn't get a real good look at it, but I think it's a painting. Old man looked happy to see it. Randolph and the girl followed him into a back room."

Jules grunted. "Maybe that's where the store's safe is. Guess we know now where the little runaways are gettin' their funds from. That mansion they live in, it's so crammed with art and fancy crap, they could regularly steal stuff for the next ten years and nobody would ever notice it's missing. You said they went into a back room. Any chance there's a rear exit?"

"Don't think so. The whole block's got stores on every side. Might be a courtyard in the middle, but unless they plan on busting down some other store's courtyard door, they won't be walkin' out on Bourbon. We gonna tail 'em on foot?"

Jules thought about that. "Let's see what they do. I'll get back in the car, in case that limo pulls up again. You stay here and follow them on foot if they take a stroll. I'll make sure to keep you in sight."

Preston looked Jules up and down and cocked an eyebrow. "Yeah. Guess there ain't too many doorways big enough for you to duck into. You be better off in the car. Take my bag, okay? And don't mess with the hat."

Jules climbed back into the Allante. He put down the window and peeled a parking ticket off the windshield. A hundred-and-fifteen bucks—he hadn't been far off. One more item on the expense account. Jules slouched low in his seat again, then thought about using Preston's hat to hide his face. Would it smell all sweaty, like old sneakers? He gave it a sniff. It didn't smell that bad—like dime-store cologne, spicy and musky, probably due to some black-guy hair goop Preston used. Jules stuck the hat on his head. It was a little tight, so he jammed it down some, then tilted the brim so his face would be shadowed.

He didn't wait long. Randolph and Pearl emerged two minutes later. Jules stuck his key in the ignition. He also made sure his passenger door was unlocked so Preston could jump in quickly if he had to.

The two young vampires began walking up Royal Street toward Canal. Jules noticed Pearl carried both backpacks; Randolph was using her like a pack mule. He walked a couple steps ahead of her, as if he didn't know (or care) she was with him. When they approached the Hotel Monteleone, Preston left his alcove and began following them.

Jules checked his mirrors for oncoming traffic. He'd need to creep up the street at a walking pace, and it wouldn't be too stealthy to have a line of taxicabs behind him blasting a symphony of impatience on their horns. He let an AMC Pacer pass by, then checked his mirror again. Royal was empty as far as his eye could see. He pulled out and began slowly tailing Preston.

Preston turned and urgently signaled Jules to come up alongside him. Jules could see Randolph and Pearl getting into a cab at the taxi stand in front of the hotel. Preston jumped in the car. He immediately did another double take. "Told you to *watch* my hat, not *wear* it!"

"It's my disguise," Jules said, not unpleased by the appalled look on his partner's face.

"Disguise, my ass. Give it here."

"You want them to make us?"

"I wanna make you eat my knuckles if that hat don't leave your head." Jules was forced to concentrate on his driving and so was unable to prevent Preston from snatching the hat. "Shee-yit. Look at this. Gonna hafta get this fucker reblocked. Whad you do, sit on it? And you got that Vitalis shit all on the inside . . ."

"Put it on the expense account," Jules said.

The cab turned right onto Canal, then turned right again at North Rampart Street. Jules passed the Goodfeller's Fried Catfish joint at the corner, then swerved to avoid a massive pothole alongside the abandoned Woolworth's. The cab drove past the Saenger Theater, Donna's Bar and Grill, and the Funky Butt, not even slowing down. So Randolph and Pearl weren't looking for a fun night out on the town.

The taxi turned right onto Esplanade Avenue, then cut left into the Faubourg Marigny neighborhood. Jules dropped back some. Traffic was scarce on most of the Marigny's narrow streets, and he didn't want to look too obvious. The Marigny was less well lit than much of the Quarter, less commercial, more residential. Some of the Creole cottages and town homes had been restored to their original antebellum grandeur. But many of their neighbors still moldered in their hundred-year decline, peeling plaster and warped weatherboards hidden by blanketing fronds of ornamental banana trees. Banana trees grew like gigantic weeds in this neighborhood, sprouting anywhere there was a patch of dirt bigger than a dinner plate. But their fruit was no more tasty than the bowl of wax fruit that had sat on Jules's mother's dining-room table for forty years.

The taxi pulled over and disgorged its passengers. Jules slowed, then pulled to the curb behind a derelict travel trailer, idling until he could see what Randolph and Pearl would do. He wondered what kind of tip Randolph gave his driver; the man drove off with his middle finger jutting out the taxi's window.

The pair opened a rusting iron gate and walked into a postage-stamp-sized front yard. Jules noticed Randolph carried a cardboard expandable folder. The two-story home was dark. Its white plaster columns looked as if they could use a few thousand dollars' worth of tender loving care. Pearl and Randolph disappeared down the narrow alley that ran between the house and its neighbor.

Jules waited to see whether any lights would come on, whether the two vampires would be welcomed inside. The house stayed dark and quiet. "You want me to hop out and see what they're doin'?" Preston asked.

"Give it another few seconds," Jules said. "Let's make sure they went inside—"

Just then, the pair returned the same way they'd come. Randolph wasn't carrying the cardboard folder anymore. They closed the iron gate behind them, then began walking in the direction of Frenchman Street and the Quarter.

"I want to see what's inside that house," Jules said.

"You don't want to follow them two?"

Jules cut the ignition and unlatched his seat belt. "You got your cell phone on you?"

"Yeah. What, you wanna split up?"

"Yeah," Jules said. "You follow them. I'll stay here and check this out. I'll call you when I'm done and you can tell me where they're at. Call me first if something important pops up."

"Like a tall dude with his face wrapped up in a scarf?"

"Right."

They exited the Allante. Randolph and Pearl were now slightly more than a block away. They didn't appear to be in a hurry. Preston stayed on the opposite sidewalk, hugging the unbroken row of parked cars that lined the street in this neighborhood without driveways. He had his hat on.

Jules opened the gate. It squeaked like a big fat rat. He thought about Daphne. She'd still looked pretty shaky earlier tonight. He'd suggested she take the night off from rat hunting, but she'd insisted on sticking with her work. Hank volunteered to miss a work shift so he could watch over her. Maybe this younger generation wasn't a total loss, after all.

The side alley was a tight squeeze. Jules was fortunate that the iron fence leaned away from him, over the neighbor's property line. Even so, his belly oozed around fence posts and his back rubbed the house's uneven weatherboards as he slowly crawfished toward the rear yard. Good thing the neighbor's lights were dark, too.

Jules reached the backyard, glad to be free of the constriction. The small yard was clogged with banana trees, many of them tall enough to rest their fronds against the house's screened-in second-story balcony. The uneven brick floor that surrounded the trees' roots was slick from the recent rains. The worn bricks were discolored with a thick layer of black mold, which gave the yard the fragrance of a neglected state-park men's room.

Jules found a sagging utility shed between some of the banana trees. Its mildewed wooden doors were shut tightly with a chain and padlock that looked rusted in place. Randolph hadn't slipped anything in there, unless he was a magician. Jules climbed the steps to the raised, screened-in porch. The door was unlatched. He stepped inside and shined his beam around the corners of the room. It looked like it had once been used as a sleeping porch, a respite from summer heat in the sweltering days before the invention of air-conditioning. The iron skeleton of an old twin-bed frame still occupied a quarter of the space. Four fancy dining-room chairs sat in a corner in varying states of decrepitude and reconstruction, surrounded by stripping tools and cans of varnish. Jules knelt down and shined his flashlight beam into all the crannies where Randolph might've left his package. He didn't find anything.

He checked the door that led into the main part of the house. It was locked. The eight-paned window was also locked tight, with no broken panes. Maybe Randolph'd had a key? Then his light beam hit an odd-colored square near the bottom of the door. Jules nudged it with his foot. It swung inward on a top hinge. A pet door. Steadying himself with the nearby iron bed frame, Jules got down on his hands and knees and stuck his arm through the little door. He felt along the floor for the folder. He was able to grab a hemp doormat, but nothing else. He pushed the pet door open with one hand and stuck his flashlight through. Halfway across the hardwood floor, well out of reach, Jules saw the folder.

What to do now? Jules didn't remember seeing any security-system warning signs posted out front. There were none here in back. He pressed his flashlight against the window, checking the sill for contact wires. None. He took off his jacket and wrapped it around his right fist, just like he'd seen Humphrey Bogart or Alan Ladd do dozens of times on the big screen. Then he bashed in one of the window panes.

No alarm. That was a relief. He cleared away the rest of the glass with his jacket, then reached inside and fumbled for a dead bolt. His fingers found two. He got the door open and stepped inside. The house smelled fresher than he would've expected—his nose was greeted by the aromas of potpourri, furniture polish, and recently baked bread.

He walked to the folder and picked it up. As he'd suspected, it was stuffed full of cash. He counted it. Six thousand dollars in hundred-dollar bills. That must've been some painting Randolph swiped.

Jules set the money folder down on an end table. He walked deeper into the house. The interior was much more opulent than the house's ramshackle exterior would suggest. His flashlight beam caught the hanging crystals of an elaborate chandelier. The light ricocheted over the ceiling and walls like a planetarium display, illuminating gleaming oak end tables, Italian landscapes in gilded frames, and sofas upholstered in quilted red velvet.

Jules opened a door and walked into what looked like a library or study. The desk wasn't tidy. It was strewn with papers and thick, leather-bound volumes, stacked high enough to partially obscure a standing photograph of a fairly young, handsome, prosperous-looking couple, posed in formal evening wear on a stone bridge in City Park. Poking around in the piles, Jules found a bronze-and-teak monogrammed paperweight. The name on the paperweight read Maurice Quentin Eustice. It didn't mean a thing to him.

A framed certificate mounted on the wall above the desk meant more. It commemorated Maurice Quentin Eustice's appointment by the mayor to the city's Historic Districts Preservation Board. Next to this certificate was a law diploma from Tulane University and a master's degree in architecture from the same institution. This guy might have a hell of a student loan bill to pay off. Not to mention the costs of restoring the outside of this house.

Jules took a closer look at the leather-bound volumes stacked on the desk. They were records of nineteenth-century construction projects in New Orleans. One of the books was open. The visible pages described a large brick cotton warehouse near the Uptown river wharfs, on Tchoupitoulas Street. Jules thought back to the community forum. Wasn't this one of the old warehouses threatened with demolition if the Goodfeller-GoodiesMart plan was approved?

A piece of black cardboard was stuck into the back of the volume. Jules opened the book to that page, which described a cotton-processing facility, also on Tchoupitoulas Street, just uptown of the warehouse. The bookmark was a familiar black invitation with red-embossed lettering. An invitation to Courane L'Enfant's Vampyres and Live Wires Soiree.

Jules's cell phone buzzed, making him jump. He set the book down. "Preston?"

"Yeah, it's me."

"Where y'at?"

"A place called Kaldi's, in the Quarter. You know it?"

"Yeah. It's on Decatur, near the French Market. That coffeehouse all the Goth kids hang out in."

"Right. Only tonight, the wannabes get to mingle with the real thing. Our lovebirds're here."

Jules ran his fingers along the invitation's glossy surface. "What're they up to?"

"They're watchin' some kinda show. A poetry readin' or somethin'. How soon can you get over here?"

"I'm just about done. Give me ten minutes. A little longer if I have to cruise around for a parking spot."

"All right. I think I saw the girl sign up to read somethin', so they'll be here a while. Meet you on the sidewalk near the back entrance."

"Great. Thanks, Preston."

Jules stuck the phone back in his pocket. What a great little gizmo. He headed for the back door, then paused by the table where he'd left the six thousand dollars. So Randolph was pretty hot to make sure the L'Enfant plan won out. Given what the punk had let drop in conversation, Jules was certain he was planning on setting up his own base of operations in the new, luxurious neighborhood. And some, if not most, of the High Krewe's youngsters were eager to follow his lead. How L'Enfant tied into this, what the musician hoped to get out of the deal, that Jules couldn't figure. Most sane human beings wouldn't be overly eager to help a colony of vampires set up shop at their doorstep.

One thing Jules knew for sure, though. He didn't like Randolph. Any garlic he could toss into the punk's plans was more spice in the red sauce. He took the money out of the folder, separated it into two piles, bound each with a rubber band, and stuck them into his jacket pockets. The money would cover a new convertible top, a new radio, and repairs to his dashboard, with plenty to spare.

Sidestepping his way back to the front yard, Jules experienced a slight pricking of his conscience. Not enough to be truly irritating, but enough to make him think. Was stealing stolen money, or money acquired from stolen goods, *really* stealing? What would the nuns at St. Joseph's have said about that?

Well, maybe what he could do . . . he could get the repairs made on his car, and then do good works with whatever money was left over. So what would make a nun happy? He couldn't very well walk into a church and drop the cash in a collection plate. Maybe he could hand out hundred-dollar bills to homeless people in the Quarter? Considering how many meals he'd gotten off the homeless over the years, he kind of owed them something. But that wasn't such a great idea, either. They'd just spend it on tons of cheap wine, and then the docs at Charity Hospital would be wringing out their livers.

He had a better idea. The New Orleans Mission. Sure. That place had been like a cafeteria for him for decades. They could do plenty with two or three grand, serve a gazillion more baloney sandwiches or something. Jules smiled, immensely pleased with himself. He'd drop off the cash in a bag with a note attached that said, "For Services Rendered."

Jules didn't find Preston waiting for him on the sidewalk outside Kaldi's. He stuck his head through the open back entrance. A petite young woman, probably high-school age, with obviously dyed midnight black hair, stood on a small raised stage near the front, nervously reciting verse. Jules recognized the backs of Randolph's and Pearl's heads. They sat at a small table close to the stage. He scanned the rest of the sprawling coffeehouse for his partner, checking the booths in back and the stools by the horseshoe counter. Unless he was holed up in the john, Preston wasn't here.

The schoolgirl finished her recital to faintly polite applause. Jules noticed that Randolph's head swiveled in her direction as she walked off the stage, her slender adolescent thighs barely hidden by torn black stockings. Maybe he was here taking stock of potential recruits? A server costumed in a ruffled white shirt and black cape, his face pierced like a Chinese pincushion, left his station next to the espresso machine and headed for the stage. Jules looked around again. Where had Preston gone? Had Elisha called him and sent him off somewhere? Had he spotted a tasty-looking meal walking by outside and decided to take five and grab a snack?

Jules shrugged his shoulders and told himself he was probably worrying for nothing. *He'll pop up in a few minutes and bum me for a cappuccino. Least now I can afford one.*

The server approached the microphone stand, set up next to a battered upright piano. "Next up," he announced, "making her eighth appearance at Blood Poetry Night, is one of your favorites and certainly one of mine, the Countess Pearl!"

Jules was surprised by the cheering that erupted when Pearl rose from her chair. When he thought about it, though, he realized he shouldn't be. In a scene characterized by phoniness and make-believe, Pearl was the real thing, whether these kids consciously realized it or not. The audience stomped their feet, banged utensils against mugs, and hissed lasciviously as she climbed the steps, haughtily ignoring their tribute. Pearl wore an ankle-length gown of black Victorian lace, a shawl dotted with glistening black ceramic beads, plus a black corset that constricted her already slender waist to barely the circumference of Jules's biceps. Unlike the rayon period re-creations sported by the audience, Pearl's outfit had been hand sewn in the days when Queen Victoria had still been alive and kicking.

She stepped up to the mike as if she owned it. Her face looked as impassive as a death mask of white marble, but Jules could tell from the sparkle in her eyes that she was secretly delighted at the adulation. Especially because it was occurring in front of Randolph. "My piece for this evening," she announced in an aristocratic tone—rather than the tarty voice Jules remembered—"is called 'My Vampire Lover.'

He glided in on mists
A child of the night
Flew silent through my window
Soft wings belied my fright
Then he took sweet form of man
And I gave my will to his dark plan
When he came to me . . ."

She laid a look of adoration on Randolph that would've melted butter at the North Pole. He seemed to be paying more attention to his coffee cup than what was transpiring on stage.

"Scented breath perfumed my neck
I was frozen by desire
Glowing white skin
Formed his sole attire
And when his fangs bit deep

I knew peace greater than sleep
When he came to me
Every blemish fell away
Swept away by tide of blood
I grew lustrous and sleek
A pearl rescued from the mud
We locked eyes and I knew trust
Surrendered to eternities of lust
And then he came
In
Me . . ."

She backed away from the microphone, a tiny, satisfied smile on her lips. The audience burst into a flurry of boisterous applause, whistles, hoots, and howls of passion. Jules backed away from the doorway until she returned to her seat. She hadn't looked in his direction; he was pretty sure she hadn't spotted him, and Randolph never turned around.

The master of ceremonies returned to the stage. "Let's hear another round of applause for Countess Pearl, who gives this joint a needed touch of class!" The audience responded generously. "Next up, we've got a blood-soaked piece from, uh . . . what's your name, guy?"

"Rude Crunchy. I, y'know, read here last week."

Jules looked for the owner of the soft, high-pitched voice—an overweight kid sitting by himself at a tiny table jammed into a back corner. He got up and made his way unsteadily to the front, trying unsuccessfully not to jostle other patrons at the closely spaced tables. Jules figured he couldn't be much older than sixteen. His hair was dirty and long, twisted into the rough beginnings of a set of dreadlocks. Weight wise, he was maybe half Jules's poundage, maybe a little less. But that still added up to a substantial kid.

Behind the mike, the boy slumped like a sack of potatoes that had just fallen off the back of a truck. His black sportcoat clashed badly with his worn brown pants, whose unraveling hems hid his sneakers in a mass of muddy threads. He squinted at the spotlight. "Geez, Countess Pearl is a tough act to follow. Tell you what—anybody out there who claps for me, they get a year's worth of free fried catfish from Goodfeller's." The remark elicited one weak chuckle. The boy smiled tentatively, then let the smile drop. "Aww, forget that. My dad's an asshole, anyway."

He rubbed his left eye and accidentally smeared black eyeliner across his cheek. "Anyway, my name's Rude Crunchy. And the name of this poem is 'GASH!' " If he'd been expecting a murmur of appreciation for his title, he didn't get it. Someone coughed. The espresso machine hissed. "Uh, here it is." He gathered a deep breath, then began.

"Even in the womb I was an evil twin
So nefarious that my very own kin
Swam away and sneered and wouldn't let me touch him
But you'd better believe I found a way to fix him
GASH! SLASH! My claws on his face!
GASH! SLASH! Then his eyeballs weren't in place!"

This wasn't what Jules was expecting; given the boy's soft voice and initial shyness, he'd figured on something damp and weepy, maybe a romantic dirge dedicated to Pearl. But the kid's entire demeanor had changed the instant he'd started, and he was picking up momentum with every word.

"Then my Mommy Dearest got her labor cramps
But when my brother came out, his face was red and damp
When it was my turn to come, I swore I'd have my say
Took a note from Sinatra, sang "I'll Do It My Way"
GASH! SLASH! My claws pierced her womb!
GASH! SLASH! I sent Mommy to her tomb!
Daddy freaked out and sent me to the orphan school
But I hated that gig and drowned the nuns all in a pool
Then I met Lizzy Borden, she was an angel from above
Licked the blood from her axe and knew it was true love
GASH! SLASH! My claws raked her cheek!
GASH! SLASH! Her blood fed me for a week!
GASH! SLASH! GASH! SLASH!"

He pulled a foil packet from his coat pocket, tore it open with his teeth, and sprayed fake blood all over his face and hair. Then he fell to the stage, rolled onto his back, and spasmed—his grand finale, meant to get the audience on its feet. The only audience members who rose, however, were a couple who walked straight out the back door.

After a few seconds of writhing on the floor, the kid must've noticed the lack of applause; indeed, the lack of any sound in the room at all, aside from a muffled belch from one of the *barristas.* He stood, dusted off his unraveling pants, and sheepishly approached the microphone again, all of his performance confidence gone. "Thank you. Thank you very much." The mike crackled with earsplitting feedback.

Jules hadn't liked the poem; he wasn't a fan of blood and gore in the arts. But he certainly appreciated the kid's guts. It took a mighty big set of balls to get up there and make an ass of yourself. He really wanted to applaud, loudly, too, but he couldn't risk calling attention to himself. Instead, he waited until the kid, shuffling toward the back, glanced over at the rear entrance. Then Jules flashed him a double thumbs-up.

The boy's face brightened. He grabbed a handful of napkins from the counter, mopped some of the fake blood off his face, and walked over to the back entrance. "You liked it?"

Jules stepped away from the exit so the boy could come out. "Yeah, sure I liked it."

"Really?"

"Really. You're a good performer. You knocked 'em dead. That's how come nobody clapped; they were too, y'know, stunned."

The kid looked dubious for a second, but then he beamed. "Thanks."

Now that they were in closer proximity, Jules noticed something else about the kid. He stank. Bad enough to get a dog's tail wagging. Jules wondered whether he'd been sleeping in a doorway somewhere. Why had he said what he did about Goodfeller's Fried Catfish? Could he really be Van Goodfeller's son? Jules peeled a twenty off his roll of working cash. "Hey. Have a cup of coffee on me. 'Cause I enjoyed the poem. All right?"

The kid's eyes widened as he looked at the bill. "Serious?"

"Serious. And get yourself somethin' to eat, too. They got bagels in there, don't they?"

The kid took the twenty. He stared up at his benefactor. Jules felt the boy's eyes scour him. Then they narrowed thoughtfully. "Hey. Tell me something. You're one of them, aren't you?"

"Them?" Chubby chasers? Child molesters?

"You know. A vampire."

Shit. Has Daphne been publishin' a newsletter? "That's dumb. What makes you say that?"

"It's not dumb. I've been around enough vampires to know what one looks like. Although I've never seen one bigger than me before. I thought only thin, beautiful people got to be vampires."

"Maybe they start out thin and beautiful," Jules mused. "But after drinkin' enough blood in this town, they don't stay that way. Thin, that is."

The boy grinned. "So I was right. You *are* one."

Yeah, he'd let it slip. Not that this was necessarily a bad thing; if the kid knew Randolph and Pearl, and if he was actually Van Goodfeller's son, maybe he could be useful. "Sure, sure. You got me. Just keep your voice down, okay?"

"Okay. Sure. Y'know, you seem really down-to-earth, for a—what you are. The others, they're so *snobby.* They won't even talk to me. I've been hoping . . . well, maybe it sounds stupid, but I was hoping that if, like, maybe if my poems were good enough, they'd invite me to, y'know, join the club."

"What? You wanna be undead?"

The kid pushed dirty locks from his face and stared up hopefully. "Well, yeah! Sure! It'd be the coolest!"

Jules leaned back against the wall. He was suddenly very conscious of his aching knees. If only the kid knew . . . if only he knew what creeps up on you with the passing decades. "You don't want that. Really, you don't."

"Sure I do!"

"No, you don't. And forget about convincin' Pearl or Randolph to make you a you-know-what. You might get one of them to fang you, maybe, if they was feelin' they could handle the calories. But you won't end up no playboy in a silk cape. You'll end up a corpse with its brains blown out, sunk to the bottom of a drainage canal."

The kid appeared to think about this. "Well, if not Pearl or Randolph, then how about you?"

Jules sidestepped the question. First Daphne wanted to jump in bed with him, and now this—Doodlebug redux. Mr. Popularity—next they'd be drafting him for king of Carnival. "Ain't you Van Goodfeller's kid? If that's the case, what's with the livin' rough and hangin' with these Goth punks?"

The kid's face drooped. "Yeah, I'm heir to the throne. Rudy Goodfeller. But call me Crunchy, okay? My dad's a complete bozo. I don't live with him anymore. I've had, what, eighteen different stepmoms since my real mom took off? He doesn't give a shit about me. He's got his speedboats and his Ferraris and his companies. Not to mention *Tif-fany.* She's, like, three years older than me. I totally blew off their fucking designer wedding at the yacht club."

"Well, whatever you think of your stepmom, wouldn't livin' in a nice mansion beat sleepin' on the streets?"

Crunchy shrugged his shoulders. "Aww, sleeping raw, it's not so bad. The tourists'll give you money, long as you don't say it's for beer."

"Your dad got any idea where you're at?"

Crunchy shook his head and grinned. "Uh-uh. He thinks I ran away to New York City. He'd freak if he found out I was here, right under his nose, hanging with a bunch of vampires."

"Yeah. I'll bet."

Crunchy leaned against the wall next to Jules. "Hey, you going to that Vampyres and Live Wires Soiree in three nights?"

Was anybody in the city *not* going to that damn party? Jules decided to play along. "Well, sure. Why wouldn't I be goin'? Isn't every you-know-what in town invited?"

"I guess. Only reason I'm asking is, I've never seen you around any of Courane L'Enfant's houses before."

Jules tried to keep from sounding too dubious. "You hang out with Courane L'Enfant?"

Crunchy stared at the sidewalk. "Uh, no, not really. But I *do* hang out with his wife. Sometimes. Her name's Edith. She's really, really cool. I help her out with stuff. She's got this big workshop with a little apartment attached. Sometimes she lets me take showers there, after we've been working on her cars."

"So you're a mechanic, too?"

Crunchy laughed. "No. See, she's an artist. She buys these really old, junky cars and turns them into, like, drivable art. That's what she calls it. I've got this shopping cart I ripped off from Winn-Dixie, and I go digging through people's trash, looking for good junk for her. People leave the best stuff out on the curb. Busted religious statues, doll heads, weird soda bottles from South America. I bring Edith a good haul, I can walk away with maybe ten, twelve bucks."

"I like art," Jules said. "I really like old cars, too. I think I'd enjoy meetin' this friend of yours. Any chance you could introduce me?"

Crunchy smiled eagerly. "Well yeah, yeah, sure. I could do that. I'm supposed to go over there tomorrow afternoon, to the place on Race Street, drop her off another cart of stuff. But I could make it for the evening, if you want. 'Cause I guess you wouldn't, y'know, make it over there in the daytime."

"Good thinkin'. How about around nine?"

"Yeah! That'd be great!"

Jules's phone began vibrating. He hoped it was Preston calling. "I've gotta take this call. See you tomorrow night, okay?"

"You know where their Race Street house is?"

Jules reached in his pocket for the phone, then waved Crunchy off. "Yeah, I been there."

The kid unfolded the twenty. "What about your change?"

"Keep it, kid. Buy yourself a muffaletta."

He pressed the phone against his ear and jammed his opposite ear closed with his pinky. "Hello?" Nobody answered on the other end. "Hello? Who's calling?"

Jules heard something guttural and raspy. "Juh . . . *Jewwl* . . ." Then it faded. An instant later, Jules heard a loud clatter, violent enough to make him jerk the phone away from his ear. The voice had sounded like Preston's. "Preston? Hey Preston, you there?"

No response. The clattering could've been the sound of the phone on the other end being dropped. Jules pressed his phone to his ear again. The connection hadn't been lost. Listening closely, he could hear street sounds. Several cars honked in succession. An electric guitar and saxophone launched into the opening chords of "Proud Mary."

Bourbon Street. It had to be. That was the only place a band would bother playing a crowd-pleasing old warhorse like "Proud Mary."

Jules hustled toward Bourbon Street. He kept the phone on one ear, while the other listened for "Left a good job in the city . . ." Preston hadn't sounded too healthy. There weren't too many things around that could make a vampire sound like that.

Between Chartres and Royal Streets, the Quarter looked like a sleepy French provincial capital, windows dark, sidewalks nearly deserted. Just two blocks away, thousands of tourists mobbed Bourbon Street, a separate world. Jules swiveled his head, trying to get a fix on "Proud Mary." He crossed Royal. What if he didn't hear it? What if he couldn't find Preston? Too many gift shops projected too much canned music onto the sidewalks. Cajun two-steps, as native to New Orleans as polar bears. "Wonderful World," Louis Armstrong's all-time worst song. It'd be a fucking wonderful world, all right, if he couldn't find his partner in time.

Then he heard it. Distant but discernible—"big wheels keep on turnin', Proud Mary keep on churnin' "—a block to his left, maybe a block and a half.

He turned up Bourbon, waddling as fast as he could, pushing tourists aside. Soon he was hearing the song clearly in stereo, both live and through the phone. He spotted the corner bar where an R&B quartet in sequined jumpsuits was pounding out the song for a small group of dancers and drinkers.

Preston was somewhere in a one-block radius. Jules wiped the sweat from the back of his neck. He listened to the phone again. The band sounded echoey, as if the receiving phone was in a warehouse or an alleyway, somewhere with plenty of space and hard walls for the music to bounce off.

He circled the block the R&B bar was located in. Heavy wrought-iron gates led into hidden inner courtyards. He tried each gate he came across. They were all locked tight. Most were topped with barbed wire or broken glass set in concrete. That wouldn't have stopped Preston. He'd come back to these gates. But first he'd check the next block over, the one across Bourbon from the club.

The crowds quickly thinned out on the west side of Bourbon. The farther Jules hurried from Bourbon Street, the more closely the sounds in his two ears matched. He came to the entrance of a parking garage. Its concrete ramp sloped downward into shadows. The lone attendant booth was dark and empty.

Jules ran down the ramp, breathing heavily. His footsteps echoed sharply. He heard the echoes through the phone. Puddles of oily rainwater had collected at the bottom of the ramp. Most of the fluorescent lamps overhead had burned out. One flickered on and off, like a streetwalker's smile.

Many of the spaces were empty. But the ones that weren't were filled with hulking pickups and SUVs, tall enough to hide a platoon of killers in the shadows between them.

Jules put his phone back in his pocket. He wished Doodlebug were here. Hell, he even wished Daphne were here. The parking spaces were each numbered in red paint. He glanced down at the numbers as he walked past them and stared into the dark spaces between the trucks. Twenty-six. Twenty-five. Twenty-four. Was he counting down the seconds and the breaths he had left to him?

He found Preston between spaces nineteen and eighteen. His partner's body was pinned to the wood and masonry wall like a note stuck on a corkboard.

EIGHTEEN

He's not a pile of dust. Not like Maureen.

Jules told himself this over and over as he approached Preston's body. The orange plank that jutted from his chest looked as if it had been torn from a street barricade. Weirdly, he couldn't see any blood where Preston's upper rib cage was caved in.

Not a pile of dust. So maybe he's not gone. Not yet.

Preston hung like an old trench coat on a hook while Jules slowly worked the plank loose from the decayed, crumbly masonry wall. He supported his partner's torso with his shoulder. Jules felt numb. He couldn't hear any breathing. Amazingly, the buckskin jacket hadn't been pierced. The crude weapon had threaded it through the hole in Preston's body and into the wall. That's why there was so little blood.

As soon as Jules tossed the plank aside, the blood came. Jules felt his half-digested dinner climbing back up his throat. Nausea and fear hit him like twin linebackers, nearly buckling his knees. But before he could set Preston's body down, his partner spasmed.

The spasm dispelled Jules's shock. Preston's eyes were open. He was staring up into Jules's face, eyes bulging. He tried holding on to Jules's shoulder, but the effort made him silently cry out.

Jules eased him down onto the concrete floor. The hole in Preston's chest gurgled. His mouth moved, trembling with effort, but no sound came out. At least none Jules could hear. He knelt so that his ear was closer to his partner's lips. "Mih-missed," the whisper came at last. "He missed. . . ."

"He missed 'cause you got no heart to run through," Jules said, hoping it might make Preston grin through the pain. But his partner's eyes flickered closed, and his face went slack.

Jules forced himself to look at the wound. It looked like a torn mouth, broken ribs jutting like busted teeth. Something was interfering with Preston's automatic regenerative powers—the hole wasn't closing anywhere near as fast as it should. At the rate his partner's lifeblood was spurting, it wouldn't be long before Preston's tank read "E." Jules had to get him back to the black vampires' underground lair. But that meant carrying him back through the Quarter. Could Preston survive the trip?

If the hole wouldn't close on its own, Jules would have to close it. The jacket. Its waterproof buckskin had kept the blood contained before. Jules removed the jacket from his unconscious partner as gently as he could. Then he wadded up one corner of the buckskin and jammed it into the wound. Preston stiffened, but his eyes didn't open. Jules packed the wound as securely as he could, berating himself for not bothering to get a little training in basic first aid sometime during his hundred-plus years.

He wrapped his jacket around Preston's torso and tied its stained sleeves together, hoping this would keep the crude buckskin dressing in place. Something was beeping. Preston's phone. He scooped it up from the floor. Preston could keep it as a lucky charm, if he pulled through. Jules fished Preston's hat from beneath a Chevy Suburban. Not knowing how he'd carry it, he stuck it on his own head.

He lifted Preston carefully, listening to his own knees popping. It'd be easiest to sling Preston over his shoulder. And that would leave his arms free, in case he needed them. But lugging Preston that way would dislodge the "bandage" for sure. No, he'd have to carry him honeymoon style.

Jules realized he must look like fat Tor Johnson in *Plan 9 from Outer Space,* carrying the strangled body of a police detective across a shoddy graveyard. The echoes of his footsteps reminded him how alone he was. The overhead fluorescent lamp cut out with a final dying buzz, leaving only the dim light from the street above to guide him. The attacker could be hiding anywhere. Behind a car. In the bed of a pickup. Inside the dark attendant's booth. And cradling Preston, Jules was as defenseless as an armless circus freak.

He needed to give his courage a kick in the ass. "Hidin' somewheres, dickhead? Might as well show your ugly face right now." He felt stupid, issuing threats to the echoing dark. It was what a little kid would do. But spouting off also made him feel less likely to freeze up. "Come on out! I'll be ready for ya! Maybe you got the drop on Preston, but Jules Duchon ain't no ninety-pound pushover!"

He reached the top of the ramp and remembered to breathe. Barely a block away was the jam-packed commotion of Bourbon Street. Jules had never been so happy to see a crowd of drunken tourists in all his life.

He pushed his way into the mass of people, walking as fast as he could. Hardly anyone stared at the tremendously obese white man in a cowboy hat carrying a black man wrapped in a bloody suit jacket. They were down near the gay section of the Quarter. Jules figured most onlookers must assume they were boyfriends on their way to some fabulous post-Carnival party.

Yeah, us happy homos. Not a care in the world.

Jules banged on the sliding steel gate. "I got an emergency here! Let me through!" He'd plowed through the barricade that guarded the entrance to the black vampires' vehicular tunnel, hidden away in a corner of the casino's multistory parking garage. But that had been a wooden pole. The Allante wasn't equipped to ram through two-inch-thick steel bars.

At last, the intercom next to the gate squawked to life. "This is a restricted area. State your name and purpose, or you will be forcibly removed."

"Just look through your gate, asshole! It's Jules Duchon!" Now wasn't the time to be dicking him around. Preston was dyeing his tan leather seat dark red. Dyeing and dying both. "I got your buddy here. He's got a hole in his chest I can stick my foot through. Get him some blood *right now*!"

That brought a pair of black vampires and a white security guard running from the main house. The security guard pressed a button that made the gate clatter open. The two vampires approached the car, but Jules mashed his accelerator and drove past them as soon as the gate had opened far enough to let the Allante through. Screw the explanations. His partner needed blood.

He screeched to a halt just outside the main house's glassed-in courtyard. Before he could climb out of the car, the Allante was surrounded by vampires, most of whom looked as though they'd gladly tear him a new hole. Elisha pushed through the crowd of bodyguards and pulled open his passenger door. Her grayish-brown face lost all semblance of normal coloration when she saw the state Preston was in. She almost swallowed her fist. The last time he'd seen her look like this, he'd just killed her brother.

"My God! What have you *done* to him!?!"

"Lady, I didn't do nuthin' to him. It was that maniac we were both after—"

"You *lie*!" She reached over her fallen lover and seized Jules's arm, hard enough to cut off his blood flow. Her eyes glistened like the feral eyes of a bird of prey. "You filthy fat *animal*! Everything I love, you rip it to pieces!"

Jules removed her hand as gently as he could. "Elisha, screw your head on straight. If I'd whacked Preston, you think I'd bring him back here? Let's cut the dramatics and get the man some help."

She recovered her composure, although fire still blazed behind her eyes. "Get Preston out of the car," she told two of her companions. "Gently. Bring him to the den next to the commissary. Harold?"

A middle-aged, stocky vampire answered. "Yes, ma'am?"

"You know how to transfuse, as well as extract?"

"I surely do."

"Set up a blood drip next to the couch in the den." The two bodyguards lifted Preston from the car. She stared at the wound, still plugged with the now-bloody buckskin jacket, and shivered.

Jules left the car and began following the men carrying his partner. "Why the hell did you do that?" she asked him, catching his arm. "His wound should've closed on its own."

"It should've. But it didn't."

"Any idea why?"

Jules walked with her through the courtyard and into the house. "I got a notion. I won't know for sure until he's able to talk, but I think maybe he got injected with the same drug this mutilator's been injecting into the High Krewe's women. Doesn't seem like any victims put up a fight, or much of one, so I'm thinkin' this drug is somethin' that paralyzes vampires. And maybe if it does that, maybe it shuts down a vampire's healin' powers, too."

"Tell me what happened."

The house was a hive of frantic activity. Harold wheeled in his blood-handling equipment from the courtyard. The white security guard spread a set of sheets over the couch in the den before the two bodyguards set Preston down. Other vampires hurried in with plastic containers of refrigerated blood from the commissary. Jules told Elisha the evening's events, ending with an unavoidably graphic description of Preston's impalement.

Elisha's eyes narrowed. "Those youngsters you were following—you think *they* made this happen? Did they set him up?"

Jules knew he needed to be careful. It wouldn't take much of a spark to set off a full-fledged war between the black vampires and the High Krewe. Just one poorly chosen word. And he'd find himself trapped in the middle. "I seriously doubt it," Jules said. "The only reason I can figure for Preston wanderin' off is him spottin' somebody who looked like the mutilator. Considerin' that this mutilator's been bumpin' off High Krewe vampires pretty much exclusively, I can't imagine those youngsters workin' a deal with him against Preston. More likely the mutilator was tailin' the youngsters, same as we were, and his and Preston's tracks got crossed."

Unless it hadn't been the mutilator who'd attacked Preston. In which case, Randolph conceivably *could've* set up a hit.

Elisha turned to Harold, who had just finished inserting an IV into Preston's left forearm. "Harold, can you sew him up? Do you know how to do that?"

Jules watched the life-giving blood flow from its plastic receptacle into Preston's forearm. But just as fast or faster, Preston's own blood burbled out of the still-open wound. Harold glanced at the red cavity and looked forlorn. "I could maybe do a passable job, ma'am. But we don't have nothin' here in the house I could use."

Jules thought back to the hundreds of hours of medical shows he and Maureen had watched on TV together. *Dr. Kildare. Marcus Welby, M.D. M*A*S*H.* What would Hawkeye Pierce do? "Hey, Harold, you guys got some kinda workshop down here? A metal-working shop? A garage?"

"Some of the guys like to tinker on their rides, yeah. We got a garage. Why?"

"Have somebody grab a few clamps. Shit, even the clamps on the ends of jumper cables might work. Just somethin' to hold him together until his healin' powers kick back in. If he got injected with somethin', I'm willin' to bet it'll wear off sooner or later."

Harold looked to Elisha. She nodded grimly. "Zimpel," she told the security guard, "go find what Mr. Duchon suggested. And be damn quick about it."

The security guard hustled out of the room, speaking into his radio. Harold went to the kitchen to boil a big pot of water, so that he could sterilize any implements when they arrived. Jules wondered whether a little motor oil seeping into his insides would do Preston any harm. A few tense minutes later, the guard returned, carrying four screw clamps and a set of jumper cables. They all went in the boiling pot.

Harold tossed Jules a pair of disposable latex gloves. "What're these for?"

"Put 'em on," Harold said. "Your idea, so you're gonna help me squeeze that wound shut."

Harold brought in the sterilized clamps. Jules pulled on his gloves. He never enjoyed being reminded that a body wasn't a solid, indivisible thing, but instead a fragile bag of blood, muscle, bone, and miscellaneous goo. He leaned over Preston's body and tried pinching the lower sides of the wound together so Harold could apply one of the clamps. It wasn't easy. The slick flesh, coated with partially congealed blood, slipped out of his fingers like squirming goldfish. It took him three tries before he managed to get a decent grip, squeezing the edges of skin together so that they looked like pale, puckered lips. The wound might not heal pretty. But at least now it would have a chance to heal.

Jules felt dizzy when he finally stood up. He blinked rapidly, trying to banish the swirling spots of color. Elisha steadied him. "This works," she said, "you'll be able to call yourself 'Doctor' Duchon."

"It's gotta pay better than drivin' a cab," Jules muttered.

He sat on a chair opposite the sofa to see how Preston would do. Harold stripped off his gloves and switched a full container of blood for the nearly empty one that had been draining into Preston's arm. With each passing second, Preston's color looked healthier—healthier for a vampire, anyway. Jules wiped his forehead, then realized he hadn't taken off his own latex gloves. He stripped them off, turning them inside out so the messy bits were hidden.

Elisha looked at him with what might almost pass for approval. Maybe even gratitude. "Go get the man some refreshment, Zimpel," she said.

"A beer?" the security guard asked.

"No. The good stuff."

Zimpel returned shortly and handed Jules a tall glass tumbler. It was filled with cold blood. "Let that stand a minute," Elisha suggested. "It'll taste better at room temperature."

"Thanks," Jules said. He was thirsty as hell, but he wasn't about to insult her sudden hospitality by scarfing down the blood straight from the cooler.

♠

When Jules had finished his glass of blood (it tasted much, *much* better than the bland, dietetic stuff the High Krewe had been paying him with), Preston opened his eyes. "How ya doin' there, slugger?" Jules asked.

"Buh . . . better," Preston managed to gasp.

Elisha sat on the arm of the couch and held Preston's hand. "Thought for a minute there we were gonna lose you," she said. She squeezed his hand. "Didn't like that. Try not to scare me like that again, okay?"

Preston tried to nod. But he could barely move his head.

"Your big friend there," Elisha said, "he pretty much saved your life."

Preston's eyes moved in Jules's direction. Jules was sure he saw a grin hiding behind those partially paralyzed facial muscles. "Can barely . . . save . . . his own ass," Preston said.

"You feel up to tellin' us what happened?" Jules said.

Preston closed his eyes and breathed in deeply, gathering his strength. "Felt him nearby," he said. "Like a buzzin' . . . back of my head."

Jules swallowed hard. This confirmed that their foe was a vampire. He'd almost forgotten how, when he'd been younger, he'd been able to sense Maureen's presence somehow, even when she'd been half a block away. She'd always complained of being hyperaware of him, her "pup." For a while, during the war, he'd experienced much the same thing with Doodlebug. Yet this extrasensory awareness had faded over the years, the way normal hearing becomes less acute with time. Jules hadn't felt it recently around Maureen, or the High Krewe vampires, or Doodlebug. But as a vampire, Preston had a lot less mileage on his odometer than Jules did, far fewer years of the pleasurable dissipation brought on by calorie-rich blood. Maybe his sensitivity to others of his kind hadn't yet attenuated.

"Spotted him . . . block away from Kaldi's," Preston continued.

Judging from the strain on his face, the effort of forming words looked equivalent to bench-pressing a bus engine. "Looked . . . just like . . . Daphne said. Went . . . after him—"

"You shoulda waited for me," Jules said.

"Preston's always been pigheaded," Elisha said fondly. She rubbed his hand briskly between hers, trying to restore some warmth to it. "He don't wait for nobody, 'less *I* tell him to."

"Thought I'd . . . cornered him . . . in that garage. Didn't. Got the—jump on me. Stuck me with somethin'. Tore it . . . outta my neck. But too late. Felt myself . . . freezin' up, like. Got me 'gainst the wall. Saw that busted—plank. Thought I was . . . y'know . . . gone pecan. But cop car. Went by. Siren. Noise musta . . . spoiled his aim. Ran away. Rest . . . you know."

"Did he say anything?" Jules asked. "Brag about his master plan or somethin'?"

"Nu-nuthin'."

"You didn't recognize him, baby?" Elisha asked.

Preston attempted to shake his head again, more successfully this time. "No. But . . . but when he staked me . . . was like he *hated* me. Hate comin' outta—his throat. No words."

Jules thought about that. Wordless hate. Could have been the frothings of a homicidal maniac. Maybe the efforts of a coldly rational assassin to steel himself for a kill. Or it could've been the vocalizations of someone who really hated Preston, simple as that.

Vampire, drug pusher, strong arm for a series of gang leaders—these were all hats Preston wore. Any number of people could hate Preston. Jules tried to comfort himself with that fact. But it didn't fly. No run-of-the-mill hater would carry a hypodermic that could drop a vampire in his tracks. Jules's gut told him there was one potential hater who he couldn't avoid checking out, no matter how much he wanted his suspicions to be wrong . . . a kindly, deceased physician whom Jules wouldn't have thought capable of hurting a soul.

"Jules."

"Huh?" He'd zoned out. Elisha was trying to get his attention.

"Preston's got a question for you."

He turned back to his partner. Preston's color was better. Jules looked at the wound. The jagged, pulpy fissure, closed by the clamps, was beginning to reknit itself. Preston's healing ability was slowly picking itself up off the mat. Jules leaned closer so Preston wouldn't have to talk too loudly. "Whad you find . . . at that house?" his partner whispered.

Jules told him about the payoff money he'd found shoved through Maurice Quentin Eustice's pet door, and that Eustice was a member of the city's Historic Districts Preservation Board, the body that would decide the fate of the old cotton warehouses on Tchoupitoulas Street. Preston's face grew animated. "You gotta go see Goodfeller," he said with a burst of energy. "Tell him. He's got the political con-connections. Has the best chance a . . . shinin' a light on the backroom stuff. Do that for me?"

"Yeah. Sure. I'll go see him."

"Hat." Preston smiled, this time unmistakably. "My hat. Still on your fat head."

Jules reached his hand up to his brow. Sure enough, the hat was still there. "Keep it," Preston said, still smiling. "Just get me another one."

"It's a deal."

Jules said he'd go see Goodfeller tomorrow night. Elisha added that she'd call the Reverend Tonqelle and have him alert Goodfeller to expect a visit from Jules. She also said she'd pull some of her men off their Horse-X details and restation them in the Quarter, on the lookout for the mutilator.

Jules didn't think that'd do much good, although he didn't say so. The mutilator had either been uncannily lucky so far, or pretty damn smart. Elisha's minions, if they were to catch sight of him, would have to get pretty lucky themselves. And their presumed sensitivity to other vampires wouldn't help, because their radars would be buzzing and pinging on each other.

What was buzzing and pinging around his own head was dread of where he knew he had to go next. Jules finished the last few swallows remaining in his glass. A small pleasure. Maybe the last he'd be enjoying for a while.

♠

Doc Landrieu's front porch was as tidy as it always had been. Its columns and plank flooring were freshly painted. Someone had installed a brand-new porch swing, a sweetener for potential buyers.

Jules rang the buzzer. The contact gave his finger a slight shock. He hoped it wasn't a foretaste of things to come. He checked his watch.

About two and a half hours until sunup. Jules didn't see any lights on inside. But that didn't mean Doc Landrieu couldn't be home, relaxing, listening to music in a dark room. One didn't yearn to chase away the dark so much when one was a vampire.

Jules rang the buzzer again. He didn't want to break in if Doc Landrieu was inside. He wanted to be able to pretend this was an ordinary social call. At four o'clock in the morning.

If he *did* come to the door, what would Jules say to him? *Hi, Doc Landrieu—cut up any young women recently?* Would his old mentor know that Jules had been hired by the High Krewe as their investigator? If so, could Jules count on their years of friendship to avert a hypodermic in the neck?

If Doc Landrieu opened the door, Jules would play it simple. He'd say he'd seen the "For Sale" sign and called the realtor, wanting to find out what had happened to the old research files. He'd found out that Doc Landrieu was still among the breathing and walking. Naturally, he'd been interested in talking with his old friend again. Particularly now that they shared so much more in common.

Simple. Easy. So how come his big frame was shaking as violently as if he'd been locked in a meat freezer?

No one answered the door. He was both relieved and surprisingly let down. He realized he'd been both terrified and anxious to see his old friend. Anxious to find some rationale, some excuse, no matter how flimsy, to cross Doc Landrieu off his short list of suspects.

Now he'd get to repay his old boss's years of kindnesses by breaking into his home. Wonderful. The streets were deserted. Jules descended the porch steps and crept around the corner into the tree-shaded backyard. He wanted to pick a window to break that wouldn't be immediately noticed, nothing on the ground floor. Even if Doc Landrieu weren't living here anymore, the realtor probably visited the property regularly.

He approached the back wall of the house. Just as he'd hoped, the wheelchair lift was still there, the one Doc Landrieu had installed for his ailing wife during her final decade. A sturdy steel mechanism, it led from the back patio to a specially built second-story landing. The lifting platform was in its elevated position. Jules checked out the gears and pulleys. They looked freshly oiled, clean, in good shape. Experimentally, he pressed the Down button. The mechanism whirred into motion and the platform began to descend, the whole thing almost as silent as the engine in his Cadillac. Looked like he'd be taking a ride.

The platform met the patio with a muffled clank. Could it lift him without stripping its gears? Doc Landrieu'd had money. He wouldn't have bought cheap machinery. These kinds of things were always overbuilt, anyway. Jules climbed aboard, shut the safety gate behind him, and pressed the Up button. The mechanism hesitated for a second, as though it were trying to make up its mind whether Jules was a liftable burden. Then, slowly but steadily, he began to rise.

As soon as he was above the top of the wooden fence that surrounded the yard, Jules found himself looking down into the Jewish cemetery, rows of headstones planted in their raised plots of earth with not a single cross in sight. A few seconds later the whole panorama of the Canal Street cemetery district came into view—the Odd Fellows cemetery, the Firemen's Memorial (the fireman statue's stone head and hose, stolen a few years back, had been replaced), the clock tower, even a corner of Metairie Cemetery on the far side of the Pontchartrain Expressway.

His mother would've liked this view. She'd always said that visiting cemeteries helped calm her nerves. She wasn't buried far from here. But he couldn't see her final resting place, the paupers' cemetery next to Delgado College; it was blocked from view by a row of tall houses. Jules had been cash poor when his mother passed, back in 1962. Doc Landrieu might've loaned him enough to bury his mother in a classier cemetery, if Jules had asked him, but Jules hadn't felt comfortable asking that big a favor. He wasn't thrilled with the notion of Mother Duchon spending an eternity in the paupers' cemetery, but at least it was consecrated ground. Paupers' cemetery or St. Louis Cemetery Number Three, Jules could only visit her from afar, kept at a distance by the forest of crosses.

Doc Landrieu had always been kind to Jules's mother. Jules hadn't been working for him too many years when his mother went into her final decline, but Doc Landrieu visited their house several times after he'd heard Jules's mother was unwell. Mother and boss struck up a surprising friendship; Doc Landrieu sometimes lingered long hours to drink coffee and play cards with her, two of Jules's mother's primary passions. Jules had never cared for card playing, himself. Unless you were playing for money (which his mother'd considered sinful), he'd never seen the point.

The lift reached the second-story landing and halted with an abrupt thud. Jules tested the knob of the door that led into a spare bedroom. Locked. Two slender frosted-glass windows flanked the doorway. How was it he could go thirty years without breaking a window, and then twice in one night have to bust one? He waited until a bus passed along Canal Street, then put Preston's hat over his knuckles and broke the lower half of a window with a fast punch.

Jules froze, listening for any sounds of movement. If Doc Landrieu *was* here and had ignored the bell before, Jules would have to come up with a damn good excuse. He could claim to be looking for the files; information such as that research shouldn't fall into the wrong hands, et cetera. Telling him he needed the files wouldn't even be a lie.

He stood stock still while his shoulders and jaw muscles grew painfully tight. He didn't hear anything; only the solitary trilling of a songbird in the Jewish cemetery, anticipating dawn by a few hours. After a few seconds, he felt safe enough to unbolt the door and begin looking around. The spare bedroom was empty. Jules clicked on his flashlight. The beige carpet still showed the imprints of furniture that had occupied the room. A painting still hung on the wall, above where the bed had rested. Jules took the painting down, then leaned it against the broken bottom portion of the window, covering it. Maybe if the realtor weren't too observant, she wouldn't notice anything was amiss for a few days.

Jules went on a coffin hunt. Finding a coffin, empty or (Jules shuddered at this thought) occupied, would be proof positive that Doc Landrieu now walked the streets of New Orleans as a vampire. A wan ray of moonlight dimly illuminated the hallway. Jules opened all of the doors on the second floor, holding his breath as each swung inward. All of the rooms were empty. In what Jules guessed was the master bedroom, he opened a walk-in closet. All he found were three sets of mildew-stained wooden blinds, all broken, and a mousetrap that held a deceased rodent.

Jules descended the stairs. The ground floor was less empty. A sofa and two side chairs still occupied the living room, covered with white sheets. He entered the kitchen. It wasn't a big room; houses of this vintage never had big kitchens, unless they'd been extensively renovated. His flashlight's beam reflected off a coffeemaker; hospitality for house shoppers, Jules figured.

A Slimline phone was mounted on the wall next to the refrigerator. Jules spotted a pad of notepaper and a pen on the counter below the phone. The paper wasn't written on. However, when he picked up the pad and held it close to the light, Jules could see faint cursive grooves, imprints left by the pressure of a pen writing on a sheet or sheets that were now gone. He remembered from one of his old pulps (maybe the issue that had mysteriously appeared in Maureen's mailbox) that Lamont Cranston, the Shadow, had made the imprints on an empty notepad readable by rubbing the creased page with a soft charcoal pencil. He tore off the top page and put it in his pocket. Just in case.

The last place to check was the basement. Jules had accumulated a lot of memories of that basement. Dozens of times over the years, his old boss had taken blood and tissue samples from him, in hopes of conjuring a cure for Jules's hunger for the red stuff. The steps were narrow and steep. They creaked ominously beneath his weight, just as they had eight months before. Back then, he'd come down here twice in a span of two weeks. The first time, he'd sought relief from what he'd feared was creeping arthritis and diabetes; Doc Landrieu had conned him with placebos, aspirin, really, in an attempt to convince Jules to leave New Orleans and accompany him to Argentina. The second visit . . . that time Jules had discovered Doc Landrieu strapped to his own examination table, a cold, stiff pincushion.

What would he find at the bottom of the stairs this time?

An empty room. The examination table was gone. The microscope, centrifuge, beakers, and tubes, plus the tables that had held them, were gone. And so were the filing cabinets that had contained decades' worth of research on the physiology of vampirism.

Jules's heart sank. He wouldn't be shipping Doodlebug any materials that might help Maureen. He hadn't found Doc Landrieu or evidence of his ex-boss's undead status. So breaking a second window tonight hadn't brought him any closer to solving either of his twin puzzles. They still harried and taunted him, hovering at his throat like a pair of fangs.

NINETEEN

When Jules woke up from an uneasy day's sleep, Daphne was already gone. *Good for her,* Jules thought. *If she's gettin' out in the daytime, maybe she's doin' some fun stuff, insteada spendin' all her time chasin' after my runaway testicles.* He also noticed that the cot she'd been sleeping in had been moved from next to his doorway back into the guest room. Maybe her brief infatuation with him was coming to an end, which made sense, because she'd just had the wits scared out of her by a vampire. He wasn't sure whether to be relieved or disappointed.

It was time to call that Realtor lady back. Jules mulled strategy as he stood over the bathroom sink and spread lime shaving cream all over his neck and cheeks. He really didn't *need* to shave—ever since his resurrection, his beard had hardly grown a bit—but it was a comforting old habit that helped him think. Come to think of it, though, could the reason for his slow beard growth be his missing parts? Would his voice begin changing? He grunted and stroked the razor more vigorously across his left cheek. One more damn thing to worry about.

Should he give his real name to the Realtor? He remembered that he'd already left his name and cell phone number with her; that'd been how she'd been able to contact him two nights back. But if he wanted Doc Landrieu to show up for a meeting (assuming Doc Landrieu was back among the living, more or less), would it be smart to have the Realtor ask him to meet with "Jules Duchon"? If Jules's most-feared suspicions were true, then Doc Landrieu could possibly know Jules was working for the High Krewe. If that were the case, he could either duck a meeting with Jules . . . or worse, arrange for a meeting Jules wouldn't walk away from.

He rinsed the remaining flecks of shaving cream from his face and toweled off. Jules didn't want to think about that latter possibility. He went to the hall phone and dialed the Realtor. She answered on the third ring; no answering machine this time. "Hello? This is Chip Newton," Jules said, raising his voice an octave (disturbingly easy to do, Jules realized). Chip Newton was an old coworker from the morgue, who'd also been under Doc Landrieu's supervision.

"Yes, Mr. Newton? What can I do for you?"

"I got your number off a 'For Sale' sign in front of a house near the corner of South Bernadotte and Cleveland Avenue. I know the owner, Amos Landrieu. Used to work for him back when he was the coroner. Anyway, I'd like to take a look at the property. That's a great neighborhood to invest in, what with the streetcar heading that way soon. Plus, I'd love to catch up with Dr. Amos. It's been years."

Doc Landrieu'd always liked Chip Newton, Jules figured, so the prospect of seeing him again should provide a sufficient draw. Then, when Jules would show up in Chip's place, he could claim he'd run into Chip, heard about his house-hunting appointment, and asked if he could tag along and make it a bigger reunion. He'd act mystified when Chip failed to show.

"So you'd like to set up an appointment to see the property?" the Realtor asked, her voice hopeful.

"Yeah. And I'd like to see Dr. Amos at the same time. Just one more thing, though. My wife and I, we're taking a three-week cruise down to, uh, the Caribbean later this week. I know this is awfully short notice, but if you could make the appointment for the next night or two, I'd really appreciate it."

"It has to be a nighttime appointment?"

"Yeah. Is that a problem?"

"No, no problem. It's just that you're the second person this week who's requested the same thing. Actually, since you want to meet with Dr. Landrieu, it works out quite well. He prefers nights, too."

Jules gave her Maureen's number this time, rather than his cell phone number. Maureen's phone was hooked up to an answering machine.

Jules checked his watch. Seven twenty-three. Too early to call

Doodlebug, given the two-hour time difference between New Orleans and California. He was dying to learn whether his friend had made any progress concerning Maureen, but that would have to wait.

He was supposed to meet Rudy Goodfeller over at the L'Enfant compound sometime after nine o'clock. He'd also promised Preston he'd go see Goodfeller Senior as soon as possible. He'd go visit the father first; Rudy would just have to wait.

Jules called Preston's number. Harold, the black vampires' resident phlebotomist, answered. He put Elisha on the line. Elisha told him Preston was out of danger, but he was still weak, barely able to walk on his own; it would probably be several nights before he'd be feeling like himself again. Reverend Tonqelle had spoken with Van Goodfeller. Goodfeller was expecting a visit from Jules tonight. She gave Jules his address. Then, surprisingly, she wished him luck.

Jules was putting on his shoes when the hall phone rang. On the chance it might be the realtor calling back, Jules answered in his Chip Newton voice. He guessed right. She told him Dr. Landrieu could meet with him tomorrow night at 8:30. Jules told her that would be perfect.

His dance card was filling up. Tonight, Van Goodfeller and Edith L'Enfant. Tomorrow night, Doc Landrieu. The night after, Courane L'Enfant's Vampyres' ball. Something would shake loose at one of those meetings. He was sure of it.

♠

It was drizzling when Jules went outside, so he spent a few minutes applying strips of duct tape to his torn convertible roof. He should've done it while the weather was still dry; now, there was no way the tape would stick more than a day or two.

From the back of the Quarter, he drove up Elysian Fields Avenue, the only road that provided a direct route from the river to Lake Pontchartrain. It was one of those streets that showed a driver wildly divergent faces. Down near the Quarter, Elysian Fields looked quaint and genteel, lined with Spanish town houses and their lacy ironwork. But once you crossed St. Claude Avenue, it got slummy real fast, not turning respectable again until two miles later, above Gentilly Boulevard. Even then, the middle-class, suburban-style houses, masked pockets of poverty, little war zones scattered between the London Avenue Canal and Industrial Canal. It wasn't until you crossed Robert E. Lee Boulevard, almost all the way to the lake, that the fancy facades no longer hid urban ills, like pancake makeup slathered over acne. Then you were in Lakeview. Silk-stocking territory.

Van Goodfeller's house was definitely in silk-stocking territory. Walls of glass met towering slabs of pink-and-gray stucco at acute angles. Illuminated alcoves of glass block were rimmed with strips of polished aluminum and chrome. To Jules, the house looked like a cross between a modern art museum and a snooty Lexus dealership.

At least the drizzle hadn't turned into anything heavier. He found an intercom near the front door. He pressed the intercom button and stared at a sculpted grinning catfish nearly as big and round as he was. The whole fish was studded with fake gemstones, which gleamed in the light of revolving multicolored beams. Jules ran his fingers along the little crown on the catfish's head. At least, he *thought* they were fake gemstones. . . .

The intercom crackled. "Yeah, who is it?" a voice asked. Jules was pretty sure it was Goodfeller himself.

"Jules Duchon. Reverend Tonqelle called and said I'd be comin' over."

"Yeah, that's right. Hang on a minute."

Three minutes later, the front door opened. Jules experienced that slight rip in the fabric of reality that occurs whenever an American sees a celebrity in the flesh. This was the same Van Goodfeller he'd seen up onstage at Laurel Elementary, the same Van Goodfeller from years of fast-food commercials, televised speedboat races, and celebrity charity telethons—tall, muscled, broad-shouldered, with a face that encapsulated both the millionaire businessman and the rough-and-tumble kid from the housing projects. Only this Van Goodfeller looked like he could use a shave and shower. Not to mention a good night's sleep.

"C'mon in. Sorry to keep you waiting." His silk shirt was rumpled, and his chinos were stained with dots of what might've been gravy. His breath smelled potent enough to sterilize medical equipment.

"No problem," Jules said. "Nice to meet you."

They shook hands. Jules stepped inside. "Hey," Goodfeller said, "didn't I see you at that forum the other night? The elementary-school thing?"

"Yeah, I was there."

"Thought so. Didn't think I'd mistake you for too many other guys."

They walked down four steps into a sunken living room. The peaked ceiling was so high, Jules felt like he was a kid again, back in St. Joseph's Church on Tulane Avenue. "So Tonq said you had something important to tell me. About St. Thomas."

" 'Tonq'?"

"The good reverend. We're buds."

Jules stared up at a quartet of gigantic paintings, each nearly fifteen feet tall. Jane Russell, Marilyn, Jayne Mansfield, and Mamie Van Doren, all done in a pop art style. Lots and lots of thigh and cleavage, all way bigger than life. "Nice paintings," he said.

"Thanks. I like movies, and I like art. So why not? It's just money." Goodfeller stopped walking. He stared at the paintings, then stared out the panoramic windows that lined the back of the house. In the glow of floodlights, Jules could see the edge of a landscaped swimming grotto and a boat dock, and the upper levels of a cabin cruiser. When Goodfeller looked at him again, he didn't have a smile on his face, satisfied or otherwise. "You want a drink?"

Jules could use a cup of coffee, but he figured Goodfeller wasn't the type to brew a pot later than nine in the morning. "No, thanks," he said.

"No?" Goodfeller looked surprised. "I'll get myself something. Then we'll go back to my office."

He walked over to a wet bar next to a towering fireplace made of black volcanic rock. Jules waited beneath Mamie Van Doren's crotch while Goodfeller mixed himself a drink. Then they walked back to Goodfeller's office.

The office, big as the whole first floor of Jules's old house, was a combination screening room, trophy room, and spare bedroom. Jules glanced at the trophies in the illuminated glass cases along the walls. Some of them were for achievements in high-school and college athletics; numerous plaques celebrated business accomplishments or were tokens of appreciation from successful franchisees. The biggest trophies, the ones on the central shelves, denoted victories in speedboat races.

The television screen was on. It was the biggest set Jules had ever seen, a flat-panel screen easily seven feet across. Just before Goodfeller turned the sound down, Jules heard a familiar voice. He stared at the screen. A vaguely familiar chubby kid, maybe eight years old, led a parade of children and a brass marching band down a typical New Orleans street of shotgun houses, wooden stoops, and tiny front yards. They ended up at a Goodfeller's Fried Catfish restaurant. The screen flashed with special deals on family boxes and side dishes, the prices about a decade out of date. Then it hit him—the cute, smiling, chubby eight-year-old was Rudy Goodfeller.

Goodfeller settled himself behind his desk. He motioned for Jules to sit on a leather love seat facing the huge TV. "So," Goodfeller said after taking a slow sip from his drink, "tell me what Tonq thought was so important for me to hear."

Jules told the story of Randolph's and Pearl's exchange of an antique painting at J. Wiltz & Sons for six thousand dollars cash. He didn't mention a word about the High Krewe. He only said that he had strong suspicions that Randolph and Pearl were part of a group who were trying to tilt the St. Thomas playing board in Courane L'Enfant's favor. They'd delivered that six thousand dollars to the home of Maurice Quentin Eustice, member of the Historic Districts Preservation Board. One of the city agencies that would rule on the fate of the 150-year-old cotton warehouses that occupied the land where Goodfeller wanted to build his distribution center.

But only half Jules's mind was occupied with telling his tale. The other half watched the cavalcade of Goodfeller's Fried Catfish commercials play on the big screen. They all featured Rudy. The early ones, the ones where Rudy was four or five years old, were relatively crude, almost like home movies, but full of happy vitality, ending with the little boy opening wide and stuffing an entire fried catfish filet in his mouth. Others, shot when Rudy was older and the ad budgets were bigger, featured Rudy steering one of his dad's speedboats on Lake Pontchartrain, huge smile on his round face, or Rudy dancing with an animated catfish. Lots of the commercials had Rudy leading a parade, with bouncing text extolling viewers to "Follow that Crunchy kid to the nearest Goodfeller's Fried Catfish Cafe!"

When the tape looped back to the first commercial Jules had seen, he realized that he hadn't said anything in a few minutes. Neither had Goodfeller. His host was watching the screen, too, taking slow sips from his drink, his eyes looking tired and sad. He set his drink down and turned to Jules. "What you just told me . . . you willing to tell the same story under oath, to a judge?"

Jules thought about that. Any hearing would likely be held in the daytime; that was obstacle enough. Worse, he might be forced to reveal information about the High Krewe and himself that could compromise the covert nature of the night-bound community. He shook his head. "No," he said. "Couldn't do that."

Jules watched the line of his host's jaw tighten. Goodfeller's eyes hardened until all hints of boozy dissolution were gone. "Then what the fuck good are you?" he said in a flat tone. "Why drive out here to dangle this shit in front of me if you aren't willing to deliver? You angling for a payday? Is that it? I didn't think Tonq would send me a bottom feeder."

Jules felt himself redden. He hated that he couldn't explain himself. "I don't want your money," he said. "That's not it at all. I've just got . . . reasons. Personal reasons for not wanting to go in front of a judge. I figured, with your resources, if I'd point you in the right direction, you could follow up on Eustice on your own. Him and the other members of the Preservation Board, the Zoning Board, too—I'll bet lots of them are taking cash under the table."

Some of the anger drained out of Goodfeller's expression. "So what's your stake in this, Mr. Duchon? Civic-minded citizen?"

"This St. Thomas thing . . . it's important to a couple of friends of mine." Goodfeller was the Catfish King. Jules figured he might as well go fishing. "And it ties in with some disappearances and violent attacks I'm investigatin'. Those people who dropped the payoff to Eustice, they're associates of some of the victims."

Goodfeller's eyebrows lifted slightly. "You're a private investigator? Tonq didn't mention that."

Jules couldn't help but grin. "If one paid case makes you a professional, then I'm a private dick, yeah. My friend told me you've got pretty good connections in city government. You pick up anything on the murders of those black preachers who supported your redevelopment plan? Tonq's friends?"

Goodfeller leaned back in his chair and rubbed his neck. "Not much more than what showed up in the papers, before the cops lowered the curtain." He leaned across the desk, his face growing dark. "I'll tell you this, though. That whole business . . . the blood, the holes in the neck . . . it's got Courane L'Enfant's *stink* all over it." He pronounced L'Enfant's name with the cold fury of an exorcist uttering the name of the devil. "How decent people could have anything to do with that piece of shit . . . knowing what he's done . . . what he sucks *children* into . . . All his rich Uptown neighbors, they look at him and laugh. So long as he makes his annual donations to their favorite charities, he's an okay guy. A little 'eccentric,' yeah. This town loves its characters. But the satanic rituals, the vampire worship . . . sure, none of it's *real.* But try telling that to a gullible sixteen-year-old kid. Try telling that to a drug addict who can't pull it together enough to keep her baby's diapers clean. Maybe it's not *real,* but it's real enough to fuck up people's lives."

Jules hadn't known what his fishing expedition might dredge up. He certainly hadn't expected this. Goodfeller steadied himself, ran his fingers through his hair, reached for his drink again but set it down. His eyes wandered back to the big screen, to the silent commercials, endlessly repeating. He sighed bitterly. "Sorry if I went off on a tear. You mentioned L'Enfant before. You said you thought those two characters were trying to tilt the board in L'Enfant's favor. I got my hopes up. I thought maybe you were gonna give me something to nail that bastard's ass to the wall with."

"Why do you want it nailed?" Jules leaned forward, struggling against the pull of the love seat. "What's your beef with L'Enfant? I thought what was between you two was just business."

"Just business?" His laugh was as mirthful as a car crash. He shook his head. "My kid . . ."

Jules tilted his head at the big screen. "That's your son up there?"

Goodfeller's eyes followed Jules's gaze to the parade of children, led by the smiling, chubby youngster. "Yeah. That's Rudy. From about ten years back. Better than home movies, these commercials."

"What's he got to do with L'Enfant?"

"Nothing." He spat out the word like a hot pepper burning his tongue. "Not if I can help it. Problem is, maybe I can't." He picked up his drink again, took a swig from it this time. "Kid's seventeen now. Practically an adult. Maybe it's too late. Maybe anything I do or try now is too fucking late."

Jules decided to fish some more. "But if he's livin' under your roof, he's gotta follow your rules, right? With all the toys you got around here, I figure you can always bribe the kid to stay in line."

Goodfeller shot him a look both sour and sad. "He's a runaway. Kid left this—all *this*—to live like a bum on the streets. Last I heard from him, he was up in New York. Maybe he went up there looking for his mother."

"How's this tied into L'Enfant?"

"Our last fight, the one that pushed him over the edge, was over that bastard. I found out Rudy'd been hanging out at L'Enfant's compound in the Lower Garden District, making friends with those 'vampire' creeps that leech off him. I grounded him, forbade him from going so much as two miles near the bastard." He rubbed the sides of his head, maybe anticipating the hangover to come. Maybe experiencing the headache already. "I hired a detective to follow him around. That's what really pissed him off; he's got a nose for those guys, can spot them a mile off. But I had my reasons. He ain't getting a chance to do to Rudy what he did to Christine. My first wife."

"Rudy's mother?"

"Yeah. I married her back before I had any of this. Before the first catfish shack, even. She was a wild one. Guess I was, too, back then. Only problem was, she wouldn't calm down when things started changing for us. When I was building a business and she was a new mother. The drinking, that was bad enough. But then we met L'Enfant and his wife, the big pretty hunchback, what's her name . . . Edith, Aubrey, something like that. Think it was at a charity luncheon. I didn't care for them, but Christine took to them, big time. They'd just bought their place in the Garden District, the first house in their collection. Christine started hanging out there, taking Rudy with her. I was working fourteen-, fifteen-hour days then, so it took me a while to notice what was happening. Longer than it should've."

"What was going on?"

Goodfeller scowled. "The kid wasn't getting fed. He was dirty. Diaper rash all the time. Couldn't ask Christine about it, 'cause whenever I was with her, she was passed out. Dead to the world." He took another sip. "The L'Enfants got her hooked on the hard stuff. And it all happened right under my nose. I hired a full-time nanny. I shipped Christine off to rehab. Three times. The longest she managed to stay straight was seven weeks and three days."

Goodfeller went silent for a while, staring again at the TV. "So what then?" Jules asked. "You got divorced?"

"It was messy," Goodfeller said. "I got her declared an unfit mother. Got sole custody of Rudy. He was four then. She could only have supervised visitation. Thing was, after ten months or so, she didn't even bother with that. She got some money in the settlement and took off. Parts unknown."

"And Rudy? He hasn't seen her since?"

"No. Not since he was five years old."

Jules looked at Goodfeller with fresh eyes. What was the man capable of, now that he saw his family threatened by the L'Enfants again? Violence? Hiring someone to cut up his enemy's allies?

Jules put on a casual smile. "Those preacher murders," he said. "The cops haven't made too much progress. But I guess that doesn't matter, huh? Not like the killers got away with it."

Goodfeller's face acquired sudden focus. "What do you mean?"

"I happen to know the killers won't be catchin' beads at Carnival parades anytime soon."

Goodfeller looked surprised. "You telling me they're dead?"

"Somethin' like that." Jules was quiet for a few seconds, trying to gauge Goodfeller's reaction. "Must feel good, huh?"

Goodfeller didn't look the slightest bit inebriated anymore. "If you're asking me whether it feels good to hear that the killers of friends of my friend are out of commission, well yeah, sure. Sure it feels good. If you're asking me, in a roundabout way, whether I had something to do with it . . ." He smiled. Jules got a strong dose of the personal charm that had carried Goodfeller so far in the local business world. "No, Mr. Duchon. As emotionally satisfying as that would be, I've got too damn much to lose. I'll be putting the squeeze on the L'Enfants. But I'll be doing it all aboveboard, on the real-estate market, in the arena of public opinion. And maybe, if what you told me before is on the level, in the courts." He pushed his drink aside and wheeled his chair closer to Jules. "I understand why you might have reasons against testifying in person. But how about a sworn deposition? We get that into the hands of a grand jury, that could get things rolling."

Jules considered this. Maybe, given the time to write things in his own words, he could come up with an account that wouldn't have cops or the district attorney sniffing around the High Krewe's gates. "Lemme think about that," Jules said.

"Here's something else I'd like you to think over," Goodfeller said. "Certain parties have suggested my son might've returned to New Orleans. Or maybe he never left. Problem is, these parties are the kind of sidewalk scum that'll say anything. For enough cash."

"Can't you have the cops look for Rudy? He's still a minor, right?"

"Not discreet enough. I go to the cops, in a week my household's dirty laundry gets aired on *A Current Affair.* Fucks my stock price something awful. I've been through it before."

"How about private detectives? You could afford to hire a small army, I'll bet."

Goodfeller shook his head. "I told you, he can sniff those guys out a mile away. He's had so much practice, he's practically supernatural. And if he *is* back in town, I don't want to do anything to make him leave again." Jules felt Goodfeller's sea blue eyes appraising him. "You're already poking your nose into L'Enfant's affairs, and you don't look or talk like any of the other dicks I've sicced on Rudy before. I'd like to put you on retainer."

"I'm already—"

"I know. I'm not asking you to drop whatever else you're working on. I just want you to keep your eyes open. Let me know if you come across him. Do that, and there's a couple easy grand in it for you."

Why not play along? Jules might need Goodfeller's help at some point. Revealing Rudy's whereabouts would be an easy way to buy it. In the meantime, he could see what he could do to keep the kid away from serious trouble. "You have a recent photo?"

"So you're willing to help me?"

"I'll keep my eyes open, sure."

Goodfeller pushed a framed photograph over to the edge of the desk. "This is maybe a year old. He's gotten a little heavier since then, unless he's lost weight living rough on the streets. Kid gets his weight problems from his mother's side of the family."

Or from all the free fried catfish and hush puppies, Jules thought.

"You want to take the photo with you?" Goodfeller asked.

"Naww. I've got his face memorized." Jules got up from the love seat, not without difficulty. "Thanks for seein' me. I know my buddy'll be glad to hear we spoke."

"No problem," Goodfeller said. "Let me know what you decide about that deposition."

"I will. And I'll keep my eyes open for Rudy."

"Thanks. Sure I can't fix you a drink before I show you out?"

"No. That's all right."

Near the back of the office, next to the entrance, was an architect's rendering of the Goodfeller's Fried Catfish distribution center planned for the St. Thomas site. Jules paused to take a look at it. Tacked to the architect's drawings were photographs of the decaying brick buildings the new center was meant to replace.

Jules stared at the photographs. The old warehouses looked hauntingly familiar. Their worn redbrick walls, surrounded by sloping roofs of green Spanish tile, were decorated with faded logos of defunct shipping companies. Jules realized they looked familiar because they were older versions of buildings he'd grown up with, the sugar and coffee warehouses that lined Decatur Street along the levee near his Montegut Street home, part of the landscape of his childhood.

He looked at the architect's rendering. The big, brown, windowless box could be anywhere . . . the suburbs of Baton Rouge, an industrial park in Amarillo. The surface of the moon.

It didn't remind him of anything at all.

"There you are! I was afraid you'd totally blown me off!"

Rudy "Crunchy" Goodfeller opened the gate, an eager smile on his round face. He wore the same clothes from last night—the threadbare black sportcoat, the brown corduroy pants unraveling at the bottoms. He smelled slightly cleaner, though.

"Sorry I'm late, Crunchy," Jules said. "I had another appointment."

"That's okay. It's not like I had anyplace else to go or anything. And Edith always stays up late working on her cars, anyway."

Jules stepped into the yard behind the looming battlements of L'Enfant's orphanage compound. The huge fenced-in space, close to an acre in size, looked like an auto-salvage yard. But an unusual auto-salvage yard. The cars all had strange growths popping from their sheet metal.

Jules walked closer to one. It was a 1966 Oldsmobile 98, about the same size and shape as his beloved old Fleetwood, now in Hank's possession. This Oldsmobile had three periscopes poking out of its black vinyl roof. Two pink torpedoes protruded from its front fenders. He walked around the back. The car had two five-foot-long Polaris missiles welded to its trunk, sticking out like spines on the back of a dinosaur. He bent down and looked underneath the bodywork. Sure enough, a rudder and twin propellers were squeezed between the tailpipes.

Rudy walked up behind him. "Pretty neat, huh? Edith's really pushing to get a bunch of new cars ready. She's got a big show scheduled at the Contemporary Art Center in June. You wanna go meet her?"

"Sure," Jules said.

Rudy led him toward a large corrugated-steel shed, big enough to fit five or six cars inside. Its windows glowed with the blue-orange flame of a welding torch. Jules stared at his young companion. He wondered how much Rudy knew about the L'Enfants' involvement with his family when Rudy had been a baby. How much had Goodfeller told him when he'd warned his son against going anywhere near Courane and Edith? Had Rudy persisted because he'd known befriending the L'Enfants was the surest way to cut his father to the quick?

They entered the garage. Blue sparks flew from the bed of a small pickup truck. The person in the bed, wearing a welding helmet and bulky protective clothing, was welding an iron frame to the truck's bed, the kind a vendor could use to hang baskets of fruit. She spotted Jules and Rudy and cut off her torch, then jumped down from the truck's bed. The thick, quilted jacket she wore didn't hide her hump.

She took off her welding helmet. Her face surprised Jules. With some years knocked off and more attentive care for her hair and skin, she could be a cover model. Shocks of silver-gray ran through her unruly black hair, but these, along with the tiny lines around her eyes and mouth, only enhanced her natural, unadorned beauty.

She set her helmet down on the tailgate and casually looked Jules over. "So you're Crunchy's new friend from Kaldi's," she said. She extended her hand after removing her glove. "I'm Edith Aubrey L'Enfant."

Jules shook her hand. Her grip was strong. She was a big, husky woman; about five inches shorter than he was, but if it weren't for the hump bending her spine, Jules figured she'd be every bit as tall as he was. For the sake of consistency, he tried recalling the false name he'd given her husband. "Nice to meet you. I'm, uh, Frederick Melon."

"Do you prefer Fred, or Rick?"

"I'll answer to both, I guess."

She smiled. "I prefer Rick. If that's all right."

"Sure." He took a look at the vehicle she was customizing. "Nice old pickup. I don't see too many Falcon Rancheros around anymore. What are you doin' with it? Another submarine?"

"No. I don't repeat myself. Come around the other side and take a look." Jules followed her. The Ranchero's other flank was covered with hundreds of multicolored bottle caps, interspersed with bits and pieces of 45 rpm vinyl records.

"It's a tribute to the city's youth tap-dancing culture," Edith said. "Crunchy's been collecting old shoes for me, worn-out canvas tennis shoes, mostly. I'll convert them into tap shoes by gluing bottle caps to the soles, then hang them from that rack. For my show at the CAC, I plan to hire a couple of dancers from the Quarter, have them tap right there in the back of the truck."

Jules wandered over to the next car, an early 1970s Coupe de Ville that was missing its hood, grille, front bumper, and windshield. "What's up with this one? I used to drive a car a lot like this once."

Edith ran her long, slender index finger down the Cadillac's empty windshield frame. "I'm making her roadworthy again. All my cars are drivable; I won't sell one that isn't. What I do is, I take things that used to be beautiful, like this Cadillac. And I make them beautiful again, but in a new way, an unexpected way. Unconventional beauty has always interested me much more than the conventional kind."

Why did her voice sound so familiar? Edith *Aubrey* . . . even the name was familiar . . . "Say, you wouldn't happen to be related to Elizabeth Aubrey, would you? The movie actress from the forties? She was in, let's see, *Fortress of Frankenstein, Fortress of Dracula*—"

Edith smiled a little more shyly. "*Fighting Angels of the Philippines, Forbidden Love of the Moors.* She was my mother. The silver screen's only real-life hunchback. 'Face of an angel, body of a monster' . . . she *loved* that particular tag line the publicity department pinned on her."

"I was a big fan of your mother's. I saw all her pictures as soon as they hit the Canal Street theaters—" He stopped short, realizing he'd just given away his advanced age. Edith didn't react with anything more than a slightly raised eyebrow. "Anyway, your mom was a tiny little thing, from what I remember. How come—"

"Where do I get my size?" Now her smile was unabashed. "That would be from my father. Since you're a fan of my mother's movies, you probably remember Glenn Strong."

Now Jules was *really* impressed. "The guy who played Frankenstein's monster after Karloff, Lugosi, and Lon Chaney, Jr.? Sure, he woulda been six-foot-seven, six-foot-eight. But I never read that he ever got married—"

"Oh, he didn't. Not from lack of encouragement on my mother's part, though." She smoothed a strand of gray hair from her face. "But that's enough about my family history. Why don't we talk about you for a bit? You needn't be shy about your age; I'm not at all surprised you saw Mother's pictures when they first came out. Crunchy's told me a bit about you. I can only assume you've come to talk with me about real estate."

"Real estate?"

Her smile was more arch this time. "Come, come, Rick. You aren't the first of your little fraternity to attempt an end run around my husband, looking for a better deal from me."

Jules smiled back. He didn't have much idea what she was talking about, but she'd sure captured his interest. "So what kind of a deal did this other guy get?"

"Him? Nothing. He was an asshole. Unless my husband decides to bargain, he'll be paying the standard one-third market rate."

Subsidized housing for *vampires*? "Any chance of my doin' better? I sure do like your Ranchero."

Edith laughed. It was the brightest sound to grace Jules's ears since Daphne's initial emergence from her cocoon five nights ago. "Flattery may not get you *everything,* Rick. But it certainly earns you points. I can't promise you much, though. My influence with my husband . . . isn't what it used to be." The shadows of age, previously kept at bay by the radiance of her expressions, crept across her face. "But I like you. You're . . . different from the others. I'll see what I can do. I assume you don't plan to live in the congregate mansion?"

"Congregate mansion? You mean, like a dormitory?"

She looked surprised by his ignorance. "You really *aren't* a member of their exclusive little club, are you? It's been part of the plan since the beginning. One of the biggest mansions in the development, with each of your 'night people' buying a share. It'll have all the amenities they've become accustomed to—private swimming grotto, Jacuzzi baths, the works. Not to mention a nice little staff to keep it spiffy. Honestly, though, given the 'sparkling' personalities of all those folks I've met, you're better off on your own. Will we be talking about a condo unit? The houses, even given the big discounts my husband is offering, are pretty steep."

Jules felt his excitement building. "What about those units for poor people? Aren't those still part of the L'Enfant redevelopment plan?"

"Of course. They have to be part of the mix, or the whole thing falls apart, both financially and otherwise. But you weren't thinking about getting into one of *those* units, were you? They're reserved for ex-residents of public housing. And, judging from your pigment, or lack of same, you don't look like you've lived in an Orleans Parish housing project recently."

She should've seen my old neighborhood, Jules thought. *With the shape it was in by the time my house burned down, some of the projects would've looked like a step up.* "I guess a condo unit would do me, then. Don't have much stuff nowadays." One thing was bugging him. A few things, actually. Given the soft life they already enjoyed, there had to be more than just subsidized luxury living to attract Randolph and company away from their current digs. Jules decided to take a stab in the dark. "Hey, even though I won't be livin' in that congregate mansion, how about the, uh, other benefits? Am I still in line for those?"

Now she'd either look mystified, or she'd tell him more. She didn't look mystified. "You mean the blood from the on-site health clinic?"

Bingo. "Yeah. That's pretty damn important. Tell me more about how that'll work."

"Well, of course it'll be part of your amenities. You needn't worry there won't be enough of the red stuff to go around. It's a stipulation written into the leases of all the subsidized, ex-public housing residents that they attend monthly health screenings at the clinic. Those screenings, incidentally, will include regular blood extractions. For testing purposes, of course." She grinned.

"Wow. That sounds great. Like a dream, or somethin'." He didn't have to work hard to feign enthusiasm. It *did* sound like a vampire's dream come true. Given what he'd just heard, the question wasn't why Randolph and company would want to move in. The question was why L'Enfant would want them to—and why he'd pay big money out of his own pocket to make it happen.

Jules glanced over at the garage's entrance to see whether Rudy was still hanging around. The less the kid overheard about vampires and vampire politics, the better. Jules saw that he was out of earshot, wandering around the yard. "Y'know, there's just one thing I've been wonderin' about. Your husband, well . . . what's the attraction for him? Why the special deals for vampires? Most people, they'd be payin' money to keep us *away.* Not keep us close."

Edith didn't smile. Jules wasn't sure whether the stark look on her face was fright, worry . . . or a wounded look of pain. "Courane's not like other people. If you've met him, I'm sure you know that. He has . . . aesthetic reasons for desiring your kind as neighbors. You inspire him. And he has great sympathy for people who are different." Her voice gathered strength. "I don't know what your personal situation is, Rick, but Courane has responded very warmly to the difficult home life your fellows are facing. He wants to provide them with an alternative, and do so in such a way that they won't need to harm anyone else. That's not so terribly mysterious, is it?"

She was good. If it weren't for that grimace earlier, he might be tempted to swallow her story whole, without chewing. "So what you're tellin' me is, your husband, he's a real big-hearted guy."

Now she smiled. "Yes. Courane has tremendous capacity for love." She slipped on her gloves again. "It's been good talking with you, Rick, but I'm afraid I must excuse myself. I need to finish another half dozen sculptures before my show, and I'm running way behind."

Jules shook her hand. "Yeah, good meetin' you, Edith. If you could put in a good word for me with your husband, I'd appreciate it. Am I gonna see you at that big party two nights from now?"

Her eyes focused on him with renewed interest. "You'll be there?"

"Yeah, I was plannin' on showing my face. I don't get to go to too many parties."

She smiled and nodded her head. "I'll see you in two nights, then."

Jules headed out of the garage. Rudy was sitting behind the wheel of a Plymouth Valiant. It was up on concrete blocks. He figured he'd offer the kid a ride back to the Quarter, since Rudy wouldn't get there in the Plymouth. Before he reached the car, his vest pocket began buzzing.

Jules flipped open his cell phone. "Yeah? This is Jules."

"Jules, it's Doodlebug. How are you?"

Jules grinned. "You got ESP or somethin'? I was plannin' on calling you in an hour or so. Hey, you aren't back in town, are you?"

"No, I'm still in California. Why? Do you want me to come back?"

"Come back when you can fix up Maureen. Until then, stick where you're at and keep with what you're doin'."

"Right . . ."

Jules didn't like the sound of this "right." It sounded discouraged. "Hey, is everything okay out there? You makin' progress?"

"Progress of a sort. Not the kind of progress that'll make you happy, though. More the kind of progress that lets us cross options off the list. Have you found the rat?"

Jules scowled. "No. My dick's still AWOL."

"Well, don't sweat it. I mean, worry about finding it insomuch as you'd like to be, you know, anatomically whole. But don't worry about it as regards Maureen's situation."

Jules felt himself begin to sweat. He didn't like the direction the conversation was heading in. "Stop beatin' around the bush, Doodlebug. If you've got somethin' to tell me, spit it out."

"All right. The last three nights haven't been all wasted effort. I found a way to significantly decrease the pain Maureen will feel on reintegration . . . should we get to the point of wanting to resurrect her again. But that idea you had, the one you wanted me to investigate—"

"You mean me donatin' some of my excess mass to her? Once I'm able to pull those kinda tricks again?"

"Yes. It's . . . a nonstarter, Jules. It won't work. Physically, you might be able to accomplish it for a very brief time. But mentally . . . it's just impossible. Your mind couldn't handle the load of simultaneously maintaining your own reduced form, being consciously 'you,' and ensuring that any donated mass stays in the exact shapes needed to sustain Maureen's life. You'd need a mental capacity approximately 6.8 times what you have in order to pull it off."

Jules's head throbbed with the awful thunder of doors slamming shut. "But—but I was able to turn myself into 187 rats. One hundred and eighty-*seven,* and that didn't take no Einstein-size brain—"

"That was different. You were essentially subdividing your mind then, putting a little piece of your consciousness into every one of those rats. Maureen has, or would have, a mind of her own. No part of your consciousness would be going along with that excess mass you'd be donating. I've talked this over with experts. I've thought it through from every direction possible. I'm sorry, Jules."

Jules leaned his forehead against the roof of a Ford Galaxie, letting its jagged vinyl dig into his skin. Strands of his silver-white hair fell into his eyes. He felt like grabbing it and pulling it until his skull ripped open, until his too-small brain flopped out onto the torn vinyl roof. "That's . . . that's all right," he heard himself say. "Don't feel bad. Thanks for tryin'."

"This isn't a brick wall, Jules. It's a setback, yes. But there may be other ways. I just need to let you know we may find our answer *later,* rather than sooner. But I won't stop looking until I find that answer. I promise."

"Yeah. I know you won't. Thanks, buddy. Talk to you later." Jules shut the phone and put it back in his pocket. Walking over to Rudy in the Valiant, he felt as if he were dragging five thousand pounds, rather than five hundred. But he put on the bravest face he could. "Hey. Squirt. You wanna ride with me back to the Quarter?"

Rudy's smile faded into a concerned frown when he saw Jules's face. "You okay? Did you have a bad talk with Edith? I thought you'd like each other—"

"Naww. That's not it. It's somethin' else." He started walking toward the gate, staring at the rutted ground. "So, you comin' or not?"

"Well, I really, *really* appreciate the offer. But Edith offered me a place to crash tonight. A spare cot in her studio. Besides, my Winn-Dixie cart, it, y'know, it wouldn't fit in your trunk." He ran a few steps to get in front of Jules. "Hey! You know what? Edith said she's gonna help me search for my real mother. They used to know each other. I haven't seen my mom since I was little. Isn't that great?"

"Yeah, that's really good, kid," Jules said, not stopping.

"Hey." Rudy stopped in front of Jules, blocking his way. "You thought any more about, y'know, maybe putting the bite on me? It's, like, free blood."

Jules sighed. "You don't want to be a vampire," he said slowly.

"But I could be, like, I dunno, your scout or something. Your sidekick, sorta."

Jules shook his head. "Been there, done that. Once was enough."

Rudy's face screwed up into an imploring whine. "Oh, come on, come *on*—"

Jules felt himself getting angry. But he didn't want to blow up at the kid. "Look. Didn't you just say you're gonna go lookin' for your mother? What do you want to become a vampire for? That's nuts."

"No it's not." The kid's expression turned earnest as a sidewalk prophet's. "See, maybe my mom . . . maybe *she'd* like to be a vampire, too. That way she wouldn't get any older. And we'd have lots of time together. Eternity, y'know? Enough time to make up for all the years we've been apart."

Jules rubbed the sides of his head. He felt very tired. "I see where you're comin' from," he said. "But that's not the way to have a family again. You wanna do the right thing? Give your father a call. Let him know you're all right. Patch things up with him, Crunchy."

The boy's face turned suspicious. "What do you know about my dad and me?"

"Enough. Enough to know he loves you, and he misses you."

"How do you *know* my dad loves me?" Rudy shot back.

"Look. I'm involved in stuff. Some of that stuff, it involves your father. I met him, not too long ago. The whole time we were talkin', he was watchin' videos of your old commercials. Couldn't keep his eyes off them. I swear."

Now Rudy looked fearful. "Is . . . is he *paying* you?"

Jules smiled. He didn't have to lie. "Naww. He hasn't paid me a cent. What I just told you, I told you for free."

Rudy backed away and let Jules pass. Jules opened the gate. "I still want to be a vampire!" Rudy shouted after him.

Jules swung the gate shut behind him. "Keep pesterin' me, kid, and you'll end up at the bottom of a canal. Don't poke a rattlesnake with a stick, okay?"

He trudged off to his car. Jules was disappointed the kid hadn't accepted his offer of a ride. His babble would've kept Jules distracted, at least for the next twenty minutes or so. But now the only driving companions he had were his thoughts. Thoughts of Maureen.

He turned onto Camp Street, headed for downtown. The dimly lit green space of Coliseum Square Park drifted by on his left, an oasis of centuries-old live oaks. He remembered how much fun he and Maureen had had back in the late sixties together, when the big urban crime wave had begun rolling over New Orleans. They'd come up with a game they loved. They'd go to Audubon Park together, after ten P.M., when the park was shunned by everyone except criminals and the occasional idiot college student. They'd stroll down the Meditation Walk, beneath dark trees, until they found an isolated bench. They'd talk overly loud and laugh the whole way in, making sure any lurkers were well aware of their presence. Then they'd make out on the bench until they were accosted.

Jules's eyes misted over as he thought about it. Those picnic dinners . . . they'd been the best. And afterward, he'd always gotten some well-needed exercise, carrying the body over to the river, weighing down its clothing with levee stones so it would sink. On a really good night, they'd attract two, sometimes even three muggers. And there was the pleasure of trying to match his bite holes to Maureen's . . . another way to taste her lips.

He forced himself to stop thinking about her. After discovering that Doc Landrieu's research notes were gone, and then tonight . . . it was too painful. Instead, he focused on the question that had gnawed at him earlier. What was in this whole deal for Courane L'Enfant? Despite Edith's efforts to explain, her husband's actions didn't make a shred of sense.

Inviting vampires to be your neighbors, *bribing* them with subsidized housing and blood to come live close by—it was like putting down a pet cushion at the foot of your bed for cobras to snuggle into.

Jules's right front tire slammed into a pothole as he cruised past the Confederate Museum. His damaged dashboard buzzed like a mutated mosquito. Then his digital gauges went black. Jules found himself driving in the dark.

TWENTY

It was a new night. The rat was determined he wouldn't lose his new playmates again, not like last night. Last night, he'd followed them for blocks after they left the crowded, smoky place, attracted by their dead-flower scent and their skin, white as spilled sugar. They interested him. He wanted to see what they'd do. He wanted to see if the medicine-smelling man, the man who'd seemed so familiar, who'd frightened Daphne, would return, attracted by them just like the rat was. But last night, they'd given the rat the slip, jumping into a rolling house (*taxicab*) before he could get too close.

Tonight, he'd be more careful. If they jumped into a *taxicab,* so would he.

Daphne wasn't being any fun. He'd gone by the food alley earlier, hoping to get her to chase him again. She was there, but she would hardly move at all. She sat on a chair in the doorway of the delicious-smelling room that overlooked the food alley. Now and then, her eyebrows would jump, as though she'd heard some startling sound so high pitched that even the rat's ears couldn't detect it. She didn't look happy. The rat tried making her more like her old self by scampering around the little food house with the see-through walls, jumping up and down, chittering. Once or twice, she'd gotten up from her chair and come after him. But she'd moved so slowly, as if she wasn't really awake. And she wouldn't take even one step outside the food alley.

It had made the rat sad. He'd decided Daphne needed to rest for a while. Then, maybe she'd be her old self. And she would chase him through the streets again, and it would be fun.

In the meantime, he had his new playmates. Picking up their scent tonight was easy, because it was so strong, and a breeze was blowing through the Quarter. Even last night, the woman had had a distinctive aroma. The usual dead-flower odor the rat associated with the pale people was mixed in her case with orange rind (a little off, like it'd been marinated in disinfectant) and the musky excretions of some animal that was feeling very frisky. Tonight her scent was even stronger, more pungent and penetrating. Something was making her feel very nervous. Her body was a factory pumping out clouds of nervous sweat.

The rat followed the clouds. He found his two playmates waiting beneath the awning of a dark drugstore. The nervous-sweat woman was much taller than her male companion. He tried to make up the difference by wearing a tall hat and boots with heels, but she still was taller. The rat hid himself between two garbage cans. The man lit a smoking stick (it smelled bad, like grease catching fire in the usually delicious-smelling room), and he put it in his mouth. But the woman snatched it away from him and put it in her own mouth, sucking on it like a straw, belching out exhaust like a tour bus.

A rolling house swerved to the curb and stopped. It wasn't a *taxicab.* It was black and squarish, with a tall, upright window in front and a shiny nose. A strange name popped into the rat's head. *Mercedesbenz.* The woman tossed her smoking stick onto the sidewalk and crushed it with her shoe. She was smelling very, very nervous, much more nervous now that the *Mercedesbenz* was here.

The man opened the back door of the rolling house and started to get inside, but the woman grabbed his arm. "Why don't you ever open up car doors for me, Randolph?"

The man looked at her with a sneer the rat didn't like. " 'Cause you've got your own two arms, that's why."

She didn't let go of his arm. "Be a fucking gentleman for once, won't you?"

He partially closed the door and moved them away from the car. He grabbed her shoulders hard enough that she squealed. His sneer was gone, but what had replaced it was worse. "Don't you louse this up, Pearl," he said in a low tone. "I don't want anything to spook this guy."

The rat took this brief window of opportunity to scamper out from his hiding place and jump through the narrow opening into the rolling house. He hid beneath the front seat. Wherever this Randolph and Pearl were going, that's where he was going, too.

They got into the car and closed the door. Pearl's feet were suddenly near the rat's nose. They smelled very interesting. "Is everything all right?" a man in the front said. The rat jumped, startled, and banged his head against a seat spring. He'd forgotten that someone would have to be in front—the "driver."

"Sure, sure," Randolph said. "Everything's jake. Happy to meet you, finally."

The springs in the front seat groaned as the driver moved. "Here are my letters of introduction," he said. "From both the National Council and the Southwest Federation of Night-bound Communities. I thought you might like to look them over."

That voice, so familiar. The rat remembered it from long ago, but he'd heard it more recently, too. Was this the medicinal-smelling man? The rat stretched his nostrils and breathed deeply, concentrating all his thinking powers on the scents pouring in. There were so many, though—the oiled leather scent of the seats, Pearl's orange musk, her nervous sweat, her feet. He couldn't detect any of the medicine scent that he remembered. Apart from the leather odor, all he could pick up from the driver's direction was a strong scent of bitter lemons, powerful enough to cover up almost anything else.

"Yeah, these papers, they look on the up-and-up, just fine," Randolph said. "But how did you find out about me?"

The *Mercedesbenz* began to move. The rat sank his claws into the carpet so he wouldn't accidentally roll out from beneath his hiding place. "The National Council has many resources," the driver said. "They have ways of finding out where the ambitious young vampires are, and when those young vampires are dissatisfied with their current circumstances. It's very important to them that this power vacuum in northern New Mexico be filled, quickly and efficiently. For someone in your situation, this is an unprecedented opportunity. The chance to ascend to leadership of a community in mere weeks, rather than struggling toward it for decades, if not centuries."

"So you told me," Randolph said. "How about giving me more details about this problem in Santa Fe? Pearl and me, we wouldn't want to stick our noses into an oven that's too hot."

Pearl shifted her feet nervously, almost kicking the rat in the snout.

"Of course not," the driver said. "I have more information on Santa Fe at the house I'm renting, where I'm taking you. And my colleague has a number of questions she'll want to ask you both. The situation is volatile. But I have little doubt that young people with your reputed talents can stamp out the current anarchy and return the community to its prior prosperity."

"Anarchy? I thought you said it was problems with the Indians."

"That's how the troubles began, yes. Joachin and Zarabella, the founders of the modern Santa Fe colony, became too aggressive in harvesting members of the surrounding Native American tribes, against the firm advisement of the National Council. One or two, now and then, that could be overlooked, explained away as the work of wolves. However, they became overconfident, forgetting or ignoring that Native Americans number among their kind some of the fiercest and most skilled vampire hunters in North America. When they encroached on the lands and people of Taos Pueblo, they essentially wrote their own death warrants."

"Sounds nasty," Randolph said. "So how come Pearl and I should want to stick our noses into that?"

"You have the opportunity to learn from Joachin's and Zarabella's poor example. Stay clear of the Indians, and you shouldn't face any serious trouble."

"Well, why come to us?" Pearl asked, speaking for the first time since she'd entered the car. "Why not just pick leaders from the vampires that're already out there?"

Randolph slapped her leg. The rat heard her whimper. The driver didn't seem to take any notice. "They're very young and immature," he said. "All of them were turned within the last ten years. They have no experience curbing their appetites—without Joachin and Zarabella to rein them in, they're like a pack of feral children. They need a firm hand. Apply that firm hand, and the benefits you stand to reap are enormous."

"Work harder to convince me," Randolph said. "Right now, what you're describing sounds like a big pain. Is the National Council offering any incentives for us to pick up and move halfway across the damn country?"

"Not that I'm aware of, no," the driver said. "But perhaps an incentive or two might be . . . negotiated. Please keep in mind that the Santa Fe territory is very rich. Thousands of wealthy tourists visit every year, many of them single, unattached. During the winter, the surrounding mountain trails teem with isolated skiers. Plus, many of the locals cultivate an interest in Wiccan and pagan spirituality . . . including bloodletting rituals."

The *Mercedesbenz* rolled to a stop. "We're here," the driver said. He opened his door. The rat immediately smelled the scents of the river—coffee, mud, eye-watering clouds that almost made him cough (from "refineries"?). Pearl opened her door and stepped out. The rat saw that it was dark outside, darker than the Quarter. Before Randolph could slide toward the open door, the rat scampered out into the darkness.

He landed on cool asphalt next to a tall curb. The street was narrow, made even more narrow by the long rows of cars parked on both sides. Something bellowed nearby, a low, resonant rumble that ruffled each of the rat's thousands of hairs and made them stand on end. It was a sound he had heard uncountable times, a sound he remembered falling asleep by—a ship's horn?

"This way, please," the driver said. He was tall, easily a foot taller than Randolph. He led them along the sidewalk about a quarter of the block. The rat kept pace, darting around car tires, shielding himself with the curb. The trio stopped in front of a white wrought-iron gate, smelling of fresh paint.

The driver opened the gate. The three walked through into a narrow front yard shadowed by a long, raised porch. Pearl smelled extremely afraid now, even more than she had in the *Mercedesbenz.* The rat wiggled through the posts of the iron fence. He knew he had to position himself to get through the front door when it was opened, and to do so unseen. But how?

Two sets of steps led up to the porch. The trio walked up the steps closest to the door. The rat hopped up the second set a second later. He hid in the narrow cranny between the wall and a porch swing that had not yet been suspended from the ceiling.

The driver pulled a set of keys from his pocket. "Lovely old house," he said. "New Orleans is so rich with these. We could've rented a place in the Quarter, my colleague and I, but this seemed so much more charming, and far from the noisy, touristy crowds."

He unlocked the door. The rat braced himself for a sudden dash through the shifting maze of feet. But at the last instant, his nerve failed him—the likelihood of his getting kicked or brushing against someone's ankle leg was too great. He'd be noticed. That wouldn't be a good thing. Not good at all.

The door shut. The rat would have to find another way in.

He pressed his nose against the wavy glass of a tall French window. He watched the driver and Randolph and Pearl walk past into another room. The parlor on the other side of the window looked warm and inviting. Standing lamps cast a dim but friendly glow through shades that dripped with beaded fringe. A striped sofa and a matching easy chair held open magazines and bundles of yarn. A fire crackled in the fireplace. A voice deep in the rat's brain told him he shouldn't try crawling down the chimney.

Still, there had to be another way inside. The rat crept to the edge of the porch. He began climbing up the weatherboards on the side of the house. His claws found precarious purchase in the grooves between boards and on loose nail heads. The windows on the second story were sealed shut. The sole window on the third level, however . . . its twin panes swayed with the breeze, and the mesh screen meant to keep out squirrels (and rats) was torn.

The rat wiggled his way inside. The dark room, barely visible by moonlight, smelled of sawdust and mildew. It had a tall, pointed roof, and the floor that the rat landed upon was uneven and squishy in places. As he crept along the floor of the attic (yes, an *attic,* that's what this room was called, the rat remembered), climbing over rafters and joists, he noticed a long, slender ray of light projecting from the floor onto the sloping ceiling.

He crawled to where the light was. A jumble of wooden steps and metal struts, folded up like an accordion, rested on top of a large wooden panel. The weight of this contraption had depressed the panel, hinged on one side. The rat poked his face through the opening. The gleaming hardwood floor below looked frighteningly far away—a leap from this high up was a one-way ticket to a broken neck. The rat heard distant voices. He was missing it, missing whatever was going on below, and the thought made his furry chest swell with frustration.

The rat stuck his head farther through the opening. His movements caused the contraption above the trapdoor to groan ominously, but the rat ignored this. His attention was captured by a possible way down—a woven rope that hung from the edge of the trapdoor, only inches away from the opening. The rope, as best the rat could tell, descended more than halfway to the floor. If he could reach it and crawl down it, he could drop the rest of the way without getting hurt. He hoped.

The rat stepped onto the trapdoor. He'd have to wiggle his way through the opening, then crawl upside down to the rope, trusting that his claws could dig into the underside of the door long enough for him to reach his dangling destination. The contraption above him groaned again. His head fit easily through the opening, but his plump midsection got caught. He worked his hind legs into the space between the lip of the trapdoor and the attic's floor. Then he pushed. The opening grew a little wider, but not wide enough. The overhead contraption shuddered, creaked, and moaned. The rat pushed harder. The moaning now sounded like the caterwauling of a dozen fornicating cats. Suddenly, the trapdoor yawned wide, and a mechanical monster pursued him from the attic. His perch tilted crazily. Metallic screeching deafened him as steps began unfolding toward the floor.

Unplanned free fall twisted his stomach into knots. He grabbed hold of a step with all his strength while the staircase unfolded like a moth emerging from its cocoon. The bottom step hit the floor with a resounding thud that the rat felt in every bone.

"What the hell was that?" It was Randolph's voice, coming from a room one level below.

"I don't know." The driver's voice. "Pardon me; I'll just be a moment."

Steps and banister creaked as someone began climbing to the second story. The rat shook off his shock-borne paralysis. Even though his heart was still beating five times faster than it was meant to, he scampered down the remaining steps and hid beside a wicker planter.

The driver reached the second story. "Ah, nothing to worry about," he called to his guests downstairs. "The attic stairs fell down. They've never closed properly. Old and creaky, just like me. I'll have to call a repairman." He leaned down, grabbed the bottom step, and pushed it toward the ceiling. The steps obediently folded back into the attic, leaving only the hanging rope behind.

The rat waited until the driver went back downstairs. Then he left his hiding place and descended the staircase himself. Sliding pocket doors that led from the stair foyer and parlor into a dining room were partially open. The rat crept through the gap and hid beneath the curving legs of a china cabinet. The three of them were seated around a long wooden table. Not just the three of them—a fourth person sat at the table, an elderly woman, short and broad, with curled mauve hair, who wore cat's-eye glasses with silver rims. She sat at the opposite end of the table from where the rat hid. Her scent was beguilingly familiar . . . sweet and overripe, like a mango left in the sun too long.

"Pearl, dear, tell me about your parents," the older woman said. A big smile deepened the creases on her lined face.

Pearl looked confused and slightly embarrassed. "There's not much to tell," she said. "They didn't have much to do with me. I got shipped around to a lot of aunts and grandparents."

"But they were nice people, your parents? Did they go to church? Send you to music lessons? I love the piano. My, my, how I *wish* I'd learned to play as a young girl! Do you play the piano, dear?"

Pearl frowned. As best the rat could tell from her scent, her nervousness was shading into irritation. "No. I'm not what you'd call musical."

"You can say that again," Randolph said. He laughed. But then his face turned hard as he glanced at the driver, sitting next to the elderly woman.

The older woman clucked her tongue. "What a shame," she said, shaking her head. "Music, it's such a comfort. It *soothes* you. My boy, I could never get him to take any music lessons. He wanted to be outside all the time, playing games with all them dirty, nasty boys in the neighborhood. Tell me, where did you go to school?"

Pearl looked more puzzled than ever. "College? I didn't go to college."

"No, no, *high* school, dear. You said you grew up in New Orleans. Did you study with the nuns?"

This brought a tight smile to Pearl's face. "Actually, yeah, I did. My aunt Gertrude, she sent me to the Academy of the Sacred Heart."

The elderly woman's eyes grew wide, her expression magnified by the glasses. *"Sacred Heart!"* She clapped her hands with delight. "On St. Charles Avenue? That beautiful building what looks like a palace?"

"That's the one, yeah. I was there a year and a half. Until the nuns decided they didn't want me back for the next semester."

"How lovely, how simply *lovely.*" The older woman reached across the table and patted Pearl on the hand. "If my boy had been a girl, well, I woulda moved heaven and *Earth* to get him into Sacred Heart. If we'd had the money. And if he'd had brains enough."

The table fell silent for a few seconds. The driver lightly touched the elderly woman on the arm. "Well, dear? What do you think of her?"

The older woman removed her glasses and wiped them with a tissue.

Then she put them back on and took a long, steady look at Pearl. "She has a lovely face. Beautiful lips, nice eyes. Nice, healthy hair. Pleasant voice, when she's not smirking. A little smirky-*sour,* maybe. But nothing I couldn't put up with. And I *love* the fact that she studied with the nuns—"

"Hey!" Pearl's tight smile was completely gone. "What's my face got to do with anything?"

"Pearl," Randolph said tightly, "don't go hysterical—"

"I told you this was an interview process," the driver said. "Before I can make my recommendation to the National Council—"

"So how come you aren't asking anything about Randolph?" Pearl said. "How come all the questions have been about *me*?"

The elderly woman clucked her tongue, more loudly this time. "Bad attitude. *Very* bad attitude. But we can change that." She smiled at the driver; rather sweetly, the rat thought. "Can't we, dear?"

The driver stroked her wrinkled hand. "Of course, sweetest. Everyone is trainable."

"Trainable?!?" Pearl looked truly hysterical now. Her sweat smelled hysterical, too. "Randolph, make them stop this right now!"

Randolph sighed and rose from his chair. He stuck his hands inside his jacket. "All right, goof time's over." His hands emerged holding a revolver and a sharpened stake. Pearl also stood, trembling, and removed two similar weapons from her purse. Randolph pointed the stake at the driver and the pistol at the elderly woman. The latter gesture made the rat angry, almost angry enough to bolt from beneath his hiding place. "We'll do the talking now," Randolph said.

"This is outrageous," the driver said. He gripped the sides of the table tightly, turning his pale knuckles even whiter. "You can't threaten us into recommending you for the Santa Fe position—"

"Oh, cut the crap, old man," Randolph said. He was smelling nervous now, almost as nervous as Pearl. "All that New Mexico talk, it's the biggest load of bullshit I ever heard."

Despite the driver's tight grip on the table, he didn't smell nervous or afraid. "Is it?"

"Course it is," Randolph said. "You're the goddamn mutilator guy. I figured it ever since you first phoned me. All those crazy questions Grandma there's been asking Pearl, that just cinched it. You two buzzards, you're coming back with us to our compound. Even if I can't get you to talk, Master Besthoff will for sure. This'll make me a big man, maybe bump off that old fuck Katz as Number Three. No more taking it up the ass. Hell, maybe I'll even become Number Two. Why the fuck should I bust my balls to start a new colony if I can be king of the palace, huh?"

Pearl's gaze darted from the driver to the old woman to Randolph. "And I'll be queen, right? 'Cause I'll be your consort?"

Although a stake was pointed at his chest, the driver smiled a wry smile. "Oh, you'll be someone's consort all right, young miss. Just not in the way you'd expected." He glanced at the old woman. "Dear, your glasses."

She fumbled for the bridge of her nose. "But I'm wearing my glasses—"

"Your other glasses, dear."

"Oh."

She reached into her stiff hairdo and pulled down a pair of blue-tinted glasses, which she placed in front of her cat's-eye lenses. The driver pulled a pair of identical tinted glasses from beneath the table. Then the rat watched him push a red button underneath the table, which was attached to wires that led down the table's leg.

Suddenly, blue crosses appeared all over the room. On the walls, the ceiling, the draperies, the cabinets, and chairs. Pearl shrieked. Randolph screamed and threw his arms across his face. His weapons clattered to the floor. The rat hissed involuntarily as his skin and fur sizzled with heat. He backed more deeply beneath the china cabinet, trying to hide from the omnipresent crosses. The air smelled like burning matches.

Randolph stumbled toward the partially open pocket doors. But the driver moved more quickly to shut them. The largest blue cross of all appeared on the huge screen formed by the closed doors. Randolph cried out and stumbled backward, knocking over a chair. He cowered against the table, trembling as he struggled to shield his face with his jacket.

"It's really incredible what one can do with video-projection equipment nowadays," the driver said. "And prices have come down so much." He turned to his companion. "Sweetest, why don't you go upstairs and have yourself a nice rest? What I have to do next won't be pleasant."

The elderly woman frowned. "But I don't want to leave you. What if you need help?"

"You know I'll be fine. Go rest. Do some knitting. Weren't you working on a wonderful pair of mittens?"

"Well, yes, I suppose . . ." She stared down at Pearl, who had crawled partially under the table. "You won't hurt her face any, will you? It's such a pretty face."

"Her face will remain flawless. I promise."

"Okay. But don't be too long."

The elderly woman left the room through the other door. The driver knelt down and picked up the stake and gun Randolph had dropped. He stood over the cowering young vampire and held the gun as though it were a hammer, hefting it, judging its weight. "Take away your fangs and your powers," he said quietly, "and you're nothing but a cheap, scared little punk. Heck, even with your fangs, you're nothing but a cheap little—"

"Nooo!!"

A gun discharged. A vase next to the window shattered. Chairs clattered to the floor as Pearl erupted blindly from beneath the table and grabbed for the driver's legs. He stepped backward, trying to avoid her grasp.

The pocket doors slid open. The rat poked his head out from beneath the cabinet, despite the intensified pain. A tall man entered, as tall or taller than the driver. He also wore blue glasses. The new man grabbed Pearl and pulled her away from the driver.

"I could've handled her," the driver said.

"Of course," the new man said. "But why take any unnecessary chances?"

Pearl's eyes, tightly shut, now popped wide open. *"You!"* She struggled to turn her head so she could see the man who'd wrapped her in his long arms. "*You!* You back-stabbing bastard! You'll rot in hell for this! I'll make you pay! I'll make you—"

"Cover her mouth, won't you?" the driver said. "There's a lady resting upstairs who has a delicate constitution." The new man complied. The rat couldn't detect his scent because of the overwhelming odor of burning matches.

Randolph continued whimpering against the tabletop. The driver shoved him onto his back. "Wherever you're going next, I hope it's at least as unpleasant as these last three minutes have been," the driver said. He rested the stake's point against Randolph's chest, then struck the blunt end with the butt of the gun.

Randolph screamed. The wave of sound shook the windows and the cabinet's glass doors. The rat watched, fascinated and horrified, as the outer layers of Randolph's body peeled away in a shower of flecks and dust. His scream crumbled, too, until it was a withered peep the rat could barely hear. By that time, Randolph was a shifting pile of particles on the floor, looking like a spilled ten-pound bag of sugar someone had tried covering up with a jacket and a fedora.

"I enjoyed that," the new man said.

"I rather thought you would," the driver said. He placed the stake and gun on the table.

A voice echoed from upstairs. "You okay down there?"

"Yes, sweetest," the driver cried out. "Everything's fine. Go back to your knitting."

"I heard something break before."

"It was just a vase. We'll buy another one. I'll be up to see you in a few minutes."

"All right. Don't be too long."

Pearl struggled a few seconds in the new man's arms, but then she slumped, quivering and quietly moaning. Tears poured from her downcast eyes. "Hurry it up with her, won't you?" the new man said. "I've never handled a woman's crying very well."

The driver approached the china cabinet. The rat backed more deeply beneath its legs. As soon as he opened the cabinet, the rat smelled a medicinal scent he hadn't detected before. The medicinal scent he remembered following through the Quarter. The driver approached Pearl holding a small glass cylinder with a long, gleaming point. He inserted the point into her neck and pressed a plunger on the cylinder. A second later, her legs went limp. Then she wasn't moving at all.

The driver pressed the red button beneath the table again. To the rat's enormous relief, all the blue crosses vanished. The driver removed his blue-tinted glasses and accepted an identical pair from his companion. "Would you mind taking her downstairs before you leave?" he said.

"Of course not," the new man said. He gathered Pearl into his arms. The driver helped him by opening the pocket doors to their fully open position. "Thank you," the new man said. "This has been a most productive evening."

"You're very welcome. And thank *you.*"

The driver vanished into the next room, which smelled like a kitchen. He returned a few seconds later with a broom and a gold-colored dustpan. He picked up Randolph's jacket, shirt, and pants and hung them over the top of a chair. He put the shoes, socks, and underwear on the window seat beside the shattered vase. He picked up the hat, looked it over, then tried it on. It was too small. He shrugged his shoulders and set it down on the table.

The door to the kitchen opened again. "Is the coast clear?" It was the old woman, still wearing her blue glasses.

"Sweetest, you didn't give me time to clean up." He walked over to her, removed the blue glasses from her nose, and kissed her forehead. Then he began sweeping pieces of the broken vase into the dustpan.

"Nonsense!" she said, grabbing the broom away from him. "Keeping things spick-and-span around here is *my* job." While he continued picking up pieces of the vase, she knelt down and began sweeping up the Randolph particles.

And then she saw the rat, whose twitching nose was poking out from beneath the china cabinet.

"Say! Look who's come to pay a visit," she said, her eyes widening. She set down the broom and crouched on her hands and knees, staring at him intently. "Don't think I've ever seen one like *that* before."

The rat didn't try to run or hide. Something about the woman was profoundly comforting. He mirrored her stare just as intently.

"Disgusting vermin," the driver muttered. "This is what we get for moving so close to the river. I'll head over to the all-night GoodiesMart in Chalmette and pick up some traps."

"He ain't no *vermin*!" the woman snapped. "He's *cute.*" She smiled sweetly at the rat, showing off slightly yellowed front teeth. "I think I wanna keep him for a pet." She clucked her tongue at him as though he were a chicken, beseeching him to come out from under the cabinet with little waving motions of her hands. "C'mere, boy. Come to Mama. Mama won't hurt you. I'll get you some nice cheese or something."

The rat left his sanctuary. He was very curious about this woman. She certainly didn't look frightening, not with her warmly glistening eyes behind those oversized glasses and her pale cheeks furrowed with laugh lines. The rat walked slowly across the floor, never taking his eyes off hers.

"Oh, look at this!" she crowed. "He's comin' straight for me! Just like he could understand every word I was sayin'."

He sniffed her hand. It smelled like cocoa-butter hand cream and cooking oil. They were good scents. He crawled onto her hand and let her pick him up. She held him against her bosom, then steadied herself against the table and stood up. "Isn't he *sweet*?" she said, stroking the top of his head with her index finger. "What a tame little thing. Why, it's like him and me've known each other all our lives."

The driver came closer. "His fur is singed," he said. "See? He looks like he's just run through a fire. I've got a funny feeling about this animal. Would you mind if I examined him?"

"No!" the woman cried, clutching the rat tightly to her breast and turning away. "I mean, yes I *would* mind! You've got enough toys downstairs without messin' with my pet. So don't you lay a *finger* on him." She stroked the rat's head again and cooed.

"Very well," the driver said. He did not look happy. "But keep a close eye on that one. I wouldn't want him turning into something else when neither of us is looking."

The woman rocked the rat in her arms. "Now, why would he want to turn into something else when he's so happy bein' just what he is?" She lifted him close to her face, so that his muzzle was an inch from her nose. "Hey, what should I call you, huh? How about 'Richard'? Short for 'Richard Rodent'? How's that?"

She laughed and carried him into the kitchen. He nuzzled closer to her bosom and stroked her plump arm by wagging his tail. As her overripe mango scent filled his nostrils, the rat began falling happily asleep.

TWENTY-ONE

"I'm so *sorry,* Mr. Newton. Usually Dr. Landrieu has been extremely punctual. I simply don't know what to say."

Jules checked his watch. Again. This time, it read 9:02 P.M. He'd been standing out here on his ex-boss's porch for almost twenty minutes. He'd been waiting at the house since 8:25.

The company wasn't anything to write home about, either. Ever since he'd arrived, realtor Fannie Yishinsky had been chirping nonstop like a toy parakeet. Judging from her petite size, Vegas showgirl makeup, feathered hair (long ago gray, but dyed electric blond), and garish green-and-orange pants suit, the image wasn't far off the mark.

"Well, at least it's a *lovely* evening, isn't it?" she said. "A little wait out on a beautiful porch like this, on a beautiful *street* like this, that's nothing to get bothered about, is it?"

Jules had wanted to wait for Doc Landrieu inside, so his old mentor wouldn't spot him from a block distant and possibly decide to stay away. He'd gotten her to go inside for a while, and they'd sat briefly on one of the shrouded sofas still left in the living room. But her nervous energy had been irresistible, and she'd badgered him into stepping outside, wanting him to experience the tree-shaded beauty of the neighborhood and its peacefulness after dark. It *was* peaceful and quiet. Or it would be, if only she'd just shut up.

"Let me try calling him again," she said. "Maybe he got hung up somewhere. He drives that old vintage car, you know? A doctor should have something newer than that. It could have broken down. A piston or something, maybe."

She pulled a cell phone from her purse and began punching in numbers. Jules tried watching and memorizing the number she dialed, but once he'd gotten the last four digits lodged in his brain, the first three were gone. While she waited with the tiny phone pressed against her ear, her free hand patted and smoothed her hair. After thirty seconds, she slammed the phone shut with a disgusted expression. "Not even an answering service! What *century* is the man living in?"

He scanned the street, wondering if hidden eyes were watching him from around a corner. "Could we go back inside? Please? I'd rather wait in there." Jules fought down a distressing suspicion that the night was a lost cause. Maybe Doc Landrieu *had* gotten held up somewhere. It wasn't impossible.

"Well, I suppose . . ." She smiled suddenly. "Actually, would you mind if I gave you the grand tour *before* Dr. Landrieu arrives? I know it's not exactly kosher, but it's a *lovely* house, with so many attractive features—"

"Sure, sure, whatever. You lead, I'll follow."

They went back inside. She took him into the kitchen first, singing the praises of recently installed marbleized countertops and the virtues of the refrigerator/freezer unit. He was only half listening. By the time she launched into an explanation of the house's termite-damage warranty, he'd retreated entirely into the dank environs of his own skull.

He'd called Besthoff before heading over here tonight. Jules felt honor-bound to give him something, to prove he wasn't wasting Besthoff's money. He told Besthoff about Randolph's and Pearl's payoff to the Historic Districts Preservation commissioner. He told him about the attack on Preston, how it had been both similar to and different from the attacks on the High Krewe's young women. And he told him what he'd learned from Edith L'Enfant about the young vampires' real-estate plans. Jules withheld his suspicions about Doc Landrieu. He didn't want to point Besthoff in that direction until Jules was absolutely sure of his ex-boss's involvement . . . or as close to absolutely sure as he could get.

Besthoff's reaction justified Jules's earlier stinginess with information. The High Krewe's leader demanded that L'Enfant be kidnapped without delay. He actually ordered Jules to meet Besthoff's servants at

L'Enfant's home and haul him back to the High Krewe's compound. Then he revealed the wellspring of his impetuousness—Randolph and Pearl hadn't come home last night.

With a flurry of fast talking, Jules was able to—barely, just barely—steer Besthoff onto a more cautious course. The two youngsters probably had a satellite nest hidden in the city, he said; given that they were planning an exodus to town, it made sense that they'd have sleeping quarters close at hand, maybe even in one of the musician's mansions. L'Enfant's ball was tomorrow night. Presumably, all the players would be gathered under his roof. Jules had his best chance then and there to discover what was going on. Kidnapping L'Enfant now would be pouring boiling water on the anthill, scattering the players so widely Jules would never catch up with all of them. Besides, if Jules failed to learn anything, there was always time for torture and mayhem the night after.

". . . second level has two cozy bathrooms, and the guest room has a lovely view of the quaint Jewish cemetery. Would you like to go upstairs?"

"Huh?" Jules blinked himself back to the present.

"I asked, Mr. Newton, if you'd like to accompany me upstairs."

Upstairs. Where the broken window was. He didn't want her to see that. Finding out his home had been broken into could make Doc Landrieu suspicious—assuming he wasn't suspicious already.

Jules made a big production out of checking his watch. "Uh, actually, it's gettin' really late. My wife and me, we've got lots of packing to do. For that cruise. So I'm afraid I gotta take a rain check, Ms. Yishinsky."

The small woman looked crestfallen. Jules almost felt sorry for her. "Of course," she said reluctantly. "I can't ask you to wait around here all night. I'm sure Dr. Landrieu will telephone his regrets as soon as he's able. In any case, can we reschedule?"

Jules was all too aware that his time was limited, and not by a cruise. Besthoff had given him just one more night to show some results. L'Enfant's shindig wouldn't get rolling until after nine P.M., so Jules had ninety minutes or so of free time beforehand. "How about tomorrow night? A little earlier, maybe eight o'clock? And I'll give you my cell phone number, just in case Doc Landrieu shows up tonight after I leave."

She looked cautiously hopeful. "I'm so glad you're willing to try again. I'll do my best to reach him. Here, why don't you write me that number. I can't tell you how much I appreciate your patience, Mr. Newton." She handed him the same notepad near the refrigerator that Jules had torn a sheet from two nights earlier. "How do you like the house so far?"

"Lovely, just lovely." Jules had another idea. "Hey, any chance you could give me Doc Landrieu's new home phone number? He's a real night owl, like me. I might have a better chance of reaching him real late tonight. Or if you've got his address, I could even stop over there—"

Fannie smiled and shook her head. "I wish I could, Mr. Newton. Especially since you're being so accommodating. But that would violate my company's confidentiality policies. And I like my job."

Back outside, Jules couldn't shake the feeling he was being watched. *Good,* he thought, bitter in his disappointment. *If you're out there watchin' me, that means we'll hook up, eventually. Hopefully before Besthoff gives ME the hook.*

Climbing into his car, Jules realized he didn't have a clue where to go next. No, that wasn't right; not exactly. He stared at the bagged copy of *The Shadow Magazine* lying in the space between the two seats. He still hadn't taken the pulp out of its protective plastic, but he remembered the stories inside, almost as clearly as when the magazine had first hit the newsstand, back in 1943. Back when he'd still been living with his mother, listening to radio shows such as *The Shadow* with her.

Jules knew where he wanted to go, even if it didn't have a thing to do with this damn investigation. He wished he could tell himself he couldn't remember the last time he'd visited his mother's grave site. Problem was, he *could* remember. And it was embarrassing. Six years ago. He'd gone on living, or existing, in New Orleans for six whole years without paying his mother the simple, basic courtesy of visiting her resting place, barely four miles from his house.

Why? Sheer laziness might've had something to do with it. But Jules hadn't been too lazy to catalog his collection of jazz records or learn how to use a computer. Oh, sure, there was the physical discomfort of walking into the cemetery, surrounded by all those modest little crosses. After even a few minutes near his mother's grave, Jules felt like a sharecropper who'd stood bare-chested in the Alabama sun all day. But discomfort was an old, familiar companion, one Jules knew how to tolerate.

Oh, there was one other thing . . . seeing his mother's grave revisited on him the sickly embarrassment, the bone-deep humiliation of having buried his mother in a paupers' cemetery. Especially after everything she'd done for him. Especially after her last instructions, her final motherly sacrifice. How many times had Jules told himself to get her coffin exhumed and moved to a classier resting place? But other things had always gotten in the way—his transmission falling out after hitting a crater on St. Claude Avenue, drying up his funds. Or a big blowout with Maureen, sending him into a major funk.

Maureen. If Jules had one biggest regret, it would be that his mother and Maureen had never been able to get along. Now they were both gone. But when they'd had their chance to be friends during the forty-plus years they'd shared his company, they'd both poisoned what could've been an unconventional but satisfactory relationship. Jules felt his head begin to pound just from the memories. Maureen had hated Jules's devotion to his mother, his insistence on living with her at least part of every week. *"She's gonna strangle the life out of you with those damn apron strings, Jules!"*

And his mother's feelings toward Maureen? They'd been . . . interesting. Oddly enough, his mother hadn't hated Maureen for turning Jules into a vampire. He'd never come out and told her Maureen had done the deed, of course, but his mother must've suspected, especially since Jules and Maureen were the only two vampires, for all she knew, that existed in the whole world. No, what had gotten his mother's dander up about Maureen had been Maureen's lack of proper upbringing, epitomized by her choice of professions—first, a chorus girl in vaudeville shows, and later, an exotic dancer in some of Bourbon Street's lower-end burlesque clubs. If she hadn't already been dead, Jules's mother would've had a coronary had she seen Maureen's career finale at Jezebel's Joy Room.

Jules parked his car in the small lot behind Delgado College's recycling bins. The cemetery, much older than the college, was just beyond the bins. Standing near the rusted, leaning fence that surrounded the paupers' cemetery, Jules was again struck by how different it was from most other New Orleans burial places. Typically, being buried in New Orleans was an expensive, complicated procedure; bodies had to be laid to rest in aboveground crypts or vaults, due to the below-sea-level elevation of much of the town. But the city fathers, in their penny-pinching wisdom, had chosen this field as the repository for the poor because it rested upon one of the higher ridges in the area, eight to twelve feet above sea level. No need for expensive crypts. Stick 'em right in the ground.

A native son of New Orleans might not even recognize the field as a cemetery at first. To the casual eye, it looked like a weed-strewn lot, most of the modest tombstones hidden by the voracious foliage. Only the cheap wooden crosses were noticeable above the weeds.

Jules walked to the spot in the fence where the gate had once been. Walking into this cemetery, with all its crosses, was like stepping into a steaming hot bath. He tried sticking to the central path, even though it wasn't clearly marked. Stepping accidentally on one of the grave sites was almost as painful as hugging one of the crosses; it was consecrated ground, and he invariably got a hotfoot. Maneuvering around Metairie Cemetery had been infinitely easier; there, the immaculate rows of crypts had causeways between them big enough to drive a Hummer through, and the snooty families that found their final rest there mostly shied away from garish displays of large crosses.

His mother was buried somewhere in the northeast section of the cemetery. Lighting was sparse; Jules had only the dim glow of distant street lamps to guide him. Five yards into the grass, he found himself surrounded by the chirpings of hundreds of crickets and the deep groanings of bullfrogs, as if a tiny piece of Honey Island Swamp had been dropped into the center of the city. He felt himself heating up. Maybe all the critter noises would cover up the coming *snap!, crackle!,* and *pop!* of his skin. If he couldn't hear it, maybe it wouldn't hurt as much.

"Mother, I don't know if you're watchin' me or if you can hear me, but I'm sorry I been away so long." He hoped talking to himself would take his mind off his increasing discomfort. "I just lucked into six thousand dollars. How about that, huh? I gotta make some repairs on this new car I got—some punks messed it up—but any leftover money, I'm gonna use it for a down payment on a new burial plot for you. St. Louis Cemetery Number Three. Top of the line. About time, huh?"

His skin was getting that itchy, heartbreak-of-psoriasis feeling. He knew if he started scratching, though, he'd be scratching all night, filling his car and clothes with ashy flakes. He kept pushing his way through the weeds, some knee high, some taller, keeping to the path by steering clear of the crosses. " 'Cause you deserve the best, Mother. I could never give you the best when you were alive. But you never complained about that. You were always happy with whatever kinda pay I brought home, just so long as I was workin' somewheres. You didn't complain when I came home with blood on my clothes. You just washed 'em. And you usually got the stains out. And then, when you knew it was your time to go, you—you . . ."

Jules felt himself choke up. He couldn't finish the sentence. A stray tear cooled his hot face before evaporating. She'd *insisted.* She wouldn't take no for an answer. With her last burst of strength, she'd made him promise he'd do it. . . .

"Jules, listen to me, boy. You know I always looked after you. Always done everything I could for you, especially after your daddy left us. So I don't want no squeamishness about this. As soon as I'm gone, Jules, I want you to drink my blood. Every last drop, you hear? Not one second before I'm gone, 'cause I don't wanna miss my appointment with Saint Peter at the pearly gates. But don't wait too long, neither, 'cause I'd feel bad knowin' I didn't give my son a hot meal."

Who else had ever willingly given him so much? He'd do better by her this time. This time, he wouldn't let *anything* get in the way of his providing his sainted mother with the resting place she deserved.

He knew he was getting close. Her little grave marker, a modest tablet of granite he'd had inscribed:

DOROTHY EDNA DUCHON
LOVING MOTHER
SHE GAVE TO HER LAST DROP

—it was around here someplace, not far from that emaciated sweet olive tree by the fence. Someone needed to get a lawn tractor back here. Damn city administration—they wouldn't shell out a hundred bucks a month to keep this cemetery from looking like a jungle.

He hated the thought of stepping off the path and burning his feet, but he needed to make sure no vandals had tipped over his mother's stone. Or worse, stolen it. The crickets and frogs were even louder back here. Their noises covered up Jules's "ahh!"s and "oww!"s as he cleared away tufts of high grass, bumping into crosses and stumbling over consecrated earth.

He found her marker. His heart lurched. Something was wrong. The last time he'd been here, the ground in front of her marker had been flat, covered with old, tough grass. Now the earth was mounded, freshly crumbled, with no grass other than a few isolated green shoots growing out of it. As if someone had been buried there recently, not almost forty years ago.

Was this even the right spot? Had someone moved his mother's marker? Who the hell would do such a thing? Jules ransacked his memory, trying to remember who had been buried next to his mother. A man with a funny name. Frantically, Jules cleared away the high grass to the left of his mother's marker. Lying on the ground was a weathered, cracked wooden cross. Jules could barely make out the faded name in the moonlight. Mack Poosay.

This was it. The right spot.

Someone had tampered with his mother's grave.

Time ground to a halt. A dumb little voice inside his head told him that even vampires could be stunned senseless with horror. He was just beginning to wrap his shredded consciousness around the pulverizing notion that his mother might no longer be where he left her, when something stung his neck.

His involuntary response was to slap whatever it was away. But his arm didn't move right. It moved as if he were deep underwater, or rubber hoses were tying it down. He tried swiveling his head around to see what was wrong with his arm, but his head wouldn't move right, either. Everything was so slow. . . . Now his legs were giving up the ghost, too, folding under his weight.

Was he having a heart attack? Was *this* what a heart attack felt like? The physical vitality he'd lost along with his vampiric powers, the added weight, the shock of seeing his mother's grave defiled—sure, nature had taken its course. He was falling, and that seemed like slow motion, too. This was the end of him; his glazed eyes would watch the sunrise, and that would be that. He was amazed he could think so clearly. Weird—there wasn't any stabbing pain in his chest, not like he'd expected at all.

He hit the ground, but he didn't feel it. His veins were pumping novocaine, not blood. He rolled onto his belly and face, lips brushing the rough grass. But he didn't stay that way. Something pushed him, rolled him over onto his back. The toe of a black shoe.

He was still able to move his eyes. When his gaze rose from the shoe to gray-striped pants, then a long, black cashmere overcoat, and finally a face shadowed by a black fedora and wrapped with a brown scarf, Jules realized he hadn't collapsed from a heart attack. Seeing this person standing over him, however, he nearly suffered a heart failure for real.

Doc Landrieu? He was tall enough to be his old boss. His eyes were hidden by dark glasses. In the dim light, Jules couldn't see even a strip of the man's face. His attacker removed the needle he'd used to disable Jules from his hypodermic, tossed it into the grass, and pocketed the plunger.

Jules wished he'd say something. Anything, even just one word. That way, Jules would know. For all the good it would do him now.

Jules saw that he held a cane in his right hand. A handsome wooden cane, maple or cherry wood, crowned with a brass alligator head. Jules racked his brain, trying to remember if he'd ever seen his old boss use such a cane. His attacker lifted the cane in the air. Then, almost faster than Jules's eyes could follow, he smashed it over Jules's mother's headstone. The resulting point looked very sharp. Very sharp indeed.

The man straddled Jules's body. His tall black form blocked all light, even the moon. As the man raised the broken cane in both fists, Jules asked himself what he'd regret most. *Not seein' Doodlebug again. Not havin' one last cuppa joe with Erato. Not solvin' this damn mystery.*

And most painful of all . . .

Never holdin' Maureen in my arms again.

If he weren't paralyzed, Jules would've tensed every muscle waiting for the killing stroke. What was taking the silent bastard so long? Why was he hesitating? Almost as if he were waiting for something—

"Stop! Don't hurt that man!"

Where had that voice come from? Jules would've traded his Cadillac for the ability to move his head even six inches. His attacker stepped away from Jules's body and hissed. He pointed the broken cane in front of him like a sword. To Jules's limited vision, what happened next was a blur. A pale hand struck the cane, sending it soaring away into the night. Arms grabbed Jules's attacker and yanked him out of Jules's range of sight. Less than a second later, a dark-draped body rocketed above Jules's head, crashing into a row of crosses. Jules heard an agonized shriek, as though the man had been scalded; then he heard the fading impact of retreating footfalls.

More footsteps. Coming closer. Another man stood above him. A tall man. This man wore a tweed sport coat and glasses that weren't dark at all. Jules could see his face in the moonlight.

Doc Landrieu.

"Are you hurt, Jules? Can you move?"

Jules, of course, could offer no reply. Even if he hadn't been paralyzed, he'd now be stunned into silence.

His old boss knelt beside him and probed Jules's throat with his fore- and middle fingers. "Pulse is strong," he muttered. He pulled a small flashlight from his pocket and shined it on Jules's face. "Small wound to your throat. A needle mark. Looks like he injected you with something. It'd have to be an elephant tranquilizer to take you down so fast." He shifted his ray onto the grass near Jules's feet. "I saw him fiddling with a hypodermic when I was coming closer. Caught a reflection off something shiny that he tossed in the grass. Maybe I can find it, figure out what he dosed you with."

He crisscrossed the trampled weeds with his light. "Ah. Here it is. Assuming this isn't a heroin needle some junkie dropped. They need better security in these old cemeteries." He took a handkerchief from his pocket and wrapped the needle with it. Then he knelt down again.

"I know what must be running through your mind," he said, laying his hand on Jules's chest in a comforting gesture. "Why didn't I show up at the house? Why did I follow you here, to your mother's grave site? There's not much to it. I was expecting to see Chip Newton at the house tonight, not you. When I spotted you standing out on the porch with Ms. Yishinsky, I froze. You see, things have changed considerably with me since we last spoke."

Jules heard him sigh, a long and heavy sound. He stood and turned away, facing the moon. "*I've* changed, Jules. I didn't know if you already knew, somehow. But even if you didn't, I feared you'd know as soon as you saw me. And I couldn't risk your blurting out some . . . indiscreet comment in front of Ms. Yishinsky."

He turned back again, his face full of embarrassed solicitude. "I'm sorry, old friend. I've no right to mull over my fate and waste precious seconds, not when you've got Lord-knows-what coursing through your veins. I've got to get you back to my house. I may be able to help you there. In any case, I certainly can't leave you lying here. That man who attacked you could return at any moment."

He partially rolled Jules onto his side, then slid his arms beneath Jules's body. Jules could only assume he'd now be getting irrefutable proof that his old boss was now a vampire. Even expecting it, he was still mutely amazed when Doc Landrieu rose with Jules in his arms. His old boss didn't even breathe hard.

"It's still incredible to me that I can do such things, Jules. This new reality of mine—it has its unique horrors, but it's not without its consolations."

They began moving slowly toward the cemetery's main entrance. Doc Landrieu shifted Jules in his arms, trying to find the least awkward way to carry him. He slung the top half of Jules's body over his left shoulder and leaned to the right so Jules wouldn't roll off. Jules felt blood rushing to his head. "Please forgive this indignity," Doc Landrieu said as he dug his fingers deeply into Jules's rear end, seeking a good grip. "I can . . . handle your weight. Your size . . . that's . . . another matter. But we should reach your car in just a moment. It's closer than mine."

They reached Jules's Allante. Doc Landrieu set him down as gently as he could, but Jules's head bounced off the car's front bumper. "Oh. Terribly sorry. Here, let's see which pocket you've got your keys in." Jules tried telling him they were in his right vest pocket, but all that came out was a tiny, strangled gurgle. "Don't bother trying to talk. Nasty bit of business that attacker pulled on you. Hopefully, we'll find out soon enough what he used. Ah, here they are."

He opened the passenger-side door. "Jules, I'm shocked you're driving such a small car. You must barely fit inside this convertible." He lifted Jules and did his best to position him comfortably on the passenger seat. "Good heavens . . . Why on earth did you get rid of your old car? Some kind of midlife crisis? Well, when you get to be my age, you learn that practicality comes before everything. Heh. Of course, you're even older than I am, aren't you?"

He started the car, rolled down both windows, and shut Jules in, taking care to arrange the seat belt around his old subordinate's middle. Then they pulled out of the parking lot. "Ignore my babbling, Jules. It's all this excitement. Eight months ago, who would've thought I'd be tossing around a masked killer in a cemetery? Anyway, as I was saying before, I felt I couldn't risk seeing you at the house. But I knew I had to talk with you. That's why I followed you to the cemetery. Considering what happened, it's a good thing I did."

He turned onto City Park Avenue, then onto Canal Street. "Too many people know me around here. That's why I'm selling the house. I need to move on. After what those . . . men did to me."

He was silent for a moment while they waited for a light to change. "They said they were doing it to get at you. Their leader's name was Malice X. I suppose you know that. He hated you fiercely. He and those punks . . . I don't like to think about what they did to me, Jules. But I think they made a mistake. I don't believe they meant to turn me into what they were, into what you are. I believe they meant to drink my blood in the most gruesome way possible, then leave my corpse for you to find. I don't know why they left before destroying my brain stem so I wouldn't rise again, changed . . . Maybe a police siren chased them off. Maybe they just got sloppy. Or maybe that Malice X was more subtle than I give him credit for. Maybe he realized that for someone like me, who'd studied a vampire and knew the physical and spiritual degradations of a vampire's existence, becoming one myself would be a fate much worse than a painful but quick death."

He turned onto the side street next to the Jewish cemetery. *Doc, there are worse things than being a vampire,* Jules wanted to say. He wished he could manage even a word or two to comfort his friend, but speaking was still as far out of reach as a flight to the next solar system. They pulled into Doc Landrieu's driveway, close to his front steps. Doc Landrieu opened the house's front door and returned to Jules's side of the car.

"You'll have to forgive me, Jules," he said, pulling Jules out of the car. "I'm going to have to drag you up those steps. Carrying you the way I did before, I nearly threw out my back. Even a vampire has his limits."

Jules felt himself bobbing in and out of consciousness. Doc Landrieu got him inside and pulled him onto one of the shrouded sofas. "You rest here. I'm going downstairs, to my lab, and run some tests on whatever residue's left on this needle I found. If I can't obtain a good enough sample of the compound, I'll need to draw some blood from you. Just like old times."

Old times . . . ? If only the doc could really make it so. Inject him with some magic liquid, a time-travel drug; bring back Jules's house, his old cab, Maureen. Jules felt his eyelids grow heavy. Heck, while he was at it, why not bring back department stores on Canal Street; ten-cent Jimmy Cagney movies; Carnival parades through the French Quarter; that streetcar named for Desire Street; a decent nickel cup of coffee? Bring back those funny little Italian mayors, like Vic Schiro. Bring back Louis Armstrong and Louie Prima. Bring back Jules's record collection. Bring back his mother . . .

Jules was sitting at his kitchen table. His old kitchen table—the one in the house he'd shared with his mother. His mother was in the kitchen, and so was Maureen. They were both wearing gingham aprons, chatting gaily together while they prepared a Thanksgiving meal. Sunlight streamed through the open windows, giving the room a warm glow. Maureen stirred the turnips while they boiled down, adding a little more seasoning, tasting her cooking and smiling. Maureen *hated* turnips, but since this was obviously a dream, this discrepancy didn't bother Jules too much. That turkey smelled damn good. Jules felt his stomach rumble. Maybe in this dream, he could eat solid food?

The doorbell rang. His mother was checking on the turkey, so Jules went to answer the door. It was Doodlebug and Doc Landrieu and Erato and Daphne, all carrying casseroles of more food.

Jules put their casseroles on the dining room table. Then they sat around in the living room, waiting for the turkey to be done. Jules turned on the TV. They watched the end of an episode of *The Phil Silvers Show.* It was a good one.

Maureen carried out bowls of turnips and gumbo and cranberries. Jules's mother carried out the turkey, half as big as she was. Jules stood with the carving knife in hand and gave the benediction. His mouth didn't burn when he invoked the Lord's name. When he began carving the turkey, however, the whole bird started trembling. A pink nose poked through the oyster dressing that filled the turkey's open end. The rat emerged, shaking himself briskly until greasy bread crumbs flew off his fur in all directions.

Everyone applauded.

"Jules . . ."

Jules's eyes popped open. He was on the sofa, still unable to move or speak. Doc Landrieu's hand was on his shoulder.

"Jules, we were in luck. I was able to get a good read on that compound. Better yet, I've been able to devise a counteragent. I'm not sure how quickly it'll work, or whether you'll get complete remission of the paralysis all at once. Obviously, I haven't been able to test it. But combined with your natural healing abilities, this counteragent should give you most of your mobility back, well before sunrise."

He rolled up Jules's sleeve, dabbed his biceps with alcohol, and injected Jules with a pinkish liquid that looked like weak lemonade. Jules barely felt the needle pierce his flesh. He was sad that Doc Landrieu had awakened him before Jules had a chance to taste the turkey.

Doc Landrieu pulled a chair closer to the sofa and sat down. "I made an intriguing discovery, Jules. Completely inadvertently. When I awoke after the attack, and I saw the blood-stained tubes sticking out of my veins, I knew immediately what I'd become. I felt the bloodlust . . . a horrible thirst, a hunger like a wild animal's. My first thought was to do myself in. Destroy myself before I could hurt someone. I steeled myself to wait for the sunrise. But an hour before dawn, I'm ashamed to say I completely lost my nerve.

"I spent my first day as a vampire curled up on the floor of a closet, slumbering on dirt from the backyard; I stuffed newspapers beneath the door to keep out the light. The next few nights, I still couldn't bring myself to actively destroy myself, but I believed I could do so passively. I didn't let myself leave the house. I felt the bloodlust build, and build, until I thought for certain I'd run screaming into the streets. But somehow, I hung on, secure in the belief that it would soon all be over.

"And it *was* over soon—simply not in the way I'd expected. Five nights after I became a vampire, the bloodlust began receding, like a slowly departing tide. It's never left me entirely—I still need to maintain strict self-control, particularly in situations where . . . opportunity comes knocking. But I learned I could sustain myself on ordinary food, that roast beef—a bit bloody, perhaps—and a glass of red wine would dampen the fires of my hunger as they always had."

He touched Jules's shoulder again, and his eyes were terribly sad. "Isn't it a shame that I couldn't have been there for you with this knowledge, that night in 1917 when you first became a vampire? How many hundreds of living souls might we have saved? But I'm more than eighty years too late. Your system has so completely adapted to a blood diet by now, I'm certain your bloodlust is as much physiological as it is psychological."

Jules tried moving his hand to touch Doc Landrieu's arm. He was surprised to find he was able to move his hand several inches; painfully slowly, but it was progress. His ex-boss noticed. "Good. You're overcoming the paralysis. I expect within an hour or two, you'll be back on your feet."

He rose from his chair. "I'm afraid I have to leave you now. There are a number of things I need to take care of before sunrise."

Jules tried talking. He had so many questions. He was able to grunt—his lips and tongue were moving, at least—but the coordination required for speech was still maybe a half hour away.

"A word of advice from your doctor," Doc Landrieu said. "I'd suggest walking around the block a few times before getting in your car. Or do some simple calisthenics in here—touch your nose with your fingertips a few dozen times. Your coordination and response time won't snap back to normal immediately. And you wouldn't want to compound tonight's events with a car wreck."

He moved toward the door. "One more thing, Jules. About your mother . . . don't worry yourself too much. She's in a better place now. You'll remember to lock up when you leave, won't you? Just push the button in. We'll talk more soon; I'll be in touch."

He left Jules's car keys on a small table in the foyer. And then Amos Landrieu shut the front door behind him.

TWENTY-TWO

The sounds of a circus greeted Jules's weary ears as he walked through the gates of Courane L'Enfant's Lower Garden District compound. Jules still felt funky. A full day's sleep (and it had been the sleep of the dead, or close to it) hadn't cleared away the cobwebs, or flushed all of the paralyzing drug out of his system. Jules was still one speed too slow. Not a good night for productive detecting . . . but the world didn't revolve around him and his needs.

Something soft and quick brushed the top of his head. A laughing bird buzzed him. Jules looked up in time to see a blur of pink feathers soar by in a long arc. The feathers were attached to a woman. She hung upside down from a trapeze, naked except for the feathered headdress and a G-string. Her partners atop one of two trapeze platforms readied her to greet the next guest to walk through the gates.

A quicksilver sideshow occupied L'Enfant's front lawn. Performers dressed in little more than tattoos and silver piercings mingled with guests dressed in formal evening wear. A snake charmer approached Jules, a woman younger than Daphne, but with eyes as cold as Besthoff's. She wordlessly offered Jules her boa, mischief enlivening her face. The big snake wound itself more tightly around her thighs and trunk, its body gliding along her shaved pubis, clearly not eager to attempt wrapping itself around Jules's gargantuan form. The feeling was mutual; the snake reminded him too much of the vampire deities in the High Krewe's chapel. "No thanks," Jules said with rubbery lips.

He pushed his way to the porch, trying to avoid a human pincushion who insisted on handing him a cloudy blue liquid to drink. The middle-aged carny, long, thin nails protruding from all parts of his hairy torso, made Jules think of how he'd discovered Doc Landrieu eight months ago; not a memory he wanted to relive. Eager to get rid of him, Jules accepted the drink, then poured it into a bush as soon as the carny's back was turned.

He climbed the steps to the porch. A matronly woman in a long black gown exited the front door with a drink in her hand, laughing, very drunk. She pulled a much younger man through the door after her, dragging him into the shadows; judging from his bemused smile, he didn't go unwillingly. Jules wasn't positive, but he thought the lady might be a city councilwoman.

Music escaped from inside. The stately tones of a baroque ensemble flowed around the stone columns before being obliterated by the Gypsy music pouring from the circus troupe's sound system. Jules had been curious what kind of music L'Enfant would showcase at his party. Jazz? Swamp pop? His own brand of thrash-Goth-Cajun blitz music? But the shock-rocker had decided to go classy. Actually, since the guy was pushing estate homes that cost as much as the annual budgets of small Latin American republics, going classy made sense.

A man built like a commercial refrigerator politely blocked Jules's path when he approached the front door. Jules remembered seeing him in the parking lot out back of Laurel Elementary School. "May I see your invitation, sir?" Jules pulled his crimson invitation from his jacket pocket. The security guard opened the front door.

Despite the orphanage's high vaulted ceilings, Jules was engulfed by a wave of claustrophobia as soon as he entered the foyer. This was not an event planned with the needs of a person of size in mind. The rooms were packed. Jules wondered how the ensemble's violinists managed to slide their bows across their strings without putting guests' eyes out. A tuxedoed server sidestepped behind Jules's back, lifting his tray of champagne glasses above Jules's head; at the same time, a tipsy young thing, dressed in a black minidress made of spidery fringe, bounced off Jules's stomach. She giggled, mumbled an incoherent apology, then patted his belly and cooed at it.

Jules began slowly making his way toward the old cafeteria dining hall, the room where L'Enfant had boasted about his scale model of the planned development. Jules wanted to see whether the shrouded, glassed-in diorama had been unveiled yet. Pushing past so many tightly packed bodies reminded him of walking through the hip-deep murk of Manchac Swamp, those times he'd been trying to make sure a victim's body sank beneath the sawgrass before daylight. As he approached the old dining hall, the scent of food grew stronger. Jambalaya, crab dip, foie gras—all forbidden treats. Jules was glad he'd imbibed before he came; otherwise, the scents of all this untouchable food would really be making him suffer. He couldn't rely on deliveries of the High Krewe's blood much longer, however. Besthoff had warned him in the strongest terms possible that tomorrow night was the deadline for answers. What then? Back to his old habits, now that he was half the vampire he used to be? And could he even stomach the old lifestyle now that Maureen was gone?

The crowd he elbowed his way through was an interesting assortment of old money, new money, no money, and antimoney. Mixed in with the Cartier watches and gold cuff links were a good number of nose rings and nipple piercings. Jules bumped into an attractive if disheveled young lady with a circle of Dr. Seuss characters tattooed around her upper arm—

"Daphne?!?"

"Jules? What are you doing here?"

"What are *you* doin' here?"

Daphne turned bright red. "I—I'm sorry," she stammered. "We weren't going to stay long—"

Hank stood next to her. He glared at Jules. "Hey, don't even *think* about giving her a hard time," Hank said. "She's been bustin' her butt, trying to trap that crazy rat of yours. You know what she went through, with those maniacs nearly attackin' her. She needed a break. She needed to be around some normal people."

"*Normal* people?" Jules glanced quickly at the crowd of faux vampires, politicians, and voyeurs with too much money on their hands. After Daphne's run-in with that High Krewe vampiress, this was one of the last places she should go for a breath of "normalcy." "Hey, how'd you rate an invite to this high-rent Halloween ball, anyway?"

Hank looked like he was burning to ask Jules the same question, in far more belligerent terms, but a tug on his sleeve from Daphne dissuaded him. "I'm a past president of the Agatha Longrain fan club, okay?"

Why any red-blooded American male would rather read Agatha Longrain than Mickey Spillane, Jules couldn't figure. There was no accounting for the tastes of the young. Daphne stared up at him with anxious eyes. "Jules, you aren't, you know, *upset* with me or anything?"

Just then, a pair of bright, pale faces at the edge of the crowd caught Jules's attention. Two of the young women from the High Krewe's compound; he remembered interviewing them only a few nights ago. They scanned the crowd, probably selecting the tastiest morsels for cultivation. What if they should take a shine to Daphne? "Uh, why would I be mad at you?" Jules stammered. "I *want* you to go out and have a good time. Here, I'll prove I'm not sore." He pulled four twenties from his wallet and shoved them into Hank's hand. "This party's a big snoozer. Take her out for a nice meal and a show, okay? Some good jazz; maybe Porkchop Chambonne's playin' over at the Palm Court tonight."

Hank looked uncertain. "I don't know . . . it feels weird, takin' money from you—"

"It's not for *you,* dummy. It's for her. Go ahead. My treat. Just get outta here before all the decent restaurants close."

Daphne tugged Hank's sleeve again. "Let's do it. Can we go? Please? I just don't feel comfortable around here."

Hank frowned. "But we haven't even been here twenty minutes yet. We haven't gotten any free food. We haven't seen them unveil the model of the new neighborhood—"

"I don't care. Jules can tell us all about it later. Can't you, Jules?" Jules nodded with alacrity. "So can we go? *Please?* Let's have a nice, quiet dinner. Okay, Hanky-panky?"

"Welllll . . ." Hank grinned, then tightened his fist around the eighty bucks. "Sure. Okay. How about La Peniche? That's nicer than the Trolley Stop, and I can get a steak."

Daphne smiled. "Any place you take me will be wonderful, Hanky-panky." She turned her smile on Jules. "Thanks so much, Jules. That's so sweet. I promise, tomorrow night, I'm back on rat patrol."

"Sure, kid. Just have a good time tonight, okay?"

The two of them headed for the front door. Just before they went out, Daphne turned and waved. Not a word of thanks from Hank; the son-of-a-gun hadn't said "thank you" when Jules had given him the Cadillac, either. Oh, well; so long as he was decent to Daphne, that was what really mattered.

Still . . . *Hanky-panky*? Jules felt slightly sick to his stomach. In any case, he wouldn't have to worry about Daphne getting ambushed by some pale, thirsty partyer tonight. One worry he could cross off his list.

The baroque ensemble stopped playing. A voice crackled from hidden speakers. "Thank you all for coming. I hope everyone's been having a marvelous time." Jules recognized the voice as L'Enfant's. "The centerpiece of our evening will occur shortly. Please join me in the dining hall for the unveiling of the reborn heart of Uptown New Orleans."

Jules was already at the edge of the dining hall. By being aggressive with his shoulders and stomach, he was able to secure a position only ten feet away from the shrouded display case. A tall, distinguished-looking black man, with a laurel of white hair and a white mustache, stood on a small platform in one corner of the room. He held the end of the rope attached, through a system of pulleys, to the corners of the cloth hiding the model. Jules recognized him. It was the ex-mayor; not the most recent mayor, but the one before that, the one with the name straight out of a Charles Dickens novel. So L'Enfant had lined up some local heavyweights behind his version of the St. Thomas. Jules wondered whether the current mayor was in the Goodfeller-GoodiesMart camp, or whether he was staying on the sidelines. How many of the politicos here tonight had seen their wallets quietly fattened?

L'Enfant climbed the platform and stood next to the ex-mayor. The host was dressed in a skintight black tuxedo, his hair slicked radically back, his face smoothed over with a thick scrim of creamy white powder. He looked like that creepy master of ceremonies from *Cabaret.* "Your honor, if you would do the honors, please," he said. The ex-mayor dutifully pulled the rope, hand over hand, and the white shroud began rising from the table.

What would the model be like? Given Courane L'Enfant's tastes, would his dream neighborhood look like something out of an old Charles Addams cartoon ("most homes come complete with a three-hearse garage; all belfries are well stocked with bats")? A housing tract only a James Whale or Shirley Jackson could love?

As the last corners of the shroud left the table, all around him, Jules heard a low moaning of appreciation. And desire.

It was beautiful. Simply beautiful. A dream neighborhood that some utopian architect might've displayed at a nineteenth-century World's Fair. At the model's center was a lush, green park, rows of oaks lining lagoons spanned by Japanese footbridges. The development was bisected by two grand avenues, each with a landscaped neutral ground at its center. Jules was surprised to see model streetcars, just like those on St. Charles Avenue, running up and down both neutral grounds. The model houses looked just like the real houses of the Garden District, Greek Revival and Italianate mansions with small front gardens and expansive backyards with greenhouses or swimming pools or goldfish ponds. Low-rise apartment houses clustered at the tract's corners, arranged around smaller green spaces and playgrounds. Bordering Tchoupitoulas Street and the Mississippi River, the old cotton warehouses were transformed into shops and cafés, with tiny umbrellas and tables in a flower-filled courtyard.

Jules was no architect. But he knew what he liked. He liked this neighborhood. A lot. To his eyes, eyes that had seen too much of what was good and beautiful in New Orleans disappear beneath Progress's concrete slabs, this model looked like a masterpiece. A home run; and he hadn't even expected L'Enfant to hit a single.

"Isn't it gorgeous?" L'Enfant asked the crowd. "Is there anyone out there tonight who would not want to live in this wonderful place?" The entranced crowd murmured its agreement; Jules was almost ready to pull out his checkbook himself. "Who can deny that a neighborhood like this one, located only three minutes from downtown, would spark a renaissance of our beloved city? Our opponents speak of the need to attract new businesses to New Orleans's depressed core. But if you were an entrepreneur, if you were the head of a Fortune 500 company, wouldn't you want to be here, live here, right here in this magical place, and find a way to bring your company here as well? We have the opportunity to build something unique in all the nation—a re-creation of the grandeur of antebellum New Orleans, gated and secure, with the finest shopping and modern amenities, but with the modernity hidden behind a veneer of New Orleans charm. *Any* city can have a GoodiesMart. But only *New Orleans* can have *this*!"

Much as he hated to admit it, Jules found himself agreeing with L'Enfant. Never in a thousand years would he have expected that. But the longer he stared at the model, the longer he imagined little people riding those streetcars, walking beside those lagoons, and holding hands as they stood on those Japanese footbridges, the more his heart yearned for it all to happen.

And yet . . . and yet Erato had a point, too. What about all those project residents who'd been shoved out of their homes so the land could be cleared? Hadn't the government money that had been spent on this been appropriated primarily for their benefit? This gorgeous plan only threw the old residents a few crumbs, a sprinkling of apartments at the edges of the development. Erato would look at this model and see only the unfairness. Jules's dilemma was that, when he looked at it, he saw it with two sets of eyes. He saw the unfairness of the rich grabbing land from the poor, but he also saw the return of a kind of beauty that had been slowly disappearing from the city for nearly a century. People mattered; that was Erato's argument, and Jules didn't disagree. But so did other things—the songs of birds in old oak trees, the soothing hum of an approaching streetcar, the quiet patter of leaves falling onto the rippling surface of a lagoon.

Maybe Jules could never afford to live there himself, but he'd be happy to know it existed, to drive by and admire it now and then.

"You sure are some lucky guy," a voice said near his elbow. Jules turned around. It was Rudy Goodfeller. "I'll bet you can't wait to move in once they build it, huh? You think maybe when I'm a vampire, too, they'll invite me to come live?"

"I ain't movin' in there, kid," Jules said. "And neither are you. So put it out of your head, okay?"

"But you need a partner," Rudy insisted. "Somebody to help you find victims and stuff."

"Kid, I need a new partner like I need a third eyeball on a stalk stickin' outta my forehead—"

If Jules'd had such a third eyeball, at that instant it would've sprung open and pointed like a hunting dog. He blinked twice to make sure what he saw wasn't a trick of the light. Descending the curving staircase in the next room was a woman Jules had never expected to see again. Certainly not here. Maybe it was a look-alike? No . . . those cartoonish curves, those monumental, gravity-defying hips and breasts, created by taxpayer-funded experimental science . . . they could only belong to one woman.

Veronika. The crazy vampire-hunting Federal agent he thought he'd put out of his life forever eight months ago.

"Jules? You okay? You look kinda weird . . ."

Jules moved the boy aside. "Crunchy, I'm sorry, kid. But I gotta go. I see someone I gotta talk with."

Making his way back to the foyer wasn't easy; guests were pouring in from all over the house to look at the unveiled model. He hoped she hadn't seen him. Although the crowd made it hard for him to move, he was suddenly thankful for the crush of people—they provided him cover, an advantage someone of his bulk usually couldn't count on.

Veronika paused on a landing, then began descending the rest of the stairs. Would she come in his direction or move away? With her being as big as she was, at least she wouldn't be able to move through the crowd any faster than he could. She reached the floor and then, with a quick glance behind her—had she recognized him?—began walking away from the dining hall.

She had about a fifty-foot lead on him. Jules began pushing more aggressively through the crowd, absorbing the dirty looks and the droplets of champagne that splashed from bumped glasses onto his jacket.

She turned a corner into another room. Jules reached that corner about ten seconds later. He entered a sunroom, lined with windows from floor to high ceiling. It was much less crowded than either the foyer or dining hall; just four couples lingered in the candlelit corners, all young vampire wannabes, absorbed in their free drinks and in each other. Veronika wasn't there.

Two additional sets of doors led to other parts of the house. Jules opened the first set. Cool, damp outside air poured in. The doors opened onto a brick pathway that led between twin galleries of columns and archways. The covered but open-air pathway led to a separate wing of the orphanage, about thirty yards distant. That wing was dark, its doorway shut. Jules guessed that Veronika couldn't have gotten across and possibly unlocked those doors this soon.

That left the other set of doors. The self-absorbed couples paid him no mind as he bulled past. The second set led to an interior hallway. Gas jets hissed on the walls; their wavering flames illuminated dark oil paintings of long-dead priests and nuns. This passageway looked like certain hallways in the High Krewe's mansion; Jules figured the two gargantuan structures had been built around the same time, maybe even by the same architects and craftsmen.

The hallway was deserted. Jules began trying doors. Nothing would've stopped her from locking a door behind her, of course. The first doorknob he turned didn't offer any resistance. He pushed it open, then fumbled for a light switch. He didn't find either a switch or a cord hanging from the ceiling. Maybe in this wing, L'Enfant hadn't bothered converting from gas to electric lights at all. He opened the door as wide as it would go. The hall jets showed him, just barely, that the room was empty.

The next two doors he tried were locked. Jules placed his ear against both doors. He didn't hear any breathing, but the hiss of the gas lamps made detecting such a subtle sound very unlikely. Jules found himself wishing he had the power to transform into his wolf form. Veronika's scent would stand out like sulphur to a wolf's nose, and a wolf's ears would detect her smallest movements. But he might as well wish for all walls surrounding him to suddenly change into glass.

His heart felt as if it were beating in an echo chamber. Wild, stray thoughts scurried across his mind. Was it sheer coincidence that Doc Landrieu had been in just the right spot at the right time last night to save Jules from the mutilator? What had his old boss meant about Jules's mother being "in a better place"?

Turning the next doorknob, Jules forced himself to focus on the situation at hand. Mildew and mustiness assaulted his nose as soon as he opened the door. The room was crammed full of books, stacked six or seven feet high, probably ancient textbooks the orphans had once used.

Frustration welled up inside him. He'd rip this whole place open if he had to, disassemble it brick by moldering brick. He hadn't been off base when he'd tried picking up Veronika's trail a few nights ago. Now that he'd spotted her here, he was certain she and her spook agency tied into the disappearances and mutilations. The orderlies at Charity Hospital said she'd been released into the care of some local celebrity, a strange-looking man with long hair. That much made sense now—it had been L'Enfant. But why had he hooked up with her? What did a Goth-Cajun musician with a taste for vampire theatrics have to do with a posse of vampire hunters? And what about that business of her supposedly aging a decade a day—

A metallic clanking, sudden and sharp, cut Jules's questions short. He held his breath, waiting for the noise to be repeated. It wasn't. Where had it come from? From beneath his feet, it had sounded like. Did this castle have a basement? A dungeon?

Jules got his answer when he tried the next door. It didn't open onto a room. It opened onto a staircase. A staircase that went down. The orphanage was close enough to the Mississippi levee, high enough on the rim of the "bowl" of soggy land that dipped between the river and Lake Pontchartrain, to be maybe ten feet above sea level. High enough to have a basement. Or dungeon.

Jules stared down the steps. The space below was dark, but not completely dark. The walls of the descending shaft were wet with condensation, and the tiny droplets reflected a weak, wavering glow. To check the possibility that maybe the glow was reflected from the hall lamps, Jules closed the door until it was only open the width of his fingertip, then peered inside. The walls still glowed dimly. The light was coming from below.

That meant someone was down there.

Electric adrenaline surged through Jules's veins. He might be on the cusp of solving his mystery. He stepped gingerly onto the first stair. It was slick; he almost lost his footing. He grabbed the railing. It twisted away from the wall, but it held. Unfortunately, its mounting bracket thudded against the bricks. The noise echoed downward. Whoever was at the bottom now knew he was coming.

Shit. Well, stealth had never been his strong suit.

He continued his descent, holding the rickety railing tightly. His eyes began itching, then watering. What could be—? Then he smelled something. Smoke. Sweet-smelling smoke, like incense. The smoke burned his nostrils and throat. It shouldn't have bothered him—he'd smelled much worse things in the Quarter—but he was getting nauseated. He felt himself begin to sweat. He was getting light-headed. It got worse the lower he descended. Every nerve ending in his body shouted for him to turn around. If Veronika were down there, waiting for him, with her knowledge of a hundred ways to make a vampire scream . . . But he forced his legs to descend the final few steps.

He thought he'd settled with her eight months ago. Gotten even with her for Veronika's role in Maureen's death. But like a big, fat bad penny, she kept turning up to torment him. Well, tonight . . . tonight they'd sort things out between them once and for all.

At the bottom of the steps, another odor hit him, one that cut through the sickly-sweet stench of the smoke like a rapier. An odor any vampire would be exquisitely sensitive to. The scent of blood.

A looming shadow blocked his path. Jules reached out and ran his fingertips across the barrier. It was some kind of room divider, built of rough, cheap plywood. It didn't extend all the way to the low ceiling;

Jules could see flickering lights from the far side reflecting off the damp roof less than two feet from his head. He shoved the divider with his palm. It rocked slightly. He could knock it down, even as weak and queasy as he was feeling right now. But he didn't have to. Three strides later, he was able to step around it.

Immediately, he wished he hadn't.

Jules realized why his eyes and lungs had been burning. A ring of lit holy candles, sticks of incense, and crucifixes, reinforced with massed strings of garlic, surrounded an emaciated, prone figure. It almost looked like a tableau of peasant piety, a deathly ill rural Italian or Mexican who'd surrounded himself with symbols of his faith in an effort to ward off the Grim Reaper. Except the pale, almost skeletal figure lying on a mat on the floor was chained to the wall with shackles that could restrain a tiger.

He felt his knees weakening, but he forced himself to move closer. The prone figure was an unconscious young man. Jules watched his chest closely for a few seconds to ascertain he was still breathing. He didn't recognize him. But Jules was sure he'd found one of the High Krewe's missing youngsters. He'd been so focused on the mutilated young women, he'd almost forgotten about the two young men who'd gone missing.

A red-stained plastic tube jutted from beneath a piece of surgical tape on the prisoner's forearm. The tube led to a hunk of medical equipment mounted on the wall. A second tube snaked from the suspended device into an old-fashioned, claw-footed bathtub.

Jules skirted the crucifixes and holy candles and garlic to look inside the bathtub. He noticed a second set of shackles mounted on the wall on the other side of the tub. Those shackles were empty. The smoke grew thicker, more noxious. Jules felt the room swimming around him.

He looked down into the bathtub. Its white enamel was stained with multiple rings of dried gore . . . the blood of a vampire.

Jules felt it coming. It was like a rolling freight train; there was no stopping it. He upchucked his most recent meal into the stained tub.

Too late, he heard a soft footstep behind him. Something flat and heavy hammered the back of his skull. He saw a broken piece of wood fly by his head. Then, vision fading, he felt himself falling toward the tub.

Shanghaied twice in two nights, he thought just before his forehead struck the enamel-coated iron rim. *I really suck at this detective biz. . . .*

TWENTY-THREE

Jules heard somebody groaning. After a second or two, he realized the pitiable sounds were coming from his own throat. His forehead felt as if he'd just been head-butted by Joe Louis (not that the Brown Bomber would ever do such a thing). An execrable taste filled his mouth. His hands felt tingly. Something was keeping them from rubbing his head to find out how badly he'd been hurt.

"Rick, I'm sorry I had to be so rough. But there's no sense taking chances when you're messing with a vampire."

Rick? A woman's voice. But not Veronika's. Jules forced his eyes to open. It was like opening a pair of windows that had been painted shut.

The voice belonged to Edith Aubrey L'Enfant.

"I'm really sorry about this, Rick. I can't tell you how sorry I am." The tall, gracefully aging hunchback stood in front of him, looking considerably taller than she usually did. Jules realized this was because he was lying on the floor. She held a large wooden crucifix in her hands. Jules tried turning his head away, but his neck was painfully stiff. The effort was wasted, in any case. Like the skeletal young man on the far side of the bathtub, he was surrounded by a Maginot Line of burning holy candles, strings of garlic, and crosses and crucifixes of all sizes. His arms were suspended above his head, and he couldn't feel his hands. The steel shackles had been meant for much thinner vampires, obviously.

"If . . . if you're so sorry," Jules said, trying to force his mouth to work right, "how about lettin' me outta this bargain-basement chamber of horrors?"

Edith didn't smile. "That's not an option, I'm afraid. After you've hooked a shark, you can't just let him go. He might turn around and bite you." She held her crucifix more tightly to her chest. "I'm being very honest when I tell you I wish this hadn't happened this way. Did you know that most crimes are crimes of opportunity? You simply provided me with too good an opportunity when you came down here. It meant I could dispense with setting up one of those tiresome traps. And dragging you down those steps would've been an ordeal." She sighed. "This may not make things seem better, but you're the least obnoxious vampire I've ever met. I'd have to say you're definitely my favorite of your kind. So I truly wish it had been one of the others that had come down the stairs an hour ago."

Jules felt himself begin to sweat. The next question was an obvious one. "What are you plannin' . . . on doin' with me?"

"This is going to sound terribly ironic. I need your blood." She paused. Even though the smoke was making his eyes tear up again, Jules thought he saw her lower lip tremble. "No, that's not right. Truthfully, *I* don't need your blood. It's Courane . . . Courane's, ah, lady friend. She . . . you see, she has this . . . this condition, this *problem* . . ."

Edith did maybe the only thing that would've surprised Jules at this point. She started weeping. Big, fat tears rolled down her cheeks, landing on her crucifix like a rain shower. She turned away from him. Then she punched the plywood room divider with shocking force.

"Do you have any idea how *hard* this is for me? How much I *hate* myself? Here I am, getting older and grayer with every month that goes by. Courane never even *touches* me anymore. And here comes this—this *freak*—who's getting decrepit even faster than I am, and she crawls to Courane, begging for help. Does she get the cold shoulder, the icy cold shoulder I've been getting for years? Hell, no. Hell, *no*! He finds a way to fix *her.* Finds a way to give her her fucking *youth* back, again and again. And what am I? I'm the flunky. They get to be Romeo and goddamn Juliet, and I get to be the old, ugly friar."

Jules didn't understand everything. But he was beginning to put the pieces together. So vampire blood could be a fountain of youth? That was a new wrinkle. He actually felt pity for Edith. However many vampires she'd given the shaft to, she'd been getting the shaft herself all along.

And her undisguised pain maybe gave him an opening. "How about . . . 'stead of hatin' yourself, you let me outta here? Give that philanderin' husband of yours . . . a big surprise. She's a real loon, that Veronika. I know her. You talk about a shark . . . but I'll take care of her for you. How about it?"

Edith's tear-wet face turned contemptuous. Whether of him or herself, Jules wasn't sure. "Have you ever been in love? Can you people even *fall* in love? Or is it all about the next meal?" She flung the words like knives. "Well, let me tell you something about love. Love isn't blind—it makes *you* blind. And you want to be blind. When Courane and I got married eighteen years ago, the preacher said, 'For richer or for poorer, 'til death do you part.' That was a contract, a binding moral contract. Do you know that my mother never betrayed my father? Never demanded that he acknowledge paternity. Never dragged him in front of a judge. Relied on him to do the right thing by me, his daughter. My whole childhood, she defended him, until the day she died. Because she loved him. And they weren't even *married*!"

For one of the few times in his long existence, Jules regretted having only an eighth-grade education. To untangle this knot, he'd need a doctorate in psychology. "Look, let me outta here, I promise I won't lay a finger on your husband. Just Veronika. That bitch'll be history. Ancient history. Then you can have Courane all . . . back to yourself again, okay?"

Edith's face wavered for an instant. But she shook her head. "No. I'll never do anything to hurt Courane. If he . . . if he wants *her* . . . then it's my responsibility to make that possible."

"Edith, that's *nuts*—"

She turned away from him again. "I'm going now. I'm going to get them. Courane can break away from his guests and come see what I've done. He'll be . . . pleased. Maybe tonight—maybe I won't spend all night working on my cars, alone."

She hurried around the plywood divider, not letting him see her face.

"Edith—!"

But her footsteps were already quickly receding up the stairs. The door slammed behind her.

Okay. He was in a fix. There was no arguing with that. He'd just had maybe his best chance to get out of this clean, and he'd blown it. It was time for Plan B.

If only he *had* a Plan B.

Maybe the kid on the other side of the bathtub could help. Maybe he knew something useful. Maybe they could get out of this together. If Jules could wake him up.

Jules tried remembering the names of the two missing young men. "Hey, kid? Kid? You awake?" One name came to him, then another. "Hey, Maxim? Jonathan?" No response. He stretched his leg so he could bang on the tub with his knee. But his effort produced more pain than noise.

"Kid, you gotta . . . get with it. Or we're both gonna look like toothpaste tubes after all the paste got squeezed out. Do they ever loosen these chains? Maybe when they're stickin' you with that tube? How about when they're feedin' you? They gotta feed you *sometime,* don't they? Don't they, kid?"

No answer. Not even the tiniest clanking of steel links to indicate his companion was stirring. Jules was on his own.

After a coughing fit brought on by the holy candle smoke, Jules fell into an exhausted but restless sleep. Voices from the top of the stairs woke him up.

"Courane, you're going to be so happy with me! Wait until you see him! His name's Rick. He's *tremendous.* You should be able to get quarts of blood from him for months and months. Now that we've learned from our mistakes with the first one, maybe I'll never need to catch you another vampire again. Maybe we can just keep this one going indefinitely—"

"You may have done even better than that, my dear. But we shall see."

Jules shook himself fully awake. He recognized the voices—Edith and Courane L'Enfant. And there was someone else with them, too. Jules thought he heard a much heavier tread descending the steps. Seconds later, his suspicions were confirmed. Three people walked around the plywood divider into the ersatz dungeon—Edith; her husband, still dressed in his creepy *Cabaret* outfit; and Veronika. Only this was a much different Veronika than he'd ever seen before. He hadn't gotten a good look at her earlier tonight, not with the crowds between them. This Veronika looked like she'd reached the deep end of middle age. The glowing blond hair he remembered was now lusterless, streaked with coarse gray. Her strawberries-and-cream complexion was marred with wrinkles and age spots. Even her artificially exaggerated curves were sagging, surrendering to the onslaught of gravity.

She clutched L'Enfant's hand tightly. Jules noticed L'Enfant wasn't holding his wife's hand. "Courane," Veronika said, her voice husky with emotion. "It's him. It's really him. The one who did this to me. It's Jules Duchon."

"What do you mean?" Edith said, her eyes questioning her husband, not Veronika. Jules noticed she tried hard not to look at the other woman in the room. "His name's Rick, not Jules—"

"No, Veronika's right, dear," L'Enfant said. "She knows this man a good deal better than you do. For some reason, when he made our acquaintance, he gave us a false name. Isn't that correct, Jules?"

There was no reason for Jules to try maintaining the charade any longer. "Sure," Jules said. He felt a bit stronger after his short rest. "So now she's got you workin' for the Feds, L'Enfant? Sellin' out to the establishment? I'll bet your fans wouldn't like that."

L'Enfant smiled his thin reed smile. "I'm not working for the government. Whatever gave you that impression?"

"That's where your new girlfriend draws her paychecks from. And not just paychecks, neither. She ever showed you them nifty wooden stakes that pop outta her bazooms? Wouldn't surprise me none if she pees holy water, too."

"I'm no longer associated with the Strategic Helium Reserve," Veronika said coldly. "After what you did to me . . . I severed my ties. I know my old superiors. If they had gotten their hands on me, they would've hooked me up to banks of machines and studied me. Watched me shrivel up into a pitiful ancient hag at the age of twenty-two. They wouldn't have tried to save me. Their brilliant scientific minds would've been too engrossed with finding out what happens to a human being when she's bled by a vampire almost, but not quite, to the point of death. Would I have stayed alive forever, even as my body became more and more decrepit? What would I have turned into at the end? Bones? Dust? Dust that thinks, that would scream if it still had a mouth?" She released L'Enfant's hand and stood over Jules, her round frame shimmering with hate. "When you wouldn't turn me into a vampire . . . did you have any idea what you were condemning me to, you ugly bastard?"

"Hell, no," Jules said. "I just wanted to piss you off."

Veronika shrieked.

"Hey, calm down," Jules said. "Old ladies shouldn't let their blood pressure get too high."

She kicked at his legs, showing little sign of diminished sprightliness. "Just drain him dry, Courane! Squeeze out every last drop! I don't *want* him to bite me!"

"Don't be hasty," L'Enfant said. "Our original plan may not be viable anymore. Did you get a look at the crowd upstairs tonight? I counted only three vampires. We haven't seen Victoria or Alexandra in weeks. And now even Randolph and Pearl have snubbed us." He turned to Jules. "You 'night people' are a fickle bunch, aren't you? To hear Randolph prattle on, conditions had become intolerable inside the High Krewe's mansion. What I was offering was a godsend; I practically had him licking dog chow from my hand. And now their interest has apparently evaporated. Can you tell me what has happened to my once-lengthy list of tenants?"

Was L'Enfant putting him on? After seeing Maxim (or Jonathan) stretched out on the floor looking like a poster child for Feed the Children, Jules had jumped to the fast conclusion that L'Enfant was behind all the attacks. But now that his head was slightly clearer, he reexamined that quick assumption. It didn't fit. If what L'Enfant and Veronika wanted was vampire *blood,* what good did it do them to hack off body parts and then dump the leftovers with the High Krewe? Maxim (or Jonathan), shriveled as he was, still had all his parts attached. And L'Enfant had no reason at this point to lie, not when he had Jules at his mercy.

"You want insider dope?" Jules said, fighting off an urge to fly into another coughing fit. "Maybe I can oblige you. Maybe not. But you give with the dope first. How did all this get started?"

L'Enfant smiled, black lipstick a thin dark gash on his paper-white face. "You really aren't in any position to bargain, Jules. You know that. But I have my own reasons for wanting you in the know, so I'm happy to tell you. I assume you remember in what condition you left Veronika the last time you saw her."

"Oh, he *remembers*—," Veronika spat.

"Darling, don't interrupt. She was on the verge of death, tantalizingly close to death, but with enough of her own blood left to sustain her life. Your self-control must've been prodigious; I believe not one vampire in a thousand could've managed to keep himself from drinking that final draught. Veronika tells me you transformed into several hundred rats before scurrying out the window. Most impressive. Don't think about repeating that here, though; we've found that the combination of holy objects you're surrounded with is quite effective at destroying a vampire's powers of concentration, not to mention draining his strength."

If he knew what shape I'm in, Jules thought, *he wouldn't have to bother with all the candles and crap. These chains alone could pin me here until New Orleans sinks back into the ocean.*

"As soon as Veronika recovered consciousness at Charity Hospital," L'Enfant continued, "she knew something was dreadfully wrong. She was aging, she later estimated, at a rate of one year per every three hours. For reasons she's already mentioned, she couldn't turn to her superiors for help. Instead, she called the only local expert on vampiric phenomena she knew. My friend, Agatha Longrain. Unbeknownst to Veronika, Agatha actually collects all of her background data from me. Esoteric researches into the supernatural, especially vampirism, have long been a hobby of mine. Agatha referred Veronika to me. I rescued the poor girl from the not-so-tender mercies of Charity Hospital; although I'll remain forever curious as to what the interns and residents would've made of her condition.

"Fortunately for Veronika, I own one of the world's greatest libraries on the subject of vampirism. I also have a considerable fan base in Europe, as well as plentiful funds to encourage their searches for a cure. Two solutions presented themselves. Veronika's body would snap back to its proper age if her interrupted transformation to a vampiress was completed. Or, failing that, her youth could be tenuously maintained through regular immersions in a vampire's blood."

"And you," Jules said, "just happened to know a few vampires, didn't you?"

"Indeed," L'Enfant said, sounding very satisfied with himself. "For years, several of your kind have been popping up at my concerts or my Vampyres' Balls. It was a fairly simple matter to establish contact with one of them—Maxim, a rather empty-headed young man. I introduced him to Veronika and offered him the opportunity to complete her transformation. You can't imagine how disappointed I was when he said he wouldn't touch her. Another vampire had already marked her as his own, he said, like a cat who sprays his territory. Apparently, beyond a certain point, vampires won't eat after one another. Presented with this setback, I quickly proceeded to the next option. My resourceful spouse quickly jury-rigged a trap for him, and finicky Maxim ended up down here, hooked up to a pump that drained his blood into that bathtub."

Jules jerked his head in the direction of his unconscious fellow prisoner. "That Maxim?"

L'Enfant looked bemused. "Unfortunately, no. That's Jonathan. Maxim didn't last very long, I'm afraid. Our efforts to determine just how much blood we could safely drain were terribly trial and error. I think Veronika got maybe all of three baths from the boy, and those were more sponge baths than nice, warm soaks. At least disposing of him was easy. He baked down to a fine white powder in the sun. Jonathan over there has lasted a good bit longer, thanks to forced feedings of cow blood. Although he looks like he's on his last legs, to be honest."

Jules smelled the burnt-bacon stench of his own skin baking from the nearness of so many crucifixes. He shook his head with disgusted amazement as the full absurdity of L'Enfant's project dawned on him. "You mean to tell me, all this . . . this whole St. Thomas thing, this whole mega-monster real-estate deal . . . you set all this up so you could make sure Ms. *Portrait of Dorian Gray* would have enough vampire blood to wash herself with?"

L'Enfant laughed. It sounded more like the laugh of a pimply pubescent who liked pouring salt on slugs. "Of course not! That's preposterously silly. One doesn't plan a whole neighborhood, then line up seventy million dollars in financing and tax abatements, in just eight months. The St. Thomas redevelopment has taken me years to set up. The notion of setting aside one of the larger houses as a vampires' co-op was a relatively recent addition. Actually, adding the free clinic for the ex-project residents has made my version of the redevelopment more palatable to certain liberal members of the City Council."

"Goody for you," Jules said. "I'm glad you didn't do all that work just on ol' Veronika's account. Take it from me—she ain't worth it."

Veronika leveled another kick against Jules's helpless torso. "Why you despicable—!"

L'Enfant pulled her back. "I wouldn't kick in his teeth just yet, my dear. Distasteful as it may be, we need to make Jules a proposition. And he'll need his teeth to fulfill his part of the bargain."

He stood over Jules. "Well? Even a dull-witted mushroom like yourself should anticipate what I'm about to suggest. Now that we have you, all this business of setting up a convenient vampire colony is moot, wouldn't you say? Finish the job you started on Veronika, and I will restore your freedom."

Jules felt his anger gather in his face and smolder there. Savoring every syllable, he said, "Go to hell."

L'Enfant's carefully plucked eyebrows peaked. "Perhaps you didn't understand. Drink Veronika's blood—that really shouldn't be a difficult concept—make *all gone,* and I will let you go."

Jules's skin burned and smelled like smoldering charcoal, but he didn't care. "Maybe you didn't understand what *I* just said. Go to hell, and take that overstuffed bitch with you. After what she did to Maureen—tippin' off Malice, makin' goddamn sure he'd shove a stake through Maureen's heart—I wouldn't piss on her if she were on fire."

L'Enfant's thin lips puckered into a slight frown. "Really? Are you truly that monumentally stupid? You would actually subject yourself to a lingering, wasting death, purely out of spite? Have no illusions about this. Although you'll probably last far longer than Maxim or Jonathan, you will die eventually. Oh, it may not be death in the form of final oblivion—I'm not sure Maxim was truly dead before we laid him out in the sun—but you will be no more alive than a desiccated vegetable, a husk. And getting there won't be a pleasure cruise. I wish Jonathan were feeling up to conversation. I'm sure he could tell you quite vividly what you have to look forward to."

Jules didn't say anything. His righteous anger had felt so good just a minute ago. Now, as the warm flush of that surge of emotion faded, Jules felt doubt's tiny, sharp teeth nibbling away at his certitude. Before, he could tell himself he was refusing to help Veronika out of love for Maureen. But what chance would Maureen ever have of being resurrected if Jules spent the rest of his time on earth moldering away in this basement?

"You know," L'Enfant said, "this isn't all about you and Veronika and your sordid little history together. After you're drained and gone, how many more young vampires will Edith set traps for? How many others of your kind will you condemn to horrible sufferings? I could understand your not feeling pity for normal humans; we're just food to you, after all. But what about your own kind? Have you no pity for them?"

Jules would've loved nothing better than to tell L'Enfant to go fuck himself. But his ungracious host was making too much sense for Jules to ignore. Not in the way L'Enfant had intended—Jules felt shockingly little empathy for any of the vampires of the High Krewe, with the possible exception of Straussman. But there were others for whom Jules did feel a debt of loyalty. His kind, his people—who were they, really? Were they just those who happened to be like him in some way, vampires or cab-drivers or working-class white males? Or were they that crazy quilt of personalities who'd bonded themselves to him somehow, who'd be-friended him or stuck their necks out for him?

His kind, his people? He could make a list, and it wasn't a very long one. Doodlebug. He'd be tops on the list, for so many reasons. Maureen; he wasn't willing to give up on her, not yet. Erato. Doc Landrieu. Daphne. Porkchop Chambonne. Maybe Rudy Goodfeller; the kid might be a bit of a pest, but he was all right. Hell, Jules would even stick Preston on the list, even though Preston had been firmly in his "Enemies" col-umn as recently as five nights ago.

He could make things better for his kind of people, all right. He had the leverage. He had the responsibility. Much as he detested saving Veronika's bacon, he'd have to shove his pride aside and cut the best deal he could. Besides, the stench of his burning skin was making him nause-ated; he had his *own* bacon to save, too.

"All right," Jules said. "I'll turn Granny back into a cover girl for *Big Cheeks Pictorial,* and I'll make sure she stays that way. But before one drop of my saliva hits that fat neck of hers, I got conditions."

"Don't bargain with this slug," Veronika told L'Enfant. "Make him suffer a few weeks, and then he'll be begging to do whatever you say—"

"Veronika, let me deal with this," L'Enfant said. He turned to Jules. "Tell me what you want. I'll consider it."

"First off, when I walk out of here, free and clear, I take Jonathan with me."

"Certainly," L'Enfant said with no hesitation. "We won't be needing him any longer, and it'll save us the bother of disposing of him."

"Second, I want you to cancel your sweetheart deal with the High Krewe's Little Rascals. They don't need to be out here in the middle of town, tempted to go noshin' on preachers and whatnot."

"Again, fine. Complete the job on Veronika, and I have as much use for those ancient brats as I would a colony of Formosan termites."

"Third, I get an honest answer to this question—did you have Vic-toria or Alexandra or Pearl or any of the others kill two black ministers for you?"

L'Enfant's expression oscillated between wariness and curiosity. "Why? What does it mean to you? You don't strike me as the church-going type. Certainly not Full Gospel Baptist."

"They were friends of friends of mine. I want to know."

L'Enfant shrugged his shoulders. "They were in the way. In this town, an outraged black Baptist preacher gets a City Councilman's attention almost as effectively as a generous bribe does. And there I was, real-estate maven for a coven of vampires—you really can't blame me for wanting to get some use out of them. Although I must say, I truly thought they'd be more professional about it. First Victoria couldn't be bothered with carting her victim outside the city limits, so she dumped him in a City Park lagoon. And Alexandra—! She was even sloppier than Victoria had been. Leaving a bloodless minister in the middle of the French Quarter—how appallingly gauche, not to mention stupid."

"Oh, Courane," Edith said in a small, hushed voice. "You never told me you were planning on killing *ministers.*"

"Don't be such a ridiculous wet blanket," L'Enfant shot back. "If you've ever been Mother Teresa, it certainly hasn't been in the eighteen years we've been married." He turned to Jules again. "Done with stating conditions? Can we get on with the blood sucking? I still have over a hundred guests upstairs, and I'd prefer to be a decent host."

"I ain't done yet."

L'Enfant rolled his eyes and sighed. "What, then? What else? You want an autographed guitar?"

"No guitar." Jules had another goal in mind.

Win one for Erato and Preston.

"Fourth," Jules said, blinking away tears of pain, "you're gonna cut a deal with Van Goodfeller's group. The catfish-distribution warehouse and the GoodiesMart, they both get squeezed into your development, 'cause folks 'round here need jobs. And them low-income residents who got pushed out when the St. Thomas got knocked down? They get fifty percent of the housing, at rents they can manage."

L'Enfant recoiled as though Jules had just shoved a votive candle up the musician's nose. "You have no idea what you're asking for. You don't know the first thing about urban-core redevelopment, the economics and aesthetics of a project of this magnitude. How do you think I plan to attract upper-income investors? By offering them a splendid view of a GoodiesMart parking lot? The opportunity to be close neighbors to a significant mass of malcontents and drug abusers?" He laughed. "Maybe your chains are too tight. You're out of your undead mind."

"Maybe. But those are my terms."

L'Enfant scowled. "Maybe Veronika had the best idea after all. She can bathe in your blood for the next few weeks. Or months. And then we'll see how flexible you are with these 'terms.' " He turned to his two companions. "Come. Let's return to our party."

They headed for the stairs. It was time to get creative. "I wouldn't go back to your party just yet, Corey Lawrence," Jules said loudly, fighting off a murderous cough.

L'Enfant visibly stiffened. Veronika noticed his consternation. "What did that gargoyle just call you?" she asked.

Jules noticed Edith looked confused, too. This was better than he could've hoped. L'Enfant had hidden his pedestrian origins not only from the general public, but from the women who were closer to him than anyone. "I think you better play ball with me, Corey," Jules said.

L'Enfant turned back to Jules. "Where did you hear that name?" His voice was flat and airless, lacking the jaunty menace of only a few seconds ago.

"That ain't all I heard," Jules said, ignoring the question for now. He smiled, even though a coughing fit knocked tears from his eyes. "And that ain't all I *know,* either. You remember my partner, Preston? The black guy?"

"Yes," L'Enfant said slowly. "The other vampire who pretended to be a reporter."

"Right. Both of us saw Randolph and Pearl make a payoff to Maurice Eustice. Eustice wasn't home when they slipped the six grand under his back door. Preston and me recovered the money, plus a note that tied the payoff back to you." That part wasn't true, but it sure as hell sounded good. "And Preston knows all about Mr. Corey Lawrence from Ontario. The dipshit Canadian who thought so little of his own real background, he ran away to South Louisiana—dreamed up a new life and a whole new history for himself. It helped that he had a little musical talent."

Jules enjoyed watching his words hit L'Enfant's face like drippy spitballs. "Preston's watchin' my back. He knew I was comin' to your party tonight. If I don't check in with him before dawn, he goes public with all your little secrets. The press, the Municipal Corruption Commission, his buddies in the black church. *OffBeat Magazine,* too. The works."

Jules sensed L'Enfant's stare trying to bore through to the truth. "You're bluffing," his captor said after a few seconds. "Your friend's a vampire. He can't expose himself. There's no way he'd risk going to the authorities."

"Who said he'd hafta blow the whistle on his own? Vampires got friends in high places, too; not just fake-ass Cajun musicians. You said it yourself a few minutes ago—a pissed-off black preacher has plenty of clout in this town."

L'Enfant continued to stare, his mouth a tight black line. "I ain't bluffing, Corey," Jules said. He'd almost convinced even himself.

"Thirty percent moderate-income units," L'Enfant said at last.

Veronika's face grew livid. "Courane! I thought you said you wouldn't bargain with this cockroach!"

"Shut up, Veronika," L'Enfant said with more weariness than anger. "I've gotten myself in a bloody hole trying to save you. Now let me climb out my own damn way."

Veronika pouted. Jules thought he saw Edith smile. "Thirty percent don't hack it," he said. His skin was itching and flaking like crazy. "It's *fifty* percent moderate income, and the GoodiesMart and the warehouse are both in the mix."

"Impossible," L'Enfant said. "You can't squeeze twenty eggs into a carton made for a dozen. Have you seen the plans for that warehouse and that store? The GoodiesMart parking lot alone eats up land that I'd planned to devote to a dozen estate homes. The only reason they're able to squeeze in as many units as they do is that their plan is so heavily tilted toward higher-density, low-income apartments." He smoothed back several strands of hair that had strayed from the shellacked mass. "Thirty-five percent. Any higher than that, and both the economics and the harmony of my development sink into the mud."

"That ain't fuckin' good enough, Corey. But I'm willin' to be a little flexible. Fifty percent, and the Goodfeller warehouse gets stuck inside them old historic cotton warehouses you like so much." He was improvising now. "And . . . and the GoodiesMart builds a parking garage instead of a big, sprawling surface lot, and they make the garage match them old warehouses."

L'Enfant's expression subtly changed. A flicker of interest shone through the hostility. "And why would Goodfeller and his partners agree to this? The changes you just listed don't come free. I've seen their renderings. They'll argue that such changes would make their plan economically unfeasible."

Jules realized his mouth had been moving faster than his brain. He'd been offering concessions on Goodfeller's part without having any notion of how he'd make those concessions stick. And Goodfeller *should* make some concessions. Jules had seen his renderings, too. They were mule-ass *ugly.*

But then Jules came up with a new idea. It made him smile so broadly, his fangs must be gleaming in the candlelight. "You leave Goodfeller to me," he said. "I'll get him to come around. You got my word on that. How about it?"

L'Enfant's eyes glazed over; Jules figured he was performing intricate financial calculations in his head. "Fifty percent, or anything near it, is impossible," L'Enfant said. "I'll go this far—thirty-eight percent moderate income, the changes you specified, plus the GoodiesMart is built as a two-story structure to lessen its footprint. All concessions on the Goodfeller-GoodiesMart end are to be put in writing, with the stipulation that if such changes are not fully implemented, the percentage of moderate-income housing units drops back to twenty percent. That is my final offer."

Jules's head was throbbing again where he'd hit it against the tub. If this went on too much longer, he wouldn't be able to think, much less bargain. "You can do better than that," he said, trying not to groan. "Keepin' the warehouse and the big store, that brings in more of that sales-tax abatement stuff, don't it? More cash. Forty-eight percent low-income, Corey."

"*Forty* percent."

"Forty-*six* percent."

L'Enfant's face grew livid beneath the mask of white makeup. "Forty-two percent! And that! Is! *Final!* One more word of argument, and you can rot down here for the next ten years! I don't care *what* your allies leak to the press!"

"Deal," Jules said. He made a motion to shake hands, but the chains only let him wiggle his numb, flaking fingers.

TWENTY-FOUR

L'Enfant demanded two more things before he released Jules from the chains—Jules was not to retaliate against L'Enfant or his associates, and he was not to tell the authorities about L'Enfant's connection to the preacher murders. Jules agreed to both conditions. Keeping the cops in the dark about the circumstances of the ministers' deaths was in both L'Enfant's and Jules's interests. However, the stipulation didn't preclude Jules from telling Preston at some point.

It made sense to try to get the deal done tonight, despite the late hour. L'Enfant's architects, money people, and political backers were upstairs at the party, and Veronika wasn't getting any younger. However, Jules insisted that the parley between L'Enfant's supporters and Goodfeller's group take place before he'd give Veronika the gift of fangs and bloodlust.

Edith returned Jules's cell phone. Despite not yet being fully recovered, Jules carried Jonathan to one of the empty rooms upstairs. The kid felt like a bundle of dry sticks. Later, Jules would have to try getting some blood down his throat. But right now, Jules had calls to make.

The first person he called was Van Goodfeller. Jules checked his watch while the line was ringing. Half past midnight. He wondered what shape Goodfeller would be in when he answered.

The catfish king picked up on the fifth ring. Jules was relieved Goodfeller's voice didn't sound slurred. He told him the relevant (nonvampire-related) details of what had just transpired.

"So now the bastard wants to deal," Goodfeller said. "What changed? At that community forum, even though the whole fucking crowd was against him, he acted like a cat licking cream from his whiskers. Like he had the whole thing sewn up somehow. What do you have on him that's forcing him to the table? You mentioned that business about the bribes, but I doubt that'd get him to cave like this. Not by itself."

"I can't give you all the details," Jules said. "All you need to know is, I got my fingers pinched on some pretty short hairs of his."

"Yeah? Well, great. More power to you. So how come I need to belly up to the bar with the kinds of changes you mentioned? If you've got him crawling, how come he can't crawl all the way to me, and polish my shoes when he gets here? You got any idea what those changes would cost? Millions. Tens of millions, maybe, right outta my pockets and the pockets of my partners and investors. Those old cotton warehouses you say I should renovate into my distribution facility? It'd be like renovating a Sopwith Camel into a space shuttle. Stuff like that, it just doesn't make sense, doesn't get done."

"It's gonna get done this time," Jules said. "With this project, nobody gets everything they want. Everybody gives on something. And that includes you."

"Whose fucking side are you on?"

"My own side. And my friends' side."

The phone was silent for a few seconds. "What if I tell you to take a fucking hike, mystery man? If L'Enfant's position has gotten as weak as you say, then maybe all I have to do is wait until he crumbles. Then I get a hundred percent of what I want, instead of just sixty percent. Give me one good reason I should drag myself out of bed and over to this goddamn vampires' ball at twelve-thirty in the goddamn morning."

Here came Jules's best shot. "You want one good reason? Rudy Goodfeller."

The line went silent again. Goodfeller's voice was much different when he spoke again. "What about Rudy? What about my son?"

"That informer was right. Rudy's back in town again, and he's hangin' with Courane and Edith L'Enfant. I've seen Rudy. I've talked with him. Play ball with me, Mr. Goodfeller, and I can make one of your biggest fears go away. Vanish like Michael Jackson's original nose."

"What are you talking about?"

"What do you think makes the L'Enfants so attractive to Rudy? It's all this vampire shit. He sees this neato community of these punk-vampire wannabes, and he wants to be part of that. He figures bein' pals with Edith L'Enfant gives him a little somethin' extra, somethin' special, makes it more likely that this gang of wannabes'll take him in. Typical kid behavior, far as I can see."

"Yeah? So what can you do about it?"

"I can pop the kid's bubble is what I can do. Drop a ton of horse manure on this vampire nonsense. Give me the go-ahead, Mr. Goodfeller, and I'll promise you one thing for sure—your son will never *think* the word 'vampire' ever again without shudderin' all the way down to his toenails."

♠

Jules got Goodfeller on board. Then he called Erato and Preston. They both agreed to come immediately. Erato was mystified at Jules's power to make such momentous events happen, but any chance to help his neighbors was too good a chance to pass up. Preston still wasn't getting around too well, but he wasn't about to miss the parley, either; he also said he'd call in the Reverend Tonqelle.

Everyone arrived at the orphanage by a quarter past two. Preston walked up the steps with the aid of a cane, a real nice number with African ceremonial masks carved along its length. Jules was pleased to see his partner up and walking, cane or no cane. Van Goodfeller didn't look happy when he walked past. That was all right. Jules didn't want him happy—just cooperative.

Erato found a good spot for his cab, right near the front entrance. He approached Jules full of eager, excited questions. Jules told him there wasn't time. He ushered him past the string quartet, still playing for the gradually diminishing crowd, and past the picked-over remains on the buffet tables. Together, they entered L'Enfant's library. More than a dozen people were already sitting around an oblong conference table in the center of the room. Jules recognized faces he'd seen on the evening news—city councilmen, executives of prominent local banks, top assistants to the mayor.

He stood in the back of the room, where he could see both L'Enfant's and Goodfeller's faces. There wasn't room for him at the closely packed table, anyway. Jules hoped he wouldn't have to say much. He hoped he wouldn't have to say anything at this point, just ensure by his silent presence a willingness on both sides to make the concessions that hurt.

Had he done the right thing? He was no urban planner. Certainly no fortune-teller. How could he know for sure that the results of his arm twisting, the mushing together of both sides' plans, would end up being any better than either plan would've been on its own? All he could go by was his gut. And his gut told him that neither side should get everything it wanted, but both sides should get some of what they wanted most.

The players were all formally dressed, but the atmosphere around the table felt more like a Saints-Falcons play-off match than a night at the opera. The lawyer from GoodiesMart's corporate headquarters in Kentucky looked shell-shocked at being awake at this hour, much less negotiating a multimillion-dollar deal. His disorientation didn't preclude combativeness, however, especially when he was presented with the alterations to his client's building plans. "It's completely out of the question," he said. "A two-tiered store would boost our cost profile by nearly a quarter—"

"What about Dallas?" L'Enfant interjected. "You were happy to build two-tiered in downtown Dallas. Their planning commission insisted on it. And your shareholders' report now lists the Dallas store as one of your most profitable. If two-tiered is good enough for Dallas, why not New Orleans?"

"The New Orleans market and the Dallas market are two entirely different animals—you damn well know that—"

Erato rose from the table, surprising Jules by jumping into the fray. "How about this? Mr. L'Enfant, wasn't a free health clinic part of your original plan?"

"Yes . . ." L'Enfant stared at Jules. "But that element is no longer required. Why bring it up?"

"Keep it in," Erato said. "It's a sweetener. You pay to build and staff the clinic, GoodiesMart pays to build a more compact store, and you both benefit from good press. Buildin' that clinic'll help cover up the fact that fewer subsidized apartments are gettin' built."

Heads nodded in unison around the table. The GoodiesMart lawyer saw the public-relations benefits of Erato's suggestion and agreed to the two-tiered store if L'Enfant's people would build the clinic. Jules was proud his pal had scored a winning basket, a clean shot that barely ruffled the net.

Jules found out why these spaces where backroom deals were cut were called "smoke-filled rooms"—the library filled with the corrosive odors of cigarette and cigar smoke, rewarmed coffee, nervous sweat. Now that the ball had begun rolling, the rest of the negotiating session didn't last nearly as long as Jules thought it would. Two sets of architects sketched out rough drawings of the huge site, and as they revised their sketches, their visions of the project grew more alike, until Jules could barely notice any differences at all. Goodfeller grumbled; L'Enfant grumbled; but piercing glances from Jules kept them both on track, heading for the final shaking of hands.

It was all done by 4:20 A.M., little more than two hours before sunrise. L'Enfant and Goodfeller approached Jules almost simultaneously as the others around the table were gathering their things. L'Enfant's eyes darted upward, in the direction of an upstairs bedroom where Jules presumed Veronika was waiting. Goodfeller was more direct. "You and me, we've gotta talk," he said, pulling Jules away from the other man. "Now."

"I got me an appointment upstairs," Jules said.

"You've got an appointment with me right now," Goodfeller said. "Tell me where my son is. Take me to him. Do what you said you're gonna do, or my lawyers are gonna find a way to blow this whole deal out of the water, signed papers or no signed papers."

"Give me fifteen minutes," Jules said. "Just fifteen lousy minutes. Wait for me in the foyer. Then we'll go find Rudy together."

Goodfeller shot Jules a hard look. "We'd better, mystery man."

Jules followed L'Enfant up the long, winding staircase. The living quarters had been thoroughly renovated, unlike the shabby rooms in the other wing. L'Enfant led Jules into one of the largest bedrooms Jules had ever seen, almost the size of the converted ballroom downstairs. Jules figured this had once been a dormitory; maybe two adjoining dormitories. The room's centerpiece was a tremendous four-poster bed. Hanging swathes of gauze and muslin, woven with golden threads, glowed in the cathedral light of surrounding Tiffany lamps.

L'Enfant pulled the curtain aside. Veronika was waiting. She wasn't glowing. Glowering was more like it. Staring at her hard, cruel face, gray as ashes in the pit of a fireplace hours after the last embers had faded, Jules wondered how he'd ever been attracted to her. Sure, she'd been gorgeous, even before the artificial curves ancient fertility fetishists would've worshipped as divine. But all that surface beauty had encompassed an emptiness, a cold void. Maureen, for all her constant nagging, had never been cold. In fact, it had been the warmth of her heart, her need for connection and companionship, that had indirectly led to her and Jules's terrible grief this past year.

Veronika settled onto the mass of pillows and turned her face away from Jules. She pulled her dull gray hair away from her neck. Jules could see two florid scars there, puncture wounds from eight months ago that still hadn't healed. "Get it over with, cockroach," she said in a flat voice.

Jules crawled through the curtains onto the bed. The expensive mattress and box spring groaned like a cheap flophouse cot under his weight. Didn't L'Enfant realize the silk bedspread and satin pillows would get ruined, irrevocably stained with gore? Jules glanced at his erstwhile captor's face and saw an almost pornographic hunger there. L'Enfant was going to watch. He was going to watch the whole thing. Jules suddenly realized how Maureen must've felt all those nights she danced naked on the stage at Jezebel's Joy Room, staring out at dozens of glazed, horny faces. Of course L'Enfant didn't care about ruined sheets and pillows. He wanted them as souvenirs.

They were going to make quite a pair, these two.

Approaching her passively aggressive form, with the pressure of L'Enfant's eyes on him, Jules felt the pangs of what could only be described as performance anxiety. He wondered whether he could produce the necessary suction—would he jab his fangs through her fleshy neck and then experience psychosomatic paralysis, letting the blood dribble down his chin? Would her blood be undrinkably bitter? After all these months, had it gone rancid, like leftover milk forgotten in the back of a refrigerator?

Aww, fuck it, he thought. *Just get it over with, cockroach.* He aimed for the unhealed puncture wounds, focusing on the mechanics of angling his mouth for the most efficient bite, so that he could finish off this stomach-churning chore as quickly as possible. He bit deeply, nicking the vertebrae of her neck, feeling horribly out of practice. He heard and felt her sharp intake of breath. All pain this time, no pleasure. *Good.* Unlike their last bout, this unavoidably intimate encounter failed to budge his sexual voltometer's needle off zero . . . although not having a certain piece of equipment undoubtedly helped.

Jules hated to admit it, but her blood actually tasted pretty darn good. He'd been getting used to the thin gruel of the High Krewe's donated blood, that low-fat, reduced-cholesterol juice squeezed from their herd of cowlike mental defectives. But Veronika had obviously been eating well during her months in L'Enfant's company. Her rich blood held traces of dinners at Commander's Palace and Galatoire's, big repasts of classic Creole dishes larded with cream sauces.

He needn't have worried about not being able to do the job. Once a few swallows of this elixir slid down his gullet, instinct and appetite took over. He held her head and shoulder in a tightening grip, sucking fiercely now. She actually started struggling—Jules heard excited little gasps from L'Enfant, and if his victim were any other woman than Veronika, he would've gotten excited, too—but Jules pushed her deeply into the mattress, growing stronger as her struggles grew weaker. Finally, her whole body jerked convulsively, went stiff, and then fell limp.

Jules continued sucking until he was swallowing more air than blood. Then he yanked his fangs from her cooling neck and sat up on the bed. The sudden shift in position made him dizzy. He'd overindulged, just like the old days when he'd troll the homeless shelters looking for lonely, corpulent cuties. But when he remembered whose lifeblood he'd just consumed, he was tempted to stick his finger down his throat and *really* stain L'Enfant's bedspread.

He glanced down at Veronika, wondering whether her youth had started returning. No, not yet; she was still just a fat, middle-aged corpse, stiffening in an unnaturally splayed position, her throat glistening with her own blood. Jules wiped his mouth with his sleeve. Now that he was in control of himself again, he had zero desire to lick his sticky lips. He wanted to wash his mouth out with a gallon of Listerine.

"How was it?" L'Enfant asked, voice thick with emotions Jules didn't care to speculate about.

"You been feedin' her pretty darn good," Jules said. "I think I just added four pounds to my dainty waistline."

"How long will it take?"

"Not much more than a couple of hours. You got a coffin for her?"

"I have one that Edith and I used to sleep in, one of our games from when she still excited me. It's in the next room over."

"Stick some dirt from the backyard in the bottom. Dump Veronika in it before sunrise. Make sure she don't pop out before sundown, unless that room's got storm shutters that're closed tight. If you're right about what you figured, she'll be back in her early twenties the next time you see her up and walkin'." Jules hoped L'Enfant's researches were junk. He pictured Veronika waking up tomorrow night the same age she was now, realizing she'd have to spend all eternity as a wrinkled, gray hag, screaming loud enough for the whole Garden District to hear—that would be delicious. Probably too delicious to come true, though.

L'Enfant stared at Veronika's corpse. Jules tried reading his expression. Anticipation, intense curiosity, and something else . . . love, near as Jules could tell. It was the only explanation Jules could come up with for why the musician had done everything he'd done. But it was hardly an answer at all, barely more edifying than his mother's long-ago, one-word answer to Jules's petulant, never-ending queries as to why his father had never returned home: *"Because."*

It was none of his business, and it didn't really matter to him, not in any material way, but Jules decided to press the issue, anyway. "I think you're strikin' a bum bargain," he said, "tradin' Edith for Veronika."

L'Enfant shook himself out of his reverie. "Who said anything about trading one for the other? I'll have both."

Jules smirked. "Not for long, you won't. Those are two strong-willed women. Edith may've convinced herself for now that she can live with this, that only your happiness matters. But I'd lay money on her not feelin' that way six months from now. And Veronika, her I know way better than I know Edith. There's no way in hell she's gonna put up with a female rival, wife or no wife. And I'll bet she's gonna come outta that coffin even more stiff-necked than she was before."

L'Enfant appeared to consider this. "If she manages to drive Edith away, then so be it. I was a far different man when I married Edith Aubrey eighteen years ago. Even though I'd already changed my name to Courane L'Enfant, I was still very much Corey Lawrence inside. I haven't been Corey Lawrence for a very long time. I've snuffed out that anonymous, insignificant little man. I'm long overdue for a new consort, one of unique beauty, power, and agelessness. I've earned it."

Shit, Jules thought, *a guy gets a platinum American Express card, he figures he deserves the whole fuckin' world.* "Yeah, maybe. But you won't be breakin' young Goth girls' hearts forever. You gotta be pushin' forty-five or so. What happens when Veronika gets tired of *you*?"

L'Enfant smiled. "When the bounds of human decay begin chafing me, Veronika will usher me into the kingdom of immortality."

Now it was Jules's turn to smile. Sure, L'Enfant might become a big, bad, immortal vampire. But if Veronika was to be his blood-mother, she'd always be one rung up in that relationship. Jules had experienced it with Maureen. Maureen could nag him raw, nag him from sundown to sunup because not only was she his lover, she was his mother, too. He'd always borne it with good humor, mostly, because down deep, Maureen was a peach. Veronika, on the other hand, was a lemon.

Jules's smile grew even wider. L'Enfant, the lucky guy, had bought himself an eternity of pussy whippings.

♠

Jules found Goodfeller waiting for him in the foyer downstairs. "C'mon," Jules said. "I got a pretty good idea where Rudy'll be hangin' out."

Goodfeller turned around. His tired eyes grew wide. "Jesus! Your face—!"

Jules rubbed his mouth again. Large flecks of dried blood flaked off onto the back of his hand. He noticed his jacket sleeves and the front of his shirt were covered with the stuff. "Jesus had nothin' to do with it," he mumbled. "Just takin' care of some old business. Let's go outside."

Jules shoved the heavy front doors open. He didn't care that Goodfeller had seen the blood on his face. Maybe seeing evidence of Jules's true, frightful nature would make Goodfeller swallow hard before contemplating reneging on their bargain once Jules had carried out his end.

He led Goodfeller toward the auto yard behind the main building. The night had turned cooler since Jules had first arrived eight long hours ago. A fog was gathering. Jules caught the scent of roasting coffee from a plant somewhere upriver. A cup of java would go down real good right about now. "Look," he said. "I can get rid of Rudy's fascination with vampires, like I told you. But vampires ain't the only hold the L'Enfants got on your kid. Edith L'Enfant, she promised him she'll start searchin' for his natural mother. You wanna have a decent relationship with your kid again? You gotta match Edith's offer."

"This another demand from you?" Goodfeller did his best to look defiant, but Jules could tell his companion's confidence wasn't what it had been. "You don't know what you're talking about. Christine? She's poison, pure poison. Even if we could manage to dig her up from whatever rathole she's crawled into, all she'd do is break his heart again. I'm Rudy's father. I know what's best for him. And *nobody* is gonna make me go against my best judgment where Rudy's concerned. Not even you."

The man was scared. Profoundly frightened. Jules could see it in his eyes. But he wasn't about to back down. Jules respected that. "It's not a demand. It's a piece of friendly advice. If you'd heard the excitement in Rudy's voice when he was talkin' about findin' his mother, if you'd seen the hope in his face, you might be whistlin' a different tune. It's a gift you can give him. What he does with that gift, whether it's a big soggy disappointment that busts as soon as he takes it outta the box, that's Rudy's business. But he'll always be grateful you offered it to him. Think about it."

They walked through a small side courtyard. Then Jules pushed open a weathered door that led to the yard. He spotted Rudy about fifty yards away, sitting in the front seat of a Chevy Impala coupe, reading a magazine beneath the lit dome light. Goodfeller saw him, too. He started rushing into the yard, but Jules grabbed him and pulled him back.

"Hey!" Jules whispered. "You want me to hold up my end of our bargain or not?"

"But he's right there, I've got to see him, talk with him—"

"Yeah, yeah, sure. But you go out there right now, that kid bolts. Let me talk to him first. After I'm done with him, I'll bet a family reunion won't seem like such a bad option to the kid. So give me two, three minutes with him, and stay out of sight."

Jules walked out into the yard. When he was about twenty feet from the Chevy, Rudy looked up from his magazine. The kid smiled and rolled down the window. "Hey," he said.

"Hey, Crunchy," Jules answered.

"The party over with?"

"Yeah. It's dead in there."

"You find that person you were looking for?"

"Yeah," Jules said. "I caught up with her." He moved into the small circle of light cast by the Chevy's dome lamp. Rudy's eyes grew large, just like his father's had three minutes earlier. Only the expression that followed was one of admiration approaching hero worship.

"Whoa!" Rudy said. "You *bit* somebody? Here at the party?"

"I killed Courane L'Enfant's lover," Jules said in a flat voice.

Rudy's eyes expanded again. "Was he, like, pissed?"

"Naww. He wanted me to do it."

Rudy's round face split with a tremendous grin. "That totally *rules.* Was it fun? Was it, y'know, sexy and all? None of the other vampires would ever talk to me about their kills. The closest I ever came to hearing about it was listening to Pearl's dumb poetry."

Jules stuck his head partially through the open window. "You think that sounds sexy, huh, drainin' a woman of all her blood? You think bein' a vampire helps you score with the ladies?"

Rudy blushed, and his smile withered a little. "Well, uh, sure! Doesn't it? I mean, y'know, Randolph, he always has lots of beautiful women hanging all over him—"

"Let me tell you somethin', kid." He leaned further into the window, sticking his face with its ugly scabs of dried blood close to Rudy's. "This here's a big secret. I'm only lettin' you in on this 'cause I kinda like you. 'Cause I don't want to see you make the same horrible mistake I made. What I'm about to tell you, you won't never read it in a vampire novel, see it in a vampire movie, or ever hear any other real vampire tell it. You ever speak a word of this to another soul, long as you live, I'll know about it. And your life won't be worth a Confederate dollar."

Rudy's face had blanched almost as white as Jules's. "Whu-what? What is it?"

"A man's body goes through lots of changes when he turns into a vampire. Some of them you know about. Skin turns white or gray. Body don't produce its own heat no more. You can't bear the light of the sun. But there's one other change that never gets publicized. No male vampire ever finds out until it's too late. Way too late."

Jules backed away from the car and unbuckled his belt. He unbuttoned and unzipped his trousers, letting them fall around his knees. Then he worked his thumbs into the elastic of his underpants, pulled it from beneath his belly's great overhang, and rolled his underpants down until they were just above his trousers. Then Jules opened the Chevy's door.

The kid's face said it all.

One unhealthy obsession: demolished.

TWENTY-FIVE

Jules rubbed his sore eyes. If he could look at himself in the mirror, he was sure he'd see dark, puffy circles beneath bloodshot orbs.

He'd tossed on Maureen's big waterbed almost the entire day, unable to drive obsessively gloomy thoughts from his brain. His big disappointment hadn't been that he'd been forced to grant the "gift" of vampirehood on Veronika. No . . . it was his discovery that L'Enfant and Veronika were responsible for only a portion of the crimes against the High Krewe.

And that left only one likely suspect. No; not *likely. Definite.* Much as he hated to face that word, he couldn't escape it.

Jules was going to have to confront one of the best friends he'd ever had. And the thought of it was driving him nuts.

He forced himself to stop pacing. He checked his watch. Seven twenty-seven P.M. Almost an hour of darkness had already slipped away. He couldn't procrastinate any longer. He walked into the hallway outside Maureen's bedroom and dialed Fanny Yishinsky's number.

The realtor answered on the third ring. "Yishinsky's Real Estate Services, Incorporated. How may we help you?"

"Mizz Yishinsky, this is Jules Duchon." No funny voice this time; no false name. There was no need for any of that nonsense now. "We talked about a week ago. I told you I was interested in lookin' at Dr. Amos Landrieu's house in Mid-City."

"Oh, yes! I remember. Didn't our conversation get cut off somehow?"

"Yeah. That was me."

"Would you still like to see the property? We've had an uptick in interest recently, but the house isn't under contract yet—"

"Actually, I'm not callin' about the house. I need to reach Amos Landrieu. I need you to have Dr. Landrieu call me."

There was a brief silence on the other end. "Well, I have to tell you, this is very irregular. I'm not Dr. Landrieu's message service, you know—"

"Mizz Yishinsky, listen. This is real important. This is—" What was about to spill out of his mouth was a threadbare cliché, but it was also literally, harrowingly true. "This is a matter of life and death."

"Well, if that's the case . . ."

He gave her his cell phone number and got off the phone. Then he carried the piece of paper he'd taken from the kitchen in Doc Landrieu's house into the bathroom. He pulled open the drawers that held Maureen's makeup and shoved aside lipsticks and mascaras and dainty jars of face creams until he found what he was looking for—an eyeliner pencil. Then he lightly rubbed the eyeliner over the indented parts of the paper until a phone number and address became clearly readable. The address, surprisingly, wasn't very far from his old home on Montegut Street. Three thousand forty-six Royal Street, in the heart of the Bywater neighborhood.

He stuck the paper in his pocket, next to his cell phone. Then he went into the guest room to check on Jonathan. Decades ago, when Doodlebug had been in the habit of occasionally flying in from California for a social visit, Maureen had invested in a guest coffin. That's where Jules had stashed Jonathan last night, after he'd messily poured a pint or two of blood down the comatose youngster's throat. Jules was glad he hadn't had to share the master bedroom. The kid was close enough to *dead*-dead to give Jules the creeps.

Tonight, though, he looked a little less dead. His breathing seemed stronger, more regular. Jules went downstairs to the kitchen to get the kid some more blood. Just as he was about to pull a bottle from the refrigerator, his cell phone buzzed against his thigh.

Jules pulled the phone and the paper from his pocket. He pressed the button that would let him answer, his heartbeat accelerating like a supercharged Corvette. "Hello?"

"Jules? This is Amos Landrieu. How are you feeling?"

Jules held the phone away from his ear and compared the phone number glowing on the tiny, green screen with the number reverse-highlighted on the paper. They were identical.

"I'm, uh, I'm doin' all right, Doc."

"You are? Ms. Yishinsky told me this was a matter of life and death. I was afraid you'd suffered some negative reaction to the antidote. You're *sure* you're feeling well?"

Jules squeezed his eyes shut. He hated this. The concern in his friend's voice was genuine. Jules hated what he was going to have to do.

"Yeah, yeah. That stuff you gave me really did the trick. After two hours, I was practically good as new."

"I'm glad to hear it. So what's the emergency? Don't tell me you frightened my Realtor half out of her wits just so we could chat."

"No. I mean, yeah. I mean . . ." The words weren't coming easily. And if they were this hard now, over the phone, Jules could barely imagine how difficult it would be speaking with his old mentor face-to-face. "What I mean is . . . Doc, we gotta talk about some stuff."

The phone was silent for a few seconds. "Yes, Jules, I suppose we do." The phone's poor reception made it difficult for Jules to determine whether Doc Landrieu was shocked, angry, or resigned. "Would you like to meet somewhere?"

"You know where the Trolley Stop Cafe is, on St. Charles?"

"I know it, yes. Busy place. Is it private enough for what you'd like to talk about?"

"It'll do," Jules said.

"What time would you like to meet?"

"I can be over there in about twenty minutes. How about you?"

"Give me a half hour. Will that be all right?"

"That'll be fine. I'll see you there."

"Right." Another brief silence; Jules wasn't sure if Doc Landrieu had hung up the phone. "I'm glad you're feeling well, Jules." Then the phone definitely clicked.

Jules headed for the door. His vest hung on the coat rack, next to one of his sport coats. The vest could hold a small armory . . . a hammer, a sharpened stake, a vial of holy water, even (if Jules could find a church open at this hour of night). But could he picture himself actually using any of those weapons against his old boss? He took the sport coat off the rack and slipped it on.

He locked the door behind him, wondering whether he'd ever use the key again. Would some of his parts get delivered to the High Krewe's mansion before sunrise? He got in his car. The digital dashboard was still dead. He turned onto North Rampart and headed downriver, away from the Trolley Stop.

Jules stared up at the house on Royal Street. The turreted Victorian was big, the biggest residence on this mostly gentrified block. It had a ground-level basement, a first and second story, and a spacious attic with dormer windows, tall enough to convert into a proper third story. An odd thought skittered through Jules's mind—was Doc Landrieu planning to open a bed-and-breakfast inn? Was that why his old boss was selling a perfectly good house in Mid-City? Running an inn might not be a bad occupation for a vampire. Maybe Jules would ask him about it sometime. After he'd asked him what he'd been doing with all those female vampire body parts.

A strong breeze off the nearby river rustled the leaves of the sweet olive trees in the darkened house's front yard. Jules checked the narrow gravel driveway for Doc Landrieu's car. The driveway was empty all the way back to a heavily shadowed wooden shed. The shed didn't look big enough to hold a car. He glanced up and down the street. Doc Landrieu's well-preserved old Mercedes sedan was nowhere in sight.

Jules heard a faint pitter-pattering above his head. He looked up. A large rat ran along a suspended power line, graceful and surefooted as a tightrope walker. A black rat. *Wrong color,* Jules thought sourly.

He checked his watch. He'd gotten off the phone with Doc Landrieu about twenty minutes ago. Jules figured he had forty-five minutes, at most, to get in and out before his old boss got suspicious and returned home from the Trolley Stop. Forty-five minutes to retrieve the missing body parts, assuming they still existed and were hidden here.

The front gate wasn't locked. Jules looked up and down the street again. No one was outside walking a dog or fiddling with his car. The two nearest houses were dark. He walked quickly through the small front yard and up the steps to the porch. A porch swing hung in front of three ten-foot-high French windows. It looked and smelled brand-new, probably just installed. Jules wondered who Doc Landrieu sat out here with. An image flashed into his head—his old friend slowly rocking with Flora Ann's limbless and headless torso on his lap. *Sick.* Jules clicked off his mental TV set as fast as he could, before the movie got even worse.

Jules stared at the sturdy front door, then glanced at the nearest

French window. Its panes were wavy and irregular, probably the original glass. Beautiful, and undoubtedly expensive to replace. But Jules didn't have time to be careful. He wrapped his coat around his fist and smashed the pane just above the window's latch. The crash of the old glass shattering sounded three times as loud as Jules would've expected. But no lights flared, either in this house or others on the block. No neighbors stuck their heads out front doors. Maybe they were used to loud noises from the nearby docks.

If I had a dime for every window I've broken in the last week, Jules thought . . . well, he'd have forty cents.

Jules unlatched the window. If it was painted shut, he was screwed. It wasn't—with a few hard yanks, the lower half of the window slid upward, knocking more chunks of broken glass to the parlor's hardwood floor.

It was going to be a damned tight fit. The opening was about three feet wide by five tall. He hunched down and turned sideways. His head, right shoulder, and right leg fit through. The belly would be the biggest challenge. He sucked it in as far as it would go. That still left about eight inches of him flopping against the outside wall like an elephant seal's blubbery flipper. Being able to transform into mist would be mighty handy right about now. But he might as well wish for the Tooth Fairy to give him a good shove.

He stared into the parlor. Damned if it didn't look just like his mother's old parlor, only with much finer pieces than she'd ever been able to afford. He looked for something to grab so he could pull himself through. The chairs and sofas were all out of reach. The only piece of furniture close enough for him to grab was a slender end table . . . that held a bottle of hand lotion.

It wasn't the Tooth Fairy. But it was the next best thing. He slathered the window's wooden frame with lotion, then unbuttoned his shirt and did the same to his blindingly white belly. Now he smelled like a gigantic coconut. But so long as there were no Hawaiian cannibals hiding inside, that was all right. He slid through the window frame relatively painlessly.

In the other house, Doc Landrieu's lab had been down in the basement. And if the limbs were anywhere, they'd probably be in the lab . . . assuming Doc Landrieu hadn't stashed them in some tremendous freezer in the shed, hidden away beneath Winn-Dixie rump roasts and legs of lamb. But Jules reminded himself that vampire body parts didn't require refrigeration.

In most of the old houses he'd been in, the door to the basement was located in the kitchen. He stepped around the parlor furniture, rebuttoning his shirt by touch as he tried acclimating to the darkness. This house smelled really good, not at all like the musty, dusty odor that had permeated his boss's other house (or Jules's old house, for that matter). He tried distinguishing the various pleasing scents. Fresh bread, sweet baked apples, copious amounts of furniture polish . . . not the scents of a bachelor's home, that was certain; at least not a *straight* bachelor.

The quickest way to find the kitchen in the dark was to follow the food scents. A center hall led into a dining room with a large wooden table surrounded by straight-backed chairs and china cabinets filled with dishes. The next room over was the kitchen. Hazy moonlight spilled through lacy curtained windows. Almost every square inch of wall space was taken up by hanging copper pots and pans. Pots big enough to bathe fat infants in sat on top of a gleaming range. Had Doc Landrieu had all this stuff in his old place? He'd never been a cook. Jules hoped he hadn't deciphered the wrong address from that piece of paper. Maybe he'd mistakenly broken into Chef Paul Prudhomme's house?

Jules looked for an entrance to the basement. One door led to the backyard. Another led into a bountifully stocked walk-in pantry. The last door belonged to the broom closet.

Frustrated, Jules headed back to the center hall. He found a second parlor on the other side of the front door. This parlor was crammed with home electronics. All the modern stuff, TV and computer and audio stack, had been ghettoized in this one room; as if whoever lived here didn't want to be reminded that time had passed since Tom Edison's day. Beyond this second parlor, Jules found an alcove with a door.

Jules opened it. Steps led down into darkness. *Bingo.* He clicked on his flashlight and began descending. The purple bruise on his forehead suddenly throbbed. He froze. Having just been set upon in a basement like this last night, his body wasn't eager for more punishment. Jules told his frozen legs they were being silly. He was alone. The faster he found the body parts, the better chance he'd have of staying alone.

His nose told him he was on the right track. The odors rising from below were similar to what he'd smelled at Charity Hospital—disinfectants, other harsh medicinal scents he couldn't identify.

He reached the bottom step. The flashlight's beam glittered back at him from dozens of reflective surfaces. Racks of test tubes and beakers. Something else, too . . . metallic. Jules moved closer. It was a tray filled with stainless-steel surgical instruments, scalpels and clamps, and other things.

Jules found an autopsy table. It was similar to tables he remembered from forensic rooms at the morgue. It had leather straps and buckles, meant to keep the corpse from shifting. Corpses moved; Jules remembered that. Cavities in their torsos filled with the gases of decay, expanding their chests like balloons. Muscles tightened with rigor mortis, a final, awkward semblance of life.

He leaned closer to the table's smooth white surface. In the indirect light, he saw what looked like spilled chocolate syrup. He bit his lip, then forced himself to direct his light there. Dried blood. A lot of it.

Even up to a minute ago, he'd hoped he'd been wrong. He'd hoped against all logic that his old friend and benefactor had clean hands. But now that hope was just as dead as those involuntary guests of the morgue had been.

"Aww, Doc . . . why'd ya hafta get yourself tangled up in this . . . ?"

He checked the spaces beneath the double sink. Nothing there, except for some power tools. Jules tried not to think what Doc had done with that circular saw. He opened cabinets, peered behind equipment racks, even went into the tiny bathroom in the corner and pulled back the floral shower curtain . . . nothing. Just as he was trying to decide which room he should search next, he heard a creak directly above his head.

A paralyzing chill spread from the base of his skull. He heard it again. The weight of a footstep on the hardwood floor overhead. Doc Landrieu couldn't be home yet—could he? *Could he?* One thing for sure—he couldn't let himself be caught down here. If Doc Landrieu came down those stairs, the only way out would be straight through his old friend . . . and now that Landrieu was a vampire himself, going through him would be like boring uphill through an M1 Abrams battle tank.

Jules hustled up the stairs, trying to combine stealth and speed. Not an easy combination for a five-hundred-pound man with trick knees. Amazingly, he reached the top landing unopposed. The only opposition came from his overburdened heart, now beating hard enough to make lights flash inside his skull like a demented disco display. He forced his breathing to settle down before he dared open the door.

The foyer and the rooms beyond it were still dark. Jules listened for any additional footfalls. He didn't hear anything, apart from the sounding of a distant Klaxon somewhere on the riverfront. Cautiously, he moved into the center hall. The media room was empty. He stared through its windows into the driveway. The Mercedes wasn't there; he breathed more easily, seeing that. Jules peered into the main parlor. The French window was still open, bits of broken glass dimly glittering with light reflected from the street lamp across the road.

He turned back toward the kitchen. Then he heard it. A squeak of compressed bedsprings from upstairs.

Jules considered his options. He could get the heck out, abandoning his best chance of retrieving the body parts without violence. Then his only recourse would be calling in the High Krewe's strong-arms and blowing the whole situation to hell. Or he could go upstairs and meet whoever was up there; maybe force that person to reveal what had happened to the severed limbs.

Jules began climbing the stairs. He sure was getting his exercise these last few days . . . he might've even lost a pound or two. But all thoughts of weight loss vanished as soon as he heard the scurrying. A light, quick scurrying, like a small animal's nails clicking on a hardwood floor. It came from behind the first closed door beyond the stair landing. He moved close to the door, put his hand on the knob. Then he heard a hushed whisper from inside, a woman's voice—

"—now you come back here, you bad boy, right this *instant*—"

He was about to open the door and see who the voice belonged to when he heard tires crunch over gravel.

Shit.

Was there another way out, aside from the window? Both the front and back doors were secured with dead bolts—the only way out was the way he'd come in. He plunged down the stairs. The old cyprus groaned with every panicked step. He could still escape. If he could just get through that window—

Except now there was a man standing in front of the window. He bent down and stepped through, kicking aside broken glass. It was Doc Landrieu.

He turned on a lamp. "Hello, Jules," he said, not sounding terribly surprised. He ran a finger over the globs of yellow hand lotion that stained the window frame, then tapped a piece of broken glass with the toe of his shoe. "You've made a bit of a mess, I see. You know, if you'd wanted to visit my new home, all you needed to do was ask. I would've invited you. I would've even opened up the front door."

"How did you know I was here?" The words tumbled out of Jules's mouth before he could think.

Doc Landrieu removed a cell phone from his pocket. "I got a call that someone was breaking into my home. I'd just gotten to the restaurant, hadn't even had a chance to turn off my engine. These little phones truly come in handy." He stepped around a sofa and began walking toward Jules.

Jules backed toward the stairway. "Don't come any closer, Doc." He felt behind him for the railing. He only had a fraction of his former strength, but maybe desperation could empower him to break off one of the wooden spokes. "I been a vampire a whole lot longer than you. I know stuff. Ways to take you down, if I have to."

Doc Landrieu frowned. He paused about twenty feet from Jules. "Why this hostility, Jules? Haven't I always been a friend to you? I helped you just two nights ago. We wouldn't be having this discussion right now if I hadn't defended you from that maniac, then come up with a remedy for his poison."

Jules swallowed hard. "Yeah, you always been my friend. One of the few friends I ever had. But that was when you were a normal. Now that you're a vampire, I don't know what kind of man you are. When the change happened to me, I wanted it, I chose it. But it got forced on you. Forced on you in a terrible kinda way, maybe terrible enough to twist you all up inside. Twist you into somebody who cuts up women and steals their body parts. Maybe somebody who'd like to cut me into chunks of meat, too."

The older man's forehead crinkled slightly, as if he were embarrassed to have been painted in such terms. He held his hands out in a gesture of supplication. "How can you think that of me? Was I the one who attacked you in the cemetery two nights ago? If there's been any violence, surely the culprit is that awful man who paralyzed you."

"You can drop the act, Doc." Jules's grip tightened on the wooden spoke. He jiggled it, hoping it was loose. It felt solid. "The two of you were in cahoots. Workin' together to pull the wool over my eyes." He took a wild-ass guess, based on a gut feeling he'd had all along. "It was Straussman under that getup, wasn't it? Maybe not always, but it was that night."

Doc Landrieu's hands fell to his sides. He smiled. The laugh lines at the corners of his brows deepened, nearly hiding his eyes. Jules thought he looked almost proud. "All right, Jules. Very good. I'll stop pretending. There's no need for all of that sleight of hand anymore. I've accomplished what I wanted to. And I've never liked lying to you. But tell me how you figured things out. I'm very curious."

This was too weird. Way too weird. Jules stared at the man he'd assumed was a deadly antagonist. Doc Landrieu's stance was relaxed, his tone of voice friendly and casual, as if they were standing next to the watercooler at the morgue, having a chat about last night's Tulane-LSU football game. But Jules didn't let go of the spoke. "A couple of clues got me going. The first was that painted coconut I found next to Micholson's tomb in Metairie Cemetery. The one that got left for me to find. Either the black vampires had left it, or somebody who wanted to stir up trouble between the black vampires and the High Krewe. I took it to the people who'd made it. They said they'd stopped using that design more than six months ago—"

"And you believed them? Aren't they the ones who killed your girlfriend?"

"I ain't forgotten that, Doc. But I could tell they weren't makin' this shit up. And you were one of the folks who would've had one of them old coconuts, assumin' you'd risen again as a vampire. Then there was the attack on Preston—"

"Who?"

"One of the black vampires. The one you ran through in the Quarter. Him and me kinda partnered up about a week ago."

Doc Landrieu shook his head with quiet disgust. "Now you're on a first-name basis with those despicable creatures?"

Surprisingly, Jules experienced a tiny twinge of shame. "Yeah, I am. Things change sometimes. Look, I know Preston had a hand in what got done to you. But leavin' that off to one side, he's really a pretty decent guy. And besides, if it hadn't been for these mutilation attacks, I never woulda had no incentive to buddy up with him. So the way I see it, you can lay that in your own lap."

Doc Landrieu frowned with patrician disappointment. "I can't say I don't feel a little betrayed. I mean, I wouldn't have made common cause with *your* murderers. Well . . . go on."

Jules blinked. Here he was, facing down the mutilator, and he felt bad that he'd just hurt his feelings. "That attack on Preston . . . it didn't fit the pattern. And Preston said his attacker had a real mad on. So that made me think of you. But that wasn't the kicker. The kicker didn't occur to me until last night, when I was at Courane L'Enfant's house, tryin' to find out if maybe *he* was the mutilator."

"And this 'kicker' was . . . ?"

"I shoulda realized it while you were workin' on me. But my brain was too fuzzed out. Sure, your antidote worked real well. But you didn't mix it up in your lab downstairs. You didn't analyze my blood in your lab, either. 'Cause you didn't have no lab at that house no more. See, I busted in there two nights before we met up, lookin' for the files you'd kept on me. That basement was bare as a baby's bottom. When I got attacked, you already had that antidote on you. You had it on you 'cause you'd planned out everything that would happen. And you knew the antidote would work, 'cause you were the one who'd come up with the poison in the first place."

Doc Landrieu smiled again. "Ah, there's never a perfect crime, is there? There's always one possible glitch that gets overlooked. So you've burglarized two of my properties in one week? Your dear mother would be mortified at such hooliganism." He grinned more broadly. "Well, even though you've pieced things together faster than I would've expected, I still managed to delay you long enough to finish my work. Now that you've unmasked me as your nefarious criminal, what do you plan to do next?"

Jules stared at his old boss's seemingly friendly smile and shook his head. "This ain't no game, Doc. I like you, and I guess I owe you from years back, but I owe Doodlebug, too. And I been given a job to do. If our friendship still means somethin' . . . let's not make this really awful. Tell me where you've stashed the body parts. Hand 'em over to me. I'll return them to their owners, and there won't be no need for me to tell the High Krewe where I got them from."

"That's a kind gesture, Jules. Worthy of an old friend. But I can't take you up on your offer."

Jules's face twisted with pain. "Why the hell *not,* Doc? You realize what kinda position you're puttin' me in? You insist on stickin' with whatever kinda crazy plan you've got, and I got no choice but to call in Besthoff and whatever nasties he's got holed up in that mansion of his. They'll take you apart. And if Straussman really was workin' with you, they'll take him apart, too, only way worse—"

Doc Landrieu stepped closer. "Oh, Jules, *really,* there's no need for these histrionics—"

Jules yanked the spoke as hard as he could. The old wood surrendered with an ear-bludgeoning crack.

"Good heavens!" Doc Landrieu said. "Was that additional vandalism really necessary? Do you have any notion what a decent carpenter costs these days?"

Jules brandished the impromptu stake, dimly aware of pain in his shoulder. Sweat rolled down his sides. "I told you to keep back, Doc. And I meant it." With his free hand, he pulled his cell phone from his pocket and held it high. "I got Besthoff's private number on speed dial. Either you agree to hand over them body parts, or I press this button and get him and his goons on the line."

Amos Landrieu's large, intelligent eyes weren't laughing anymore. Instead, they seemed full of sympathy. "You aren't going to make that call, Jules. Not after I introduce my companion upstairs."

Jules couldn't risk glancing over his shoulder, up the stairs. "Who you got up there? Straussman? If Straussman comes creepin' down those stairs—"

Another smile. "Now why would I have *Straussman* lurking about? Really, that man is way too busy to be hanging around here. Do you know how many rooms he has to dust each evening just to keep that palace of theirs looking halfway presentable?" He cupped his hands around his mouth and aimed his voice up the stairs. "Dear? Everything's fine down here. I believe it's time for you to make your grand entrance."

Jules heard a door open on the second floor. He edged away from the bottom stair, keeping his back to the wall. That business about speed dial had been a bluff. If this were Straussman descending, or someone like him, Jules was in the soup. A very hot and spicy soup.

Jules listened to the descending footsteps. They were faint, almost inaudible. Whoever was coming down couldn't weigh much more than a hundred pounds and was either barefoot or wearing slippers. *Who—?*

Jules couldn't stand it anymore. He had to look up, even though it meant taking his eyes off Doc Landrieu. The top part of the stairway was dark, bereft of even the weak light that came through the windows from the street. The descending figure was petite, not much bigger than a ten- or eleven-year-old. Jules saw a flash of what looked like curled, purple hair, possibly glasses. The figure paused. Jules heard a high-pitched keening, an expression of unbearable anticipation. She pulled a large purse off her shoulder (she was definitely a she), dropped it on the stair, and ran down the rest of the steps, tottering like an antique windup toy.

"Jules!!"

That voice—! She was on him in an instant, throwing her arms around him, squeezing him, burying her face in his gargantuan middle. Then she looked up, and he saw her face clearly in the glow of the parlor lamp.

Reality took a ten-count.

"MOTHER!!!"

"Oh baby boy! Baby boy!" Her glasses were half off her face, and tears streamed from her eyes. "I been waitin' forty years to see you! *Forty years!* I thought this night would *never* come!" She squeezed him harder. He felt his ribs begin to crack.

Before she managed to pulverize him to jelly, she let go and stepped back to get a better look at him. Her adoring look turned disapproving. Her mouth fell agape. "Boy, you gotten big as a *house*! A St. Charles Avenue mansion! What you been eatin' these past forty years? An ice cream factory? You was always chubby, but this—this takes the cake! Wasn't I always on you to do them calisthenics exercises? Even your Grandpa Jacques never got so gosh-durned *tremendous,* and he was one heck of an eater—"

Jules's mind was blank. Blank as a freshly scrubbed chalkboard. He tried to compose thoughts, simple thoughts, childlike thoughts, but he could manage only one syllable of even vaguely human cogitation—"Hah . . . *how*?"

His mother stared at him quizzically. " 'How' what? How did Grandpa Jacques get so fat? I told you, until you came along, he was the family's cham-*peen* eater, and one heck of a cook, too—"

Doc Landrieu walked quietly to her side and put his arm gently around her shoulders. "No, dear. I believe what Jules wants to know is, how did you come to be here, forty years after you supposedly died and were buried?"

She pushed her cat's-eye glasses back up onto the bridge of her nose. "Oh. *That.*" She visibly shivered. "Ohhh, I don't like thinkin' about all them years . . ."

Doc Landrieu hugged her more tightly. "It's all right. It's all over now, all in the past. Tell Jules what happened. He needs to hear it."

"Well . . ." She looked up at Doc Landrieu, smiled hesitantly, then turned back to Jules with a steely expression. "I should tan that battleship-size behind of yours, boy. Didn't I tell you to wait until I was good and dead before you drank my blood? Didn't I tell you to make absolutely, positively *sure*? But did you listen?"

"Buh-but you told me not to let you go cold before—"

She bulldozed right over his shaky objection. "Did you listen to my instructions? Heck *no*! Next thing I knew, I woke up inside my box, and I couldn't so much as wiggle my nose. I was caught in, in . . . oh, what was that fancy word you used, Amos?"

"Stasis, dear."

"Yeah, that's right. Stasis. I couldn't move none at all. Amos explained that was 'cause my body got blessed by a priest and I got buried in consecrated ground. Otherwise, maybe I coulda dug myself outta there, although scratchin' through that cheap coffin and all that dirt woulda done my poor fingernails somethin' horrible. So there I was, stuck in that cheap pine box for forty years. I tell you, if I didn't have my card games to play in my head, and my *Lucy* episodes, I woulda gone stark ravin' bonkers. I can't tell you how many times I played that same durn game of solitaire. And it's a good thing CBS repeated them episodes of *Lucy* so many times before I got buried. I remembered them real good. Although that episode with Lucy and Ethel in the candy factory, that was one I coulda done without remembering so sharp . . . I got so hungry, I thought my stomach was gonna up and eat itself. And then . . . well, Amos, you tell the rest of it."

"You've probably experienced this yourself, Jules," Doc Landrieu said in a breezy tone of voice. "I would be in a crowd of people, say at a performance of the opera, when a strange buzzing in my sinuses would start up. It would grow stronger and stronger the closer I came to a certain individual. Through careful observation and trial and error, I determined that this sensation was an exquisite sensitivity to the proximity of fellow vampires. That's how I first met your Mr. Straussman, a fellow opera fan.

"About your mother . . . well, even before my transformation, I'd often take long walks along the fringes of City Park and Delgado College. For exercise, and to stimulate my thinking. Not very long after my change, I began to notice that almost painful sensation in my sinuses whenever I'd walk anywhere close to the paupers' cemetery behind the college. Once I'd learned what that sensation meant, I became extremely curious, of course, as to who might be buried there. One evening, I decided to brave the discomforts of Christian paraphernalia in order to systematically read all the grave markers. Such thoroughness wasn't necessary; my sensitivity led me directly to one particular grave site. I can't tell you how delighted I was to recall, upon seeing the stone, that you'd buried your mother there. A very sweet lady whom I remembered very fondly. Once I'd made that discovery, it was a fairly simple matter to hire a couple of neighborhood layabouts to dig—"

Jules's mother wiggled out of Doc Landrieu's embrace and grabbed her son's hand. "Now, Amos, stop right there. Jules don't need to hear about how his own mother got dug out from her grave. We got much more *important* things to talk about!" She pulled Jules toward the staircase.

Jules felt like Dorothy from *The Wizard of Oz,* whirling around in a flying farmhouse caught in the middle of a tornado. Except when this house finally crashed back to earth, it wouldn't land on the Wicked Witch of the East—it'd land on top of his own sanity, squishing it like an unlucky tree roach. Doc Landrieu grinned at him like the Wizard, having stepped out from behind the curtain to reveal himself as a dapper and benevolent traveling salesman. His mother (Dorothy herself, although she always went by Edna) pulled him up the steps, yanking on his arm with the strength of a team of Busch Beer Clydesdales.

One horrible thought pulsed in his head like a blood-red neon sign—*I turned my mother into a vampire. My own mother . . .*

He almost didn't notice the furry little white head and pink nose that popped out of his mother's purse when he passed it on the stairs. He would've missed it entirely if it hadn't been for a sudden buzzing in his sinuses, a buzzing Jules hadn't felt in decades.

Jules paused next to the purse and stared down at the rat. After all he'd experienced tonight, this reunion with a missing piece of himself barely elicited the slightest sensation of amazement or surprise. Everything was proceeding with the curious logic of a deranged dream. "Mother, uh, pardon my French, but why do you have my dick in your purse?"

"*Your* Dick?" She stared back at him with a pinched mixture of confusion, consternation, and impatience. "That's *my* Dick. He's my little pet, goes with me everywhere. But how'd you know I'd named him Richard?"

Jules squeezed his eyes shut and sighed. "It's a long, *looong* story," he said.

"Well, it'll have to wait for later," she said, tightening her grip on his wrist and pulling him higher with renewed determination. "I've got somebody to introduce you to. Somebody special. Someone who's gonna change your life, get you to shape up once and for all."

Jules didn't dare ask.

She pulled him onto the top step and down the corridor. "All those years I was stuck in that box," his mother continued, "there was just one thing I was thinkin' of, aside from card games and *Lucy* episodes. And that was how much I'd always wanted you to settle down with a nice girl. Not like that Maureen trash you always hung around. The biggest disappointment of my life as a mother was that I'd never picked you out a real nice girl, somebody I could approve of. Someone from a good background, a girl who'd make me a nice daughter-in-law, be a comfort to me in my old age. Well, Amos, bless his heart, he decided, not too long after he dug me up, that he was gonna help make my dream come true."

She stopped in front of a closed bedroom door and rapped three times with her tiny, wrinkled knuckles. "Dear? You decent in there? That prowler wasn't a thief at all, and no rapist neither. Look, I'm gonna come in there with somebody. Got a big surprise for you, honey!"

She pushed open the door without waiting for a response and stepped into the room. Jules hung back, but he peered inside, vacillating between dread and curiosity. The bedroom was dark. His mother walked over to the far wall and switched on a light. The room held a small four-poster bed, a chest of drawers, a nightstand, two reading chairs, and a standing lamp, whose weak bulb was dimmed further by a fringed canvas shade. A book sat open on one of the chairs by the lamp.

Jules's mother walked to the closet. "Honey," she said, putting her hand on the doorknob, "I told you the coast was clear. You can come out now."

"Edna, I don't want to meet anyone," a female voice replied from inside the closet. "I'm in my nightgown, and I'm not feeling that great. Just leave me alone, okay?"

"That's *not* okay, young lady! Now, I told you, I got someone very important for you to meet. And don't worry none about him seein' you in your nightgown. He's gonna be seein' you all sorts of ways from now on, so you might as well get used to it."

Jules's mother pulled the door open, overcoming some resistance from the other side. A tall young woman walked reluctantly out of the closet, as unsteady on her legs as a newborn colt. Her long auburn hair partly obscured her face. But when she brushed the hair from her eyes with a brusque, awkward, gesture, Jules had no doubt who he was looking at.

"Aww, shit . . . ," Jules said, feeling his weakened tethers to reality become shakier still.

It was Pearl. There was no mistaking that pale, heart-shaped face. But it wasn't Pearl. Or it wasn't *just* Pearl. This woman was much taller than he remembered Pearl having been. The top of her nightgown fell slightly open, and even in the dim light, Jules could see the pinkish, slightly raised seam of flesh, crisscrossed with suture marks, where Pearl's neck was attached to shoulders not originally her own . . .

Flora Ann's shoulders and torso. Which Jules had no doubt were also attached to Alexandra's arms, shimmering with fine, ivory down, and Victoria's long, muscular dancer's legs.

TWENTY-SIX

"It's Fatty Arbuckle! It's that awful detective!"

"No—," Jules said, "this ain't happenin'—"

"What are you backin' away for?" Jules's mother said, pursuing him into the hall. "Come on in here and meet your future bride!"

"Mother, get your hands off me—!"

"What the heck are you bein' so *shy* for? You were never shy around girls before. And this one's a real nice *sweet* young girl. I should know—I made her myself! Well, not by *myself,* maybe—I mean, Amos did the actual work—but I gave the okay on all the pieces before they got put together!" She locked a Herculean grip on both his wrists and yanked him back toward the bedroom. "Now you stop this stallin' and get in there and say a proper hello!"

Stumbling on legs made of sawdust and Jell-O, Jules allowed himself to be led back into the room. The look on Pearl/not-Pearl's face wasn't exactly welcoming. Jules could only inadequately describe it as extreme horror, peppered with a liberal helping of disgust.

"Oh, no," her pretty lips said as they curled back. "No no no no *no.* Not *him.* Not *HIM*!" Her hands (Alexandra's hands) flew to her mouth, then covered her eyes. But she couldn't help splaying her fingers and looking, if only to convince herself of the depths of her misfortune. "I—I've been asking myself for hours if this nightmare could get any worse. It can't possibly get *worse,* I told myself. But it has! It *HAS*!"

"Now look, Pearl," Jules said, fighting down a sense of panic that was beginning to match Pearl's own rising hysteria. "None of this was my idea. I been tryin' to prevent this whole thing all along—"

Jules's mother came between them. "Now see here, missy," she hissed at Pearl, "you just shut your nasty little mouth about my boy! I've *told* you to watch that witchy tongue of yours. My Jules is one *heck* of a catch—"

"He's a *monstrosity*!" Pearl shrieked. "How can you expect me to feel anything but *revulsion* for such a gross, vulgar, human *whale*? For *this* you took away my Randolph? For this nightmare version of *The Dating Game*?" She looked wildly around the room. "Where's Bachelor Number Two? Bachelor Number Three? *Anyone* else would be a prince by comparison! That horrible old man who carved me up, even—"

"Amos is *taken,*" Jules's mother growled.

Jules took his mother gently by the shoulders and led her away from Pearl's fury. "Mother, you gotta understand, you can't just take two people—or in this case, five or six people—shove 'em together and say it's a match. Maybe back in Europe, that's how things got done. But this is America, y'know? Land of the *free*? People got a right to make their own choices—"

Her lower lip began trembling, and before Jules knew what had hit him, he was watching his mother bawl. "How—how can you talk about chuh-*choices* and *freedom* when I ain't seen you in forty years, and here the only thing I wanted, the only thing I puh-*PRAYED* for was your happiness . . ."

Tears always got him. Whether they were his mother's or Maureen's or even some potential victim's in his cab, the sight and sound of a woman crying squeezed his heart in a vice. "Oh cripes . . . yeah, I know, honey . . . I *know* you always only wanted the best for me . . ." He tried embracing her, to calm her down, but she pulled away. "I appreciate what you're tryin' to do for me—look, could you maybe cut off the waterworks, please? *Please?* Really, I appreciate it, I know you gone to a lot of trouble, but this just ain't gonna work out—"

Her tears magically stopped, and her mouth set itself in a firm, defiant line. "Give me one good reason why it won't, Jules Augustine Duchon."

Jules gulped. He was in trouble now. She'd used his middle name, never a good sign. "First of all, she hates my guts." As if on cue, Pearl hissed, spraying tiny droplets of saliva in his direction. "Is that the expression of a woman even a smidgen in love?"

His mother's expression didn't change. "That's a weak excuse not to try. Love or no love, it don't matter much, not in the long run. I could barely stand your father, but we ended up with a pretty decent marriage."

"Until he left and never came back, maybe—"

Her face grew livid. "*Don't* you throw that back in my face, boy! Your father left us because he liked booze and foreign cigars and South Seas hotties more than he liked responsibility. It had *nothin'* to do with the quality of our marriage!"

Pearl stomped her foot. "I'd stand out in the sun and *dissolve* before I'd even touch him, much less *marry* him!"

"You shut your trap if you know what's good for you, missy!"

Jules felt himself rapidly losing patience. He stared at his mother. This was just like their old arguments about his leaving dirty coffee mugs in the sink, only a million times worse. "Mother, even if she worshiped the ground I walk on, this *still* couldn't work. 'Cause *I* can't stand *her,* neither. Can you try to get that through your head? I'm the captain of my own ship, and I *been* captain for more than eighty years now, with no cocaptain. And I done just fine. The only woman I ever came close to marryin', ever, was Maureen. And as far as I'm concerned, she's still the only woman for me, alive or dead or undead—"

The tears started again, this time undergirded by ball-shriveling maternal fury. "Don't you toss that *hussy's* name in my face! I was never so ashamed in all my life as when you started bringin' that sleazy burlesque dancer into my home! I raised you for better than that, Jules Augustine! How can you even *think* about throwin' away this beautiful gift I done made for you? Huh? How *can* you? After all those years I lay trapped in that cheap pine box in the ground, in that awful paupers' cemetery, not even one of the St. Louis Cemeteries like what I wanted—"

This was a low blow. "I was gonna move you! I *swear*! If it hadn't been for Doc Landrieu diggin' you up, I woulda saved up enough cash in a few months—"

"Don't try changin' the subject! You *owe* me, boy! You owe me for those forty years I spent in that pine box! Now you and Pearl are gonna go downstairs together and sit on a sofa and get properly acquainted. Or I'm gonna knock your two thick heads together so hard, you'll both think you're pins in a bowling alley!"

The last vestiges of any sense of control or propriety were slipping from his fingers like blowing sand. "Mother, *I'd* rather stand out in the sun and dissolve before sittin' on the couch with Miss Spare Parts over there—"

Jules felt a firm grip on his shoulder. Doc Landrieu stepped between him and his mother. "Jules, simmer down before you have an embolism." He took Edna's hand, and Jules couldn't help but be impressed by how quickly his mother's expression shifted from full boil to something approaching worshipfulness. "Edna, dear, you know how I hate seeing you get so worked up. Let me speak with Jules privately. We'll talk things out, man to man. I'm sure his seeing you tonight has been a considerable shock. He's probably not thinking straight yet. Give me a few minutes to straighten him out."

Edna's expression wavered between trust in her companion and exasperation with her son. "If you think it's best, Amos . . . well, all right, then. But I gotta warn you—my boy is stubborn as burnt gravy in the bottom of an old pot."

Jules wasn't especially eager to spend quality time with Doc Landrieu. But any excuse to escape the emotional pressure cooker of Pearl's bedroom was welcome. He followed his mentor into the next room. As soon as Doc Landrieu shut the door behind them, Jules whirled on him. "What kinda sick business have you yanked my mother into, you son of a bitch?"

"Your mother's in complete agreement with everything I've done, Jules—"

"I don't believe that! How can she be in favor of something like—like *this*? She was stuck under six feet of dirt for forty years—she's confused, her mind's addled. For all I know, maybe she went a little nuts down there. Maybe *more* than a little nuts. You're just takin' advantage of her—"

Doc Landrieu shook his head. "I am *not* taking advantage of Edna. I was fond of your mother before she died, and in the months since she's returned, I've grown extremely fond of her. It's Fate, Jules. Kismet. Edna and I are meant to be with each other. Why else was I the one to answer her distress call? Why else would she have been held in stasis just long enough for me to catch up to her in age, so that now we'll remain the same age for the rest of time? It's miraculous. You should be happy for us."

Jules exploded. "*Happy?!?* Happy my mother's a vampire? Happy she's shacked up with a knife-crazy psycho I thought was my friend? Happy that it turns out I'm somehow the cause of every goddamn crime I been investigatin' the past two weeks?"

"Keep your voice down." Doc Landrieu's face turned hard. "Show some consideration. Your mother's in the next room." He lowered his own voice to just above a whisper. "First of all, you're off base, calling me a 'knife-crazy psycho.' You and I worked together in the morgue for twenty-seven years. We saw the handiwork of many a *genuine* knife-crazy psycho, so you should know the difference. What I've done regarding the young woman next door, I did for two reasons, both of which are eminently logical and defensible. I took four vicious killers and reduced them to one being. In her present state, that of a consciousness struggling to control the bodily components of three other vampires, Pearl is tractable, easily manageable. Her condition robs her of any supernormal abilities. I can sustain her on a diet of animal-blood and human-blood products I obtain from my medical contacts. She doesn't like it, but she has no choice in the matter. So I've essentially taken four killers off the streets of New Orleans—"

"But—"

"Whisper, Jules."

Jules lowered his voice. "But that don't wash. Those four gals were all livin' off the blood of them pet retards at the High Krewe's compound."

"You're wrong. They'd all wandered off the reservation; otherwise, I never could've captured them. Never would've even known they existed, aside from a few statements you had made over the years about a High Krewe of vampires. Mr. Straussman wasn't the first fellow vampire I noticed due to that odd buzzing in my sinus passages; he was just the first one I spoke with. But I'd passed by others in the Quarter, mostly young women. I first became aware of their activities when I read a newspaper account of the dead black pastor who was dredged from the mud of a City Park lagoon, drained of blood. It could've been your work, but you had disappeared. I also thought of the black vampires who'd attacked me, but this particular killing seemed unlike them.

"After I struck up a friendly acquaintance with Mr. Straussman at the opera—he was very amenable to showing a new member of the fraternity the ropes, particularly a fellow opera fan—I asked him about the young women I'd sensed in the Quarter, and the murder of the pastor. He told me that many of the younger members of his household had been making unauthorized visits to the city, and he strongly suspected that they had been involved in the pastor's death. There was little love lost between Mr. Straussman and the High Krewe's youngsters. Even though he'd been a vampire for several centuries, he'd gotten stuck in his original role as butler, and he'd been obligated to play the degrading role for a succession of more junior vampires. The most recent cohort has posed a severe challenge to Mr. Straussman's considerable stoicism, however. When the time came, he was more than happy to help me push a few of the brats out of the picture . . . letting me know when they had left the compound, for example, so I'd know to expect them down in the Quarter. He also informed me of your return, and your forced recruitment as the High Krewe's private investigator."

Jules grunted. This explained that business with Flora Ann, how Jules had been outsmarted even when he'd thought he had an edge on the mutilator. "You said you had two reasons for doin' what you did."

"Yes. You've already alluded to the other reason yourself. Your mother's mental state when I rescued her from her coffin was extremely fragile. It still is, for that matter. The reason I purchased this house was to try to ground her by returning her to her old, familiar neighborhood. It's helped, but not enough. And her terrible hunger for blood hasn't helped matters at all. Whenever we're out in public, I have to watch her like a hawk—otherwise, she's liable to jump onto the back of the closest pedestrian and try to sink her teeth into his neck."

"So she hasn't—"

"No. So far, I've been able to keep her completely away from blood; Lord willing, I'll always be able to do so." Jules remembered what Doodlebug had told him about the vampire monks in Tibet who'd existed for millennia without ever downing a drop of blood. "The best thing for her would've been to reunite with you, but you'd gone missing. I was afraid you'd been destroyed by the black vampires, but Mr. Straussman had heard you'd beaten Malice X. So I could only assume you'd gone away for some reason. Your mother never lost faith that you'd return. She left that old pulp magazine at Maureen's house with the hope that you'd come home and find it."

So *that's* who that *Shadow Magazine* had come from. "I never went away. I was in the French Quarter the whole damn time. But I'll explain later. Go on."

"Of course, all your mother wanted was to see you. Each night that passed without you here, she grew more disconsolate. She needed a project, something she could focus on until you eventually returned. Actually, Edna provided the idea for this whole endeavor. She complained to me nightly about her terrible disappointment that you'd never found a decent woman to marry. One thing she said again and again was that, if she couldn't find you a nice girl—"

"She'd have to go out and make me one. Yeah, I used to hear it, too."

The two men were quiet for a minute. Jules shifted his feet, stared at the floor, and sighed. "Okay, Doc. I'm willin' to give you the benefit of the doubt. I'll grant that what you done, you ain't done it outta maliciousness or bein' a knife-crazy psycho. You done it for what you figured were good reasons." He looked his old friend in the eyes. "But that still don't make it *right.* And even if it *were* right, it won't work. Pearl and me, we can't stand each other. Put us in the same city block, much less the same bedroom, and we'll be tearin' each other new assholes inside of one week. What happened to the rest of her, anyway?"

"I kept it as a possible source of spares. In case any of the other parts turned out to be incompatible with each other."

"That's good news, at least. You gotta do the right thing, Doc. Stick Pearl's head back on her regular body, where it belongs. Take the rest of the patchwork body apart and let me take Pearl and the pieces back to the High Krewe. I won't tell them a thing about you or Straussman. Maybe I could get Straussman to hypnotize Pearl, so she wouldn't remember what got done to her. I'd do it myself, but my, uh, vampire powers, they ain't workin' too great right now."

Doc Landrieu shook his head. "Jules, I can't do that. Your mother's pinned all her hopes on this. I told you how fragile her mental state is."

Jules grimaced. "Just—just let *me* handle my mother, okay? I'll think of something. I got no fuckin' idea *what,* but I'll think of *something*—"

A knock on the door interrupted them. "Aren't you boys done in there yet?"

Edna entered the room without bothering to wait for an answer. Jules noticed she'd brought her purse. The rat's white head popped out of the top. Edna absently stroked his head with her index finger. His little pink eyes froze on Jules's face, and his nose twitched with sudden agitation. Seeing the rat gave Jules an idea . . . maybe a way to slither out from beneath the maternal trap he was caught in.

"Edna, we'll be just a few more minutes," Doc Landrieu said. "Why don't you go downstairs—"

"No, Mother, stick around," Jules said. "There's somethin' I gotta tell you about your pet rat there."

Edna glanced down at her purse. "You mean Richard?"

"Yeah. Y'see, I wasn't kiddin' around before when I said he belongs to me . . ."

Jules proceeded to tell his mother and Doc Landrieu the story of how he'd become 187 white rats, only to end up eight months later as a man who'd suffered a severe supernatural circumcision.

". . . so Mother, y'see, I *can't* get married. I can't be a husband to no woman. I mean, I appreciate what you've tried doin' for me, really I do. You done it outta love. And I love you for it. But, y'know, it just wouldn't be fair to poor Pearl to stick her with a man who can't satisfy her womanly needs."

Edna's mouth had fallen open. Now she closed it, and her lips puckered into an incredulous scowl. "Jules Augustine Duchon, that is the most *outlandish* story you have ever told me. And you've told me some whoppers. Why, this even tops that time you tried gettin' outta school by tellin' me the King of Spain blowed up the schoolhouse like he did the *Maine*—"

"Mother, what do I gotta do to prove this, drop my pants? Do I hafta do *that*?"

"Well, I certainly wouldn't be seeing' nothin' I ain't seen a thousand times before!"

Doc Landrieu gently put his arms around her shoulders. "Edna, would you mind if I took a closer look at your pet?"

"Don't tell me you actually put any credence in this nonsense?"

Doc Landrieu smiled slightly. "Do you remember the very first time we encountered your pet? I sensed something odd about him then, remember? I just want to see if I still feel that way."

"Well . . . I guess there's no harm in that. Just as long as you don't stick him with no scalpel or nothin'."

"I'll be very gentle."

She handed him her purse. Doc Landrieu removed the rat; the creature didn't bite or try to squirm out of his hands. He examined the animal very closely. As soon as the rat was six inches from his nose, Doc Landrieu winced. He rubbed the ridges above his eyes, as if trying to banish sinus pain, then put the rat back in the purse.

"This is a vampire rat," he said. "Jules is telling the truth, Edna."

Jules pressed his advantage. "Here's what Doodlebug told me about gettin' my parts back. You remember Doodlebug, don't you? Rory Richelieu?"

His mother's front of certainty wavered. "You mean that boy that used to hang around you during the war years? The pale, skinny boy?"

"Yeah. The one I changed into a vampire, and now he's a big expert on everything to do with vampires. What he told me was, in order for little Richard and me to, y'know, get it together again, both of us gotta want it. *Both* of us. And that means, no matter how much I might want to make you happy by bein' a husband for Pearl, it's not up to just me. Richard's got a vote, too. And he don't look too eager to give up his cozy life—gettin' petted all the time, bein' hand-fed, sleepin' on his own little pillow. It's gotta be a helluvah lot better than havin' pee come outta the top of his head three or four times a night."

"Why don't we give the little creature a say in the matter?" Doc Landrieu said.

Now it was Jules's turn to wince. He wasn't sure what his old boss was up to. "Whadda you got in mind, Doc?"

Doc Landrieu hugged Edna close. "Something out of a fairy tale. You know 'The Princess and the Pea'? Well, this little test I have in mind, we'll call it 'The Princess, the Prince, and the Pee-er.' "

♠

"This is a complete and utter *nightmare,*" Pearl said in a constricted voice.

"Y'know, Pearl, this ain't no day at the races for me, neither."

Jules lay on the small four-poster bed, taking up four-fifths of it. Pearl occupied the remaining fifth. Despite her extremely limited space, she somehow managed to avoid having any molecule of her skin touch his. They were both naked. A sheet covered them only up to their mid-thighs. The rat sat on Jules's midsection. He looked as though he'd climbed a small mountain of hairy, moldy Limburger cheese.

Pearl stared obstinately at the clock on the wall. "How long did that horrible old couple say we have to stay like this?"

"A half hour. You got thirteen minutes to go."

"It's only been seventeen minutes?!? It feels like seventeen *centuries*!"

"Well, just close your eyes and imagine I'm Richard Gere."

"Richard the *Third* is more like it."

Edna stuck her head into the room for the second time. "Has it happened yet?"

Jules grabbed for the sheets. "Mother! Gawd dang it! Keep your nose *outta* here! Or nothing'll happen for *sure*!"

His mother retreated after making a sour face. Jules pushed the sheets back down onto his legs, then reached for the rat, who'd scurried up his chest and was now hiding behind his pillow. Pearl sighed like a braking locomotive and turned on her side, away from him.

Jules put the rat back on his belly. He couldn't read the little creature's mood. When the three of them first occupied the bed, the rat had shown definite interest in Pearl, sniffing vigorously at her armpits and crotch, despite the young woman's squirming and protestations. Jules had gotten scared—he'd expected to see the rat's form begin to waver and smoke at any second. For the last five minutes or so, however, the rat had been sitting quietly on Jules's stomach, hardly moving. If Jules didn't know better, he'd say the rat looked contemplative, as if he were waiting for *Jules* to make up his mind.

That possibility scared Jules. What if the rat had made up *its* mind? What if it was ready to go, one hundred percent, and was just waiting for Jules's subconscious to accept the inevitable? Despite himself, Jules glanced over at Pearl. He had to admit, the body Doc Landrieu had pieced together had aesthetic appeal. The arms and legs and torso went together real nice. Sure, Jules had always preferred meatier women, but at least Flora Ann'd had wide hips. And now those swelling hips were only inches away from his fingers, daring them to reach over and caress cool white flesh.

Jules started sweating. What if his subconscious mind really did want this? Who the heck could know what went on in the deepest, dankest corners of their own innermost mind? What if he secretly found hectoring bitches irresistibly attractive? What if, buried deep inside him, there was a little momma's boy who'd do *anything* to please his mother? Was the rat locked and loaded, ready to become a penis again the second the pins of Jules's subconscious longings tumbled into place?

Jules sensed a minute vibration on his belly. He heard a tiny wheezing. Was the moment of transformation at hand?

He stared down at his stomach. The rat had fallen asleep.

Jules let himself breathe again. Yeah, Richard had had a vote, all right. And he'd just cast it. Now Jules could disabuse his mother of her matchmaking notions and get Doc Landrieu to let him put all the pieces back where they were supposed to be. One nagging problem remained; Jules would still be dropping ostrich turds for the foreseeable future.

Or would he?

The idea hit him with the force of a thunderclap. He stared at the pale pink seam, now mostly healed, between Pearl's neck and Flora Ann's shoulders. If Doc Landrieu had managed to fit Pearl's head on those shoulders, why not another head? Why not—(he bit his lower lip and squeezed his eyes tightly shut, afraid that even *thinking* the thought might send him instantly to the hottest fire pits of Hell)—Maureen's head?

There. He'd let the dragon loose in his mind. And now that it was loose, he knew he'd never get that dragon back in its cage again. Because he'd never wanted anything with the passionate intensity that he wanted this.

Even if getting it meant his immortal soul was damned to the fire pits of Hell.

But his soul was *already* damned, wasn't it?

Wasn't it?

"Doodlebug, I need your advice. Your moral advice. And depending on the advice, maybe I'll need your help, too."

"Of course, Jules. Any help I can give, you've got it. Considering what you're doing for me, I could hardly do less."

The long-distance cell connection was poor. Doodlebug sounded like he was on another planet. "Don't be so fast to offer your help with this, buddy," Jules said. "After you hear what I'm about to tell ya, maybe you won't wanna touch this with a two-thousand-mile pole."

"Are you okay, Jules?"

"I'm okay, yeah. And I'm not okay. I'm not sure what the hell I am right now. I feel like my goddamn head's about to explode . . ." He told Doodlebug the story. The whole story, all the pieces, including the pieces of various vampire girls that had been stitched together into an unwilling bride. And then confronted by an equally unwilling rat.

And Jules told Doodlebug what his heart was now begging him to do.

The static on the tiny phone seemed to crackle for an eternity before Doodlebug said anything. "That's . . . quite a tale."

"You got a real gift for understatement, D.B." Jules searched for the right words. He was at war with himself. He wanted to do the right thing . . . but he wanted to do the wrong thing much, much more. "You're the only one I can turn to, y'know? I mean, aside from my mother, you're the closest thing to family I got. And aside from Doc Landrieu, you're the smartest guy I ever known. So tell me—what am I supposed to *do*? I mean, I'm the detective, right? The good guy? I'm supposed to *solve* the crimes. Not *commit* the crimes. Would Charlie Chan do what I'm thinkin' of doin'? Would Philip Marlowe even let it enter his head? But what I want . . . Doodlebug, if there's any chance on earth I can have her back, I hafta race after that chance as fast as I can run. If I don't, I won't be able to live with myself. But if I *do* . . . I'm not sure I'll be able to live with myself then, either."

"What are you really asking me for, Jules? My permission? You want me to tell you what you want to do is right?"

"Well . . . yeah, sure! You're the big philosopher, right? I mean, you studied with them monks for ten years, and you pretty much started your own religion. *And* you're a vampire. If there's anybody on the planet who can tell me this is okay, it's you."

"Well, I'm flattered by your confidence." The line was silent for a few seconds. "But I'm afraid that confidence is misplaced. I can't justify this for you. Using another person, or in this case, *persons,* as tools for your own ends is morally wrong. In this case, you wouldn't be doing so entirely for your own selfish reasons—Maureen would benefit, too, of course—so that mitigates the wrong, but only slightly. Stealing is wrong. That's a basic tenet of every system of morality. And stealing is what you'd be doing—stealing not only the flesh of three women, but stealing the rest of their existences."

The back of Jules's throat went dry. This isn't what he wanted to hear. "But, y'know, don't Victoria and Alexandra and Flora Ann kinda deserve it? I mean, they were goin' out and killin' preachers and stuff . . ."

"Hasn't Maureen been a killer, too? How many customers of that strip club did she drop down the chute to the furnace after she'd drained them of blood?"

"But, but what about what Doc Landrieu said? About takin' four killers and reducin' 'em down to just one? Isn't that a good justification?"

"You know as well as I do that's a false calculus. If those three women were to be restored to their normal states, I have no doubt that they'd never leave the High Krewe's compound ever again. They'd go back to subsisting on blood harvested from living humans. You wouldn't be removing three active killers off the streets at all."

Jules's head began to pound. This wasn't good. If Doodlebug wouldn't help him, he might have to spend years trying to learn how to work the resurrection spell on his own. He was no scholar—he might never learn what he needed to know. "So lay it out straight for me. You're tellin' me there's no way I can think of rescuin' Maureen as bein' the right thing to do, right? And . . . and that means I can forget about . . . askin' for your help?"

"No. That's not what I've said at all. What I'm saying is this: if you're going to do this thing, if you're going to take this burden on your soul, you need to be honest with yourself about what you're taking on. You can't fool yourself by thinking there's some easy moral loophole floating in the ether somewhere that'll get you off the hook. Tell me this. Let's say I'm your parish priest—that's the role you're trying to put me in—and after hearing your story, I say to you that doing what you intend to do would be a mortal sin, condemning your soul to Purgatory and the torments of Hell. Would you still go ahead and do it anyway, knowing the punishment that awaited you?"

Jules didn't have to think very long. "I'd do it. I'd do whatever I have to to get Maureen back. And I'd take whatever was comin' for me."

"There! There you are. Your mind is made up. You've made your decision. Nothing I could say, no bit of moral philosophy or religious hectoring could change your mind. You told me before that you couldn't live with yourself if you didn't bring back Maureen, and yet you couldn't live with yourself if you did do it. I believe the first part. I don't believe the second. That second assertion, that's just you morally flattering yourself. You're no St. Francis of Assisi, Jules. You'll live with your choice. Oh, it might not always be *comfortable* to live with it . . . you may have many sleepless days ahead of you. And who's to say how this will affect your relationship with Maureen, assuming everything goes successfully? She could become a very different person; as could you. But you'll live with it. I just want you to have your eyes open going in."

Jules's tried desperately to follow his friend's logic. "So you don't condemn me . . . right? 'Cause condemnin' me wouldn't do no good?" He wiped the sweat off his throbbing forehead. "But you won't get your own hands dirty with this—right? If I do this, I do it on my own?"

"Jules, why do you insist on putting words in my mouth? Of *course* I'll help you."

Jules blinked. He shook the phone to make sure it didn't have a loose microchip. "D.B., was that static, or did you just say you'll help me bring Maureen back?"

"I said of *course* I'll help you. Why did you doubt it?"

"Uh, maybe 'cause you just spent five minutes tellin' me it's, y'know, immoral and wrong?"

"Well, it *is*. That doesn't mean it's undoable. You see, we are creatures blessed, or cursed, with free will. Our Creator granted us the option to choose to do things that are objectively wrong, even immoral, so long as we understand the consequences. And if we don't understand them beforehand, we learn them soon enough. I'm choosing to do this with you, Jules. My little speech was as much for my ears as it was for yours. We'll be partaking of this sin together."

Jules's throat tightened. His eyes got heavy and wet. He wished Doodlebug weren't two thousand miles away; he'd never been this grateful to anybody, ever. "I—I don't know what to say . . . thanks. Thanks, buddy."

"I'll see you tomorrow night. I'll call as soon as I've made my flight arrangements." There was a brief pause before he spoke again. "Jules . . . I'm not doing this just for you, you know . . . I loved Maureen, too."

He'd made his choice. Now he had to make sure he could live with that choice.

Jules walked out of Doc Landrieu's house. His mother was despondent over the failure of her matchmaking. Jules decided not to tell her his intentions, not yet. He'd wait until Doodlebug got here. She'd always liked Doodlebug, even if she remembered him as a weedy little boy, not a suave young woman. Jules was pretty sure he could count on Doc Landrieu's support, too. . . . He'd certainly prefer the Maureen option to returning all the body pieces to their original owners.

There was someone else who was certain to prefer the Maureen option to the alternative. Jules walked over to his car, leaned on its long, red hood, and took out his cell phone. He'd been meaning to call Preston, in any case. Preston had a right to know who'd killed the preachers. And Jules no longer had any qualms about telling him.

He was a little surprised when Preston himself answered the phone. "Hey! How're you feelin'?"

"Jules? That you?"

"The one and only. How come you're playin' receptionist?"

"I'm still on the mend, and I wanted to be useful. Hey, that was one helluvah parley you put together last night! You ever think about runnin' for mayor?"

"Naww. Politics makes me sick to my stomach, and you gotta stand out in the sun too much, kissin' babies. Listen, I got some news to share with you. Some answers . . ."

Jules told him what he'd learned from Courane L'Enfant. And then he told him all the twisting, twisted events of this evening. Leaving out, for the time being, the part about Maureen.

Preston took a few seconds to sort it all out. "*Whoa,*" he said. "That's some pretty heavy-duty, fucked-up shit."

"That's one way of puttin' it."

"So that dude that attacked me . . . you're sayin' this is your pal the coroner, that old guy the boys and me aced way back last year? And Malice forgot to ice his brain stem?"

This was the one thing Jules regretted having to reveal to Preston. Jules didn't want to stir up a cycle of vengeance. . . . His mother was depending on Amos, and that was reason enough to be concerned for his well-being. "Yeah, that was him," Jules said reluctantly. "But Preston, look, the man had a perfect right to be pissed at you. He didn't go gunnin' for you, lookin' to rub you out. He was after the women. You just got in his way, and he remembered what you done, and he lost it."

Preston didn't say anything. Jules tried to picture what he'd do if the two of them came to blows again. The only thing he could imagine is getting between them, not a good place to be; he just prayed it wouldn't come to that.

Preston apparently decided to sidestep the issue, at least for the moment. "So we was right about that fuckin' Courane L'Enfant, huh? I *knew* that fucker was up to something. We gonna step on that guy so hard, he gonna be wearin' his hat on his shoes."

"Take a number. You guys aren't gonna be the only ones after his ass. I promised him I wouldn't tell nothin' to the authorities. I didn't promise shit about tellin' you and the High Krewe."

"But now, those women what did the actual killings, they're from the High Krewe, ain't they?"

"Yeah. But the High Krewe's bigwigs didn't have nothin' to do with any of this. They didn't know where the youngsters were sneakin' off to, what they was involved in. It was mainly Randolph's idea . . . and thanks to Doc Landrieu, Randolph's outta the picture."

"But the women who did it . . . you're sayin' they's *comatose* . . . and their *parts* got sewn together into some kinda Frankenstein bride yo' *mama* wants to set you up with? But . . . but lemme get this *straight* here . . . but yo' *dick,* in the shape of a *rat,* he won't have nuthin' to do with *nuthin'*?"

Jules took a deep breath. "That's where things stand, yeah."

"Well, what's gonna happen with this here jilted Frankenstein bride, now? You gonna take her back to the High Krewe, let them put all them womens back together the way they's meant to be? 'Cause now, see, it's one thing if Miss Frankenstein stays a Frankenstein, 'cause then all them preacher killers stay comatose, good as bein' dead, see. But it's a whole *'nother* thing if they gets put back together. Then, knowin' what I know, we'll hafta go after them. Even if that means war with the High Krewe.

"So what you gonna do, Jules? They hired you to find this mutilator guy and put those ladies back together. You gonna do it?"

"That's what I was hired to do," Jules said, a grin spreading slowly across his face. "But, see, I've come up with this other idea, and I wanted to pass it by you, get your opinion . . ."

Now Jules told Preston about Maureen.

"So if you were in my shoes," Jules asked slyly, "what would you do?"

"What would *I* do?" Preston laughed. "I'd get my woman back, is what I'd do. *Fuck* them hoity-toity fuckers! Shee-yit, man, you be doin' them High Krewe assholes a favor. Keep them preacher killers comatose, ain't gonna be no war. Let 'em off the hook, though, and there'll be a bad-ass *muthafuckin'* war. Somethin' awful like this town never seen before. Make the Battle of New Orleans look like a kiddie cap pistol fight. Y'know? But I tell you what—you keep them ladies comatose, stick your own lady friend's head on that Frankenstein body, and I'll let the High Krewe ride. Hell, as a bonus, I'll even let bygones be bygones with that Nutty Perfessor doctor buddy of yours."

A ship's horn sounded on the nearby river. A pair of gulls flew overhead, calling playfully to each other, their wings glistening as they swooped beneath a street lamp. For the first time since his resurrection, Jules felt in his breast the stirrings of happiness.

"Thanks, pal. You got no idea what your threat of war means to me. I mean that."

Preston chuckled. Jules could easily visualize the knowing grin on his partner's face. "Anytime, my man. Anytime."

♠

"Jules, I—I just can't stand to see you ruin your life like this!"

"Mother, this ain't gonna ruin my life. Just the opposite."

Doodlebug brought Edna a glass of ice water. "Mrs. Duchon, I know you've never approved of Maureen. But I spent a lot of time with them together. While they were living with each other, they were a very loving couple. They went to musical comedies together. They had the most wonderful model train set they built with each other. She took good care of Jules. I'm sure you would've approved—"

"But she's so *vulgar*!"

"Mother," Jules said, "*I'm* vulgar. It's a perfect match!"

"Edna," Doc Landrieu said, putting his arm around her shoulders, "we really should give Jules his head on this. After all, he's not a little boy anymore. He's been a grown man for a long time now, and he's perfectly capable of making informed decisions. I met this Maureen on a few occasions. Really, she wasn't so awful—"

Edna pulled away from his embrace and turned her glare on him. "Oh, you're *all* gangin' up on me! The only lady in the room! *Shameful!*"

Jules could tell Doodlebug hadn't appreciated that remark. Oh, well. "Mother, don't you want me to be happy?"

"Of *course* I want you to be happy! Just not this way!" She stormed over to the dining-room table. Richard sat there in a shoe box filled with shredded newspaper. She sat huffily in one of the dining-room chairs and began stroking the rat's head, muttering darkly to herself. Somehow, the rat had remained high in her esteem, despite his failure to ratify Edna's choice of life mate for her son (maybe due to some primal maternal memory she had of sprinkling cornstarch on him and wiping up his messes).

Jules slowly approached his mother. She pointedly refused to look in his direction. "Mother, y'know, I'm gonna do this whether you like it or not. I'm gonna bring Maureen back, and I'm gonna get down on my bum knees and beg her to marry me. I'd rather you be happy. But I ain't gonna let your unhappiness stop me. 'Cause you know how much you love me? Well, that's how much I love Maureen."

She didn't say a word. Jules sat carefully on one of the chairs next to her, then reached over and patted the rat's head himself. "You really like this little guy, don't you?"

"He's my friend. Doesn't give me any back talk."

"You trust him? I mean, trust him to do the right thing? To make the right choice?"

She looked over at him, finally. "Well, I think he's got a better head on him than you do."

Jules couldn't really argue with that. In his experience, two heads had definitely been better than one. "Well, then let's let him make his choice, okay? Can you promise me you won't stay mad if Richard gives Maureen the green light?"

"I can't make no promises, Jules Augustine." His mother's expression softened just a tiny bit. "But I'll do my best not to be unreasonable."

♠

Having his wrist slit hardly hurt at all this time. Doc Landrieu stood by with clamps and bandages to ensure that, unlike the first time, Jules's donation wouldn't veer toward unplanned suicide. Jules and Doodlebug both stood over the doctor's antique bathtub and dribbled their blood onto the pale dust that had been spread over the bottom of the tub. Just like last time, Doodlebug mixed the blood and dust into a pinkish paste, then spread the paste into a roughly woman-shaped silhouette.

Jules was so nervous that his shaking legs rubbed against the toilet seat and made it clatter like a VW Bug motor. He was light-headed from the loss of blood. The crowded bathroom felt like a tableau from a vertiginous dream. "D.B., she was in so much pain when she came back the first time. Isn't there anything you can do so she won't suffer?"

Doc Landrieu opened a small leather case and removed a hypodermic. "No need to worry, Jules. I'll immediately inject her with the same compound you were injected with. She won't feel a thing, I promise."

Doodlebug's face shifted like stop-motion clay, taking on again the eerie reptilian cast of a prehistoric vampire. When he opened his lengthened jaws, his lips replaced with a mosaic of shining scales, the words that emerged were ancient and cacophonous, as distant from the music of human speech as New Orleans was from the moons of Mars.

Jules stared into the depths of the tub, afraid to breathe. Mist began swirling above the white enamel surface. The pink paste golem began taking on more than two dimensions. Jules felt like a sea bird, circling high above the turbulent waters of the Pacific, blessed with an angel's view of God's never-ending process of creation as volcanoes spewed their lava and smoke, and newborn islands pierced the mist as they rose from the turquoise depths of the sea.

The scent of her coalesced in metastasizing molecules, and Jules's aroused olfactory brain rode a thrilling roller coaster of memories . . . Maureen's perspiration after a hot summer night's walk through the

Quarter; Maureen's long golden hair, still damp from the shower; the rich, drowsy musk of her after their lovemaking . . .

She's coming back, she's coming back, and this time it's FOREVER—

The mist began to settle, and the most gorgeous island Jules could imagine rose from the black depths of oblivion . . . the face of his beloved.

The rat was back in bed again. He was nestled between the same two people he'd been in bed with the last time—his brother rat (who wasn't a rat) and the woman of many competing scents.

Only this time was much different from last time. Last time, the swirl of angry secretions had been exciting for a while, a thrilling battle of scents, but it had also given the rat a headache, so bad a headache that he'd been forced to escape by falling asleep. Also, last time, the woman had been awake, making angry, disgusted noises, and she had shifted so far to one side of the bed the rat had been certain she would fall off. Now, the woman was asleep. Her face was softer. Was this just because she was asleep? The rat took a closer look. He didn't think so. This was a different face from before. A face that didn't match the rest of the body; it was as though a bulldog's jowly head had been placed on a poodle's body. A different scent, too. The new face and the new scent made him feel warm and good inside. They were familiar. And they were beloved. He crept closer to the face, nuzzled it with his damp muzzle.

The man (his brother rat who wasn't a rat) seemed different, too. Not physically. But his mood and scent were different. Before, he had seemed ready to attack, or maybe flee. Now, he smelled sweet, like bananas on the tree just as they were turning their most brilliant shade of green.

The woman stirred. Her long eyelashes quivered. The man's breath caught in his throat. Then her eyes opened. She turned her head toward her companion, and her eyes grew wider. "Jules . . ."

That voice . . . that wonderful voice. The sound of closeness and laughter. The rat remembered this voice very well.

"Jules . . . Your hair's gone all white . . . Are we in heaven? I don't feel any pain . . . How—?"

The man, his brother, smiled, and water was running down his face, and when he spoke, his voice was broken like an Uptown sidewalk. "Welcome back, baby. Welcome back."

His brother rolled toward her, and the rat had to shimmy up his thigh to his massive white hip in order to avoid being crushed.

"Ohh, Jules . . ."

Jules. The rat had heard this name before. Only this time, he shuddered with sudden recognition, because he realized it was his own name, too. And as the two of them embraced, and further talk was postponed by a mashing of lips and hungry intercourse of tongues, the rat remembered everything. He knew who Maureen was. He knew who Jules was. And he knew what he, himself, was.

He began to quiver and stiffen, and he knew this was right, this was the way things were meant to be. He felt the briefest instant of regret—it had been fun, running along the rooftops of the Quarter, scurrying through the streets, battling his brothers for the tastiest morsels. But it was time to say goodbye to all that. Goodbye to all that, and hello to whatever was to come.

The rat felt his flesh loosen from his bones, become light and insubstantial as feathery down. He sensed his bones running like spilled syrup, then boiling away into mist. It didn't hurt. It didn't feel like anything at all. For a microscopic eternity, he floated above the two of them, covering their passion like a sheltering cloud, and he loved them both.

Hello . . .

TWENTY-SEVEN

"You are two nights late, Mr. Duchon. Neither my colleagues nor I like being kept waiting."

Besthoff's eyes bore in on Jules's face like twin targeting lasers. *Aww, fuck him and his trick eyes,* Jules thought. *I got my Richard back, so Besthoff don't have a thing on me in the spook department.* "You can't rush quality, Mr. Besthoff," Jules said, wondering whether he sounded as insolent as he felt.

"You dare call what you have brought to us 'quality'?" Besthoff unfolded his hands and placed them flat on his desk. His right eyebrow arched, an affectation Jules found increasingly noxious. "Seven members of my household were violated or missing. You have restored to me the grand total of *two.* And where is the perpetrator? Why is this villain not here in my office, kneeling before me in chains?"

Doodlebug cleared his throat. "Mr. Besthoff, once you've listened to the entirety of Jules's report, I believe you'll find that his conduct in this matter has been both thorough and prudent."

Besthoff did not deign to look in Doodlebug's direction. He kept his gaze locked on Jules. "Why is Mr. Richelieu here? I recall giving specific instructions that he was not to be involved in this investigation."

"Doodlebug was here for the start," Jules said. "He wanted to be here for the end."

Maybe it was something in Jules's tone, some new hint of steel, but

Besthoff did not choose to press the issue further. Instead, he laced his fingers again on his marble-top desk. "Straussman is caring for Pearl and Jonathan. Give me your report. I demand a full accounting of the whereabouts of each of the others, as well as an explanation of why you have failed to follow the entirety of my instructions."

Jules silently rehearsed what he'd decided to tell Besthoff. He'd been unable to fit himself, Doodlebug, Jonathan, and Pearl in his two-seater car, so he'd had to call in Erato for an assist. Jonathan's memories of his ordeal would suit Jules's story to a tee. Pearl had been more problematic. However, thanks to her weakened physical and mental state just after Doc Landrieu reattached her head to her own body, Jules had been able to utilize his restored powers of vampiric hypnosis to ensure that her memories would essentially match and reinforce Jonathan's.

"My suspicions were dead-on," Jules said. "L'Enfant was behind everything. The truth came out at that Vampyres and Live Wires party of his. That bastard's got more tricks up his sleeve than Harry Houdini. If it hadn't been for Doodlebug, I'd still be chained up in that basement dungeon of his, tube in my arm, my blood bein' leeched off so this damn twat Veronika didn't hafta worry none about wrinkles."

He told Besthoff the actual events, up to the point when he and L'Enfant had begun bargaining. That part, he'd leave out. "They drained Maxim dry over a period of a couple of weeks, then left him out in the sun. Randolph didn't last that long. Before I got captured, they experimented on him, wantin' to see whether they could draw more blood from him faster, but still keep him alive. Didn't work too well. So his ashes and Maxim's are both blowin' around the Lower Garden District somewheres."

"You say this L'Enfant was also behind the mutilation attacks?" Besthoff said.

"Yeah. He had different bodyguards carryin' out the attacks, men that he'd gotten trained to handle vampires. Guy's got a private army, practically."

"What did he hope to gain? Surely blood extraction couldn't have been the reason behind the mutilations?"

This was the part of the story Jules was most proud of, if he could be said to be proud of any of it. "While I was at his mercy, L'Enfant bragged about his pals in the Red Chinese army. L'Enfant met these military-intelligence guys when he was over in Asia, tourin' with his band. Seems they'd been doin' research on vampires, lookin' for a way to give vampire powers to their soldiers without actually havin' them become vampires. They found out it was way too dangerous to fool with whole, live vampires, though. So L'Enfant, after he'd started hobnobbin' with your strayin' youngsters at his parties and whatnot, he came up with this idea to make some money off the Commies. He offered to send them vampire parts . . . parts are as good as whole vampires for their purposes, see, and a whole lot easier to work with. So Alexandra's and Victoria's and Flora Ann's missin' pieces, they're way the hell over on the far side of the Pacific Ocean. And L'Enfant, he's sinkin' his Red Army profits into that big real-estate development goin' up where the St. Thomas Housing Project used to be."

Jules waited for Besthoff's reaction. The whole deal hinged on the next few seconds. Jules prayed he hadn't been too outlandish. He'd chosen the Red Chinese for his fable both because of their reputation for paranormal research, and because China was remote enough that Jules could feel reasonably assured Besthoff and Co. wouldn't try verifying the story . . . or sending a team to recover the body parts.

Besthoff's eyes narrowed slightly, but otherwise his expression remained unchanged. Jules might've detected a minute stiffening of his shoulders, a slight clenching of his hands on the desk, but he couldn't be sure. "A nefarious . . . scheme," Besthoff said at last. "Tell me, how did you manage to escape?"

"A body like mine, it's got its advantages. Lotsa deep nooks and crannies where you can hide stuff. Like a cell phone. You don't wanna know where I hid it. Anyway, when I was alone down in the dungeon, I managed to get a call off to Doodlebug—"

"Why did you call Mr. Richelieu, rather than me? My people and I are much closer than California, and you were in desperate straits, surely."

Jules gulped. He hadn't thought through this part. "I, uh, I had Doodlebug's number saved on speed dial. Your number was in my pocket. And they, y'know, they took my jacket away."

"I see. And Mr. Richelieu, when he came, he helped you to rescue Pearl and Jonathan?"

"Yeah. That's right. Doodlebug's real good at sneakin' around. He, uh, she learned that from me back durin' World War Two, when we was huntin' down Nazi saboteurs together. Jonathan and Pearl, they were down there in that dungeon with me, chained to the wall like I was, surrounded by a buncha holy candles and crucifixes. Pearl was in good shape, since they hadn't started messin' with her yet, or not much, anyway—looks like they may've been screwin' with her neck, 'cause there's a mark there—but Jonathan, he was hangin' on by a thread. First thing we did once Doodlebug sprung us was burn rubber back to Maureen's house, so we could get some blood down Jonathan's throat. Then we came straight over here."

"And the two of you made no attempt to apprehend L'Enfant?"

"I told you—the guy's got a fuckin' army—"

"Mr. Besthoff," Doodlebug interjected, "in my judgment, it would've been impossible for us to both rescue your youngsters and capture Mr. L'Enfant. Jules was in a considerably weakened state. And the security forces were both numerous and very capable."

Now Besthoff leveled his intimidating stare on Doodlebug. "Mr. Richelieu, are you willing to swear that these events transpired exactly as Mr. Duchon has described them?"

"He don't hafta swear nothin'," Jules said angrily. "Just ask Pearl or Jonathan what went on. They'll tell ya. Well, Pearl will, anyway; Jonathan was pretty out of it by the time I got there. Anyhow, you don't gotta worry about nothin' anymore from L'Enfant and Veronika. They forced me to finish the job on her, so she don't need no vampire blood anymore—just regular blood, like the rest of us. And once word spreads around this shack about what happened to Pearl and Jonathan, none of your other youngsters are gonna be sneakin' out to the city for a good long time to come. Case is closed. I mean, you're certainly within your rights to go drop a horse's head in their bed, or somethin'. But I gotta warn you . . . they know I was workin' for the High Krewe, so they'll be expectin' you."

"We will retaliate, of course," Besthoff said. "No matter what preparations they might have made." His eyes narrowed once more, and he seemed to be studying Jules especially closely. "Mr. Duchon, you appear to be a changed man from the person I interviewed two weeks ago. I assume you will be at our side when we carry out our revenge?"

Jules squared his shoulders. "No. I'm out. I got other priorities right now than playin' flunky."

"A pity." All traces of humanity in Besthoff's face melted away. He now looked as reptilian as Doodlebug had when he'd chanted the ancient incantation. "You realize, of course, that this represents a breach in our verbal contract. All benefits that were to have accrued to you are henceforth canceled. No final payments, either of cash or blood, will be paid, including reimbursement for any expenses. Since you are refusing to complete the work you were contracted for, you are responsible for repaying all monies already advanced. Failure to do so within a two-week period will result in expropriation of other assets. Additionally, you are to surrender the keys for the Cadillac to Straussman, immediately."

Every muscle in Jules's body urged him to give Besthoff the finger, then shove it up his ass. But the cool voice of logic reminded him what he was getting out of this deal. Maureen. "Fine," he said, without a lick of regret. He pulled the car keys out of his vest pocket and tossed them onto the desk. But then Jules thought of something else. "What about Rory?"

Doodlebug quickly put a hand on his arm. "Jules, I won't let him use me as a lever to blackmail you anymore. If . . . if he wishes to take away my institute, I'll accept that."

Jules looked back to Besthoff. Their host, apparently realizing his last source of leverage had slipped away, shrugged his shoulders and faintly smiled, trying to look elegant in defeat. "Of course Mr. Richelieu shall retain control of his institute. My colleagues and I have an interest in seeing his success continue. Our financial support will not be withdrawn."

His trace smile vanished when he stood. "So our business is at an end. You have proven to be a disappointment, Mr. Duchon. Had you chosen to be a more enthusiastic ally, you would find our friendship invaluable; but now that door is closed to you. Some of your . . . facts . . . do not sit easily with me. The veracity of your account is still to be measured. And it will be measured, I promise . . . Pray that what we find seals your words with truth."

Besthoff pressed a button inlaid in the desk's oak trim. A few seconds later, the door opened, and Straussman ushered Jules and Doodlebug out of the office. They walked quickly toward the front entrance; Jules was eager to leave the High Krewe's compound, hopefully forever. But after Straussman opened the twelve-foot-high doors that opened onto the front gardens, Jules paused before descending the steps.

"Thanks, chief," he said to the butler in a low voice. "I appreciate what you done. Just watch your ass around here, okay?"

For the first time he could remember, Jules saw Straussman smile. "I shall indeed. Please do give my regards to Maureen. Events can sometimes transpire far better than we'd hoped. It has been a pleasure serving you, Mr. Duchon."

♠

They walked past the Allante. Jules paused to take a last look at it. It seemed forlorn in the darkness, waiting for the repossessor to come.

"Are you going to miss it?" Doodlebug asked.

"Naww. Not a bit." Jules was quietly amazed to hear himself say it and to realize it was true. "I was an idiot, thinkin' I could own a convertible in the city. Thing was turnin' to shit faster than grain in a goose's colon. I'm lucky to be rid of it."

When they reached the edge of Metairie Road, Jules called Erato and asked him to come pick them up. After he hung up, Jules saw Doodlebug looking at him strangely. "Why're you lookin' at me like that?"

"You've got a haunted look on your face. Is something the matter?"

Jules kicked a small shower of gravel into the street. "Yeah. I just realized somethin'. Now that Maureen's back in the picture, how do I explain that to Erato? I mean, he's the guy I asked to look after Maureen's ashes."

"I guess you just tell him the truth," Doodlebug said.

Jules snorted, with more sadness than disdain, however. "Erato's the best pal I got, aside from you. I don't wanna risk losin' him."

Doodlebug frowned in sympathy. "I don't see that you have much choice. Unless you want to hide Maureen in the closet for the rest of Erato's life."

Jules frowned. "That ain't gonna happen. Maureen ain't the type to stay hidden." His shoulders sagged. "I don't think I could take it. Tellin' him the truth, seeing' the horror spread on his face . . ."

Doodlebug held Jules's hand between his slender, cool palms. "If you want to keep him as a friend, a true friend, that's a risk you have to take. The other night, I told you there'd be consequences for doing what you'd chosen to do. This is one of them."

"Yeah . . . I guess."

Jules heard a familiar beeping behind him. He turned around and saw Erato's tricolored Lincoln cab pull up to the curb. "Where are we off to now?" Doodlebug asked.

Jules walked toward the cab. "Back to someplace I didn't think I'd ever go back; to do somethin' that may turn out really dumb. But when has that ever stopped me before?"

♠

"Hello, Edith."

Edith Aubrey L'Enfant looked up from the oil-stained engine of a Ford Galaxie. To her credit, her eyes barely widened when she saw Jules standing on the other side of the raised hood. She rubbed grease off her fingers with a rag.

"I figured I'd never see you again," she said.

"If you're smart," Jules said, "you'll make sure this is the last time you ever see me. You'll get the hell away from New Orleans."

She set the rag down. "And why would I want to do that? I have a life here. A good life. Is this a threat?"

Jules's expression was grim. "This ain't a threat. It's a warnin'. Edith, I was workin' for the High Krewe of Vlad Tepes. The buncha vampires that Maxim and Jonathan hailed from. I told the head of the High Krewe what your husband and Veronika did to them. This ain't a nice, sweet buncha people—they're killers. And they don't take stuff like that lying down. They're comin'."

Edith's cheek twitched as though Jules had struck her with the back of his hand. "Why—why are you telling me this? I thought there wasn't any love lost between you and Veronika. Or Courane."

"There ain't. Far as I'm concerned, the two of them can burn in the fire they started, and I'll be there to roast marshmallows. But you're a different story. The High Krewe don't know nothin' about your part in this."

Edith's eyes narrowed. "What are you saying?"

Jules looked around him, trying to make sure they weren't being watched. "Get outta here. That's what I'm sayin'. The High Krewe, they don't know you from Marie Antoinette. Drain a couple of your husband's bank accounts, then go spend a long vacation in Sweden. Vampires hate the cold."

She began shaking her head before he'd finished. "No. I'd never leave Courane. We'll run away together. All three of us. Courane has friends all over the world—"

Now it was Jules's turn to shake his head. "It won't help. Vampires, they're kinda like the Mafia. There're families in almost every part of the world. Besthoff'll put out the word. There'll be eyes watchin' for your husband and Veronika in every city, and most small towns. Stick with them, no matter where they go, and it's like punchin' your own one-way ticket to the afterlife."

Veronika closed her eyes tightly. Her chin began trembling. "It doesn't matter." Her fierce whispering was meant more for herself, he felt, than for him. "I'm guilty, too. We're guilty together, Courane and I." Her eyes shot open, like she'd bolted awake from a nightmare. "Why offer *me* safety when you've doomed my husband?"

" 'Cause I like you," Jules said.

"You have to give me a better reason than that!"

Jules ransacked his brain for the right words, the words that would make her see reason. "Because . . . because your husband and Veronika, they're *evil.* I mean, they use other people for their schemes, chew 'em up and spit 'em out like old gum. . . ." This seemingly promising line of invective petered out as Jules remembered Doodlebug's words to him the night before. Jules had used other people for his own schemes, too; he couldn't sidestep that. "Well, all three of you were involved in bad crap, but you were doin' it outta love. You just wanted your husband to be happy—"

"And why should this absolve me and not him?" Edith's face had turned calm again, as if she'd reconciled herself to what was to come. "Everything he did to you people, he did for Veronika's sake. I truly believe that he loves her, in his way. Try again, Jules."

Jules's shoulders sagged. How was what L'Enfant had done for Veronika any different from what Doc Landrieu had done for the sake of Jules's mother's sanity? Or what Jules had done for Maureen? How could he condemn L'Enfant if he wasn't condemning Edith or Doc or himself? "Yeah, well . . . far as I could tell, Courane and Veronika enjoyed what they was doin'. You hated it. And, and . . ."

His mind circled back to his original, and most heartfelt, explanation. "And I really like you, and I think you're a decent person, and I think the two of them stink."

She graced him with the smile of a woman willing to place her own neck in the gallows noose. "I think you're a decent person, too. You know, for the past two nights, I've been trying to sort out how I should feel about you. You gave immortality to my husband's lover. Should I hate you? But you also gave my husband the means to be happy, and I'm fulfilled when my husband is happy. So maybe I should be grateful, instead?"

Jules couldn't think of a reply.

She smiled anyway. "I like you very much, Jules Duchon. Now I'm going to go be with my husband, whether he wants my company or not."

Jules felt knots clenching in his stomach. "Edith, you deserve better than all this—"

She shook her head again. "Save your breath. Keep an eye on Crunchy for me, will you? He's really a good kid. Just a little lost."

She shut the Galaxie's hood with a muffled thud and walked back toward the main house.

Jules returned to the waiting cab. "How did everything go?" Doodlebug asked.

Jules slid into the front seat next to Erato. He didn't say anything. He'd tell Doodlebug some night, but not right now.

"Let's go get my old car back," he said.

Waiting for Hank to come from the back of Arnaud's Restaurant, Jules scanned the street for his beloved white Fleetwood. He could barely wait to settle his posterior into the car's well-worn, cracked leather seat, whose springs had adapted perfectly over the years to his unique shape.

Daphne stepped out of the kitchen. "Hank's coming," she said. She looked much healthier than Jules remembered; less harried, less sallow-faced, better fed for sure.

Jules waved hello, then nudged an animal trap near the Dumpster with his foot. "You can put this mess away, sweetheart. No need for it anymore. I got my rat back."

Daphne looked shocked. "How did you manage it?"

"Chalk it up to mother love," Jules said, letting Daphne's unspoken questions go unanswered. Heck, he still didn't know the full story behind his mother's and Richard's reunion himself; he'd probably never know, unless he could teach his dick to talk.

Hank appeared in his busboy uniform. "Hey, Jules! Thanks for dinner the other night. What can I do for you?"

"Hank, I wanna buy back my car from you. I'm a fair man, and I'm willin' to offer fair market value—"

Hank's smile faded to a sheepish cringe. "Gee, y'know, I'd love to sell you your car back. But that ain't possible."

Jules's heart nearly leaped out of his mouth. Terrible visions flashed through his brain. "You wrecked my Cadillac . . ."

"No, no, I didn't wreck it. I *sold* it. It was too damn hard to park around here. Wonderful car, but the thing must be twenty-two feet long. Parking fees were eatin' a quarter of my tips. So I sold it, and I used the cash to buy a really cool Kawasaki bike. *That,* I can park anywhere, and Daphne likes riding on the back."

Desperation seized Jules's soul. He grabbed Hank's shoulders. "I've gotta get that car back. It ran like a top, never gave me a minute's worth of trouble. Who'd you sell it to?"

Hank obviously didn't like being manhandled. "Hey! No need to shake the answer out of me, okay? I sold it to this little used-car joint on St. Claude Avenue, near the corner of North Rampart . . ."

Jules's heart sank to the soles of his shoes. He knew exactly where he needed to go to reclaim his Cadillac. And he knew exactly with whom he'd be forced to deal.

♠

"Hey, hey! Cadillac Jules! Long time no see, brother!"

Billy Mac waved enthusiastically as he left his tiny office. He advanced across his dusty used-car lot with the speed and rapacity of a pint-size General Sherman. Jules saw his old Fleetwood, freshly waxed and washed, sitting proudly on the display ramp under the big sign near the street, obviously the prize car on the lot.

Billy Mac shook his hand vigorously, his enormous smile showcasing his missing four front teeth without a hint of self-consciousness. Jules recalled that the little Javanese mechanic had lost the teeth years ago in an argument with a disgruntled customer; he'd been more willing to part with teeth than offer a refund.

"So where've you been hiding yourself, Jules? Baton Rouge? Hey, you still driving that cream puff Lincoln I sold you?"

Jules groaned inwardly when he recalled the Lincoln, the worst piece of shit he'd ever had the misfortune to drive. Remembering the price Billy Mac had extorted from him made Jules weak in the knees. "I donated that car to the NOPD, Billy Mac."

"Really? That's very civic-minded of you." His eyebrows floated higher with pleasure. "So I take it you're in the market for another vehicle?"

"That's the one I want." Jules pointed to the Cadillac. "I want to buy my old car back."

"That's *your* old car?" Billy Mac looked honestly surprised. "I thought those pistons looked familiar."

Jules took a deep breath. "What're you askin' for it?"

The proprietor pulled a well-worn spiral notebook from his back pocket. He put on a pair of horn-rimmed reading glasses, then thumbed through the notebook's pages with practiced ease. "Let's see . . . well, that particular vehicle has a sale price of seventy-five hundred dollars."

"Seventy-five *hundred*—! Billy Mac, the blue book value on my car is no more than two thousand bucks, tops."

Billy Mac grinned as if he'd heard a particularly funny joke. "Oh, come on, Jules. Blue book don't mean anything around here. Did you know there are four kinds of lies? Lies, damn lies, statistics, and blue book values."

Seventy-five hundred dollars. That was fifteen hundred more than the bribe payment Jules had intercepted. Plus, he owed well over a grand to Besthoff. "Billy Mac, I been a good customer of yours for a long, long time. How about you knock three grand off for me?"

Billy Mac clapped him on the back in a show of fellow feeling. "No can do, my friend. Maybe on one of my other fine vehicles, but not this one. Not the king of the lot."

Jules started to sweat. "Billy Mac, be reasonable. I got this loan I gotta pay back in two weeks, and these guys are real sharks—"

"Selling you a car you'll love? That's my problem. Fixing your financial conundrums? That's *not* my problem."

Killing him was out of the question. As Jules had decided long ago, a decent mechanic was too valuable to lose. He wheeled out his last, feeble bit of leverage. "It's not just the loan. See, I done promised the Sisters of Charity a big, fat donation. You can't have me let down the holy sisters, can you?"

Billy Mac chuckled and playfully punched Jules in the shoulder. Jules stared at his familiar old chariot, realizing that, like Jacob in the Bible, he'd probably have to slave seven years to buy back his beloved. And like Jacob, he'd do whatever he had to . . . even pay Billy Mac's usurious financing rates.

"Ahh, Cadillac Jules . . . charity's all well and good," Billy Mac said. "But don't you know that charity starts at home, brother? It starts at *home*."

TWENTY-EIGHT

Jules's hand trembled as he pushed open the office door. Maureen's mouth fell open as soon as she saw him.

"Jules! Get *out*! You aren't supposed to see me like this!"

Maureen was a vision of brideliness. The white gown, the sleeves of French lace, the garland atop her head . . . How many years had he dreamed of seeing her just like this? Okay, he'd dreamed her two hundred pounds heavier; but then, no dream come true was ever one hundred percent complete.

She pulled her veil down over her face, then tried pushing him back toward the door. "You big *doofus*! What were you thinking? You know it's bad luck for the groom to see the bride before the wedding!"

Jules held his ground. It was easier, now that he outweighed Maureen by three hundred and fifty pounds. "Mo, we gotta talk."

"Talk?!? Can't this wait until after the '*I do*'s?"

"No, babe. It can't."

Maureen sighed and gave up her struggles. She offered Jules a chair, the sturdiest chair in the Trolley Stop Cafe's office. "Okay . . . whenever you get that look on your face, I know darn well you can't be talked out of whatever notion you've gotten stuck in your head. Spill it. Just make it fast, though, 'cause the girls from Jezebel's are gonna be here any minute to do my makeup. Life without mirrors is a real pain in the ass."

Jules sank slowly into the chair. "Mo, baby, this ain't easy for me to say . . ."

Maureen gasped. She flung her veil away from her face. "Don't—don't tell me you're getting *second thoughts*!"

Jules shook his head. "No, not me, sweetheart. I could *never* get second thoughts about you. It's just . . . well . . . in case maybe *you* were havin' second thoughts . . . I wanted you to know you could, y'know, pull out, and there wouldn't be no hard feelings."

Maureen looked utterly bewildered. "Jules, what are you talking about?"

"I just—I don't want you to do this, go ahead with this, just because you feel"—he forced himself to spit out the word that had been causing him so much trepidation—"*obligated.* I mean, y'know, I brought you back from limbo or wherever—okay, Doodlebug did that, but he did it for me. And I got you a new body—yeah, yeah, that was Doc Landrieu, but I made him give it to you . . . So, y'know, maybe there's a chance that—"

"I'm only marrying you because I feel *grateful*?" She snorted, put her hand over her mouth, but couldn't keep herself from laughing so hard tears rolled down her face. "Oh, Jules . . . Jules, you wonderful, *silly* man! You heard the tape. What were the last words I spoke before Malice X turned me into a housekeeping nightmare?"

" 'Jules, I love you.' "

She wiped the laughing tears from her eyes. "That's right. Now, at that moment of time, do you think I was capable of lying? Of telling anything less than the whole blessed truth? Do you?"

"I—I guess not."

"You *guess* not." She smiled and took his hands in hers. She looked almost exactly the same as the ravishing young beauty who'd taken away his humanity and replaced it with something even better way back in 1917. The plastic surgery and facial liposuction Doc Landrieu had bought for her as an early wedding gift had sucked decades away. It had also ensured that her face wouldn't visually clash with her new, slender body. Maureen was about as thrilled as a woman could be; Doc Landrieu had earned an everlasting place in her heart. Jules hadn't told her this, and probably never would, but he missed her old jowls and wattles.

She carefully sat on his lap, arranging her dress so that it wouldn't wrinkle, and put her arms around his neck. She didn't feel any heavier than a child. "Now, Jules, honey, if I loved you with all my heart *then,* why would I love you any less *now*? Baby, you're my great big *hero.* Being grateful to somebody doesn't make you love them less, silly. It makes you love them *more.*"

Jules pulled her face close to his. His hands were still trembling, but for a different reason now. Maureen pulled away from him and placed a finger on his hungry lips. "Save some of that for later, tiger," she whispered.

He would. The fact that Richard had been such an aggressive, voracious eater during his months as a rat had provided Jules with a surprising but not at all unwelcome lagniappe.

Maureen got up and pushed him toward the door again. "Now git!" she said, swatting him on his rear.

Only after he was out of the office did he feel the full impact of his relief and joy. He leaned against the bar and stared at the covered mirrors behind the liquor bottles while he soared on wave after wave of emotion. *He was getting married to Maureen.* And not only that, but his mother was going to be here to see it.

The cafe's front door swung open. Porkchop Chambonne walked in, carrying his trumpet case and his drummer's cymbals. The handsome, elderly black bandleader paused and looked around the cafe. "Hey, Jules. They got this place fixed up right pretty. Looks like you set for a fine affair."

Jules grabbed the cymbals and walked them over to where the bandstand was set up, next to the white runner and the floral arrangements. "Chop, thanks so much for comin'. I can't tell you how much this means to me, havin' you and your boys play. Can I help you get any of the other stuff outta your car?"

The bandleader waved the suggestion aside. "Oh, don't worry 'bout that none. You the *groom.* Don't need to be totin' no drum kit and stuff." He looked at Jules with the wary fascination of a herpetologist studying a rare but poisonous snake. "Y'know, when we spoke that last time, nine months back, it sounded to me like I wasn't never gonna be seein' you no more. Givin' away all your money and all."

"Well, you know me, Chop. I got a way of turnin' up when you least expect." Jules remembered the desperate night before his final battle with Malice X, when he'd distributed his insurance-settlement money among his friends. He'd paid Chop to circle the upper French Quarter with his marching brass band, second-lining in Maureen's memory. "I'm just happy you been able to keep the band together."

"Thanks to you and your donation, in part." He sidled closer and whispered, even though the only other people around were cooks in the kitchen. "Hey. I been playin' for money since before I was shavin', and that's a long time. For a few other brides and grooms, I done played both their wedding *and* their funeral. But, y'know, this is the only time I ever played the bride's wake *before* I played her wedding."

He winked, then headed out the door to help his bandmates.

Jules made up his mind right then and there. Sometime in the very near future, while Chop was still in good health and at the height of his musical powers, he'd ask him if he wanted to undergo the big change. There weren't that many musicians of Chop's generation left in New Orleans; even at Preservation Hall, the city's living museum of classic jazz, the bandstand was filled by younger faces each year. Some people really deserved to stay on the planet forever. And Chop didn't seem to be at all averse to the existence and company of vampires. He just accepted them as part of the flavorful mix of people that made up this humid, mongrel port city.

Jules wished Erato could've been so accepting. Telling Erato his big secret had been like chewing ground glass. Watching his reaction had been like swallowing it. But there'd been no getting around it. Jules had been determined to ask Erato to be his best man. His request hadn't fallen on the most fertile ground. His friend hadn't said no, exactly; he hadn't said anything at all—just stood there in stunned silence until Jules crept out of his house, his steps heavy with chagrin and sadness.

Jules checked his watch. Erato still had forty-five minutes to put in an appearance before the ceremony started. None of the other guests were here yet; not even Doodlebug, and he was the minister. Jules fingered the small box in his jacket pocket, the box with the ring in it. Until the last possible second arrived, he wasn't surrendering that box to any of his other potential best men. Doc Landrieu would have his hands full being Jules's mother's escort. Marvin Oday, one of Jules's old coworkers from the morgue and now the city's assistant coroner, would be here, but Jules had never been as tight with him as he'd been with Erato. Preston was a possible dark-horse candidate, but Jules really didn't want to risk offending Doc Landrieu and causing a scene.

A long white limousine pulled up in front of the Trolley Stop's entrance. Rudy Goodfeller stepped out. In a new suit, yet, with no tears in the knees or pizza stains on the jacket. He looked about as comfortable in it as a nutria would in a bikini. Jules figured Van Goodfeller must've gotten back in his son's good graces, and vice versa. He was glad.

Rudy approached Jules with trepidation, staring around at the empty restaurant. "I'm here too early, aren't I? I *told* Mr. Garner he shouldn't drop me off for another half hour. Hey, should I, like, go someplace else for a while? There's a Chinese restaurant across the street—"

Jules put his hand on Rudy's shoulder. "Don't sweat it, Crunchy. I'm glad you're here. Grooms get kinda nervous before the big event."

"I know *I'd* be nervous. Hey, your wife-to-be, does she . . . y'know, does she, like, *know*?"

"Know what?" Rudy's eyes drifted down to the area below Jules's belt, and Jules understood. "Oh, *that.* Yeah, she knows. Don't worry about it. Once you get past a certain age, other stuff is more important to a couple than, y'know, *that.*" Rudy looked relieved. "So, you seen Edith L'Enfant lately?"

Rudy shook his head. "Their house is boarded up. I went to Courane's website. It said his band was on a world tour, but it didn't say which cities they'd be playing in."

A motorcycle rumbled onto the sidewalk in front of the restaurant. "Look, a couple more guests are here," Jules said. "Now you ain't the only one anymore."

Daphne and Hank pulled off their helmets and walked inside. Daphne was dressed in an ankle-length purple dress with sunburst yellow flowers; not exactly demure, but on her, it looked like a queen's coronation gown. "Jules!" She threw her arms around his neck. "We've got it all figured out! We're so happy!"

She and Hank told him about their plans to open a no-kill shelter for the city's legion of stray animals. Daphne would earn funds by training their smarter rescues as animal actors in locally made movies. Plus, Hank would learn how to apply for grants.

Rudy's face lit up. "Hey! That's really cool! Y'know, my dad's always giving away money to different charities. Maybe I could ask him to give you guys a grant?"

Daphne and Hank both looked to Jules, silently asking whether Rudy was on the level. It would've helped if they could've seen the limo he had just stepped out of, Jules thought.

Before Jules could decide what to say, a waitress emerged from the kitchen carrying a platter of finger sandwiches. The heaping pile of bread and meat immediately captured Rudy's attention. "You think it's okay if I eat a couple?" he asked Jules. "I'm starving."

"Go ahead," Jules said. "Nobody's gonna notice if a few are missin' from the top."

Rudy made a beeline for the food table, a bounce in his step. "Crunchy's a good kid," Jules said to Daphne and Hank. "I'd consider it a big favor if you two could maybe take him under your wings a little, keep him outta trouble."

"Could he actually help us with some dough?" Hank asked tentatively, watching Rudy pick through the finger sandwiches with the avidity of the recently homeless.

"Maybe," Jules said. "I just think you'd like each other. Daphne, just picture him as a big hairless rat."

Daphne smiled. "Sure, Jules. If you say he's worth knowing, then he's worth knowing. Hank, let's go grab some sandwiches."

The waitress brought out a pan of meatballs, which made both Rudy and Hank very happy. Maybe the three of them could manage to look out for each other, Jules thought. Hank could put a sidecar on his motorcycle. A big sidecar.

Some of the old regulars showed up, cabbies who'd shared the Trolley Stop's row of bar stools with Jules and Erato. Marvin Oday walked in and gave Jules a warm hug. Faces Jules recognized from Jezebel's Joy Room, Maureen's coworkers, drifted into the growing crowd. Maureen had accomplished a twofer, managing to explain with one story both her long absence and her radically different appearance. She'd told her friends she had melted away the pounds during long-term treatment at a weight-loss spa in Switzerland.

Preston showed in his usual outfit, black lizard boots, black-fringed buckskin jacket, and big black cowboy hat. Jules would've been disappointed if he'd made an appearance wearing anything else.

He checked his watch again. Ten minutes to liftoff, and still no Erato.

"Jules? Is everything okay?"

Doodlebug had come inside without Jules's even noticing. He was dressed in a conservative black gown, a soft-shouldered black linen jacket, and a diminutive cream-colored pillbox hat. "You look real nice, D.B.," Jules said. "This your uniform for whenever you do a marriage ceremony?"

"Actually, your ceremony will be the first one I've ever performed."

Jules grimaced. "Great."

Doodlebug playfully swatted his arm. "I'm going to do a terrific job, and you know it. How could I do any less? This'll virtually be like marrying my own parents."

Jules looked around the room. "Speakin' of parents, you haven't seen my mother and Doc Landrieu around anywhere, have you?"

"The good doctor was parking his Mercedes across the street when the cab dropped me off."

"Good. That's one less thing I gotta worry about. Assumin' my mother behaves. Hey, you ain't seen Erato around, huh?"

Responding to the exaggerated hope in Jules's voice, Doodlebug offered a sympathetic smile. "You haven't heard from him since your talk?"

"Nope."

Doodlebug reached over and gave his arm a squeeze. "I hope he comes through for you, Jules. I really do. Let's hope for the best."

Doc Landrieu opened the front door, and Jules's mother walked through ahead of him. As soon as she saw her son, her pale, rouged face glowed with maternal pride. Jules could tell she was trying to hide it, pinching her smile with her cheek muscles so she didn't look too enraptured; she still wasn't crazy about this particular wedding. But seeing her only son in his wedding tux—Jules hoped she'd forgive herself for letting a few flashes of joy shine through.

"You look beautiful, Mother," Jules said. And she did. "That's a swell dress. You almost look like a bride yourself."

"You look lovely, Mrs. Duchon," Doodlebug said.

"Thank you, both of you," Edna said. She flashed Doc Landrieu a quick, incandescent smile. "Amos helped me pick this out. I haven't had a dress this nice to wear since Roosevelt said the only thing we have to fear is fear itself. And you both look wonderful, too. Son, I can't tell you how relieved I am that that shop on Canal was able to special-order you a tux in your size. I was afraid you'd have to wear a barrel to your own wedding."

Jules took his mother's hands. "Mother, you're okay with this, right? I mean, you're gonna sit with Amos and enjoy the ceremony, won't you?"

Edna pulled her hands away and waved off his fears. "Sure, sure. I'll be a little lamb. Maureen's been awful sweet to me these past few weeks. *Too* sweet, if you ask me, but I'll let it pass." Her expression softened into a mischievous grin. "By the way, Amos and I have a big surprise for you later."

Jules's stomach plunged down a roller-coaster drop. "Aww geez, Ma. I sure in hell hope it's not another girl for me to marry. Polygamy's illegal in Louisiana."

"Ha, ha. Big joke. You'll just have to wait and find out, smarty-pants."

Doodlebug gestured toward the rows of white folding chairs, which were already beginning to fill. "We'll be getting started in just a minute. I made sure some seats were saved for you two up front."

Doc Landrieu shook Jules's hand in a powerful grip. "Best of luck, Jules."

"Thanks, Doc. It wouldn't be happenin' without you."

Doodlebug put his hand lightly on Jules's back. "Come on, Jules. It's time."

The walked down the aisle to where a flowered wicker trellis had been set up. Porkchop Chambonne's band, which had been playing traditional New Orleans jazz in a surprisingly subdued fashion, quieted down, waiting for the big moment when the bride would appear.

Doodlebug took his place beneath the trellis. Jules stood to Doodlebug's left, outside the shelter of daisy blooms and white wicker. Alone. He felt naked, even in his expensive custom tux. What was a groom without a best man to stand beside him? It was too late to ask Marvin or Preston to come be with him. Maureen would be walking down the aisle any second now.

Suddenly, he understood why grooms broke glasses at Jewish weddings.

His mind hurtled back to Dryades Street, to the Jewish commercial strip where Jules used to hang out and do his shopping because the stores stayed open until ten or eleven at night. Back in the forties, there'd been a kosher butcher Jules had enjoyed palling around with, maybe because they both appreciated the stench of blood. One night, he'd asked the butcher why Jewish grooms always stepped on glasses at the end of the ceremony. The man had told him this was a commemoration of the destruction of the Temple of Solomon. Jules said a wedding was a strange time to be remembering an old-time bummer. But the butcher shook his head no; a wedding was the perfect time to remember such a thing. Because no occasion, no matter how joyous, was entirely devoid of sorrow.

He hadn't gotten what the man was saying, those sixty long years ago. He got it now.

Porkchop Chambonne looked to Doodlebug for a signal to start the processional. Doodlebug looked to Jules. Jules chewed his lower lip, then nodded his head. Doodlebug nodded to Chop. The bandleader smiled broadly and launched his band into a rousing, syncopated rendition of "Here Comes the Bride."

And then Jules saw Erato standing outside the windows at the front of the restaurant.

Jules rushed over to the bandstand, waving his arms. "Chop! Wait a minute! Just wait!"

The music collapsed. The guests, who'd all turned around to witness the bride's procession, now all stared at the man outside the windows. Jules heard Maureen shout from around the corner—"Jules! What the heck's going on? A musician have a heart attack?"

"Just wait a minute, sweetheart! Erato ran late. We'll get goin' again in just a second."

Jules's closest human friend slowly pushed through the door. He swayed, tripping over the carpet when he walked inside. Jules was certain he'd been drinking. But the Dutch courage hadn't helped all that much. Erato's clay-colored face was shiny with perspiration. His lazy eye and good eye both scanned the guests fearfully, trying to pinpoint who among them were unholy killers.

Jules's spirits had soared when he saw Erato standing at the window. Now they plummeted as he saw the mental toll merely walking into the restaurant had taken on his friend. This visceral terror was so unnecessary—the moon would come crashing into the earth before Jules would allow anyone, vampire or human, to lay a fang or finger on Erato's head.

Could he ever make his friend understand this?

Staring at the floor, Erato steered an erratic path down the white runner. Jules left his station next to the trellis to steady him, but Erato flinched away from his touch.

"Just gimme the ring, okay?" Erato said quietly, not looking Jules in the face. "Then I'll give it back to you when—when Maureen comes."

"Sure thing, Erato," Jules said. He handed him the ring, trusting somehow that his friend wouldn't drop it. "Thanks so much for bein' here, for standin' with me."

Jules took his position again. Erato stood next to him, although closer to the musicians than to the groom. Jules signaled Chop to start the wedding march again.

As soon as trumpet, clarinet, trombone, and rhythm broke into the familiar music, Maureen turned the corner, escorted by Straussman. Even though Jules had seen her in her wedding dress less than an hour ago, the impact of seeing her now was nothing less than magical. All his worries were blown out to sea by a benevolent but irresistible wind.

Straussman unlocked his arm from Maureen's and placed her hand in Jules's. Jules was really pleased the older vampire had agreed to participate; he was even more pleased that Straussman wasn't jealous. After all, when he'd ushered Maureen into the ranks of the undead, he'd expected her to become his own bride. But, to his credit, all he wanted tonight was Maureen's happiness.

Jules and Maureen took their places. Jules stared into her eyes. He tried to recall if there'd ever been a time when he'd been as much in love with her as he was tonight. The first night he'd seen her? The night she'd chosen him for her consort? The night, ten months ago, when he'd visited her up at Jezebel's for the first time in ten lonely years?

It didn't matter. They were together again. And after tonight, they'd never be apart.

Doodlebug daintily cleared his throat. "Dearly beloved, family and friends, we are gathered here tonight to celebrate the union in holy matrimony of two individuals who found each other, lost each other, and then found one another once again. Jules and Maureen share a story that is a tribute to the power of patience, perseverance, and abiding love. Their story is unique; but then, aren't the stories of all lovers unique, if only in their own hearts?

"All unions such as this should be sanctified. The journey of commitment, love, and mutual support Jules and Maureen are beginning together tonight is a holy one. I call upon the loving God, Creator of all things, to bless this union. Creator of the light *and* the darkness; the good *and* the evil; the holy *and* the profane. Loving Creator of us all, I ask that you bless and sanctify this union, seeing that it is entered into not to circumvent your purposes, but to raise them up and celebrate them."

Jules cringed inwardly—he fully expected that, any second now, a thunderbolt would erase the Trolley Stop Cafe from St. Charles Avenue. Doodlebug hadn't previewed any of the ceremony for Jules. It was ballsy of the little guy to ask for a blessing, but Jules would've been a heck of a lot more comfortable if his friend had taken a big pass on the GEE-OH-DEE talk. Still, when the building hadn't exploded by the time five full seconds had passed, Jules began breathing a little easier.

"Jules Augustine Duchon, do you take Maureen Remoulade to be your lawfully wedded wife, to have and to hold, in sickness and in health, till final death do you part?"

Jules squeezed Maureen's hands, so recently not her own. "I sure as hell *do.*"

Maureen swatted his hand, but her smile didn't waver.

"Maureen Remoulade, do you take Jules Augustine Duchon to be your lawfully wedded husband, to have and to hold, in sickness and in health, till final death do you part?"

"I do."

Jules gestured for Erato to give him the ring, expecting to now put it on Maureen's finger. But he'd overlooked one part of the ceremony—

"If anyone present has any objection to this union, let him speak now or forever hold his peace."

Oh no! Jules's blood pressure spiked higher than Chop's highest trumpet note. He didn't want to look, but he had to—the crowd was already quietly gasping. Yes, his mother had shot up from her chair with the alacrity of a buck private saluting a five-star general.

"I've got something to say," she said.

Oh no. Oh no oh no oh no . . .

She removed a piece of paper from her purse and waved it to the crowd. "This here's a valid marriage license. Amos and me are gettin' hitched, too."

Jules swiveled around and glared at Doodlebug. Had he known about this? Obviously not, to judge from his expression. Jules hadn't seen Doodlebug flustered too many times, but this discombobulation was a doozy.

"Uh . . . okay, Mrs. Duchon," Doodlebug stuttered. "I'll be, uh, *happy* to accommodate you. But let's have one marriage at a time, okay?"

"Okay." Edna winked at her gape-mouthed son and took her seat again.

Maureen looked not at all pleased by her mother-in-law's antics. But she did an admirable job of maintaining her composure. "Doodle," she whispered. "The ring—? Don't forget the ring part."

Doodlebug cleared his throat and nodded. "Jules, please place the, ah, ring on Maureen's finger." Jules did so. The ring slid on much easier than it would've on Maureen's original, megaplump ring finger. "You may now kiss the bride . . ."

The good part. At last . . .

♠

It was a swell party. Chop's band played with gusto. Chop himself fired off such virtuoso solos that Jules could've sworn they'd gone back in time to the musician's youth. All their human guests had come with impressive appetites; the pots of gumbo and pans of jambalaya didn't have time to go cold. Jules wished he could've provided something special for his undead guests, maybe some chichi California blood shipped in from Doodlebug's private cache, but Doc Landrieu had insisted that no blood or blood-laced snacks be made available. He hadn't wanted to risk Jules's mother's falling off the wagon.

This also meant that Jules's stomach was doomed to whine and rumble while many of his friends chowed down with abandon. One bright spot was that Maureen, like Doc Landrieu and Jules's mother (now *Mr. and Mrs.* Landrieu), was able to enjoy the party food. Her "borrowed" body parts were young enough, in vampiric terms, to be able to tolerate solid foods; her new digestive system hadn't yet been corrupted by decades of absorbing and processing hundreds of gallons of cholesterol- and lipid-laced blood.

Jules derived considerable pleasure from watching her snarf down plate after plate of jambalaya and assorted finger sandwiches. She stabbed meatballs with a miniature plastic sword and delightedly popped them into her mouth, one after another. It was a show Jules hadn't seen Maureen perform since the Eisenhower years. He tugged on his pants, noticing that Richard found the spectacle intriguing, too.

The only bummer was that Erato sat in a corner, alone, seemingly too afraid to say a word to any of the other guests. Jules tried a few times to get him talking, but Erato would only answer in slurred, frightened monosyllables. He didn't touch any of the food Jules brought him, either. Jules pulled aside Marvin Oday and asked him to drive Erato home.

The time came to cut the wedding cake. Jules wrapped his arms around his bride and held his hand on hers as she lifted the big silver cake knife, its handle wrapped in a cloth napkin so the touch of silver wouldn't sting her fingers.

Jules let Maureen's hand guide the slicing of the cake. He let his grateful gaze wander around the room. Less than two months ago, he'd been living inside the termite-ravaged walls of the French Quarter, his only company dozens of rodent versions of himself. But now, amazingly, he had a family again. An exasperating, byzantine family, but a family, nonetheless.

Had there ever been such a twisted family tree? There was his mother; but she was also (and this was a creepy thought) his blood-daughter. That made Doc Landrieu both his stepfather *and* his son-in-law. But wait—Doc Landrieu was turned into a vampire by Malice X, Jules's blood-brother, so that meant that Doc Landrieu was also Jules's blood-*nephew.* Just like Preston. In fact, Preston and Doc Landrieu were both blood-sons of the same blood-father. Maureen was Jules's blood-mother, and now she was his legal wife, too. That meant that Strauss-man, Jules's blood-grandfather, was now also his father-in-law. And Jules's mother . . . somehow she'd ended up both Maureen's mother-in-law and Maureen's blood-*granddaughter* . . .

Jules was getting dizzy. This was like trying to trace a single strand of spaghetti through a five-liter bowl of knotted pasta.

But he had a family again. That much he knew for sure.

"Jules. Open wide, sweetie."

Maureen held a big, fat slice of cake on a plate. She dangled a fork near his lips, loaded with a frosting-slathered hunk.

Jules frowned with disappointment. "Hey, babe, you know I can't eat that. It'll start jumpin' on my GI tract like a kid on a trampoline . . ."

Maureen refused to lower the fork. "Come on, hubby mine. One little bite won't kill you."

The onlooking crowd began to chant, *"Eat! Eat! Eat!"*

Jules shrugged his shoulders and opened wide. Maureen made little airplane noises as she steered the fork toward his mouth, detouring to leave a blob of frosting on his nose before banking the cake between his lips.

Jules chewed and swallowed. It tasted good. Hell, it tasted *terrific.* His stomach quivered as the mass of sugar and flour passed through his esophagus, and he knew he might have a spot of trouble later, but he didn't care. In fact, later on, after all the guests left, he was going to change into a wolf and *really* enjoy himself.

Jules grabbed the plate and fork from Maureen. "Okay, now it's *your* turn." He speared a big chunk and aimed it straight for her lips, not bothering with the customary tomfoolery. She licked the excess frosting off the fork, showing the guests a little more tongue than was strictly ladylike. Her eyes closed with pleasure. Watching her, Jules found himself wishing all the guests were already gone. Richard wished the same thing.

"How about another piece, lover?" she mumbled with her mouth still full.

Jules fed her another piece. And then another. Already, he was anticipating the future. If her appetite stayed anything like this, she wouldn't be *Vogue* skinny forever.

Maureen hadn't become the loving armful he so lustfully remembered overnight, he reminded himself. She'd billowed and grown gradually, over the course of eighty years and thousands of rich Crescent City meals.

He could wait another eighty years if he had to. Good things come to those who wait, and a vampire could afford to wait a long, long time.

Especially a *married* vampire.

ABOUT THE AUTHOR

ANDREW JAY FOX was born in 1964 and grew up in North Miami Beach, Florida. The first movie he remembers seeing is Japanese monster fest *Destroy All Monsters,* viewed from the backseat of his stepdad's Caprice convertible. Early passions included Universal horror movies, 1950s giant monster flicks, WWII navy dramas, *Planet of the Apes,* and horror comics, particularly Marv Wolfman's and Gene Colan's "Tomb of Dracula." His earliest exposure to literary science fiction came by way of H. G. Wells, Ray Bradbury, and Anne McCaffrey's Pern series; other favorites through the years have included Robert Silverberg, J. G. Ballard, Richard Matheson, and Ursula K. Le Guin.

He attended Loyola University in New Orleans, where he studied social work and wrote a fantasy play for visually handicapped children that involved the audience rubbing their hands on a Vaseline-coated foam rubber mermaid's tail and sniffing spoiled sardines. He studied public administration at Syracuse University, then worked at a public children's psychiatric center on Long Island while continuing to write plays (none of which involved sardines). Since returning to New Orleans in 1990, he has worked as manager of the Louisiana Commodity Supplemental Food Program, a federally funded monthly nutrition program for low-income senior citizens. In 1995, he joined a monthly writing workshop founded by award-winning SF author George Alec Effinger.

His first novel to see print was *Fat White Vampire Blues* (Del Rey, 2003). *Bride of the Fat White Vampire* is his second novel.